The Radio Ham

The Radio Ham

David Fletcher

Copyright © 2024 David Fletcher

The moral right of the author has been asserted.

Apart from any fair dealing for the purposes of research or private study, or criticism or review, as permitted under the Copyright, Designs and Patents Act 1988, this publication may only be reproduced, stored or transmitted, in any form or by any means, with the prior permission in writing of the publishers, or in the case of reprographic reproduction in accordance with the terms of licences issued by the Copyright Licensing Agency. Enquiries concerning reproduction outside those terms should be sent to the publishers.

This is a work of fiction. Names, characters, businesses, places, events and incidents are either the products of the author's imagination or used in a fictitious manner. Any resemblance to actual persons, living or dead, or actual events is purely coincidental.

Troubador Publishing Ltd
Unit E2 Airfield Business Park,
Harrison Road, Market Harborough,
Leicestershire. LE16 7UL
Tel: 0116 2792299
Email: books@troubador.co.uk
Web: www.troubador.co.uk

ISBN 978 1805142 454

British Library Cataloguing in Publication Data.
A catalogue record for this book is available from the British Library.

Printed and bound in Great Britain by 4edge Limited
Typeset in 11.5pt Minion Pro by Troubador Publishing Ltd, Leicester, UK

For Mark and Christiane

Aashir, 2025 (i)

Not like this in Aleppo. There, embraced by the city. Its souks and its citadel. Vibrant. Alive. People with smiles on their faces. People with a home to return to. Polite people. And warm there. And full of the smells he'd been brought up with. But now. Now, this cold hellhole. Sand dunes, spiky grass, endless blue tents, buckets, trash, filth. And all too open. Too exposed. Too much sky. No embraces. Like being in a desert. A dirty desert. Full of dirty people with their dirty belongings. And with their despair and their anguish and their incomprehension. Their total inability to understand why those with so much were not prepared to share their bounty with so few. Good people. People who would work. People who would become model citizens of their precious model world.

And it was all so close. Aashir could see it. He could

almost reach out and touch it. White cliffs, like a tempting slab of soapwort meringue, just waiting to be devoured. Chewed and swallowed, before moving on to the next meal. The main meal of the day. Another place that would embrace him just like Aleppo had. Full of life. Full of opportunities. Full of wealth. Full of so many people like him. Outsiders who had found their way inside. Outsiders who were no longer outsiders. But citizens. Londoners as much as those Londoners he'd seen in the films. When London was in black and white and being bombed by the Germans. This was where he wanted to be. Wrapped around by concrete and stone. Immersed in that multitude of men. Sharing the lives of all those new Londoners. Those who'd made London what it was. A cosmopolitan stronghold. A citadel for all. A much bigger citadel than Aleppo's own. And richer than the whole of Aleppo by far. And safer than Aleppo by far. And a lot safer than being in a dinghy.

He'd never seen one before. But now he knew all about them. What sizes they came in. Which were the most seaworthy. Or at least which wouldn't just tip over at the first wave. And most important of all, how many souls could perch around their sides and squat down within them without their sinking in sight of the beach. Most of his maths he'd long forgotten, but he was now an expert in the calculus of dinghy-carrying capacities. And the price of a dinghy ticket. And he certainly knew how much he would have to pay to guarantee he wouldn't be floundering around in the English Channel before he got anywhere near English waters. Which meant that, with only two hours to go, he felt more confident than apprehensive. His magic carpet to England would not be blown off course by the winds or swamped by intemperate waves. And before this day was out, he would be on that large island and able to look back at where he was now. The stinking halfway house to his new life. A life that he was owed. A life that the people over there had no right to deny him. And no right even to resent his arrival. How often had they landed on other people's shores without an invitation? And not even with the intention of becoming model citizens. More to become masters and exploiters. Brigands with manners who had in life only one intention: to gobble up what they wanted and to spit out what they didn't. In fact, the more he considered their motives alongside his own, the more he thought his entitlement was absolute. An entitlement to live in the land of the pale Anglo-Saxons.

It was no more than he deserved.

1. 2154

Why, when all that technology had crashed and burnt, had the only survivors to crawl out of the wreckage been emojis? How could they have been that impervious to annihilation? And now, why were so many people ensuring these idiotic icons would survive for all time? These were questions Sidney asked himself every time a customer came to him with some childish attempts at the chosen emojis, scrawled on a scrap of paper or a piece of bark, and with the earnest request that a facsimile of the chosen symbols be inserted into the narrative where required.

Fortunately, this 'elaboration' only infrequently made its way into anything of an official nature, but even in some serious correspondence destined to be exchanged between two 'people of age', there was often a desire to display this unwarranted allegiance to the residue of a technology that neither of them could really remember. Perhaps, Sidney would tell himself, it was one of the few echoes of the past that still had some use, no matter how faint was that echo or how frivolous its use. Or, there again, maybe it was simply more evidence of a lingering yearning for the past. For a time when the world hosted all sorts of devices that enabled their users to employ countless cartoon images when communicating with their peers.

This evening, however, emojis would not put in an appearance. Sidney was sure. Old Sanjiv had booked him for a session, and old Sanjiv had never before harnessed his scribing services for anything other than 'official purposes'. Furthermore, the wrinkled old grump was just too damn sour to indulge in anything quite so waggish. Even if, one day, the unlikely occurred and he asked Sidney to write something personal, it would involve just words and definitely no pictures. Although what that might be, Sidney could not imagine. After all, Sanjiv had no friends – either in the village or, as far as was known, anywhere else. His sourness had made sure of that.

He arrived outside Sidney's cabin just after eight – and sat on the cabin's deck.

Sidney joined him immediately, sat down himself and offered a greeting. 'Mr Kumar,' he said, 'you are my most punctual customer.'

He said this with a smile, but the smile was not returned. Sanjiv just grunted and turned to look at the pond. Then he turned to face Sidney again and gave him the sort of look that Sidney had seen on so many faces before: a look of disdain mixed with resentment. He wasn't surprised. Not only was Sidney regarded more as a necessary device than a human being but most found it distasteful in the extreme that this 'device' could do what they could not: write – and write very well. Whatever Sidney's customers dictated was reproduced faithfully by his hand, albeit it often had to be cleaned up as he wrote to remove their frequent deviations from standard English. Not that he ever admitted to them that he did this.

Anyway, impatience was now overtaking disdain and resentment on Sanjiv's face, and this was Sidney's cue to invite him to commence his dictation. 'Ready when you are, Mr Kumar. Fire away.'

Judging from the look of disgust that had now arrived on Sanjiv's face, he seemed to have taken needless offence at this request, but Sidney ignored this and focused instead on the job in hand. In his lap, he had a sheaf of rough paper pinned to a rigid plastic clipboard, and in his hand, he had one of his three treasured pens. In his mind, he had something else: a concern that he might need all or even more of those waiting sheets. After all, Sanjiv was as longwinded in his dictation as he was sour in his nature, and Sidney might be in for an extended session – one of tedium… and pain.

Sidney was only forty-one, but a life of hard physical work and a poor diet had gifted him a decent amount of premature arthritis in his hands. And if, for too long, his right one had to grapple with the task of scratching line after line of inky paths across pages of coarse notepaper, its arthritic condition would make itself known. It wasn't a prospect he relished.

Fortunately, however, Sidney's concern proved completely misplaced, and his hand suffered hardly any discomfort whatsoever. Sanjiv had rattled through his dictation with barely a pause but at just the pace that Sidney could manage. Therefore, it took no more than fifteen minutes for the dictated epistle to be concluded, ready for Sanjiv's unintelligible signature to be appended to its end.

It was as though, thought Sidney, Sanjiv had been rehearsing its contents in his head for some time.

And that would hardly be surprising. Sanjiv had the role of 'village warden', and one of his main duties within this role was to inform the regional governor's office of any simmering problems in the village. Well, there was one problem that had passed the simmering stage and was now boiling away to its heart's content. It was, therefore, what formed the substance of Sanjiv's missive. And, of course, everybody in the village knew only too well what it was. Indeed, even a simple device used for committing dictation to paper knew what it was – because this device had eyes. It therefore couldn't fail to observe that the fields were full of jowar and bajra that hadn't grown as they should. The individual plants looked shrivelled and stunted, and some of the jowar had barely grown at all. There was no way that crop yields would be other than dreadful this year, and – as discussed openly in the family – it wasn't a problem in just this village. Crop yields were apparently shaping up to be dreadful everywhere, a point Sanjiv had been at pains to make clear in his report to the governor. Even though the governor would no doubt already know – and would already be wondering how he could exist on a much-reduced tithe.

Old Sanjiv was now making his spider marks in ink at the bottom of the page, and Sidney thought he detected a hint of unease in his curmudgeonly customer.

Could it be, he thought, that Sanjiv was not only concerned about how his report would be received but also a little embarrassed that the communal failure he was reporting had to be admitted so unequivocally to a mere device; a mere device that had the audacity to be the only fixture in the village capable of penning a communication?

Sidney was well aware that he was allowed to be privy to all sorts of official communications and a whole range of sensitive personal communications only because he was held in such low regard. In the minds of all of his customers – without exception – revealing anything at all to Sidney was no more than revealing something to a wooden post. After all, for them, Sidney was effectively inanimate. That way, it was so much easier to push his facility with a pen – and their total lack of this facility – to the back of their minds. And it didn't even involve their adopting any different thinking about this alien within their midst. After all, weren't all such aliens little better than objects, whether they were useful objects or not?

However, on this occasion, it was just possible, thought Sidney, that Sanjiv hadn't been able to maintain in his mind the far-from-human nature of his scribe. In which case, he might be feeling at least a little bit sheepish. The contents of his report were, after all, not something in which he could take any pride.

Sidney made quite sure that he gave no hint that he had such thoughts, and made no comment whatsoever on the contents of Sanjiv's missive. That might lead to all sorts of unpleasantness and maybe even a bout of apoplexy for Sanjiv – who was not only sour but fitted out with a very short fuse. Instead, Sidney would wait in silence until the missive was handed back, when he would then fold the sheets, ready for their sealing, and just hope that old Sanjiv would leave with them without further ado – and with or without a cheery goodbye.

It turned out well. Sanjiv left immediately, and as expected, without even a perfunctory goodbye. It was now not even eight-thirty, and Sidney was on his own in his cabin – with two speckled, brown eggs in payment for his services, and the distinct likelihood that the family wouldn't need him again for the rest of the evening. And that meant he could stow his pen and unused sheets of paper in his desk – and spend some much-needed time with his radio.

He lost no time at all in bringing his equipment to life. Battered and worn, it still worked remarkably well, and that meant it still enabled him to talk to three other worthless types around the globe – three others who had access to similar vintage technology and a similar desire to sustain a remote but reassuring relationship with like-minded souls. And as it was before nine, and that meant it was before ten in the evening in Namibia, the worthless type he would try to raise now would be Ted in Windhoek. After all, most of the snakes that Ted was called upon to catch for his Chinese clients turned up in the morning or in the heat of day. They tended to have lost their enthusiasm for invading people's homes by mid-afternoon. And that meant Ted was rarely at work in the evening – and hence, generally, no more than a few yards from his radio.

So, Ted it would be. If, that is, Sidney could once again conjure up the magic of long-distance HF radio communication. For which purpose, he would first have to recite the magical incantations. And with his ancient microphone held to his lips, this is just what he did.

'Is this frequency in use?' he asked. 'G5LMS, Golf Five Lima Mike Sierra; is this frequency in use? Is anybody using this frequency? G5LMS, Golf Five Lima Mike Sierra. Is this frequency available? Golf Five Lima Mike Sierra.'

Then he waited – in the full knowledge that, if he elicited a response to these questions, he would – in all likelihood – fall off his chair. After all, they were no more than a nod to times long past when tens of thousands of radio hams around the world checked to confirm that the frequency on which they had chosen to transmit wasn't already in use by some other radio hams deep in some radio-ham conversation. Needless to say, with the radio-ham population now an endangered species, whatever frequency he chose would inevitably be free for his use, and he ran zero risk of interrupting anybody else's conversation. That said, one had, of course, to observe all the established conventions – which after a twenty-second wait, required Sidney to continue with his incantations; incantations that would hopefully see the magic finally appear.

'G5LMS calling CQ DX – Africa,' he began. And then 'Calling CQ DX – Africa; G5LMS, Golf Five Lima Mike Sierra. G5LMS, Golf Five Lima Mike Sierra calling CQ DX – Africa. Hello. G5LMS, Golf Five Lima Mike Sierra, calling CQ DX – Africa. Hello. Golf Five Lima Mike Sierra.'

He waited again; aware this time that he still felt mildly embarrassed by having to recite this indisputably nerdy overture to a radio conversation. But it was unavoidable. It was the only way to elicit a response through the ether. And it worked. Within less than fifteen seconds, out of a wall of background noise came the unmistakable voice of Ted, the snake catcher – one of the few Caucasians tolerated in Chinese Windhoek and one of the least inhibited human beings on the planet. How his inhibitions hadn't already landed him in all sorts of trouble, Sidney could never quite understand.

He started with one of his usual greetings: 'Sid, you old bastard. I knew it was you. I can smell the curry from here. Anyway, how are you? Still on the shit detail or have things taken a turn for the worse?'

Sidney sniggered and then responded. 'Well, my dear Victor Five Eight Papa Tango, it's getting worse all the time. And soon it'll be a lot worse than any shit detail. Like when no one has anything to eat.'

'Um, it hasn't got any better then?'

'No. It's a hell of a lot worse. And they just don't seem to get it. They just don't seem to understand that crops that require high temperatures will refuse to thrive if the temperature falls. You know, like it's been doing for five or more years now. I know we've discussed all this before, but it's so blindingly obvious now that I've no idea how they can still ignore it. The climate is getting ever colder. Because of you know what. Yet they still plant stuff they grew in the Tropics. And then, bugger me, they're somehow surprised when it doesn't perform. When sometimes it doesn't grow at all, let alone ripen. And they're not just surprised; they're pretty upset. And I mean pretty upset indeed.'

'I suppose it's the same over the border?'

'Worse, from what I've heard. But no great surprise. The further north you go, the chillier it must get. And the chances of anything from the Tropics managing it up there must be just about zero.'

'So, what do you think will happen?'

'Well, there's still a little food around now. But God knows what's going to be left for over winter. Probably only that famous two-thirds of three-eighths of fuck all. And you can imagine how much of that will find its way onto my wooden platter.'

'Mmm, that don't sound so good. Pity you ain't got

more snakes around there. A nice horned adder can keep me in tucker for days. And an Angolan python… well…'

'So, you're doing OK, then? No problems with the snakes and none with the locals?'

'No. The snakes are just fine, and the locals… well, they're just behaving like the locals. You know, the occasional bout of verbal abuse; the occasional dollop of physical abuse. And worse than that, of course, some of the bastards choose not to pay me. Not so much as a dumpling or a spoonful of rice.'

'God, that stinks. And I suppose there's not much you can do?'

'Well, not a lot… other than… well, you know, maybe forgoing the odd meal of Cape cobra – and then making damn sure it finds its way back from where it came…'

'You mean their house? *And you do that?*'

'Bloody right, I do that. Especially if the snake's venomous enough – and I've had more than enough. I find it very cathartic – and quite heart-warming as well. 'Course, I don't do it immediately. They might smell a rat, as it were. So I wait a few hours or even take it back the next day. Hell, the way I see it, life's got to have at least a few pleasures. And scaring the shit out of cheapskate bastards is one of the few pleasures I've still got.'

'So, keeping your clients happy or "exceeding their expectations" isn't what you'd describe as your primary goal?'

Ted laughed in faraway Windhoek. 'Sid, what do you think? I have as much time for my clients as they have for me. Making them happy and "exceeding their expectations" couldn't be further from my mind. They're the enemy, Sid. And whatever they think of me, it doesn't matter a sod. As you know, I'm one of only three snake catchers in Windhoek and, I might say, the best of the three. So I'm never going to be out of work – no matter how they regard me. Which means there's always going to be enough of them who *do* pay for my services to keep the wolf from the door. And as regards those who don't... well, they get exactly what they deserve. And sometimes, even a repeat visit from yours truly – for which, my dear Sid, they inevitably pay – even though it's always at my "premium rate".'

Sidney laughed out loud, and even as he was laughing, he was reminded why these calls to his 'pals overseas' were so important. Indeed, they were vital. Without them, he would be lost. He suspected they would be as well. Ted and the other two 'hams' out there were all, like him, enduring what could best be described as a form of solitary confinement, and the need for mutual contact was intense. Even if the contact was necessarily sporadic, sometimes of such poor audio quality that it had to be abandoned – and always far too short. Running Sidney's equipment took very little power, but an ancient patched-together solar panel, even with a mysterious 'transmuter', delivered no more than very little. Consequently, his contact conversations had to be drawn to a close all too soon, and it wouldn't be long before this one was nearing its end.

Nevertheless, that wouldn't be before its two participants had moved on to a discussion about the growing threat to the Chinese hegemony in Namibia. This, it appeared, was being posed by those other African landlords – from India – combined with an insurgency in the north of the country being staged by the continent's original inhabitants. Many of Ted's clients, he reported with some satisfaction, were now not just alarmed by the ingress of snakes but also by the potential ingress of some real competition. Then, after this run-down of developments in Namibia, there was even time for a precis by Sidney of developments in France – provided the week before by Marc in Toulon. Ted always had difficulty in raising Marc himself, so he was quite interested to get an update – and also to learn that their mutual 'amateur doctor' friend in Toulon was keeping his head well above water by selling more home-made hooch than ever…

When he did finally sign off, Sidney felt tired from his labours of the day but greatly revived in his mind from his chat with Ted.

No doubt, he thought, had he been rendered as an emoji this evening, it would have been that really irritating one with the manic smile on its improbably round face…

Aashir, 2025 (ii)

Pebbles beneath his feet. Small pebbles. Large pebbles. Shiny pebbles. British pebbles...

He'd made it! With so many others. There were dozens. Some standing and smiling. Some still in their lifejackets, sitting and staring. Not quite believing that a new life was now theirs. No more tents. No more filth and cold. No more hide and seek with men in uniform. No more just not knowing. No more fear and no more desperation. No. Now, just a new reality. A need to offer themselves up to new experiences. As he would. The thought made him shudder. With joy.

Ten hours later, more shudders of joy. A room. A clean, airy room. His own room. And a bed – with white sheets and pillows. Lamps by the bed. A television! A huge new television. And warm. Dark outside now, but in here warm. He wanted to cry. Wanted to hug someone. Wanted to share his joy. But he was alone. In his own room!

Overwhelming. Humbling. Extraordinary.

But not for long. Why travel all this way to stare at a TV? To eat tasteless food? To count the hours of each day? And he wasn't imprisoned. He could come and go as he pleased. And it pleased him to go. To Haringey. Deeper into that embracing city. Where he had a cousin. And his cousin had friends. Others from Aleppo who could provide him with an address – and a way out of this dismal hotel.

Not easy. Not to start with. Not before you learn to evade. Not before you've chosen to dive down and out of sight. Asylum takes years. But Ghaleb wants someone now. A bright guy. A young guy. A guy who can look after himself. Who can deal with a bit of rough and tumble.

Fixed. Plugged in. Sorted. In a city that belonged to those who lived in it. From wherever they'd come. And no matter what they thought.

If only he could taste more of its fruits. If only there were more than his errands for Ghaleb. If only he could have what so many others in this honeypot already had. If only he could get in with Umar. Umar with the Merc. Umar with the Rolex. Umar who had all those girls. Umar who was looking for a smart boy to cope with a whole tide of new business.

Now, not just sorted. But properly set up. And on the up. Might not be legal. But hadn't he been helped? So why not now help others? All those others Umar was keen to help. Others who would pay more and more to land on a pebble beach. And barely a risk. As in, no risk at all. Just happy punters. Happy faces on the shores of his new home. And in due course, some of them ready to receive more of his help. And to help him get his first Rolex. It was what this place was all about. Opportunity. Ripe opportunity. Ready to be plucked by anyone. Just as anyone could come here. No one had the right to keep anyone out. He'd known that for years. But now he could see he'd been right. All along.

Yes. He and all the new Londoners were this place's future. Without them, it would wither and die. Look around. They were its new blood. Young. Eager. Fresh of mind. Not hindered by dated loyalties. Old traditions. 'Accepted practices'. Or worthless allegiances.

Its salvation was already underway...

2.

Night soil: in Sidney's opinion, it was the king of all euphemisms. But however euphemistic, it still needed to be collected each morning, before the family had risen, and carted to the pit in the wood to join all the other shit that he'd dumped there before. It was the worst possible start to the day, and it never got any easier. This morning, it was particularly bad. The stink from the bucket made him retch, and as he finally made it to the pit, he began to feel faint. He had to steady his tall frame against a tree and take several deep breaths before he could unload his cargo and then stumble back towards his cabin, a slick of sweat now gathered on his brow. And that definitely wasn't due to any heat. Despite a blanket of cloud and a total absence of wind, it was really chilly this morning. Indeed, the chill was aiding his recovery. So much so that, by the time Rishi turned up outside the cabin, he felt more or less fine – albeit entirely unprepared for such an unexpected visit. After all, Rishi conducted all his business on his home turf. Away fixtures at his 'ward's' accommodation were virtually unknown. It was as though he regarded Sidney's cabin as in some way unclean, and he rarely, if ever, came near it. Or there again, maybe it was what both the cabin and its occupant held that kept him at bay: a store of knowledge; a store of knowledge that made him feel deeply uncomfortable…

Rishi was the head of the family, a pot-bellied man of about fifty who was currently extremely concerned about his crops. When he had awoken this morning to find that they were again going to be starved of warmth, he would no doubt have been more worried than ever. And when Sidney had recovered from his surprise, this was the reason, he decided, that Rishi had beaten a path to his door. This was open, and it was where Rishi was now standing – with a look on his face that wasn't purely impassive. There was a hint of unease there as well. Just as there was in his voice when he finally addressed Sidney. It had obviously taken him even longer to come to terms with this unusual situation than it had his humble helper.

'Sidney,' he began, 'I was just wondering…' And there he stopped. Maybe he just couldn't demean himself by actually asking a question, or maybe he was regretting not preparing the ground for a question by offering at least a cursory greeting. Sidney couldn't tell.

But being Sidney, he decided immediately to come to his master's aid. Just a few words would do it: 'About the weather?'

Rishi's eyes widened and his mouth dropped open. It was as though he'd just seen a ghost – or had heard the first utterings of an oracle. Clearly, he would now need just a little more help.

'It's not getting any warmer, is it?' This was hardly the pronouncement of an oracle. Indeed, it was no less than the most banal of observations.

Nevertheless, it seemed to work, and Rishi managed to find his voice again. He posed a direct question to Sidney – indeed, the exact question that Sidney knew he'd come here to ask. 'Do you… do you know why? Do you know why the weather keeps getting colder?'

'*Me?* I don't… I mean, how could I…? How could I know? How could I possibly know? I'm just… well, you know… just your… just your… grateful servant. I… I don't know how…'

This response to Rishi's enquiry was not only peppered with plenty of fabricated hesitations but also Sidney had delivered it whilst wearing a suitably hangdog expression on his thin face, and with his shoulders bent forwards as if he expected to be struck. It was a masterclass in how to look submissive and, at the same time, to sound apologetic – for one's unavoidable and pitiful ignorance. And it worked.

A discomforted-looking Rishi instantaneously offered a series of *real* hesitations of his own. 'Yes… er, yes. Silly of me. I was just… Well, I just thought…

You know, if you'd heard... I mean, or if you'd... you know, read. But it doesn't matter. I realise... I realise. Erm. Look...' And that was the end of his hesitations. Along with his look of discomfort. He now looked on the verge of anger, and brought this most awkward and unexpected exchange to a conclusion with a drawn-out grunt and a wave of his arms that Sidney translated as 'Why did I bother? And why did I just humiliate myself in such a ridiculous manner?'

And then he was gone, and Sidney was left to his thoughts. To start with, these were his thoughts on why the weather had been on a downward temperature gradient for years. For, despite his protestations of ignorance on this matter, he did know why Britain was cooling year after year. In fact, he had known for some time now, ever since he'd come across the explanation in one of his most treasured tomes. It was an ancient book about the climate experienced in different parts of the world – and it included a comprehensive account of the part played by ocean currents in determining these local climates. So, he knew all about the Atlantic Conveyor and how this huge ocean current had been bringing warm water up from the Tropics to northern Europe for eons, thereby making Britain's climate significantly warmer than it would have been without it. Add in global warming and the result was, in place of the old temperate climate, a sub-tropical variety that provided ideal conditions for growing crops such as jowar and bajra.

However, in discussing the Atlantic Conveyor, that treasured tome had stressed just how fragile this ocean phenomenon was and how susceptible it would be to a general warming of the ocean – such as might be brought about by global warming. Then it might break down. It might simply stop working. Not immediately, but over a number of years. Which is precisely, Sidney believed, what was now happening. Britain's central heating was beginning to fail, and the country's climate – even with the impact of the increase in air temperatures due to global warming – was slipping back to temperate. He was almost certain of it. Just as he was almost certain that to have delivered this information to Rishi would not have been a good move. After all, how could the bearer of tidings that would lead to such a disastrous outcome for Rishi's family – his no longer being able to feed them – not in some way be implicated in the disaster? Sidney knew how Rishi thought – and how the majority of his family thought – and he knew, without a shadow of doubt, that to be the messenger who brought this message to their attention would not be a good choice to make. Much better to play dumb and to start to give some serious thought to how he himself might possibly avoid the catastrophe that awaited his master and his clan. And that way, keep himself alive.

Indeed, whilst he had a whole stack of chores to attend to, what had just happened had focused his mind on his own future to such an extent that he felt he had to make that start right away. Rishi wouldn't return, and it was very unlikely that any other members of the family would be dropping in any time soon. So, rather than setting about any of those chores, he sat on his bunk and he began to ponder – both his future and his survival.

It wasn't easy. Actually, it wasn't easy even to know where to start. His life up to now had been little more than a series of hardships. But now he was faced with more than just another hardship; he was faced with his probable personal extinction. It really was likely to get that bad. How could it not? When the food ran out, it ran out. And then there would be nobody in his life who would come to his aid. He would be on his own, and he would have to depend on his own resources. And it was when that thought finally found its way through the mist of his musings that he realised where he needed to start in mapping out a route to survival. It would be a consideration of the resources he had now and the resources he might be able to assemble when his world fell apart – when his world failed to provide him with even the modest amount of nourishment it did now.

So, this was what he considered, and it took him no time at all to decide that the resources he commanded now were minimal, to say the least. As regards a store of anything he could actually eat, he had nothing at all. Life nowadays made the idea of stockpiling comestibles of any sort more or less unthinkable, and in any event, doing something like that just wasn't in his nature. One lived one's life from day to day, and one was too thankful for each day's meals to give even a passing thought to putting aside a personal stash of food for the future. Even if, maybe with the help of a miracle, one could devise a way that it wouldn't just perish or rot. And that meant his only real resources were his health – of sorts – and his ingenuity.

These he could use to supplement his meagre diet, and he already did this by searching out berries and fungi and sometimes even roots. These, he could find in the 'wood'; the nearby scrappy expanse of land that was referred to as a 'wood', but that was covered mostly in scrub and that had avoided being cultivated because it was made up more of stone and rubble than it was of soil. Nobody really knew why, but there was a belief amongst some of the villagers that it had once been a dumping ground for the remains of bomb-damaged buildings back in the twentieth century. But whatever its genesis, it was a place where Sidney could forage for a modest amount of not-very-nourishing food – if, of course, he was prepared to spend the necessary time, and if he could avoid the attentions of Rishi and the rest of the family, all but one of whom tended to regard anything that could be eaten as primarily their own.

Nevertheless, no matter how much scavenging he might do, he was only too aware that it could never be enough to sustain his body. He knew he'd have to do a great deal more than just forage when the inevitable arrived, and he really had to fend for himself. But what? Health and ingenuity, even if bolstered by desperation, couldn't spirit food out of thin air.

Although, there again, he thought, maybe ingenuity on its own might be able to assist in its 'liberation' from others…

And that was it. It was the only way. He felt almost elated that he'd so quickly arrived at this obvious path to survival. When the food ran out, the obedient serf would have to become the resourceful thief. If he could no longer live on what Rishi's small patch of land could provide, he would have to live off his wits and his neighbours. Whatever he needed would be garnered by guile and at the expense of all those who had treated him with such disdain for so many years. Now it would be their turn to feel aggrieved and abused – and maybe the pangs of real hunger as their food disappeared.

It was a great idea – right up until it hit the wall of reality; something it did in no more than a minute after its conception. Elation was replaced with despair. Sidney knew he would make a terrible thief. Not only was it not in his nature but he was pretty sure that he had neither the audacity nor the skills to separate from his neighbours any of their daily bread. Furthermore, they – like him – would in all probability have little or no daily bread themselves, or if they did, they would be somewhere else. They would have moved off to wherever there was a chance of finding some food, and they would probably not take kindly to a camp follower intent on filching what little they had, even if he could bring himself to do this. It was hopeless. He couldn't exist as a thieving parasite, and he knew it.

Which rather meant that he had no way out of his predicament unless, just possibly, he joined them in their migration to who knows where and did his best to help them survive. But no, that wouldn't work either.

Even Rishi and his family would disown him, he was sure. And the likelihood of any of the other villagers allowing an alien to share their food – no matter what he might do for them – was remote in the extreme. He was staring in the face not just an uncertain future but also probably a very limited future. And as much as he might ponder his situation further and take his thinking in other directions, he knew he would only arrive at another wall of reality. At least he would today.

Yes, it was time to bring his mental juggling to an end. All he could do was file his thoughts away for now, and when he had the time, maybe recruit the assistance of his three friends before he tackled his thoughts again. His friends were no more likely to have answers themselves, but just debating his predicament with them would be more than helpful. One of them might even know how to avoid the impending catastrophe by somehow convincing a whole bunch of farmers to wake up to the inevitable and to do something practical and effective. Albeit this was highly unlikely.

Meanwhile, he would get about his business for the day and maybe even relish the fact that, however arduous it might prove to be, it wouldn't involve any more buckets of shit...

3.

'*Oui*, I can 'ardly cope. There are, as you say, not enough 'ours in the day. And I 'ave to admit, not always enough… well, let's say enough of the… essential ingredients…'

Sidney and Marc were now a few minutes into their radio exchange, and the conversation had landed on Marc's dependence on selling his 'drink' and the problems encountered in pursuing this trade.

And in response to that mention of essential ingredients, Sidney now made a necessary observation. 'The essential ingredients?' he queried. 'For hooch?'

'Sidney, 'ow often must I remind you? My English iz not good, but I do know that '"ooch" iz a… derisory term…'

'Derogatory,' corrected Sidney.

'Derisory, de… rogatory. What I'm saying iz that "'ooch" iz a name given to something of inferior quality, whereas my pastis iz anything but inferior. It'z, 'ow you say? A quality product.'

'Good or poor quality?'

'Sidney! 'Ow can you ask such a question? As I 'ave told you before, my pastis iz put together with all the traditional elements: star anise, liquorice, coriander, fennel—'

'And if you can't get the star anise or the liquorice or the coriander or the fennel, then you use a good old mix of dried egg, dried tarragon, neat ethylene and maybe a little extract of khat.'

''*Oo told you that?*'

'You did. Two weeks ago. When you were bragging about selling old rope to gullible peasants.'

There was a pause in the radio exchange. Then Marc found his voice again, but it was hardly convincing. 'Surely some mistake,' he said.

But even over the distance of several hundred miles, Sidney could tell that Marc was now smirking. 'You mean you put some benzene and some hemlock in as well?'

''Emlock? What iz 'emlock?'

'A rather poisonous plant.'

'Oh no. I don't put any poison in. And benzene's poisonous as well, izn't it? No, I just *adapt* the recipe now and again – but only with 'armless ingredients – that might be… well, a little more abundant at the time…'

'Like dandelions?'

'Did I tell you that as well?'

'Yes, you did. You even went on to explain how piss can help in achieving that essential pastis colour. And how the early morning—'

'Enough!' interrupted Marc. 'I plead… existential circumsessions.'

'Extenuating circumstances.'

'*Oui*. Extenuating circumstances. And I can't let my clients down. I 'ave to think of them.'

'Oh, I'm sure you do,' offered Sidney.

At which point, both hams burst into laughter. Because they both knew what each of them thought about Marc's indispensable clients. (Indispensable in the sense that unregulated medical services would, on their own, never be quite enough to keep Marc in the manner to which he'd now become accustomed, and certainly not whilst he remained in the cesspool that was now the south of France. So, those gullible peasants really were essential.)

When the laughter came to an end, it was Marc who picked up the conversation – by posing two questions. He appeared to have taken no offence at the aspersions cast on his 'quality product', and instead, he was clearly more interested in addressing what he suspected was the primary purpose of Sidney's contact through the ether. This was only too obvious from the nature of the questions – and their direct, not to say blunt, presentation.

'You going to starve, Sidney? Or you going to survive?'

Sidney was taken aback, and managed not much more than a mumble in response to Marc's sudden interrogation. 'Er, I... er...'

'No time for "ers", my friend. It'z time to think what you're going to do. If I've understood what you've been telling me over the past few weeks, you're... well, you're in a *situation très dangereuse*, and you can't wait around until it becomes a *situation mortelle*. You understand what I mean?'

Sidney did understand. Indeed, he understood very well that he simply couldn't hide from his predicament forever. And now here was a friend providing him with an honest and objective view of his plight – a view that he couldn't ignore. No longer could he simply ponder his dilemma and file it away for further consideration. His life, he now knew, depended on him doing something; on him doing anything other than procrastinating indefinitely and thus running out of time. But what? What could he do? And might Marc be able to help him? Might he have any ideas? Well, maybe he should just ask him. Directly. And so he did.

'Good bedside manner, Doc,' he commented. 'I'm duly impressed. And I do understand what you mean. But... well, it's one thing to recognise an ailment. It's quite another to know how to cure it. And what I mean is that I've already given my situation some serious thought. In fact, quite a lot of thought. But I've still no idea what to do. So... well, Doctor Marc, have *you* any idea what I should do? If we swapped places tomorrow, how would you go about avoiding that *situation mortelle?*'

There was silence from the other end of the connection. Marc was presumably gathering his thoughts. Then he spoke.

'Mmm, most of my patients pay me well for my services. That iz to say, all of them 'oo don't just go and die on me. But I suspect you're not looking to pay me at all. Just as well, then, that I'm in such a *humeur généreuse,* and that my pastis sales are going so well. For once, I can offer my services without any charge whatsoever...'

'And?' encouraged Sidney.

'You must watch. You must listen. You must gauge. And you must act – decidedly.'

'You mean "decisively".'

'*Oui, oui,*' responded Marc almost irritably. 'Or you may not get a second chance to act at all. And when you do act, don't do the obvious. Don't... you know, think that there izn't another way. And don't be squeamish. Be ruthless. Remember 'ow you've been treated all your life, and 'ow that gives you... 'Ow you say? Uh... a licence to do whatever you need to do – whatever you need to do to stay alive.'

This, it appeared, was to be the therapy advised for Sidney's unfortunate condition of being the unconsidered property of a family of farmers who were facing possible starvation and who would not prioritise his own well-being – or even give it a passing thought. It was clearly a studied therapy, and one with which it was difficult to find fault. However, it was entirely lacking in any specific advice, and it definitely didn't include a specific plan. It was just… well, general guidance, and Sidney couldn't help feeling a little disappointed. He had hoped for rather more.

There again, he thought, why would a pal sitting in Toulon have a ready-made plan for someone he'd never met, living in a place he'd never visited, and who was now experiencing a developing situation that could be envisaged only through its description over the airwaves? And furthermore, Marc was no fool. What he'd prescribed for Sidney's condition was not to be ignored. It might well prove to be a very effective treatment – when given a little more consideration and maybe a context in which to be applied.

Sidney therefore displayed no disappointment in his acknowledgement of Marc's counselling and instead thanked him – almost profusely. 'Marc, what can I say? That's really helpful. Especially that bit about not doing the obvious. And being ruthless. I'm sure you're right. And I won't be wasting any more time in not sorting out what I need to do. I promise. In fact, I'll be on the case straightaway. Just as soon as Rishi and Anika have brought me my breakfast, and Farid and Myra have helped me to dress.'

There was an immediate burst of laughter from Toulon. Marc knew all about Rishi and Rishi's wife, Anika, from previous discussions with Sidney – and how Anika was only ever not spiteful when she was being vicious. The idea of her being involved in delivering a meal to Sidney was simply risible. As was Farid, the pair's elder son, and Myra, their malevolent daughter, doing anything that might involve helping Sidney. After all, in respect of Sidney, their exclusive purpose was to make his life as miserable as possible. As would be confirmed only minutes after Sidney had concluded his early morning call to Marc and was setting about his chores for the day.

*

He was down on his knees, using a khurpa to hoe between the rows of sorrel in the family's veg plot. This was one of the few plants on the family's four-acre plot that was still doing well. Albeit, without something to accompany it, even a bumper crop of its leaves would do little to alleviate the family's impending shortage of food. It would make no more than a dent in their hunger. Nevertheless, the plants were still worth some serious attention. And today, this attention was being provided by a hunched-over Sidney – who hadn't heard Farid coming up behind him.

He was only aware of Farid's presence when he announced his arrival with a taunt: 'You planning on shitting or working, Sidney? Coz it looks to me as if you can't quite decide. Or maybe you're planning to do both? Have yourself a dump and then scuff up some weeds to hide what you've done. Maybe it's just as well I came when I did.'

Sidney's heart sank. He'd been taken by surprise, but that surprise had been instantly swamped by a flood of real dread. Farid hadn't hounded him for a few days now, and a full bout of torment was well overdue. Farid was here to make up for lost time.

There was nothing Sidney could do, other than play out his role as the submissive serf and just hope for the best. He first pulled himself upright, turned to face his 'better' and then, with his head slightly bowed, addressed him – meekly and politely. 'Hello Farid,' he began. 'I hope you are well.'

'And what about Myra? Why don't you hope Myra is well too?'

Sidney hadn't seen her, but Farid's eleven-year-old sister was there as well. And she'd now begun to giggle. She was already enjoying the show.

Sidney had little option other than to offer a grovelling apology, even though he knew it would be to no avail. So, with head still bowed, he addressed her directly. 'Myra, I am sorry. I didn't see you, but of course I hope you are well too.'

In response to this atonement, Myra simply giggled some more. Then she exchanged a wicked glance with her big brother, who was now ready to resume Sidney's torment.

He did this by delivering a second question to his victim. 'What did you say to our father? When he… when he saw you at the cabin? What did you say to upset him?'

'*What?*'

'You heard. You're a snivelling little runt. When you're not shitting in our veg plot, you're upsetting our father. Probably with something out of one of those fucking books of yours. I should have burnt them years ago – and you along with them.'

The word 'scapegoat' flashed across Sidney's mind. It might not have been entirely appropriate for his current status, but there was little doubt that, over the last couple of days, Rishi had failed to hide his anxiety over the future, and Farid had ascribed his father's display of heightened unease to that unexpected visit to Sidney's cabin. And whilst Farid loathed rather than loved his father, this spurious association of mood and event was more than enough to give the family's principal bully a reason to embark on yet another episode of oppression. Not that he really needed any reason at all.

In any event, the rules of such an assault meant Sidney was now obliged to mount a futile defence, and he began this with a comprehensive display of ignorance. After all, it was something that – unlike a display of any sort of knowledge – would be unlikely to antagonise Farid any more than he appeared to be antagonised already.

'Farid,' Sidney began, 'I don't know what you mean. And I don't know what you mean about me telling him anything, because I don't know anything. You know I don't know anything.'

'What do you take me for, you worm? I know you read all those books.'

'About the past, Farid. They're all about the past. There's nothing in them that's of any use for now. And nothing that would upset your father. Even if I'd told him anything. Which I didn't. I really didn't…'

'You're lying!'

'No, Farid. I swear. I didn't tell him anything. And I've no idea why he's upset.'

At this point, Sidney expected another tongue-lashing from Farid. It was how these exchanges normally went on until Farid ran out of steam or simply got bored. But instead of that verbal lashing, Sidney received a very physical kick. Without any warning at all, Farid had swung back his leg and then delivered a leather-covered foot to Sidney's left thigh with as much force as he could manage. Indeed, with so much force that Sidney toppled sideways and ended up lying across two rows of sorrel, neither of which he'd yet addressed with his khurpa.

This wasn't the way the game was normally played. Farid had occasionally punched him in the past – 'playfully' but painfully – and he sometimes slapped him around the face, more as an act of humiliation than one of violence. But he'd never kicked him like this before. And neither had he followed up one kick with another as the object of his bullying lay on the ground. Which is what he'd done now – with the vocal encouragement of his hateful sister. And it didn't stop there: Farid was just continuing to kick him, aiming all his shots at Sidney's stomach, with most of them finding their mark.

Sidney was in trouble, and he had no idea how to react, other than to curl himself up into a ball and instinctively hide his head in his hands, lest his tormentor decided to redirect his kicks to that most vulnerable part of his body. That didn't happen. Farid just continued to focus on Sidney's torso, and he only stopped when Viraj charged him and sent him sprawling onto a half-picked row of lettuces and the remains of a row of carrots.

Then there was just silence. Myra wasn't giggling any more. Sidney was too confused to make any sort of sound. Viraj was just standing there, mute and stony-eyed, above Farid. And Farid was clearly stunned and entirely speechless.

It therefore fell to Viraj to bring the silence to an end, and he did this by finding his voice and using it to condemn his brother's behaviour in the most forceful and strident manner. He simply spat out his words: 'You stupid savage! You stupid bloody halfwit! What do you think you're doing? What do you think gives you the right to treat Sidney like that? He might not be one of us, but that doesn't mean you can kick him to death. And what would father say? How do you think he'd react to you killing or maiming such a valuable possession? He'd probably kill *you*.'

Sidney had now gathered himself enough to absorb what Viraj was saying, and also to appreciate that Viraj's older, bigger brother was simply taking this verbal mugging without any attempt at retaliation. Farid had managed to raise himself from the ground, but he appeared still to be too stunned to do much more than gaze at his attacker, his eyes staring and his mouth wide open in amazement. After all, what had happened to him was just so extraordinary.

Farid was nineteen years of age. He had an intellect that was more than a little underweight, but a body that was more than a little overweight. He was a pretty big guy. Viraj, who was not quite sixteen, was much smaller – albeit he was very sturdy – and he was twice as intelligent as Farid. Quite how he and his older brother now dealt with each other, Sidney wasn't sure. Although over recent times, he had observed that Farid seemed more wary of Viraj than he had in the past, and he now never teased or goaded him; something he'd done repeatedly for years. So, the balance of power had probably been shifting for some time, and both brothers may well have known that a sturdy (and rather athletic) body was more than a match for a flabby dumpling of a body, especially one that was home to a plainly inferior brain.

And now... well, faced with a situation that called for an immediate intervention, Viraj hadn't hesitated to confirm that power shift in the most dramatic way possible. That said, Sidney was already thinking that what he'd just witnessed hadn't primarily been a confirmation of supremacy by son number two over son number one, but that this was just an inevitable aspect of what son number one had just done. Yes, the real reason Viraj had attacked his brother and then berated him so forcefully was that, unlike his parents and his two siblings, he did not despise their captive *daas,* but instead he rather admired him, and he clearly didn't like to see him attacked in this way.

Farid was never happier than when he was tormenting Sidney – often with Myra as his audience or sometimes as his active assistant. Viraj, on the other hand, had never tormented Sidney and hadn't even scolded him or reproached him – something the other family members did at every opportunity. Furthermore, over the past year or so, on those rare occasions when Sidney and Viraj were alone, Viraj would ask him about his books and his radio. He'd been showing an increasing interest in Sidney's store of knowledge and his bank of 'magic' equipment. And even though Sidney had been cautious about revealing the breadth of his knowledge or the scope of the magic afforded by the equipment, Viraj was always eager to learn more – and in doing so, he'd come to accept Sidney as his teacher. And in doing that, he'd also come to respect Sidney in a way that the rest of the family would have found unfathomable, just as they would have been unable to comprehend that respect can sometimes lead to admiration. But it had. And how could it not? In Viraj's eyes, Sidney was something special. A lowly servant, yes, but also something much more: a portal, a portal to another world beyond the scrappy four acres that was Viraj's life. And he knew things; things that were beyond the comprehension of the rest of his family – and, indeed, of the whole village – because he had looked into that other world and he had seen what it held. He had seen that it held more than rows of shrivelling crops, a once-handsome home now run-down and damp, a collection of neighbours who were surly and dense, and a culture that ruled out both wisdom and joy.

Just elements of all these thoughts went through Sidney's mind as he lay on the ground. They would all, no doubt, be explored at greater length when he was alone in his cabin. And as regards the immediate… Well, that called for a cautious stillness on Sidney's part as the other participants to the recent incident withdrew from the scene of the action. Myra was the first to leave, walking slowly away without even glancing at Farid. Then Farid himself shuffled off, wiping soil from his clothes, but failing to wipe a look of defeat from his face. And then it was Viraj's turn, but not before he'd helped Sidney to his feet and enquired of his health.

'You OK?' he asked. 'You took quite a beating.'

'I'm fine,' Sidney declared with a smile – even though he wasn't, and he wouldn't be for some time yet. Farid had hurt him a lot.

Still smiling, he then went on to offer Viraj his thanks. As he did this, he became aware that it was the first time he'd had cause to offer any of the family any real thanks for anything they'd done. And this made him ensure that Viraj understood just how grateful he was. 'Thanks. Thanks for… well, for saving my life. I don't think your brother would have known when to stop. And Viraj, I do know how you didn't hesitate for a second – and that what you've just done may… well, may have some awkward consequences. So, thank you again. I'm in your debt for all time.'

Sidney realised immediately that the ending of his expression of gratitude was possibly a little melodramatic. It had certainly given Viraj a problem in putting together a response. He was now clearly embarrassed and just as clearly wanted nothing more than to leave the scene of the action as soon as possible. This he did by nodding to Sidney – undoubtedly to signify that he'd accepted Sidney's thanks – and then advising him to keep out of Farid's way for the rest of the day.

That advice wasn't necessary. Sidney had already decided to keep out of his way for as long as he could. Even though he doubted he would be the object of Farid's feet – or fists – ever again. He now had a guardian angel – and a new factor to introduce into his calculus of how to survive the impending collapse of his world.

Imran, 2033

No rest for months. Onward and onward. By cart. By truck. By bus. But mostly by foot. Shoes worn through. Feet worn out. Legs worn out. Soul worn out. Would it ever end? Roads that snaked on forever. Tracks that went on for mile after mile. And hills. And mountains. And plains. A world so big. A world so much bigger than his home near Lahore.

But Imran had to go on. There was no turning back. No return to the place he knew. To the place he'd spent all his life. Until he couldn't anymore. Too dry. Too hot. Far, far too hot. Nothing grew anymore. No wheat for the puri. No rice for the tehri. People dying. People dying of starvation.

Had to get out. Had to head north. Had to keep heading north. Afghanistan. Different but familiar.

And hostile. Uzbekistan. More hostile. And threatening Kazakhstan. Where people died. Then Russia. And now hope more than fear.

More trucks. More buses. Organised. Purposeful. A conveyor. A conveyor taking him further north. Just as promised. Him and thousands like him. Willing munitions for an assault on the West. Not that he or the others saw it that way. For them, it was just the escape they wanted. And they were fed. Bread. Black Russian bread. And red Russian soup. Made with something called 'beetroots'. Not good, but not bad. And they were also given clothes. Musty Russian great coats. Musty padded jackets. Garments to keep out the chill of the north. And the chill of the sea!

Yes, he, like so many before him, had made it. After all those months on the move. A sprawling camp. Row after row of neat canvas tents. With soldiers. With guards. With order. With constraints. But also with a programme. A schedule. With a schedule that meant it was his turn today. His and a whole host of others. Most, like him, from those harsh and hot lands to the south. All thrown together to serve a Russian cause. All willing and eager to leave Russian shores.

So now surly seamen. All scowls and no smiles. Their fishing boat rigged for a new sort of work. For now, they didn't fish, but they ferried instead. A new catch of travellers to wherever they choose. And this lot for England. Across the North Sea.

So, then came the waves. And cries of scared men. And vomit. And stink. And no one to care. Four hundred men without any friends. Cramped on the deck or, worse, down below. And all alone. Homeless refugees in search of a home. At sea. At the mercy of the sea. Maybe it had been a mistake to come. All this way. And now all this purgatory. With laughing seamen. With scornful seamen. With nothing familiar. With a fear of the worse. With a fear of coming to grief in that most unfamiliar sea...

Yet sleep came. For Imran, it came and consoled him. And then, through the mist, there was land. Awake now. Aware of the moment. And aware of another vessel. A British flag flying. Watching. Observing the Russians, and how they would land their catch. But doing nothing. Always doing nothing. Powerless to stem this now constant beaching of men from the south.

The first dinghy, already away. Soon to return for another batch of settlers. All yearning for a new place to settle. A kind place. A cool place. Somewhere that wasn't roasting hot. And where there was food. And help. And so many others like themselves. Some of them in powerful positions. The most powerful positions in the land. So, nothing to stop them leaving that beach and starting a new life on that longed-for refuge-island.

And everyone happy. The Russian rulers happy. A new consignment of trouble for those cocky Western states. Something more to add to their growing burden. To bring them to their knees. And the Russian fishermen happy. Another bumper bonus to fund another day on land. And then the new Britons... happy beyond words. And none more so than Imran.

All those months. All those miles. All those days wondering whether the days would run out. Whether his days on this earth were numbered. But now, success! Now nirvana! Now a heaven he could touch. A heaven he could breathe in. Could revel in – till the end of his days. Yes. No going back! No longer a fear of drought. No longer a fear of famine. Or a fear of disease. And no more suffering. No more anguish. Instead, just the prospect of everything he'd ever wanted. Nothing less than the prospect of access to everything he and everybody else in this world deserved…

4.

His battered copy of the *RSPB Handbook of British Birds,* published in 2006, told him that nearly a century and a half ago, there were almost 250 species of birds that could regularly be found in the UK. Now, Sidney was aware of only five.

There were the crows and the magpies. There were always the crows and the magpies. Always searching and always foraging; the crows cocky and the magpies wary, making their escape on the wing at the first hint of a threat. Then there were the herons, as inedible as the corvids and somehow able to make a living out of almost nothing. And that left the two smaller birds that could still be seen: on odd occasions, diminutive and dowdy house sparrows, constantly hopping around in the dust; and in winter, large flocks of hardy redwings, still managing to arrive in substantial numbers from Russia and elsewhere – and presumably still able to find enough worms and berries to make their flight here worthwhile.

But that was it. No longer any flashes of strong colours. No longer any displays of sublime aerial skills. No longer any soaring on large, feathered wings. What it must have been like to have witnessed such an abundance of avian delights, Sidney could barely imagine. And when he did try to imagine it, he simply succumbed to deep gloom. That he'd been born too late to relish this kaleidoscopic spectacle made him feel despondent beyond words, and it simply reinforced his belief that the country of his birth was now more threadbare than it had ever been before. Not that it wasn't set to become more threadbare still…

Yes, it wasn't just its birds that had disappeared. So too, as the constant gnawing in his stomach reminded him, had the prospect of its ability to continue to feed him. No longer could he ignore it. Hunger and its camp follower of potential starvation may have arrived with little fanfare, but they appeared to be establishing themselves so firmly that they would soon demand his attention like never before. They would certainly eclipse his regret at the loss of Britain's birds. And they would also ensure he would spend even more time seeking comfort and advice from his trio of radio hams.

And maybe this evening it should be Sonia; Sonia the songster from Saskatoon, a woman who sometimes still sang for her supper, but was more often to be found in a soup kitchen, handing out meals to some of the more desperate inhabitants of a city that was now home to well over 10 million people. Saskatoon was, after all, one of the few places in North America that hadn't yet been submerged by the deluge from the south, and although under an increasing threat of inundation, it was still holding out. And Sonia was still able to use her radio…

Sidney had called her, but as she made very clear immediately, she had just been about to call him. She had some news about a woman. In Scotland!

'*Sidney,*' she shouted, '*you won't believe it, but I've found you a girl!*'

'*What?*'

'A girl. A woman. On your own tiny little island. And she's got a radio. She's on HF, and we've been having such a good chat—' Sonia sounded as though she were drunk. Her delivery was very excited and slightly manic at the same time. And she wasn't going to be interrupted.

'Sonia, what—?'

'Her name is Dorothy, and she's part English and part Scottish. And she was very interested in—'

'Sonia, slow down.'

'She was fascinated to hear that you had all your books and that you'd studied them so much. And that—'

'*Sonia,*' Sidney shouted into his microphone, '*I'm going to run out of juice before I know what the hell you're talking about. You've got to slow down and tell me who the heck this… Dorothy is – and where she is. I mean, how and—?*'

'Sorry,' interjected a calmer-sounding Sonia, 'but finding another ham isn't exactly an everyday event. And this one's in Scotland. I mean, Scotland! And well… with you being in England…'

Sidney was now attempting to assimilate this unexpected news from Canada, whilst, at the same time, trying to evaluate the possibility of making radio contact with anybody in Scotland. Which, he soon decided, was zero. In teaching himself about HF radio communication, he'd learnt that the HF radio signals 'bend' through the earth's ionosphere levels back down to the earth's surface and, sometimes, back up and down again. That was why he was able to talk to his friends in Namibia, France and Canada – or in theory, to anybody else on the planet – just as long as they were far enough away. However, if another ham was too close to allow for one of these 'signal skips', then perversely, he or she would be out of range, and Sidney would only ever be able to make contact if he had access to what was known as 'ground-wave propagation' – which he didn't. Talking to people thousands of miles away – or even as close as maybe just 500 miles away – was possible. Talking to people less than, say, 400 miles away was just about impossible. Sonia was in reach. This Dorothy was not in reach, and she never would be with his current equipment.

'Anyway,' Sonia continued, 'I know you probably won't be able to contact her yourself. You'll be far too close. But I'll certainly be happy to act as a go-between. And that's what Dorothy suggested: that I relay stuff between you and her, and that—'

'What stuff?' interrupted Sidney. 'And on the subject of which, what stuff has she revealed about herself? I mean, where exactly is she in Scotland? And how has she got access to a radio? As far as I know, north of the border – and I mean the new border – there just aren't any radios at all. Or any English speakers, come to that. I mean, I assume you have been talking to her in English?'

There was a brief hiatus before Sonia replied to Sidney's enquiries, and when she did, she sounded more than a little flustered. 'Er... well, yes. Of course, we were talking in English. But well, she wouldn't tell me exactly where she was, and I don't think I asked her about how she'd got a radio. In fact, I'm not too sure she told me a great deal about herself at all. But she was very interested in you.'

'You mean you've told her all about me but without knowing anything about her?'

Sonia replied to this question, sounding more flustered than ever. 'Well, I only told her where you were and what you did. You know, your scribing stuff, and all your studying stuff – and how many books you had. That sort of thing. I didn't tell her a great deal else.'

'Sonia,' Sidney pronounced, with a smile in his voice, 'there isn't a great deal else to tell.'

'Yes, I see what you mean,' responded a sheepish-sounding Sonia. 'But she just sounded so interested and so... well, very nice...'

'*Very nice?*'

If Sonia had been properly attuned to that retort, she would have recognised there was no anger in it, only a good dose of bemused delight. After all, Sidney was no less than fascinated by this unearthing of an English-speaking ham north of the border, and at the same time, no less than revelling in Sonia's trusting naïvety. It was why he found her to be such a good pal. If the devil himself had turned up to her soup kitchen, she would have first of all ladled him out some food – and then she would have asked him whether he needed to take the weight off his hooves. She was, herself, just the living manifestation of 'very nice'. As was only too apparent when she continued with her revelation.

'She seemed to be very interested in me as well. You know, where I was and how I was… you know… surviving.'

'And so, of course, you told her. I mean, why wouldn't you? After she'd told you so much about herself.'

'Well…' Here, Sonia was stuck for words. It must finally have occurred to her that she'd had a rather one-sided conversation with a woman in Scotland – if the woman was indeed in Scotland – and that she may have been just a little indiscreet, if not a little foolish, in revealing anything at all about both herself and her long-standing friend in England.

However, before she had an opportunity to decide what to say and whether an apology might be in order, Sidney stepped in to help her. 'I'm winding you up. Can't you tell? Hell, you've known me long enough by now to know that I never get angry – at least, not with you – and all you've done is to be yourself. Which means you've been open, helpful, trusting and just a teeny-weeny bit naïve. Indeed, I would have been surprised and disappointed if you'd been anything else.

'And no harm's been done, has it? All you've actually done is establish contact with another human being, who sounds as though she might well become a friend. And what's more, she's in my neighbourhood! Not quite next door, and probably no more reachable than if she lived on Saturn. However, even just knowing she's there – maybe just a few hundred miles away – is very comforting. And who knows? One day, she might even come within reach somehow. And then she can tell me a little more about herself – face to face, as it were.'

There was still a smile in Sidney's voice, and he was genuinely trying to reassure Sonia that he welcomed her news, even if the news was a little thin on any detail about 'nice Dorothy' and much thinner in content than whatever she herself had supplied to her new find. And he succeeded in his goal.

When Sonia spoke again, she no longer sounded flustered, but instead controlled – and contrite. 'I've been such a clot. I should have been so much more careful. I'm really sorry. I really am.'

Sidney hesitated briefly before he responded, largely because he wasn't quite sure what 'clot' meant. He suspected it was an archaic English word hanging on to its existence by its fingernails in Canada – and that it meant 'idiot'. And his suspicion was certainly strong enough to enable him to assume this when he did then acknowledge Sonia's contrition. 'Come on, you've given me some really good news. That's not something to be sorry about or to feel foolish about. Far from it. And what we need to do now is simply to focus on what to do next. I mean, how we develop a relationship with Dorothy: yours directly and mine very indirectly – as in via Saskatoon. And what I suggest is that, when you next speak to Dorothy, you make very clear that I'm delighted to know that she's "so close", and that I agree with her that she and I should seek to make contact and keep in contact – through you – as well as your keeping in contact with her directly. And to kick things off, why don't you tell her about the food situation here. You know, that it's looking more and more bleak. And then invite her to tell you how she's getting on with food where she is. That might even encourage her to tell you a little more about herself. Even whereabouts she is in Scotland. And if nothing else, we'll get an idea of how friendly she's prepared to become – if she's prepared to become friendly at all...'

'Oh, I'm sure she wants to become a pal. I'm really certain of it. And maybe I should have made it clearer. I mean, she wasn't just relieved to have made contact; she was *thrilled* to have made contact. Even if she wasn't very forthcoming about herself.'

'Fine. I mean, really fine. We all need all the friends we can get. I certainly do. And I suppose she does as well. Let's just hope you can ensnare her with your charm and make sure we have one more friendly ham in the team. What's more, I've never had dealings with a Dorothy before. And Dorothy sounds rather sexy...'

Immediately, a burst of laughter rang out in Sidney's ears. It was just what he'd hoped for in his campaign to relieve Sonia of any residual guilt from her exchange with Dorothy. After all, he knew Sonia was well aware that, given his solitary and cloistered existence, his reference to Dorothy sounding sexy was akin to a blind man passing comment on the beauty of a sunset. It was meant to amuse her – and it had succeeded in doing this. However, at the same time, her chortling response reminded him of how much he was at ease with this woman; a woman whom he'd never met and, in all likelihood, would never meet. It almost made him cry, and he realised straightaway that he would have to distract himself with a change of topic to make quite sure he didn't.

'Anyway, enough of new *amours*. How are you getting on? And is the enemy still at the gate, or have they decided to pack up and go home?' he queried.

'*Go home?* We should be so lucky. As far as they're concerned, this *is* their home, and we're just irritating squatters – some inconvenient reminders of the past that will soon be just a feature of the past. They're never going to give up, Sidney, and one day they will succeed. And then… well, if we're lucky, it will be reservation time for us. And if we're not… well, who can say. You might find us tipping up on the shores of your own little island. After all, you've always told me that you crave the company of like-minded souls.'

This time it was Sidney's turn to laugh. And after he'd spluttered out a chuckle, he responded to Sonia's improbable forecast with a more serious observation: 'Well, I hope it never comes to that. "Out of the frying pan and into the fire" wouldn't do it justice. As you well know. And at least you've still got some food there.'

'Yes, I suppose I shouldn't joke. I mean, I haven't forgotten your own situation. It's just that things are certainly not getting any better here, and I really don't know how long it will be before… well, you know what. And I've never fancied the idea of being a subjugated minority in my own land.'

As she'd started this exchange with Sidney, Sonia had been sounding ecstatic, bordering on the inebriated. She now sounded just deeply morose. It was therefore time for Sidney to bring the exchange to an end and to send her away with something that would lift her mood. This he did by returning to the subject of her original remarkable news, by reminding her that finding any new voices on this planet was a cause for huge optimism, and by stating he was more grateful than he could say that this particular new voice was so close to his home. Just as long as, he stipulated, its owner didn't play the bagpipes, a musical instrument of sorts that, according to one of his tomes, made a noise that was something of an acquired taste.

Sidney wasn't entirely sure whether this addendum provided a genuine uplift to his friend in Canada or simply a dose of incomprehension, but when she signed off, she sounded cheerful once again and definitely not morose. He was therefore suitably content, albeit just a little morose himself.

It was inevitable. Sonia had uncovered a new associate: a new radio-ham contact somewhere in his own back yard. But despite the relative proximity of this new contact, not only would he never be able to talk to her directly, but also he would never be able to meet her. As he himself had said to Sonia, Dorothy might as well be located on Saturn, and his fantasy of them one day being able to come face to face was just that: a fantasy. He knew all too well that he would never be able to go north of that border, the one that for years now had split Britain in two, and it was inconceivable that Dorothy would ever be able to cross this border *from* the north. Even if she ever wanted to and could, in some way, make it all the way south from Scotland. She might become an ally of sorts, but how could she become a proper friend when he couldn't talk to her directly and when he'd never, in their lifetimes, get that face-to-face encounter? Sonia's news was good news, but it was also sad news. And right now, it was its sad aspect that was dominating Sidney's thoughts. If only he'd been born when all those birds were still around – when he and people like him had the freedom to do what they chose and to meet who they chose; a state of affairs he knew existed back then, thanks primarily to his mother and since reinforced by his reading of some of his books. And what did he have now? Just voices through the ether and a possible new voice – one that was tantalisingly close, but one that he would never himself hear.

This was no good. He was beginning to feel sorry for himself when he knew full well that he should be relishing the fact that his disparate little community was about to become just a little less little. And even though he might not be able to talk to its newest member directly, any addition to his vital support group could only be welcomed – and thereafter cherished. So, it was time to slough the morose, and time to allow himself just a brief spell of rejoicing. Just before he settled down for the night – and once again pondered his predicament and whether he might soon be joining the ranks of all those birds that had disappeared. Some of whom had no doubt disappeared because they'd run out of food…

5.

When Sidney awoke, he decided to award himself just a few minutes more in his bunk – and whilst there, he would direct his thoughts to how he'd arrived where he was now. It was something he did every few weeks, as he'd promised himself long ago that he would never forget his past, and regular mental revisions were his way of making quite sure that he didn't. Soon, therefore, he was thinking about the one square mile of Herefordshire that, for the first twenty years of his life, had been his home.

It hadn't been easy there. With so many others dumped on to that same square mile and with so few resources, it had been a constant struggle to do little more than exist. But he had done more than exist – largely thanks to the efforts of his parents, who were as strong-willed as they were intelligent, and who were both intent on making sure that their one and only child didn't just have enough food for his belly but more than enough sustenance for his mind. They taught him everything they knew – and between them, they knew an awful lot. So young Sidney soon learnt to read and write, and armed with those two essential tools, he was then able to make inroads into a range of other disciplines. Unlike many of his peers, he became adept at mathematics, and with the help of his father, who had been one of the last electrical engineers in the country, he secured a good understanding of applied physics. With the assistance of his mother, he even gained an understanding of world geography and world history – two areas of knowledge that were largely neglected, even within the boundaries of the reservation. And then, without any real warning, his world hit the buffers.

The residents of the rest of Britain had decided their need for that precious square mile (and a whole string of other square miles throughout Britain) trumped the need of its existing residents, and therefore these residents had to leave. They would have to be resettled elsewhere. Which, for Sidney and his parents, meant that they ended up in Worcestershire under the 'guardianship' of an extended family there, a family that was apparently in need of three pairs of hands to support its ever-growing needs.

It was dreadful. All three of them were overworked – and underfed – for years. And this living hell only came to an end when the entire family, along with Sidney's dear parents, succumbed to an incurable dose of measles. Or at least that's what the local village elders decided it was. Just before they decided how to carve up the dead family's now-vacant property and how to dispose of the one surviving 'sentient chattel' on the property, the one who had been spared the deadly effects of whatever had killed the other two chattels and their owners – and who was now no longer needed. And that's how Sidney found himself at Hope Farm: Rishi's ironically named smallholding, Rishi being his new guardian and the man, Sidney learnt, who had paid barely a pittance for his family's new acquisition. After all, if one's primary role was to labour, it was nothing more than a drawback to have any other abilities. Not only might they cause one's betters to feel uncomfortable but they might also incubate all sorts of undesirable aspirations. And that, in turn, could lead to all sorts of problems.

Sidney, however, would be no problem whatsoever. He'd hated where he'd come from – and more so now that it had consumed his parents – but Hope Farm promised a far brighter future. There was so much to recommend it. To start with, Rishi, whilst rather aloof in his manner and sometimes short of temper, was plainly not a completely unreasonable man. He even suggested to Sidney that his unfortunate writing abilities might be put to good use – for his personal benefit. Furthermore, it soon became apparent that Rishi would act as something of a shield from the attentions of his wife and their two problem children – not an inconsiderable plus point at all. But what really made Sidney feel so optimistic about his new home had little to do with its existing occupants; rather it was much more to do with his new billet: a falling-down cabin sandwiched between a hedge and a large pond, well away from the family house – and containing the sort of treasure trove he could only ever have dreamt of.

Whoever had originally lived at Hope Farm had clearly been blessed with an enquiring mind, and one that had demanded the collection of books – when, many years ago, books had still been produced and books had still been read. And there really were hundreds of them, all dumped in this cabin, probably several decades ago, there to await their transformation into dust. However, that hadn't happened yet, and that meant Sidney had been gifted not just a very cluttered, falling-down cabin but also his very own library. He could barely believe it. Just as he could barely believe that such a store of knowledge hadn't inspired at least one of the Hope Farm family to have taught himself or herself to read. No matter how difficult that might have been. However, even Viraj hadn't done this, probably because he'd been actively discouraged by the rest of his family. And they, Sidney believed, were only interested in leading a joyless existence on their little patch of land, and their learning anything at all that might distract them from their joyless stupor would have been avoided at all costs.

It was the same with all the radio kit. It held for them no fascination whatsoever. It was just one more thing to be avoided. Yes, as well as the books, Sidney had inherited the potential ability to communicate with other people, probably other people like himself!

He'd known this wouldn't be easy, and even with the knowledge he'd acquired from his father, activating and then operating an antediluvian transmitter and receiver would be more than a minor challenge. An antenna was still in place: a 100-foot length of fourteen-gauge wire stretching from a pole on the cabin to the one remaining oak tree at the edge of the wood. But whether that would work and whether the actual kit was operable, or repairable if it wasn't, he just didn't know. Well, in the event, the antenna did work, and so too did the radio. Albeit it took him nearly six months to breathe life into the ancient apparatus, and then another six months before he'd been able to recruit his modest panel of radio correspondents: three other souls from around the planet who had similar kit and a similar desire to find some faraway pals.

And all three of them would have appreciated how a mere *chokra* could not ignore his duties indefinitely, and that, at some point, he would have to admit to himself that there was a time for recalling the past and a time to get on with disposing of a bucket load of shit. After which, there would no doubt be a whole series of chores that required his attention.

There were. The ordure having been dumped in the wood, there was then some kindling to find (an increasingly difficult task), and then there was Kaalki the *khachchar* to tend to; the family's gentle mule, who seemed to know that, in Sidney, he had a fellow servant of the family. He wasn't just gentle and docile with Sidney, he was positively friendly, often nudging his partner-in-toil with his pretty, black nose and, sometimes, even insisting that his ears were rubbed before he'd let Sidney leave him. His affection, Sidney decided, was beginning to challenge or even exceed the pleasure of his having his own library and a privileged access to a two-way radio. And it certainly helped to set him up for the more onerous demands of the day, which, on this day, would involve the repair of a crumbling and fragile roof…

Hope Farm's main building (the family's sprawling home) was not in good order. Some of it was nearly 500 years old and so decrepit that it had now been adapted (with the help of a sledgehammer) to house Kaalki and the ancient wagon he pulled, together with a large collection of discarded implements, fittings, tools and genuine detritus – all of which did little more than buttress the walls of what must once have been a desirable and comfortable home. This older part of the building was connected, via what years ago had been a conservatory (but was now a spacious hencoop), to the significantly newer part that was occupied by Rishi and his family. This being where they ate and slept – and bickered and rowed – and for which those roof repairs were now urgent. It seemed, according to Rishi, that the roof over this part of the 'mansion' was letting in a lot more water than the odd dribble that Sidney had learnt to live with in his falling-down cabin, and it was now imperative that Sidney, along with Viraj, took himself onto that failing roof and sorted out the leaks.

Sidney was no roofer, but with Viraj's help and the careful placing of some rusting sheets of corrugated iron, he at least managed to make it look as though he'd made an acceptable repair. Better still, with nobody around to eavesdrop, he and Viraj had been able to have a long conversation on the geography of the world – something of which Viraj was almost entirely ignorant – and then, even a discussion about how, in the past, people had been able to experience this geography first-hand by travelling around it in ships and in planes. Sidney was simply delighted at how Viraj was now so openly keen to be enlightened by the family's lowly helper, but at the same time, he couldn't help feeling desperately sorry that a boy of Viraj's age could be so comprehensively ignorant of the planet on which he lived.

Why, he asked himself, had what he believed to be the majority of mankind cast away so much knowledge, and why had it so little appetite for its restitution? Unless, of course, there were far more Virajs than he knew, all of them thirsting to fill their minds with a consignment of insights and facts.

Alternatively, maybe there were too many Farids in the modern world, dullards and dunces whose primary aim was to bully their peers into the same state of ignorance as themselves, and in that way, ensure that humanity continued its blinkered and miserable existence in a grossly impoverished world. And as regards the Farid of Hope Farm, well, he was only notable by his absence today. Since that physical reproach by his brother, he'd kept a very low profile, and had gone out of his way – sometimes literally – to avoid Sidney. Indeed, the only barbs that had still been thrown Sidney's way were from Myra, and these were easy to endure, especially as Myra now seemed much less confident in her spite. Without Farid, she could barely even irritate Sidney, let alone intimidate him.

So, when, towards the end of the day, Sidney finally made it to the refuge of his cabin, he was in an unusually good mood. Kaalki and Viraj had both lifted his spirits, Myra had been unable to depress them, and Farid hadn't even been around to try. Whatever fate might have in store for him hadn't gone away, but just at the moment, any fears for the future were in abeyance, and he could almost relish his existence. And he could certainly harness the power of HF radio signals to raise one or two of his real friends. Or he could when he'd dealt with Sanjiv...

Sanjiv had arrived at Sidney's door only minutes after he'd gone inside his cabin to take a brief rest on his bunk. And not only was his arrival a very unusual event, in that Sanjiv always scheduled his visits to the village scribe, but the expression on the village warden's face was also very unusual, in that it was one of alarm mixed with fear. When he then began to speak, before Sidney even had a chance to offer a greeting, it was the fear that took over almost entirely. And there was fear in his voice as well. 'I need you to write a letter,' he said. 'Immediately!'

'Of course, Mr Kumar,' responded Sidney automatically. 'I'll just get my stuff…'

Sanjiv rubbed his chin, looked more fearful than ever, and then turned around to face the pond before sitting himself down on the cabin's deck. Meanwhile, Sidney found his clipboard, took a few sheets of paper from a pile on the floor, and then rummaged around on his makeshift desk until he found one of his pens. Armed with this equipment, and more bemused than ever at the entirely unexpected nature of this visitation, he then joined his client on the deck and invited him to begin his dictation.

Sanjiv cleared his throat and then he started. He sounded nervous and as though he had aged years in just days. His voice had changed from being simply old-age thin to being hoary croaky; it was something like a creak, made to sound more ancient still by that overlay of fear. And the reason for this lay in the words he uttered. For they concerned his desire to inform the regional governor's office – without delay – of the fact that four strangers had been observed to the west of the village. And that, whilst it could not be confirmed without doubt, it was considered highly likely by the two (reliable) villagers who'd seen them – and clearly heard their speech – that they were from over the border; that they were followers of that other faith!

Sidney raised his eyebrows in surprise. How could he not? Nobody came over that border, and the idea of four people doing so, and then making it this far south of the border wasn't really credible. Hope Farm was part of a village that sat almost twenty miles from that line that divided the country in two, and a visitation from a quartet of 'northerners' was as improbable as a visitation from outer space. But here was Sanjiv reporting that it had happened, and clearly very confident that it had indeed happened. His fear was the confirmation.

However, Sidney realised he couldn't abandon his professionalism, and he now focused on committing to paper the conclusion to Sanjiv's brief missive, which concerned a request for some urgent guidance from the regional governor's office as to how to act in response to this unheard-of event – rounded off, of course, with the normal sycophantic tributes to the governor himself. With this completed, he then invited Sanjiv to append his signature to the script in the normal way, making quite sure that, at the same time, he didn't betray his thoughts that the news the script contained was anything but normal. Even though it was news that would probably have little trouble in overriding his concerns about starving to death – certainly in the short term, and probably for some time thereafter.

Sidney was very relieved when Sanjiv had left him – this time, with neither a spoken farewell nor a payment for his work – and he immediately began to process what he'd heard and what it might mean for a *chokra* whose only proven friends were a mule and a handful of pals in faraway places. And just as he was wondering whether his having a new ally in Viraj might mean he wouldn't have to face the possible consequences of this new event all on his own, his attention was caught by a light bulb. It was a small green one on his receiver, and it was blinking on and off. It was telling him that one of those faraway proven friends was now trying to call him.

It was Sonia. And after contact with her had been established, she had some more to tell him about Dorothy. 'Sidney, I've been in contact with Dorothy again, and she wanted you to know what's going on in southern Scotland—'

'Southern Scotland?' interrupted Sidney. 'Is that where she is? You mean you've pinned her down to the bottom half of Scotland?'

'Er, well, yes. Didn't I say? I meant to. It's just that I thought I ought to…' Sonia was being very Sonia again. Whenever there was information to impart, it infrequently came in a logical order – especially when there was a juicy bit in it that she wanted to impart first. Nevertheless, it was still possible to prompt her into a rather more ordered presentation, as Sidney was about to witness.

'Sorry, Sidney. I'll start again, shall I? And I'll start by telling you that Dorothy is based in a part of Scotland quite close to the border with England. That much she told me, although she just wouldn't be any more specific. She's still very wary. Anyway, what she really wanted *you* to know, was that there's been a lot of movement around where she lives. And she couldn't stress it enough. People everywhere are on the move, and all of them are on the move south.'

'Did she tell you why? You know, why they're all on the move?'

'She can't be absolutely certain, she said, but she's pretty sure it's their hunger.'

Sidney wasn't in the least surprised by that answer, but it still made him go cold. There was such an obvious connection between his own situation and what was now happening in Scotland – in addition to the reported appearance of a group of northerners near the village. And it was the appearance of those northerners, he thought, that should now be made known to Sonia – with a request that it be passed back to Dorothy.

'Sonia, I've got a little news for you. Four strangers have just been spotted passing our village. And there's little doubt they were from north of the border. I mean *the* border, not the old one between England and Scotland. And—'

'Is that a big deal?' interrupted Sonia. 'Four strangers from north of the border?'

'Yes, it's a very big deal. There've always been rumours of the odd person coming across the divide – mostly by mistake – but there's never been a case of anybody coming anything like this far south. Not one in my whole lifetime. But now four guys together – and when stories of imminent food shortages are everywhere. I'm sure you're there already, but reports of people moving south in Scotland – because of hunger – do rather underline why that quartet down here is causing so much concern. I mean, I doubt anybody believes there won't be more of them to come. And maybe an awful lot more...'

'I see,' responded a very alert-sounding Sonia. 'And

I suppose you want me to tell Dorothy about this… er, incursion? I'm sure she'll want to know.'

'Yes. Definitely. I don't know what good it'll do, but it can't do any harm, and it might help you to get her to open up some more. You know, trading information like this might help gain her trust, and one day, she might even tell you exactly where she lives and whether she's a blonde or a brunette.'

'That I won't ask her.' giggled Sonia. 'But I will certainly pass on your news ASAP. After all, it seems to me that something of import might be bubbling up on your little island, and it might not be long before it bubbles over. Or am I reading a little too much into all those people getting fidgety?'

'No, I don't think you are. And just for the record, I won't mind if she's blonde or brunette or auburn or… grey. Just as long as she has got some hair…'

And so a light-hearted note was used as a prelude to the conclusion of their sober exchange, and after a brief discussion about some unseasonably cold weather in Saskatoon, the two hams finally signed off.

Sidney was then left to ponder whether the provision of any information to a reticent human, well beyond the limit of his physical reach, could have any meaningful bearing on the fact that his life was in danger. After all, not only might he run out of food, but now he might also be run out of his cabin by a horde of invaders from the north.

Life, he eventually decided, had been far less unsettling on the reservation…

Yousaf, 2052 (i)

Bereft of its trade. Almost empty. Just pieces left. Uncleared metal scraps. Here and there, a half-dismantled hulk. But no activity. No noise. No clanging. No clatter. No sparks. No swarming masses. Gadani Beach as nearly just a beach once again. No longer a breaker's yard. And no maritime monsters awaiting their turn. No pensioned-off tankers. No past-their-time freighters. No worse-for-wear cruise ships, their charms now defunct. And Yousaf knew why. Everyone knew why. As everyone knew it was the same in Alang and Chittagong. Faraway places where, just as here, a new use beckoned for sea-going vessels. Still seaworthy vessels. No longer pristine. And no longer 'desirable'. But ideal for their new use. Whether in India. Or in Bangladesh. Or here, in nearby Karachi...

Dozens of them in the harbour. A flotilla. An unlovely armada. All sizes. All shapes. All types. And in the port, more of them. Tied to the dock – and besieged. The dock hidden. The gangplanks hidden. Beneath bodies. Squirming, shoving, sweating bodies. Frenzied souls. Anguished souls. Desperate souls. Desperate for a place on a rusty magic carpet. Any magic carpet. It didn't matter. After all, weren't they all going to the same place? The place where others had already ventured – and succeeded in their venture. The new promised land. The new, cool, green, unguarded land. Over the years, in dribs and drabs. But now in their thousands and in their tens of thousands. And nothing to stop them. No barriers. No barricades. No guns. No resolve. And no will. Beach a ship. Or dock a ship. And it wouldn't get stopped. Nor would its cargo. The new residents of Europe. The new inheritors of Europe. The new rightful owners of Europe. No wonder the ships were besieged.

And now Yousaf's turn. Yousaf's turn to push and shove. To barge his way through. To propel himself forward. To aim for a gangplank. To think only of himself. Like everyone else. Like all the other pilgrims. Like all the other pilgrims on their way to the sacred land. Just don't give up. Just don't stop. Just carry on. And this ship's ideal. The one above him. A freighter. A medium-sized freighter. The Britannica! *It couldn't be better. And now the handrail. The gangplank within reach. Then onto the gangplank. Just in time to see an old man fall. Too old. Too old to be starting a new life. And now without a life. Already dead as his head hits the side of the dock. With no need to drown. And with no heed paid to his demise by the throng up above. All now intent on making their way to the head of the gangplank. None more so than Yousaf.*

And now on. Now on the red-painted metal of the Britannica's *deck. But no time to wait. No time to savour the moment. Hurry. Find a patch of deck. Find a patch and stake a claim. Sheltered if possible. But anywhere was better than anywhere below. He'd been told. He'd been warned. Stories of weeks at sea and bodies in the unlit holds. Asphyxiated. Suffocated. Or murdered. In the dark. Just for their paltry possessions. Or their last scraps of food. No. Stay up here. Endure the elements. Maybe find a mate. Another young man like himself. Look after one another. Look after each other's stuff. Each other's rations. And whatever they could find of anybody else's…*

Done. Midship at the base of a derrick. Not perfect. But Faizan was. Not too bright. Very eager for a companion. And very strong. With muscles from his time at Gadani…

6.

Sidney's world might be about to spin off its axis, but that didn't mean he could neglect his duties. So, once again, his day started with a bucket, and soon after this, he was again busy in the veg plot – although not too busy to notice that, today, he was sharing Hope Farm with just Anika and Myra. Rishi and both his sons were nowhere to be seen.

He had a good idea of why they were all absent, and in due course, his suspicions would be confirmed when, mid-morning, Anika paid him a visit to deliver some instructions. She was, of course, her normal disagreeable self, and as always, she made no attempt to hide the fact that she found the process of direct interaction with Sidney extremely distasteful. It was all too obvious in both her screwed-up face and her tone of voice.

When she spoke, she no less than hissed out her words: 'Boy,' she began (she'd never used Sidney's name in all their long time together), 'I want carrots. Two handfuls. And make sure they're sound. Then top up the kindling. With good sticks, mind. No more of those stupid twigs you've been bringing. They're no use at all.'

Sidney wanted to tell Anika that there probably weren't two handfuls of sound carrots in the entire veg plot, and that if she could find any 'good sticks' within a mile of Hope Farm, then she would earn his enduring admiration. However, he knew that, if he imparted that information, it wouldn't be only her hiss and her disdain he would have to endure. It would be something far worse, no doubt involving her husband and the pit bull, Farid. Hence, instead of enlightening her on the poor state of their home-grown produce and the dearth of top-notch kindling in the vicinity, he simply opted for the normal deferential compliance. 'Of course, Miss Anika. I'll attend to that straightaway. And I'm sorry about the twigs…'

'Well, make sure you're not sorry again,' hissed the serpent, 'or I'll make sure you're a great deal sorrier still.'

'Yes, yes,' mumbled Sidney. 'Of course. And… and…'

'And what?'

'Well, I was just wondering…'

Anika's eyes had now widened into discs and her nostrils had flared. It happened every time Sidney even hinted that he might be about to ask her a question. Every time that he threatened to extend their one-on-one interaction by requiring her to say a few more words. So, he was well prepared to ignore that look of growing rage on her face and instead to press on with his enquiry. He was pretty sure he already knew what Anika would tell him, but he wanted to be sure. He wanted to have all the information he could gather in these increasingly uncertain times.

'I was wondering where Mr Rishi is. And Farid and Viraj. And whether their absence is something to do with those... you know, with those strangers; those men who were seen to the west?'

Anika looked as though she were about to have a seizure, but she managed to vent her apoplexy by spitting out an answer to Sidney's query, which – not that surprisingly – included an unwarranted rebuke of his own supposed inaction. 'They're doing something, something important, while you do nothing! Yes, nothing. You leave it all to others, don't you? Just like you always do. So there you are, wasting your rotten time, while up in the village, all the real men are sorting out how to defend themselves and their womenfolk – along with everything they own. Even a miserable little scut like yourself—'

'Well—'

'...and all that sorting out calls for some proper planning. And for some proper preparation. Maybe even you can understand that? And understand why all the men of the village are where they are now, while you stand here, idling away your hours and not even finding me some decent sticks for my fire. You should be ashamed of yourself. If, of course, your lot can feel any shame...'

Sidney stood, looking at his accuser and letting her slights and her insults wash over him as if they were the empty ramblings of a crone. Which they were. He'd heard so much similar stuff in the past that it now had no effect. And in this instance, it certainly didn't distract him from the substance of Anika's diatribe, which had confirmed without a doubt his belief that Rishi, Farid and Viraj were all involved in putting together whatever was thought necessary to ready the village for the arrival of maybe a lot more than just four uninvited strangers. The potential threat from the north wasn't, it seemed, just something he'd imagined. It was real – or at least real enough to warrant what was probably an unprecedented gathering of all the village's males.

This confirmation of his concerns was, in a strange way, rather comforting. So much so that Sidney couldn't even muster a well-deserved dose of loathing for his mistress when, with a torrent of real abuse, she brought their exchange to a climactic conclusion. It was Anika at her very worst. But it meant nothing to Sidney, and by the time she had quit the veg plot, he'd already put her out of his mind and was thinking about whether he should do more than just pull up some carrots and search long and hard for some decent kindling. Maybe he should also consider how he might engage with the defence of the village – if he thought it was a worthwhile pursuit? And maybe he should also think about how he might defend himself? After all, he had no desire to have to curl up into a ball again to protect his body. Indeed, in all likelihood, he would need to do a lot more than just curl up if he wanted to guarantee his survival. And as a first step, he would probably need to arm himself with a weapon...

And here was a focus for his thoughts. Why, he asked himself, hadn't he considered this already? It was just so obvious. It might be suicidal to use a weapon to defend himself from an assault by Farid. But to defend himself from an assault by one of those northerners… Well, he'd have the support of every single villager. So why not? And more to the point, what weapon should he choose?

After much deliberation – whilst scouring the wood for sticks (and dry roots) – he settled on the rusty sickle that lived in Kaalki's 'stable'. It hadn't seen service in years, and it was very unlikely that any of the family still knew of its existence. Sidney was only aware of it because he'd grazed his hand on it some months ago – before he'd then stowed it out of the way on the top of a rafter. It was out of sight and in only Sidney's mind. It would be perfect. Even if it wasn't too sharp, it would unsettle any enemy, and if employed vigorously enough, even do said enemy some genuine harm.

*

So, later that afternoon, before Rishi and his sons returned, Sidney visited Kaalki's modest quarters, and after giving his friend some irresistible affection, he removed the sickle from its hiding place, and was just about to give it an initial inspection when Myra arrived…

'*What are you doing?*' she squealed. '*And where did you find that? Why have you got it?*'

As Sidney well knew, Myra had a licence to question anything he did that was in the least way out of the ordinary, and she used this licence whenever she could. So finding him with an unfamiliar implement in his hands was more than enough reason to embark on an inquest. And in this case, it was an inquest Sidney needed to respond to immediately. He could, of course, have done this by simply explaining how he was equipping himself for a potential attack by persons unknown, which would not only be to his advantage but also to the advantage of Myra and the rest of her family. However, he strongly suspected that such an explanation would in some way be turned against him by this hateful brat, and the end result would probably involve his losing his chosen weapon. He also suspected that, in these precarious times, the conventions of the past might soon be about to crumble. So, what better way to recognise that impending disintegration than to cast off the established subservience to a horrid little child and instead give her the fright of her life?

Accordingly, Sidney did not seek to humble himself by assembling the expected deferential response to dear Myra's query, but instead he made an announcement. And for maximum effect, he did this only when he'd approached Myra and his six-foot-plus frame was towering above her with the sickle now raised in the air – and with Myra already looking encouragingly shocked…

'I'm working for the governor,' he pronounced solemnly. 'You do know who the governor is, don't you?'

Myra nodded, the expression on her face now a pleasing mix of alarm and terror.

'Good. Well, he wrote me a letter. You know. A piece of paper with marks on it. That I can read and understand. And what he's asked me to do is make sure there's nobody in the village who might be up to no good. You know, stuff like… well, like maybe helping any strangers. Stuff like that. And if I do find anyone… well, not behaving as they should, I have to deal with them. I have to make sure they won't do any bad stuff ever again. The governor made that very clear…'

At this point, Myra actually gulped. Sidney had to make a concerted effort not to burst out laughing and to remember that scaring the pants off an eleven-year-old – whilst in possession of an offensive weapon – was not only very easy but also something he needed to continue in the interests of making sure that said eleven-year-old didn't report the loss of her pants to anyone else.

'Of course, if anybody told anyone else of my secret mission… well, that wouldn't be good, would it?'

Myra nodded her head in agreement, and then she indulged in another gulp.

'Because then… Well…'

And here he stopped and turned his head to stare at his sickle. He didn't need to say any more, as was only too apparent in the look of utter distress that had now parked itself on Myra's face. Sidney had never seen anything like it before and was already feeling a little pang of guilt at having so scared the young girl before him. But only a little pang. He hadn't forgotten how this malevolent minor had treated him in the past – consistently – and she was well overdue for a dose of payback. And she certainly wouldn't be running back to tell Anika what had just happened. She had been not just terrified but demolished. It was there in her eyes. And it was there in the way she sidled back to the house when Sidney had chosen to dismiss her. No way, he knew, would she want to risk crossing the man with a secret mission – the man with the rusty sickle…

*

Later that day, Sidney and his sickle were back in his cabin, and Sidney was still relishing his defiant actions. After all, they did merit a great deal of relishing. And they almost certainly deserved to be shared with a couple of his overseas pals, along with an update on a few other events in his increasingly 'interesting' life. So, it wasn't long before Sidney was again conjuring up the marvels of HF transmissions – to talk first to his friend in France.

He kicked off the conversation with an unexpurgated account of his 'interaction' with Myra, and then he moved on to a run-down of developments in and around the village, before going on to inform Marc of the tortuous communications being conducted with the enigmatic Dorothy in Scotland. Marc appeared more than interested in everything

Sidney had to tell him, and he made sure Sidney knew he was delighted that he had followed his advice to be ruthless with his keepers – even if, so far, it was only in the form of a heartless attack on their youngest member. It nevertheless, Marc insisted, demonstrated that there was a 'worm on the turn'. And that could only be good.

As regards the communications with Scottish Dot, that, Marc pronounced, could only be good too. After all, he went on to explain, any new radio ham in the loop was extremely good news. And this one was a woman! What could possibly be better?

Furthermore, that original advice Marc had proffered had included not only the need to be ruthless but also the need to accept that there wasn't just one course of action: the obvious course. And that everything should be considered as an option. Fitting into that advice a barely known woman who lived somewhere in Scotland might not be easy, he admitted, but her existence should certainly be borne in mind. Who could tell how events might play out? And who could tell whether Sidney's circumstances might be improved by his following one of Marc's established occupations? Yes, having stayed more or less on the side of sensible, it was time for Marc to embark on one of his less than sensible flights of fancy by proposing to Sidney that, in the middle of any forthcoming mayhem, he took up the manufacture of a 'liqueur'.

'There iz no better time to start a new venture,' Marc insisted, 'than when things are in a state of flix.'

'Flux,' corrected Sidney.

'*Oui*, flux. And there iz no better venture than providing some much-needed "impulse" to all those 'oo are in need of a boost in what may be *très difficile* times. And I mean some impulse in the form of some gin...'

Sidney laughed. 'Marc, I can't think of anything more impractical than me setting up a gin distillery. There's just so much wrong with that suggestion that I don't know where to start.'

'Oh, come on, my friend. If you can't get any juniper berries, you could always just make vodka. And then put anything in it – and call it what you like. Just as long as what you make iz alcoholic, you won't 'ave a problem. I mean, in selling it – or in making lots of new friends. Just the sort of thing you should be thinking about now. Because, as you know, in troubled times, one can never 'ave too many friends.'

Marc continued to push the advantages of this new enterprise for quite some time, and he only agreed to suspend his promotion of the lunatic idea when Sidney made it clear that he wanted to have a chat with Ted in Windhoek, and for that he would need some power – all of which would soon have drained away if Marc didn't close down very soon. So he did, but not before leaving Sidney with a particularly warm glow. Not only had Marc given him further support and comfort but he had also served up another dish of the preposterous (something he often did) and this never failed to brighten up Sidney's mood.

Hence, when Sidney started his exchange with Ted, he felt better than he'd felt all day. Indeed, so much so that Ted was soon questioning his buoyant manner. Had he, Sidney, discovered a secret path to another, better world or had he been bingeing on fermented fruit?

Sidney made it clear that it was neither, and then made sure Ted was up to speed with all the developments in rural Worcestershire and southern Scotland – all before he'd given Ted any opportunity to reveal that Ted himself had made contact with that new ham in Scotland. Yes, with Sonia's help, he'd spoken to Dorothy directly, and when he was finally able to make this known, he suggested to Sidney that he had better shut up and let him tell him what he'd discovered through that contact.

Ted didn't need to suggest this twice. Sidney couldn't wait to hear more about the mysterious Dorothy.

'Well,' Ted began, 'she's not very forthcoming about herself, as you well know. But I did learn one or two things. I mean, to start with, she has a very keen interest in what's happening in Scotland. You know, all the people on the move up there. But I didn't get the impression that's she's unduly concerned about it. She just sounded so confident. And I think that means she's not in your situation. As in vulnerable. I don't know why, but I suspect it might be connected with the fact that she's not on her own—'

'Did she tell you that?' interrupted Sidney. 'I had no idea...'

'No, she didn't. But you have to be a really slippery character to fool an old snake catcher like me, and she isn't slippery. She's honest. And that honesty gave me an insight into her world. From listening to her, there were a number of things that just didn't fit in with her being on her tod, so I'd swear she's got some sort of company up there. And maybe more than just a partner or an immediate family. Which may or may not be useful information. But I thought you should know – along with the fact that she's honest, of course. And that, my friend, you should bear in mind in any future dealings with her.

'She's not devious, and I don't think she means you any harm. Trust her and give her any information she wants. I think it's really important that you keep her on your team, no matter how little she might be able to do to help you directly. And, well… you know I'm always right. So, you'd damn well better take my advice.'

Sidney assured Ted that he would indeed take his advice – just before his power supply meant that their conversation had to be drawn to a close. Although this wasn't before Sidney had thanked his African friend for his new insights and wished him a lucrative, bite-free workload over the forthcoming few days.

As soon as he had closed down his equipment, Sidney began to absorb the significance of what he'd learnt – on top of the significance of his mutinous behaviour earlier in the day. He continued to do this even when he'd retired to his bunk and his cabin was in total darkness. Indeed, he only stopped when he heard voices in the distance…

Creeping to the window of his cabin, his newly acquired sickle in his hand, he peered into the gloom. At first, he saw nothing. Nor were there any more sounds of voices. But then, at the edge of the wood, there were three moving figures; three shadowy figures who were clearly attempting to pass by Hope Farm without being seen. Sidney stared at them until they'd gone, heading past the solitary oak tree and presumably down the old bridle path that would take them further south – and presumably out of Sidney's life forever.

He returned to his bed and quickly came to two conclusions. The first was that he might have a problem in bringing himself to use a sickle as a weapon – if and when a far-off shadowy figure became a human being within sickle-striking distance. The second was that he would maintain his newly acquired subversive behaviour and not report what he'd seen. He could see about as much benefit in doing that as he could in building a still for the production of juniper-free hooch.

7.

Sidney sat on the threshold of his cabin and stared at the pond that separated his own little sanctuary from the rest of the world. He knew that long ago there had probably been some life beneath its surface – before all the fish in all the ponds, lakes and rivers in Britain had been wiped out, either by pollution or by unrestrained fishing. Other freshwater life had disappeared as well, so any pool or any flow of water in the country was now sterile – albeit very far from clean. He wondered what people's relationship with these liquid features had been when they were full of life and how that might compare with his own rather more ambivalent relationship with the smooth-surfaced expanse before him. For whilst he took pleasure every day from its serenity and its sometimes-ruffled unrest – and it provided a tangible barrier between him and 'them' – he could never completely forget that it symbolised so well what had been wreaked on the world. A planet once full of wonder and joy had been reduced to a virtual wasteland. He knew this both from his parents and from his books, and therefore every morning it was difficult not to be reminded by that expansive stretch of water of what once had been. Reminded of a time when a large pond in Worcestershire would have been a magnet for life and not just a monument to life now lost.

Not for the first time, he began to feel morose, and his mood dipped even further when he rose from his threshold and regarded the interior of his cabin. It was a mess, but a beautiful mess, one full of so much that made his life worth living. There were his books – so many books. And, of course, his precious radio. But also some stones he'd collected. And some old bottles he'd unearthed. And that pad of notes from his dad. And one of his mother's shawls; another reminder of what once had been. And even his old musty bunk and its horsehair pillow. All taken together, nothing less than his life and his very own private universe. As much a part of himself as his legs and his arms. And at the same time, succour for his soul – in physical form. And there was now every chance that soon he would lose it! That in the very near future, he would have to abandon it – for who knew what? Not another cabin like this, that was for sure. One brimming with both treasure and spiritual comfort – and, of course, with that view of a pond. Yes, that barren reservoir might be dead, but so often the view of it lifted his heart as its surface mirrored the sky or, with the help of rain, transformed itself into a sheet of splashing charm. He would miss it desperately. And he would miss his cabin beyond words.

This was no good. He couldn't just stand here indefinitely, feeling sorry for himself. He had work to do. He always had work to do, and it never did itself. So, after a long, drawn-out sigh, Sidney set about his day – starting, as usual, with a bucket and a walk to the wood. After this, it was a bout of hard manual work. There was a ditch that needed to be cleared – just the sort of job to keep a drudge with a spade busy all day. And out of the way all day.

Whatever preparations were being made for the reception of strangers would not, it seemed, be involving Sidney. Of the farm's men, Rishi was still around, but only until mid-morning. Then he disappeared, possibly to join Farid and Viraj or maybe another gathering of all the village men. Sidney had no way of knowing. After all, he had no stomach for another (single) question-and-answer session with Anika, and her daughter probably wouldn't even let him get within question-asking distance. He'd seen her when he'd gone to collect his spade – just before she'd scuttled back to the house as soon as she'd glimpsed him. She might, he thought, never speak to him again.

So, it was the ditch that would hold his attention all day, and the ditch that would require the sort of all-day effort that would leave him flagging by mid-afternoon.

Which is why, when Viraj returned from wherever he'd been and came to talk to him, Sidney was sitting, with his legs in the ditch, trying to gather what little was left of his energy in order to resume his ordeal. He hadn't seen or heard Viraj's approach until Viraj was standing above him. And when Viraj then announced his presence – with a chuckle – Sidney instinctively jumped to his feet, feeling both foolish and a little guilty.

Viraj then followed up his chuckle with some words. 'Shirking again, Sidney?' he asked, a large smile spreading across his face. 'Or are you withdrawing your services? Have you gone on strike – for better conditions and more perks?'

'No, no. I was just—'

'Sidney, I'm joking. I'm joking. I can see what you've done. And if I were you, I wouldn't just be sitting down by now; I'd be lying down – and not planning to get up again for some time. So, cool it. I'm Viraj, remember. Not Farid. And I'm only here to give you some news.'

Sidney managed to gather himself, and when he responded to Viraj's words, it was to acknowledge his rather embarrassing initial reaction. 'I'm sorry about that. I really am. It's just—'

'…the way we've made you,' finished Viraj. 'I should have known better, and it's me who should be sorry. So, I am. And with that little bit of awkwardness out of the way, why don't I get on and tell you what I came here to tell you? Which is far more interesting because it's some more news about some more of those strangers—'

'*What?*'

'Yes. Another four of them. Another four northerners. They were caught last night. Two old guys and two younger ones. And they've been questioned all day. You know. To try and find out what's going on. And whether there's more of them to come.'

'Blimey!'

'Yes, it is a bit blimey, isn't it? And it's difficult to think that there won't be more of them coming. I mean, why on earth wouldn't there be?'

'And that's what they've admitted? They've actually said that?'

'No, not as far as I'm aware. I mean, I think they're being a bit cagey. But there again, as far as I know, they're still being interrogated. So, they might admit it soon. I mean, they have to, don't they? After all, as I've said, there's no way there won't be more of them coming. Which is why we're doing all the preparing we're doing. And why Farid and me have been out patrolling all day. You know, to keep a look out for any more of them. And we'll be doing it again tomorrow—'

'Viraj, should you be telling me all this?' I'm only—'

'...family, as far as I'm concerned. And I intend to keep you up to speed with everything that's going on. In fact, as to why you've not been included... Oh, well, I suppose we both know why you've not been included. But that won't stop me telling you everything I know as often and as soon as I can. You shouldn't be kept in the dark, Sidney. That wouldn't be fair. Not in these *unpredictable* times, and not when I can do something to maybe shine a little light onto things.'

Sidney suddenly realised he was feeling a surge of delight. One of his 'owners' was expressing a concern for his well-being, and it seemed said owner was also prepared to take steps to protect his well-being. It wasn't something he'd expected – even from amiable Viraj. He barely knew how to react. But almost before he knew it, he was expressing his gratitude in the simplest way possible. With a clearly pronounced, unmistakably earnest 'Thank you,' and an instinctive bowing of his head.

Viraj acknowledged this with another broad smile and a further observation on the likelihood of hosting more 'foreigners' in the immediate future. 'Just make sure you look out for me as much as I'll try to look out for you. I really want you on my side.'

'I will do,' responded Sidney gravely. 'You have my word.'

'Good. And to start with, I think you should be looking to save your strength. No point in spending it on clearing a bloody ditch – particularly one that can't be seen from the house and one that's pretty unlikely to be visited for the rest of the day.' And here he winked at Sidney while at the same time presenting him with a final smile – just before he turned to leave his confidante with his now redundant spade.

Yes, Sidney would take his advice and maybe slink back to his cabin. He might even have a word with Sonia. He might be able to catch her before her own day got underway.

*

He did, and he lost no time at all in bringing her up to date with the emerging situation in Worcestershire and his surprise at discovering that he had a real flesh-and-blood guardian angel to stand by his side. Sonia was suitably intrigued and suitably relieved to hear the news about Viraj. But it wouldn't have been Sonia if she didn't have some news of her own to deliver. Therefore, it wasn't long before she'd taken over the agenda of their exchange.

'Sidney,' she declared, 'You need to know what Dorothy told me last night. We had quite a long chat. And you see, she's been thinking about how she might be able to help you. Not directly, you understand, but through one of her friends—'

'*What?*'

'Well, you see, she has these friends—'

'Friends? Where?'

'Well, I don't know quite where, but I think she meant much closer to you… you know, than she is. And she was thinking about what one of them might be able to do for you if you got into any sort of trouble—'

'Sonia,' Sidney interrupted, 'what exactly did she say? I mean, who is this friend? And how close is he? Or she? I'm trying to make some sort of sense out of this—'

'And I'm trying to tell you what Dorothy told me,' re-interrupted Sonia. 'You know she only tells me what she wants to tell me, and that means she hasn't told me whether she's got four or forty friends, she hasn't told me which one of them she has in mind, and she certainly hasn't told me where this friend is. And before you ask, nor has she told me how she keeps in contact with any of these friends. All she's told me is what I've already told you: that there might be another guardian angel in the offing if times are getting tough – and, of course, if you're able to tell her this – through me.'

'This all sounds so vague – and so tenuous. And I have no idea how this friend of hers could help me, even if he or she is a lot closer than southern Scotland. How would this friend even find me?'

'No idea, young man,' retorted Sonia. 'You'll presumably have to leave that to Dorothy. But the important thing to remember is that, however *vague* and *tenuous* this news might be, it is good news. I mean, I haven't just told you that a giant asteroid is on course to hit England. I've told you something rather more uplifting.'

'Point taken,' conceded an ashamed-sounding Sidney. 'I'll file your news in the good-news file, along with the news about Viraj. And please make sure that you pass my gratitude back to Dorothy. Oh, and also tell her that I'll be very happy to provide her with all and every bit of info she might require – anything that might help her help me. Just like I tell you everything you want to know...'

'You've never been prepared to tell me whether I sound sexy.'

'You've never asked me,' squawked Sidney, and then he burst out laughing. As soon as he could manage, he then went on to assure his radio correspondent that she didn't need to ask that question because he could confirm right now that her voice was definitely the sexiest voice he had ever heard. Which, rather sadly for Sidney, was nothing less than the truth. After all, she had virtually no competition.

Sonia reacted very well to this disclosure and assured Sidney that she found his voice sexy as well. Which may or may not have been the truth, but which admission did help bring their shared conversation to a pleasingly congenial conclusion – only a little while before another conversation was about to commence.

This one wasn't over the airways, but by way of an unexpected face-to-face confrontation. Because, no more than five minutes after closing down his equipment, Sidney spotted Rishi and Sanjiv making a beeline for his cabin. He needed to get outside and meet them.

*

Rishi looked flustered. Sanjiv looked simply deranged: as though his mind had been turned upside down, and as though his equilibrium had arrived at an unannounced terminus and it no longer had any idea where to go. It was therefore the flustered Rishi who had to initiate the unscheduled exchange with Sidney. He did this, after an overture of large inhalations, by announcing that Sidney needed to equip himself with pen and paper, as Sanjiv had a letter to dictate – one that needed to be dispatched to the governor at the earliest opportunity.

Sidney registered the urgency in Rishi's voice. Straightaway, he popped inside his cabin and was soon back out on the deck with his writing kit – and with his two uninvited guests. There, they all sat down crossed-legged, and with Rishi's prompting, Sanjiv finally broke out of his unsettling stupor and started to speak.

'Boy,' he commanded offensively, 'take down this letter.'

Sidney bristled at both the salutation and the tone of the command. Normally, Sanjiv wasn't openly as disdainful or as high-handed as this. Nevertheless, this was hardly the time to put in a plea for more courteous treatment, and Sidney simply waited, pen in hand, for the contents of the probably quite important letter to be revealed. He didn't have to wait too long. Nor did he have to wait too long to be shocked and appalled. This was because Sanjiv was dictating to the governor a short story concerning the capture of four 'outsiders' who had been apprehended near the village and how, through some intense interrogation, one of them had finally admitted that more of their number were massing at the border with the intention of sweeping south – and presumably everything and everyone before them. And just to ensure that the distinguished governor was left in no doubt whatsoever, he stated quite categorically that a real invasion was just about to happen – and with due respect, he would very much like to know what the governor was planning to do about it. Indeed, Sanjiv had worked himself up into such a lather by this stage of his dictation that he even made the suggestion that the esteemed governor might want to consider sending a generous number of reinforcements from Pershore, and possibly elsewhere, in order to stem what would be an inevitable tide from the north.

At this point in the proceedings, Sidney was experiencing a range of emotions. Fear was in there somewhere, but so too were shock and at least a *soupçon* of excitement. But not yet horror. That only came when Sanjiv went on to inform the governor that the four out-of-towners had now all 'been dealt with'; that they had all received the treatment that would be dished out to any other northerner who dared to sully the peace and purity of the south.

Sidney felt sick. He knew that those four men who had been interrogated for hours – and maybe tortured – hadn't died in any sort of conflict but had instead been killed in cold blood. Some of his neighbours, and maybe even Rishi and Sanjiv, had brought their lives to an end in the most despicable manner imaginable – probably whilst they were tied up, and probably whilst they were begging to be allowed to live.

*

Sidney still felt queasy when, two hours later, he was called upon to harness Kaalki to the family's venerable but sturdy wagon in readiness for its journey to somewhere near Pershore. This was because Rishi had already made the decision to evacuate Anika and Myra before the likely outbreak of hostilities, having presumably settled on the idea that the Pershore area constituted an impregnable bastion that would keep at bay any number of northern devils – some of whom would no doubt be intent on taking his home, his land, his livelihood and his women. And with these latter assets safely tucked away, he could then, no doubt, focus all his attention on the protection of those of his assets that were rather less animate and a lot less movable.

Sidney was surprised that his queasiness only really left him when it was displaced by pity at the sight of the two women being trundled off by his master to a fate unknown. As much as he despised them, he couldn't ignore their shared looks of despair nor their obvious anguish at the thought of being separated from the rest of their family – possibly never to see them again.

It was just the way he was: oversensitive and maybe even a little soft. Which is why he'd stayed up late this night to satisfy himself that the potentially murderous Rishi had finally returned safely from his destination near Pershore and, of course, that Kaalki then had a well-deserved, albeit very late, supper.

After all, weren't all mules just as deserving of a guardian angel as those who yoked them to a wagon? If not quite often rather more so.

Yousaf, 2052 (ii)

Smells. Smells mingled and mixed. Oil with sweat. Soot with piss. Incense with puke. Faeces with smoke. Always the smoke. Always fires on the deck. Always somebody cooking. And always somebody squatting. Always somebody recharging the stench. Blending the scents of excrement with the smells of chapatis. Or papadums. Or pakoras. And so, a whole ship clouded in a revolting miasma. A cloying miasma. A miasma so thick it confounded the wind. Not even a gale could make it give up its grip. So, now, out here in the middle of the ocean, Yousaf couldn't even smell the salt of the sea. Only the stink of the Britannica *and its five thousand souls. Or its six thousand. Or its seven thousand. Nobody knew. Nobody cared. Nor when one soul departed. Nor when a new one was born. Why would they? When all they ever cared about was the promised land. And maybe being free of the stink.*

A week. Then two weeks. The Suez Canal blocked. The Britannica *one of a convoy. All on their way to the Cape of Good Hope. Crawling. Plodding. Inching their way forward. A tide of humanity well on its way. And surviving. Existing. People suffering, but willingly. Even those in the bowels. Even those sharing space with the dark and with death. Without even Yousaf and Faizan's prized place on the deck. For they all, like these two, had a goal in their sights. A goal to entrance them. A goal to sustain them. A goal to assist them in dealing with dread.*

And before very long, a surge of excitement! The Cape being passed, they were on their way north! A million new settlers for those lands in such need. For those lands in such need of a fix of new blood.

Yousaf was thrilled. Faizan was stirred. Even the stink could no longer disturb them. Nor could the hunger of those all around them. Nor could the horrors now lined up before them.

As weeks turned to more weeks, the food petered out. The strong became weak and the weak became frail. And the frail then succumbed and were cast overboard. Life was now something to hold on to tightly. And those who could not would have no one to help them. Even their families could not be relied on. Such was the conduct survival demanded. For those still surviving, this wasn't a problem. Not least for young Yousaf. Who always had food. And so too did Faizan, the other king scrounger. No scruples, no feelings to get in their way. So, if someone's near death, then why not admit it. And why not relieve them of what they don't need?

They were far from unique in the way they kept going. There were Yousafs and Faizans on each single ship.

So, the convoy was now like a cortege of squalor. With pallbearers stationed on every ship's deck. Death and survival, and survival and death. A reek of real pain now combined with the stink. But still the convoy ploughed on. Not one hulk left behind. Until, on one morning, Morocco was sighted. And just after this, a new blockage announced.

The Straits of Gibraltar were no longer free. Europe's best warships were barring the way. The Med, it now seemed, was well out of bounds. The convoy would have to proceed further north. Its cargo would have to spend more time at sea. And never give up. And never say die. Not now, after weeks. Not now, near the end. Not after such hardship. Not after surviving…

Yousaf elated. A decision was made. For some it was Spain. For some it was France. But for Britannica's *folk, it was Britain first stop! And Britain was best. Britain was top. The land of his dreams. The land of his hopes. Where he knew he should go. Where he knew he should be. Where so many like him had gone to before. And the softest of all. No warships would stop him. No barriers would block him. And no fences to climb. No hurdles to jump. To start his new life. But just the reverse. A welcome. A greeting. The warmest reception. It was all they could do there. Accept. Acquiesce. Accede. And adjust. There was no other way. Not with so many folk turning up on your shores. With so many more to turn up in their turn. And so many more after that.*

Faizan was happy too. He had family in England. And now a new friend. One he had guarded as he'd guarded him. Newcomers both. To a new-come-to land. To a new way of life. One without heat and the scorch of the sun. One without fear and those dry, barren fields. And no longer a need to steal other men's food. No longer a need to help some to their end. And without that wretched miasma. That cloak of foetid air he'd had to breathe for the last ten weeks. That he could leave as soon as the Britannica *beached – near Falmouth.*

Yousaf thought it epic. An armada of fourteen rusting hulks heaving themselves onto the sands of the promised land in one final, desperate mechanical effort. Few, if any of them, could have made it much further. And few of their filthy, emaciated passengers could have made it much further. It was a joy. A joy unbounded. Even those who perished as they scrambled off the leaning wrecks would have experienced this joy. Right up until they expired. And for those who did make it safely onto England's shore, the joy would last forever.

It did so for Yousaf. And for his friend. And neither of them set foot on a ship ever again. Or left their new-found home ever again...

8.

Sidney looked at the field of jowar. It was the wrong colour: more yellowish-green than bluish-green, with here and there, even patches of brown. And every plant was stunted; every one, no more than a dwarf, each with just a small, droopy head. Under the overcast early morning sky, it was a sight to drain the cheer from any observer. Even one who'd just enjoyed two days of very welcome isolation – two days without even a hint of 'guidance' from the family. Anika and Myra were wherever they'd been taken to near Pershore – and therefore effectively 'in foreign parts'. And whilst the men of the family were still very much in the immediate locality, they were happily elsewhere in this locality. Sidney had caught only a glimpse of them on the day after Anika and Myra's evacuation, and, yesterday, he hadn't seen them at all. He essentially had Hope Farm to himself.

This meant he'd been able to ease back on his workload – very significantly. He'd also been able to chat with all his ham friends without the remotest fear of interruption, and he'd even been able to worry about what might happen at any moment.

Would a swarm of northerners descend on his world and seize it for themselves? Would they seize him as well, and would they either treat him even more harshly than his masters had or simply kill him? And would his masters have any role at all in attempting to protect both the farm and the life of its dedicated servant? And what role, if any, would his guardian angel, Viraj, play in this attempt?

He had no answers to these questions. And anyway, right now, all such musings had been pushed to the back of his mind by the spectacle of all those sickly jowar plants. They made for such a desperate sight that they'd consumed his thoughts entirely. He'd even lost track of the fact that he had some work to do – in the veg plot.

*

Then, on his way to the veg plot, he saw them. More than a hundred yards away, three men running to the scrubby wood beyond the field of jowar – with Farid and Viraj in pursuit. The calm, it seemed, had come to an end, and some sort of storm had now broken. And in view of the identity of one of those overtaken by this storm, Sidney decided immediately that he needed to brave it himself. He had to help and protect Viraj in any way he could. Which meant that, virtually before he knew it, he was running back to his cabin to gather his sickle.

When he arrived there, he realised his heart was pounding – and that he had no clear idea of what he should do next, other than pick up his sickle and take himself off in the direction of the wood. There he could, no doubt, 'play it by ear'.

So, sooner than he'd have chosen, he found himself running between the bushes and saplings that lay beyond the field of jowar, desperately trying to establish where the hunt had now moved. And this was by no means easy. After all, the scrubby growth all around him was obscuring his view in every direction, and he was therefore having to play it by ear literally in his attempt to guide himself towards the action. But was that Farid shouting or was it Rishi? He couldn't tell. And if it was Rishi, had he too joined the pursuit of the uninvited strangers or was he somewhere else? Maybe Rishi was gathering more help for the chase. And now Sidney could definitely hear two sets of voices from two distinct directions – and in one set, there were definitely the high-pitched tones of Rishi. He sounded extremely agitated and as though he was somewhere near the house. He was certainly not in the wood.

Sidney was becoming confused. He then became more confused when Rishi's voice was joined by screams of alarm, which is when Sidney decided to abandon his blind rush through the shrubs and just stand and listen. It was the only way he would be able to get a better idea of what was going on and where it was going on.

Just five seconds after he had come to a stop, this tactic delivered a result. He heard a twig break. It was clearly the sound of somebody stepping on a piece of kindling he had yet to collect, and it was a sound that had been made no more than fifteen to twenty yards from where he stood. So, with howls and shouts still evident in the distance, Sidney began to move slowly in the direction of the broken-twig sound. He was now holding his sickle above his head – as if it were a club – and his heart was pounding more than ever.

Would he really, he asked himself, be able to strike anybody with his rusty weapon? And if he did, what might the target of his assault provide as a response? Dull-edged agricultural implements, he knew, wouldn't necessarily deliver a killer blow.

He was now having to make a conscious effort to control his breathing. And this effort was abandoned only when he caught sight of Viraj between two blackthorn bushes. It was clearly him who had stepped on the twig, just as clearly as he was no longer involved in any chase. He was looking back to the house, where a commotion was still going on, and it didn't take too much thought on Sidney's part to work out that the hunted three must have doubled back to Hope Farm, where they'd then been set upon – and presumably apprehended – by a mob of village irregulars. Probably with Rishi in the lead. In fact, there were already some distinct hoots of victory coming from the direction of the farm, and Viraj's body language suggested to Sidney that Viraj had come to a similar conclusion himself. That he and Farid had somehow caused their quarry to run back into the arms of more of the hunters – and that they were now in the bag.

Then Viraj's body language changed – radically. It spoke of intense shock. Then of intense pain.

Sidney was transfixed. He didn't know what to do. If one of those northerners hadn't doubled back to the house but had instead just assaulted Viraj, how should he best proceed? Then he saw it clearly. A knife. It was just being extracted from Viraj's back – so it could be plunged in again. And again. And again. By *Farid*.

It all happened too fast. As Viraj slumped to the ground, Farid pushed his limp body to one side and, being careful to avoid the resulting awful spurt of blood, he slit his brother's throat almost literally from ear to ear.

No sooner had he done this, than he dropped the knife to the ground and set off running towards the farmhouse, screaming as he ran. He'd just murdered his brother, and Sidney was quite sure Farid had no intention of confessing to having done this. The terrible deed would no doubt be ascribed to one of those captured northerners; the one whom Farid would accuse of arriving from the north with a nine-inch blade – which Farid had then used to kill his brother – rather than it having just been dropped in the chase. After all, Farid wasn't quite that stupid. Just entirely wicked and quite prepared to turn any fluke event to his advantage if at all possible.

Sidney began to cry. Then he took the few short steps that brought him to the side of his fallen guardian angel. His guardian angel! Hell, it wasn't supposed to be like this. And if this guardian angel had himself needed guarding, why hadn't Sidney provided that service? He'd been so close. Had he thought a little more quickly, he might have been able to intervene. But he'd done nothing. He'd simply stood there with his sickle and watched the only person he really cared for in the village being robbed of his life. He was crushed. Too crushed to even feel angry. Or barely rational.

But then something kicked in: the realisation that if he were found next to the body of his dear friend, he might have more explaining to do than he could manage. No matter how difficult it might be, it was time to be a little dispassionate and take himself and his sickle back to his cabin. There, he might be able to come to terms with what he'd just witnessed – and to work out how he might deal with the knowledge that what he'd just witnessed was a clear act of fratricide: one very bad brother killing one very good brother. With the bad brother now intending to place the responsibility for the crime onto somebody else.

But what was Sidney doing? Why was he going back to his cabin? Maybe it was the shock. But how could he not process what it might mean for those captured northerners if Farid arrived to tell the gathered villagers that it was them who had killed Viraj? And to tell

Rishi that it was them who had killed his son? Hell, these people had already done away with four other strangers as a finale to their interrogation. So, if they believed they now had some assassins in their hands, they wouldn't hesitate for a second. And there was no way Farid wouldn't convince them that those they were holding were indeed assassins. After all, it was an integral part of his quickly conceived plan; his way of getting rid of an upstart brother and then blaming it on a group of convenient aliens – three of those folk from the north whom were known for their brutality and for their blind, unthinking barbarity.

So, he had to forget the cabin. He had to forget the luxury of coming to terms with the murder of his guardian angel. Instead, he had to get himself to the farmhouse – and reveal what he'd seen. Whatever the consequences.

He dropped his sickle and ran – right through the middle of the field of jowar. And ignoring any aspects of the protocol that surrounded a *chokra* approaching a gathering of his betters, he rushed into the yard at the back of the farmhouse – just in time to see a crazed looking Rishi wiping the blade of his machete on the discarded cloak of one of his victims. Farid must have been so fast and so convincing – and Rishi and the rest of the mob so inflamed – that it had taken only seconds for 'justice' to be dispensed. To the perpetrators of a terrible crime for which they were not actually responsible.

Sidney again fell into shock. He stood with his mouth open, struggling to believe what he was seeing.

He certainly didn't notice that no one was paying him much attention. Or that Farid was clearly trying to look more distraught than self-satisfied. But Sidney did eventually register that there were just two bodies on the ground. Which didn't mean that one of the *three* strangers had been spared, but that he simply hadn't been captured. It took him a little while to work it out, but as the shock began to wear off, Sidney decided that only these two poor sods had made the mistake of doubling back to the farm, and their absent third companion must have chosen a different (safer) course, which in all likelihood, had taken him due south, probably never to be seen again. Heck, if Farid had suspected he was still anywhere near, he would have thought twice about murdering his brother in the way he had. He must have been pretty sure his convenient culprits were the only convenient culprits who remained.

'Definitely stupid' Sidney reminded himself again, but not completely reckless.

So, what to do now? Blurt out that Farid was an evil killer? Denounce him for what he was and demand that he too should feel the bite of a machete? And then maybe bring the two strangers back from the dead and be congratulated by Rishi for helping him rid himself of both sons in one single day? Or might such a course of action not work out quite so well? Because in addition to discovering that reviving the dead was beyond his powers, he might also discover that, by attributing Viraj's death to his elder brother, he might well end up on the wrong side of life himself. After all, serfs were not expected to accuse their masters of such deeds – ever. And certainly not after the deeds in question had been ascribed to two others, both of whom were unable to refute the accusation on account of their having been summarily dispatched – by a group of still highly aroused masters.

It was shameful. Especially because Sidney's silence would compound the wrong that had been inflicted on… his guardian angel. But he wasn't a hero. And he knew only too well that any accusation thrown in the direction of Farid would be dismissed out of hand. It would be just a gesture, a completely meaningless gesture that would almost certainly cost Sidney his own life. If this lot were now in the habit of eliminating anybody they chose – whether or not they had been accused of a crime – how likely was it that they wouldn't add a worthless whitie to their list without a second's hesitation? Yes, it was definitely shameful, but Sidney had little choice but to withdraw quietly from the farmhouse yard and slink back to his cabin, there to ponder his shame – and there maybe to weep for his dear departed friend.

*

Within barely a minute, he was skirting the pond. He had no more than twenty paces to take to reach the cabin. That was when he saw it: a roof tile under the deck. It was in the wrong place. Of that he was absolutely certain.

The cabin and its deck were held above the ground by brick-built piers. This meant there was a ten-inch gap between the wooden construction and the earth that sat below it; a convenient space into which all sorts of 'this and that' had been stowed over the years – including, at the approach to the deck, a stack of seven grey roof tiles. Every time Sidney had returned to his cabin, since he'd lived there, those tiles had offered him a silent greeting. They were now almost hardwired into his image of his home. So when the top one was no longer the top one, but was instead leaning against its partners, Sidney had no problem noticing it was out of place. Furthermore, given the events of the day so far, he had little problem imagining what might have caused that tile to have been dislodged. Even before he stopped to crouch down to look under the deck, he knew that the missing stranger wasn't, in fact, on his way further south, but he was instead lodged under the deck, probably feeling even more frightened than the guy who was just about to confirm he was there.

When, through that planned crouching down, Sidney had indeed established that he had an uninvited and very unexpected visitor, there was then the matter of what now needed to be done. Extraction from under the deck was probably the first task to be dealt with. But what then? Should the third member of the murderous trio be handed over to those who had butchered his companions, or should Sidney devise a more considerate welcome for his visitor? Maybe one that would not involve his being attacked with a machete?

Needless to say, Sidney decided on the latter course within a microsecond. Albeit this decision did nothing to equip him for the task of extraction. This wasn't a scared dog under the deck. It was a probably very scared and possibly very aggressive northerner; a breed of human Sidney had never before met (whilst still alive), and a breed of human who might have a very different perspective on the current situation than that of the cabin's more established tenant.

He hesitated. How would he even initiate an exchange with this chap? Sidney knew absolutely no Urdu and no Bengali, and so he couldn't even tell him that he meant him no harm. It could all go terribly wrong very quickly indeed.

It was clearly time to remind himself that, on a day that had barely started, he'd already witnessed far too much death, and he had no desire to witness any more. He'd also failed to prevent any of those deaths, but now he'd been given another chance. There was somebody here who needed his protection and his help to stay alive. So, whatever the consequences, he just had to get on with it and get that fugitive from beneath the deck. Even if it meant talking to him in a language he wouldn't understand and that might just enrage him instead. He had no choice.

So, Sidney abandoned his crouching stance, walked briskly to the edge of the deck and, using the most affable tone he could manage, addressed his prone guest – in, of course, standard English: 'Hello down there. I don't think we've met before, but my name's Sidney. I was wondering whether it might be better if you got yourself out from under there, and we had a chat in my cabin?'

Sidney simply couldn't believe what he'd just said. He'd sounded as though he were playing a character not just from the last century but from the century before that – when according to one of his books, manners were more or less the essence of civilised life. However, he had no time to get properly embarrassed, because from between the slats of the deck, his enquiry was met with a response.

'Nice to meet you, Sidney. My name is Hazeem, and I've twisted my ankle.'

Sidney had to shake his head. Had he really heard that? A devil from the north sounding entirely reasonable – and sounding entirely reasonable in English? The answer, he decided, was yes.

Because the devil had then gone on to ask him – again, in English – whether Sidney might be able to pull him out. 'Because my ankle is making it rather difficult for me to move.'

Not for the first time today, Sidney 'pulled himself together'. And once he'd checked that there were no executioners about, he crouched down again, reached below the deck and felt around for the extremities of his guest. They turned out to be his sandalled feet. By grasping both of them, he soon discovered that it was the right ankle of his guest that was twisted.

'No! Not the right one,' Hazeem squeaked. 'That really hurts. Just tug on the other.'

And so, with much tugging of the left foot, aided by the strenuous use of Hazeem's arms, a diminutive body emerged from under the deck, and Sidney laid his eyes on the first living northerner he had ever encountered. It then seemed no more than proper to enquire of his health. 'Are you OK?' he said. 'It's only your foot that's hurt, isn't it?'

Hazeem laughed. 'Yes. Only my foot. But believe me, that's quite enough. It's bloody painful – and, I can tell you, it's the only reason I'm here with you now. If I hadn't twisted it, I'd be long gone. And I wouldn't have had the pleasure of meeting you. I mean, it's not very often I come across… well, you know, one of your sort. Even in my line of work.'

Sidney wanted to know what this line of work was, but that would have to wait. Passing pleasantries with 'the enemy' out in the open wasn't something to be recommended. He needed to get Hazeem into his cabin as soon as he could. It was time for some practical action.

'Look,' he said, 'I've no idea what I'm doing, but I do know we can't stay here. Anybody might see us. So, can you make it to the cabin? We really would be a lot better inside.'

'No problem. The Vale of Evesham might be beyond me, but I think I can manage a few yards.'

He could. Albeit slowly – and whilst Sidney was now pondering not only what that reference to the Vale of Evesham was all about but also what it might mean to be giving succour to an adversary; an adversary who had an inexplicable command of English.

9.

Sidney's life to date had left him ill-equipped to deal with his present situation. He didn't even know whether he should offer Hazeem a seat on either his single worse-for-wear chair or his shabby bunk, and was only able to resolve this issue by choosing the bunk for himself. This action had the desired effect.

Hazeem, his eyes still scanning the confines of the cabin, edged towards the chair – and then asked his host for permission to use it. 'May I?' he enquired politely.

'Of course. Of course. Take the weight off that ankle...'

He did. He flopped onto the chair, grimaced with what looked like a mix of pain and relief, and then addressed his host. 'Well, to start with, I think I ought to thank you—'

'What for?' interrupted Sidney. 'I haven't done anything.'

'You have,' contradicted Hazeem. 'You haven't shouted for your mates.'

'My mates?'

'The guys at the farmhouse. The ones—' And here Hazeem interrupted himself. 'Ah. Of course. They're maybe not your mates.'

Sidney said nothing. He didn't need to.

And then Hazeem carried on, 'Sidney, I hope you know what you're doing?'

'I told you outside. I have no idea what I'm doing – and I have no idea what I should do next. I mean, you are from the north, aren't you? And you were with the other two, the other two who—'

'…are now dead,' finished Hazeem, 'who have now been eliminated by your—'

'…owner,' assisted Sidney. 'Yes, I'm afraid they've both been killed. In cold blood. And I can hardly believe it. And that's why… well, why I haven't… you know, raised the alarm. I've already seen too much killing today, and I couldn't bear to see any more. I really couldn't.'

'Mmm,' murmured Hazeem. 'I can only thank you again – and I should also confirm what you think: that I am indeed from "the north". Not that far north, I might say. But north of the border. North enough to be a genuine alien in your land – and an alien who could be forgiven for wondering whether a touch more killing might be on the cards, not necessarily for today, but maybe for tomorrow or for the day after that.'

'Sorry?'

'Sidney, I'm in your hands. That is, I'm in your cabin, and your cabin is in… well, let's call it hostile territory – and just right now I can't walk more than a few yards. Which means that if I'm discovered – before this ankle has sorted itself out – I've had it. And given what you've now told me, I suspect you might not have too bright a future yourself. So far, you've only *found* me, but if you don't turn me in very soon, you'll be harbouring me. And I doubt that, taking account of what's already happened to my two associates, harbouring one of us northerners will be regarded as a minor misdemeanour.'

'I know.'

'So, what I'm saying is that I'm very, very grateful that you've not given me away already, but if I were you, I'd think very carefully about what to do next. I'm not a very nice person, believe me, but I would hate to think that the cost of maybe just deferring my… er, murder, would be your murder as well. And if you want me to spell it out, what I'm saying is that, if you want me to hobble off and away from your cabin – now – I'll quite understand. And if and when I'm captured, I won't mention our… meeting. I'll swear I've never set eyes on you. You have my word. My word as a *northerner*.'

Hazeem had delivered this last word with a theatrical emphasis, and now sat grinning at his host, waiting for a response. However, what he'd said and the way he'd said it had left Sidney with even less idea of what he should now do. Saving a life had been his prime motive for inviting Hazeem into his cabin, but he knew he couldn't ignore that he had a significant interest in saving his own life as well. And he was already putting that at serious risk. If he now chose to give shelter to his rescued northerner, that risk would only become larger. Probably, a great deal larger.

He was therefore still weighing up in his mind what he should do and what he should say to Hazeem, when he heard Rishi announcing his approach to the cabin.

'*Sidney,*' Rishi shouted. '*You in there? We could do with your help.*'

'Shit!' announced Sidney. And as he leapt off his bunk to look out of the cabin door, he repeated this expletive, but almost under his breath. Then he turned to Hazeem, who'd instinctively ducked down, and advised him with hand signals to drop to the floor. Immediately. He had no time to inform him that Rishi was walking towards the cabin with, just behind him, Farid and six other villagers. Nor did he have time to spell out that, implicit in that command to drop to the floor, was that he'd decided to risk his life to save the life of a foreigner whom he barely knew.

However, he didn't need to. Hazeem would have come to that conclusion within a couple of seconds. Even before Sidney was out of the door in a desperate bid to ensure that Rishi's posse came no closer to the cabin.

And it was a posse, a fact confirmed when Rishi continued with his shouted proclamation. '*There's another one – another northerner – and we need to find him. And that means you're coming too. Now. We have no time to lose. Understand?*'

Sidney felt a gush of relief. Rishi and his entourage were now no more than ten yards away. But they were stationary. That last question had been delivered by Rishi as he stood at the edge of the pond. It seemed highly unlikely that Sidney would have any further guests in his cabin today. But then he felt a gush of alarm. Farid was drawing closer just as Sidney was moving away from the cabin. Perhaps he'd already decided to make quite sure that their quarry wasn't very near to hand.

However, when he came face to face with Sidney, he stopped and, with a predictably sour expression on his face, he spat out four words, 'You might need this.'

As Sidney was processing what these four words might allude to, Farid presented him with his rusty sickle. It was only then that Sidney realised Farid had been carrying his discarded weapon. Fortunately, he was still able to thank Farid for returning it and to keep his hand steady as he took it back – even though he was now trying to cope with a new wave of turmoil. Had Farid assumed that a rusty sickle could only be the property of a lowly serf or was there another reason he'd assumed it was Sidney's? And had he deduced anything from where he'd found it? Had he worked out that his crime might have been witnessed – and by this servant? He certainly now looked not just sour but also threatening. But, there again, when didn't he?

Sidney would just have to ride out this latest assault on his equilibrium, assume he hadn't been rumbled as a witness to a crime, and get on with the fruitless search for the fugitive northerner. This, he discovered, he could manage. Just as, after receiving the sickle, he'd managed to respond to a direct question from Rishi with a convincing lie. When he'd been asked whether he'd seen any sign of the sought-after stranger, he'd assured his master that he'd seen nothing and heard nothing. And that, had he done so, he would, of course, already have reported it.

Rishi had accepted this assurance, and they were now free to commence the hunt. It would take all day, and, of course, it wouldn't have a successful outcome – at least not for Rishi and his men. For Sidney, however, it was something of a triumph. Not only did he see more of the countryside immediately south of his home than he'd seen in his entire lifetime but he was also able to relish the conclusion reached by the posse's leader that the missing man was now long gone and unlikely ever to return. The hunt wouldn't be resumed in the morning. No matter how much Rishi would have liked to have captured – and slaughtered – the third member of the trio of raiding bastards.

As a result, when Sidney finally made it back to the sanctuary of his cabin, he was in an unexpectedly good mood, albeit more unsure than ever of how to deal with his very foreign house guest.

*

He was sitting on the floor of the cabin when Sidney walked in, and he was smiling. And, with that smile still firmly in place, he greeted his protector: 'Sidney! Did you find me? Did you track me down and give me my just deserts? Or have I successfully slipped away? Am I still on the run?'

In response to this greeting, Sidney managed just a 'What?' He was so distracted by his visitor's playful welcome – and by his perfect English – that he could do no more. After all, neither humour nor a facility with his own language were features he'd ever associated with men from the north. Just as he'd never expected to be housing one of their number in his cabin.

'Sorry,' Hazeem continued as he rose from the floor to sit on the cabin's chair. 'You must have had an exhausting day, and all I can do is make jokes. It's just that I thought it might set you at ease. You know, assure you that I hadn't turned into some sort of threat while you were away.'

'It's fine,' Sidney responded. 'It's just… you know… I'm…'

'Yeah. Tired, still a bit *discomposed a*nd probably more than a bit anxious. I mean, not only have you taken on the role of my saviour – at least for the time being – but you know next to nothing about who you've saved.'

That was it. It was time, Sidney decided, to become a little less discomposed – and to engage with Hazeem, and in a way that would put his guest at ease.

So, as he sat down on his bed, he did this by picking up on Hazeem's last observation. 'You're right. And I don't even know whether you've had anything to eat today. For all I know, you might be starving.'

Hazeem grinned and then shook his head. 'A considerate saviour. How lucky can I get?'

'But have you eaten?' Sidney pressed.

'Not a banquet, Sidney. But the veg plot's within hobbling distance, and I've always liked salad—'

'*You've been out of the cabin?*'

'Sidney, I've come over the border, remember? I've taken risks. In fact, my whole life is about taking risks. So, I was hardly not going to venture outside, was I? Particularly when I needed some food and when I was pretty sure there was no one around. Leaving the cabin for a short spell of food-filching was barely a risk at all.'

'What do you mean about your life being all about taking risks? Have you done this sort of stuff before? I mean, have you come across the border before?' Sidney now sounded less than friendly. What Hazeem had just said had made him realise that he might have been taken for a fool. This young man in his cabin might not be quite so deserving of his protection after all.

Nevertheless, Hazeem was now grinning more than ever, and it took him no time at all to respond to Sidney's concerns. 'OK, it's confession time. I'm a smuggler. And as you can well imagine, smuggling involves taking risks. All the time.'

'A smuggler!'

'Yes. One of those guys who willingly – and for a reasonable reward – provides a service to certain people either side of a border. Whether they might want to get their hands on some affordable booze or maybe offload some… well, let's call them some shipments of *recreational medication*.'

'*You mean drugs?* Drugs… and booze. You actually take this stuff over the border? I mean, the border between—'

'Sidney, you've spent too long in your cabin. And if you think all the folk who live around here are all upstanding, God-fearing types and they're not riddled with all the failings that have afflicted our species since it first evolved, then you ought to get out a bit more. Hell, if they're quite happy to kill two of my friends in cold blood, they're hardly going to baulk at the idea of getting their hands on some illicit whisky. And it's not just your lot. Us northerners are just the same; pious on the outside, but more sinful within than you could ever imagine. And quite happy to indulge their desires in any way they can. Even if it means dealing with a no-good, rotten smuggler like me.'

'I had no idea.'

'I can see that from your face. But it's true. How else do you think I've learnt to speak English? And although I say it myself, like a native. I've been on this game since I was a kid. Hell, I even dream in English now. Quite often about boxes of booze and packages of… medications. And you know something? Maybe dreaming about them in Urdu would make me feel guilty. Turn my dreams into nightmares…'

Sidney had now been prodded into a state of wide-awake attention and was quick to pose a further question to his guest: 'Why are you here? I mean, why, as a smuggler, would you want to venture this far from the border? And with two other smugglers?'

'They weren't smugglers, Sidney. They were just a couple of my friends; two desperate people. Two desperate people among millions of desperate people. And I was just hitching a ride.'

'I don't understand.'

'Sidney, to be a smuggler, one essential thing you need is a border; some sort of frontier over which you can do your smuggling. And if that border is getting ready to move, you have to move with it. Or better still, move ahead of it. So, you're in place when it arrives. Maybe in somewhere like Evesham. Before it maybe moves on again. By which time *you'll* have moved on again.'

'Christ! You mean…?'

'Yes. The border is about to be breached. By hundreds of thousands of hungry, desperate people. My people. And in their wake, there'll be hundreds of thousands more. And then millions. The border will be washed away. Far to the south. Depending, I suppose, on how well your lot gets its act together. And I can't begin to describe how ugly it will get. Shit, there might even be a hiatus in the need for smugglers – no matter where we might position ourselves in readiness for the deluge.'

Sidney was again thrown off balance. Here was his guest once more mixing humour with an eloquent use of English. But at the same time, he was delivering the news that Hope Farm, together with an enormous swathe of the south, was about to be inundated by a tsunami of northerners. Not in the cause of conquest, but in the cause of staying alive. And the northerners' potential starvation meant that there was no way they'd be dissuaded from their plan.

Although this news was no more than a confirmation of what Sidney had already learnt from that session with Sanjiv, it was still very difficult to take in. He therefore indulged in some mental temporisation by asking his informant about his two friends and the other northerners who'd either been spotted or dispatched over the last few days. 'Why did they jump the gun?' he enquired.

'Impatience,' was the one-word response. But then Hazeem went on, 'Well, mostly impatience, but there was fear as well – and opportunism, of course. Take my two friends. They were so desperate that they'd convinced themselves they could set themselves up as scouts, as some sort of advance guard for the… well, you know, for the "invading army". And they were hoping they might even do more than just survive – if they got rewarded well enough for their services. Just like I would for mine—'

'And this "invading army",' interrupted Sidney. 'When, exactly, is it due to arrive?'

'In two days' time. That's when the dam's due to burst.'

'Two days! Jeez!'

'Yes, 2 September. It's been in the diary for weeks.'

'And what's so special about 2 September?'

'Easy. It's an anniversary.'

'Of what?'

'You don't need to know – other than it's of something that happened ages ago, and it means that 2 September this year is an auspicious day. Auspicious enough to make it the perfect day to kick off a mass migration from the north.'

'God!'

'God, my friend, has probably very little to do with all this. It's more to do with all his children here on earth and what they've been doing *to* the earth. And before you ask, I'm a lot better smuggler than I am a "follower". And I suspect we should leave it at that.'

This was overload. Too much was happening in Sidney's world, and it was all happening too fast. He needed time to think – time to make some sense out of what he'd heard. And maybe time to talk to his radio friends.

However, before he had such an opportunity, Hazeem provided him with something of a diversion from his ferment – by asking him about the equipment he used to talk to his friends, as well as about his store of books. He'd had the opportunity to study all Sidney's unusual possessions during the day, and he was now keen to learn how Sidney had acquired them and what those mysterious metal boxes did – if they did anything at all.

Sidney was happy to provide all the answers to Hazeem's questions. He also promised him that – as soon as he could after he'd had some much-needed sleep, and if it were safe – he would demonstrate the use of the radio kit. Probably, he informed Hazeem, to ask for some guidance from his radio friends – on how he might go about dealing with the end of his world.

Hazeem was amused.

Sidney, however, was just exhausted. Far too exhausted to think about what to do next and or to debate with his house guest what to do next. So, instead, he excused himself for the night and immediately lay back on his bed. There, he soon went to sleep – hoping, as he drifted off, that he would wake up well before 2 September…

Hamza, 2078

Excitement. Anticipation. So much anticipation. After all those months. Month after month, all cramped together. On top of each other. In each other's way. No peace. No room. No room to think. No way for people to live. No way for a family to thrive. No way to raise seven precious gifts from that munificent God. Hamza loathed it. Resented it. Found it truly offensive. When others had so much room. So much space. Too much space. Space they couldn't use. While he, Yalina and all his young ones had to endure. Had to live in a hutch. Had to exist in a hutch. Had to exist as they could.

And nobody helped. Nobody wanted to know. Nobody wanted to think of their plight. It just wasn't fair. It just wasn't right. It couldn't go on. And there were others like him. Thousands like him. Tens of thousands like him.

Maybe more. All of them squeezed into coops. Coops that were far too small. Far too small for a proper family. Something had to change. Something had to be done. Something had to be done to save them.

And praise be! His voice had been heard. His voice and the voice of others. For at last, their likes were firmly in charge. And they were listening. They were receptive. And they had power. More power than ever. And the power to put things to rights. To make it fair. To ensure Hamza and tens of thousands of other Hamzas could get what was rightly theirs. Space. All the space they would ever need. And it was so easy. So straightforward. So just! Even if not everyone agreed...

The diehards. The bigots. The racists. The owners of all those large houses. The owners of houses they couldn't fill. Houses with more rooms than children. Or houses with no children at all! Occupied by barren bigots. Hoarding all that space. All that valuable space. How could they do that? How could they sleep at night? How could they not be consumed with guilt?

No matter. They wouldn't prevail. Theirs was a cause that was lost. And if not willingly, then with 'persuasion' they would move. To a hutch. To a hutch that was now empty. A hutch just vacated. By a Hamza. Or by a Jaaved. Or by a Salman. All now gone to a much bigger home. With their much bigger families. Families who deserved a lot more than a miserable hutch.

And today, it was Hamza's turn! Hamza and Yalina's turn. And Hamza and Yalina's children's turn. All of them off to a new home. A fitting home. A home meant to be filled with life. Completely filled with life. So, that excitement. Unbounded excitement. And sky-high anticipation. Anticipation of an end to an existence and the beginning of a life. A proper life. A proper life in a proper house. A decent house. A large house.

And there it was. Standing alone. In its own garden. With trees. And shrubs. And a drive. A gravel drive! Palatial. Impressive. Imposing. And now theirs. Now theirs to explore. Theirs to discover that within it, it was grand. And pristine. And furnished. And all that Hamza had ever prayed for. And more. More space than he could absorb. More space than he could come to terms with. More space than even the nine of them would need. Or maybe God had some other ideas…

And maybe God even had a care for those who had been here before. Those who were now in a hutch. Feeling remorseful. And chastised. And ashamed. With only one child. How selfish they had been. And thoughtless. And heedless. And helpless…

But no. Maybe God had better things to do than care for such wretches. Such remnants. Such overstayers of their time. They were nothing now. No longer of interest. No longer in control. No longer in any way relevant. And within a couple of days of Hamza moving into their home, not even given a passing thought by their home's gleeful new tenants.

10.

'Hey! Wake up! Rouse yourself, you idle bastard.'

The shouted instruction worked. Sidney woke with a start, sprang out of bed immediately and nearly tripped over Hazeem in the process. Hazeem had spent the night on the cabin floor beneath a blanket, but he was now wide awake as well. Not that Sidney was aware of this, as Hazeem hadn't moved and it was still very dark. It must, thought Sidney, be just before dawn. And he also thought the voice he'd heard was that of someone he knew. This was confirmed when a follow-up 'Come on, move yourself' command was uttered. There was now no doubt about it. It was Farid. And Farid was just outside the cabin door.

Sidney was too surprised to be panicked. Instead, he told himself that Farid had never stepped foot in his cabin in his life – for fear of exposing himself to so much of what he didn't understand – and he was therefore highly unlikely to come in now. This meant that, even if the door of the cabin were opened, there was no way Farid would discover that Hazeem was on the cabin's floor. Just as long, that is, as Hazeem didn't move from where he was.

Sidney now knew enough about Hazeem to be confident that he wouldn't. So, with barely any hesitation, he stepped to the door, opened it and greeted his early morning caller, 'Farid, is there a problem?'

'Fucking right there's a problem. It's called all those bastards from the north.'

'Ah, I meant—'

'Look. All you need to know is that father and me will be out most of the day. We'll be taking the wagon, and we won't be back till evening. So, make sure you keep your ears and your eyes open. And if you see anything... well, use your imagination – or maybe your sickle. I don't want to come back to a houseful of heathens. And do some bloody work as well.'

Sidney would have acknowledged these thoughtful instructions if Farid hadn't immediately turned away and disappeared through the gloom. He'd clearly not enjoyed having to get out of bed quite so early – or having to carry a message to someone he so loathed.

Instead, after Farid was far enough away, Sidney turned to Hazeem and offered him a greeting. 'Morning, had a good night?'

As he lifted himself from the floor, Hazeem presented his host with a response. 'Morning to you.

And, yes, thanks; I had a very peaceful night. Right up until a few minutes ago. Talking of which, may I just say I now know you can be a very cool character. You didn't say much to that guy, but what you did say sounded calm and collected. And by the way, who was that guy? Presumably one of the family's sons.'

'Yes. That was Farid, the family's son who killed the family's other son, and the one who hastened the demise of your two friends.'

It was still too dark to see the surprise on Hazeem's face, but not too early – when Hazeem requested it – to supply him with the full story of Viraj's murder. He was therefore soon well acquainted with the behaviour of the two remaining males of Sidney's 'guardian' family – both of whom wouldn't be a cause for concern for the whole of the day.

*

Yes, it took very little time for Sidney and Hazeem to appreciate that they'd been granted a whole waking day to sort out what they might need to do next to prepare for the imminent upheaval of the world. No 'bloody work' would be done to satisfy Farid's command, but instead, some thinking and some consultation would be undertaken – concerning the expected deluge due in twenty-four hours' time.

A light breakfast came first, during which Hazeem's present incapacitation was discussed. His ankle was apparently a little better, but he was still having some trouble walking. However, with breakfast consumed, it was now time to focus on that topic of the world's upheaval – regarding which, Sidney announced that it might be better to invest in some consultation before any thinking – or planning – was tackled. As this would also mean he could demonstrate the magic of radio communication to Hazeem as he'd promised.

Hazeem agreed.

So, with the morning beginning to lighten, Sidney booted up his equipment, and after reciting his traditional radio-ham prayers, he was soon on the hunt for his mate in Windhoek. It might be a bit early for Ted, but he'd understand. His life was all about dealing with emergencies, and an imminent threat of being overwhelmed – not with snakes but with hungry foreigners – easily constituted one of the most serious emergencies imaginable.

When contact had been established, Sidney was delighted to hear Ted's voice – even though it betrayed that he'd probably had a late and *demanding* night – and he was equally delighted to observe that Hazeem was entranced by the long-standing magic of frequency modulation.

As soon as he could, Sidney asked Ted just to listen while he gave him a brief rundown of what had happened at Hope Farm and what was now due to happen.

When Ted then responded to these revelations, he sounded entirely sober – and very concerned. He clearly appreciated that his friend in England wasn't facing just the prospect of possible hunger and, ultimately, starvation, but now the prospect of death at the hands of a horde of invaders – and maybe in only twenty-four hours' time.

Ted started off by admitting he had no super powers that would enable him to whisk Sidney and his new foreign friend off to safety. He only wished he had, he confessed. But there again, he did know of this woman in Scotland. And if anybody had super powers, it might just be her. In which case, he and Sidney should terminate their radio conversation forthwith to enable one Windhoek radio ham to make contact with another in Scotland as soon as possible. And when he'd done this and as soon as he had anything to report, he'd then get back to Sidney. Although maybe without anything of any use. But it was certainly worth a try, he assured Sidney. Especially, as there were now, he emphasised, *two* lives to look out for.

When Sidney closed down the line to Ted, he couldn't fail to notice that Hazeem was wearing an expression he probably rarely wore. It betrayed an odd mix of wonder and gratitude; wonder, no doubt, at the workings of the technology he'd just observed, and gratitude, no doubt, that someone he neither knew nor with whom he had anything in common had so easily and so willingly accepted him as someone who needed help. And, of course, inherent in this acceptance was a disregard of the fact that Hazeem was from 'the wrong side of the border', but instead, there was an acknowledgement that he was Sidney's mate – and his valuable ally.

Sidney could see all this had made Hazeem feel very humble. It augured well, he thought, for their (probably) shared, immediate future.

*

However, Sidney's thoughts were soon somewhere else. Because, having assured Hazeem that, in due course, he would explain Ted's reference to a superwoman in Scotland, he was already conjuring up another virtual meeting with a faraway friend. It was now late enough in the morning, he thought, to find Marc out of bed.

Marc was out of bed. Albeit he was not in the best of moods. 'Sidney!' he exclaimed before Sidney had a chance to talk, 'I'm glad you called. I need to let off a little stream—'

'Steam,' Sidney corrected automatically.

'*Oui*, steam. You see these "clients" of mine... well, three of them – *oui*, three of them – they 'ave made some outrageous claims about my new *premiere* pastis. They 'ave claimed that it 'as affected their eyesight. That they're finding it *difficile* to focus – or, indeed, *difficile* to see anything at all. Well, they are all lying, of course. I mean, my pastis 'as never 'armed anybody's eyesight. Unless, of course, there's been some *tomber par terre* involved, if you know what I mean? After all, my stuff iz very strong, and it can cause... well, let's call them *problèmes de stabilité*. Anyway, *baise-les*. I'll sue them for deformation—'

'Defamation,' corrected Sidney again.

'*Oui*, I'll sue *les pantalons* off them, as you say. Even if I 'ave to show them the way to court.' At this point, Marc started to laugh. He'd clearly become tired of his rant, and this was confirmed when he failed to return to it, but instead enquired after Sidney's situation – and, in particular, his food situation. How were things generally, he asked, and were things any better on the food front?

When Sidney then briefed him on what had recently taken place at Hope Farm and what was now about to overwhelm it, Marc's first response was to apologise for all the nonsense he'd been spouting and to ask for Sidney's forgiveness for what had been such a stupid, self-absorbed opening to their exchange.

Sidney assured him that no forgiveness was required, and he went on to suggest that, if Marc had a recipe for any beverage that might be able to blind an advancing army of intruders, then he might want to read it over the airways – straightaway.

This suggestion made even Hazeem laugh, and it certainly brought the radio exchange back on track – and heading in the direction Sidney wanted: towards some sort of practical advice. Or, indeed, towards any sort of advice. He knew he'd been here before, but this didn't stop Sidney hoping there might be something Marc could say that in some way would be of assistance.

In the event, Marc did have something to say. And whilst it was nothing new, it was probably more relevant than ever, and in due course, it would certainly have an impact on the decisions Sidney made.

'Sidney,' Marc began, sounding graver than he'd ever sounded before, 'I feel 'elpless stuck over 'ere, and I 'ave nothing to tell you that I 'aven't told you before. But it seems to me that, given what you're now going to 'ave to face, you should not lose sight of two pieces of my home-distilled advice; two pieces I think I mentioned in a recent conversation. The first piece of advice iz "be ruthless". And if you've got a new real friend there, that goes for 'im as well. You can't afford to be otherwise. And the second piece of advice iz "don't do the obvious" – which, given that you now 'ave an admirer in *Écosse*, might be more relevant than ever. Don't ask me 'ow; I 'ave no idea. But… well, be open to any solution. Any at all. It may save your life.'

Sidney made it clear that he was grateful for this counsel, but again, he felt a little disappointed. Marc had once more proffered no specific advice, and it was now becoming more apparent than ever that Sidney and Hazeem would have to provide their own salvation. Even in the unlikely event that his distant Scottish admirer could in some way hold out a remote helping hand – within a very short period of time. And that was very unlikely indeed.

Despite the disappointment, Sidney tried to sound cheerful when he signed off, and he remembered to wish Marc well in his dealings with his aggrieved and partially or totally blinded clients – all three of whom were, of course, the owners of perfectly working peepers and deserved nothing less than the loss of their *pantalons*. And possibly a bottle or two of his standard-issue pastis if they dropped their accusations and then displayed a suitable degree of remorse.

Hazeem was now looking a little puzzled. Even with his perfect command of English, references to 'pastis' and 'peepers' had clearly left him at a loss. So too, as was apparent from his first question to Sidney, had that mention of somewhere called *Écosse*.

'Where's this Coss place? I've never heard of it,' Hazeem questioned.

Sidney responded to Hazeem's question with a smile. 'It's *É-cosse,* and it's French for Scotland.'

'Ah! I see. The woman in Scotland again. The woman Ted was going to contact. The woman you were going to tell me about.'

'Yes. And a woman who I've never met or even spoken to.' This was Sidney's opening to Hazeem's lesson on the mysterious Dorothy – a lesson that took little time to deliver in view of how little was known about her.

However, Hazeem was fascinated, not only by the fact that there was an English-speaking woman (and maybe others) living in the heart of 'his' land but also that she had access to the same long-distance communication as his host. Nonetheless, he was also perplexed. If she had the same sort of kit as Sidney's, why weren't they speaking to each other directly? Why was Sidney relying on people in other parts of the world to act as go-betweens? And furthermore, how had this technology emerged from the ashes of mobile communication? How, when the ubiquitous cell-phone disappeared, had somebody devised this new way of communicating over long distances?

Hazeem put all these questions to Sidney, and Sidney's first response had to be a broad smile. Then he began to follow up his lecture on Dorothy with another on HF radio communication, starting with the information that this form of communication actually predated mobile communication – which everybody had heard of through their older relatives – and it certainly hadn't arisen from the ashes of that defunct technology. That it was so old that it had dropped out of the collective memory of at least three generations – but that, with the right equipment, it still worked perfectly well. He then went on to explain why, with the equipment he had, he could talk to someone in Namibia but not to someone in Scotland. This inevitably got rather technical, but ultimately, Hazeem began to grasp the concept of bouncing radio waves around the world and how, to receive them, someone with the right kit would have to be beyond the length of a signal skip. If they were too close, he or she would have to employ something called 'ground-wave propagation', which wasn't something Sidney's kit was set up for.

It all made some sort of sense, Hazeem conceded as the lecture ended, although he had to admit that something called the 'ionosphere' – against which the waves apparently bounced – sounded more like a fairy story than something real. And a fairy story that was even more difficult to swallow than some of the stuff he'd been taught in his youth. Albeit, there again, he added, this fairy story did seem to have some sort of use…

When Sidney heard this view expressed, he was tempted to ask Hazeem to expand on his thoughts, but just as he was about to, a blinking, green light on his radio kit told him somebody was trying to call him, and he needed to attend to this straightaway.

It was Sonia. She had some urgent news. 'Sidney, Sidney,' she began excitedly. 'Dorothy wants you in Scotland.'

'*What?*'

'Ted called me. He couldn't get through to Scotland, so I called Dorothy and told her what was going on – you know, in your neck of the woods. And, well, I haven't got back to Ted yet as I thought I should call you first coz of what Dorothy told me. And so that's why I'm calling you now… That's… er, wait a minute. I… er…'

Sonia was racing, and it sounded as though she'd soon career off the track. It was time for Sidney to put a hand on the wheel.

'Sonia,' he said. 'Just calm down a bit. I've still got some power at this end, so you've got plenty of time.'

'Oh, sorry, Sidney, but… well, you know…'

'Just take it from the top,' advised Sidney, 'slowly and calmly.'

'Yes,' agreed Sonia. 'Slowly and calmly. I feel such a fool.'

'You're not a fool, Sonia. It's just that you've obviously got something important to tell me. Which is what I suggest you do now – slowly and calmly, remember.

And maybe even including why Dorothy wants me in Scotland.'

Sidney could hear a substantial sigh from faraway Saskatoon, and then Sonia continued. Quite slowly and relatively calmly. 'Right. Well, you see, Dorothy didn't know you were so close to… you know, a real problem. But as soon as I told her what was going on, she insisted she wanted to help. I mean, she insisted she wanted to offer you some refuge in Scotland. Sidney, she wants you up there with her. She thinks it might be the only way you'll survive.'

Sidney felt a shiver going down his spine. For a brief second, that last short sentence uttered by his friend in Canada had blotted out anything she'd said before, and he was overwhelmed by what seemed to be the extreme paucity of his survival options. Indeed, it seemed as if the only way to dodge fate's fatal bullet was to make his way to Scotland – and that would be impossible.

However, the brief second passed, and as slowly and calmly as he could manage, he then posed a question to Sonia. 'How on earth does Dorothy think I can make it all the way up to Scotland? After all, it's not only a very long way up north but, as you can well imagine, there might be a rather large… well, *army* in the way.'

'Ah,' responded Sonia, her voice sounding strangely euphoric. 'that's why I've called you. To tell you what Dorothy told me about how you might get there. And I've written it all down. So, I won't mess it up. So, if you're ready, I'll tell you now what she told me.'

Sidney doubted he'd ever been more ready for anything in his whole life, and so he invited Sonia to carry on. Not necessarily slowly, but just very calmly.

'OK,' she began 'What you have to do is get yourself to a place called "RAF Cosford" in somewhere called Shropshire. Apparently, about a century or more ago – according to Dorothy – it used to be an airfield. You know, for aeroplanes. For military flying machines. I don't know what it's used for now, but it seems that there's one of Dorothy's friends there. And he'll know the way to Dorothy's place. So, if you go there, he'll be looking out for you, and when he finds you, he'll be able to lead you further north. I mean, he'll be able to take you to where Dorothy is. And all being well, your problems will then be solved!'

Sidney wasn't sure what to say. Sonia might just as well have told him that a refuge existed on the Moon, and if he made his way there, his future would be assured. Oh, and his voyage to the Moon would be assisted by someone he'd never met in a place he'd never heard of. However, to his credit, he didn't relay these thoughts to his Canadian friend; instead, he merely asked her whether Dorothy had imparted any further uplifting news.

And she had. She'd finally admitted to Sonia that she was one of a small community. She wasn't on her own. Furthermore, the whole community was really eager to bolster its numbers with someone like Sidney. They were really keen to take in somebody who had a knowledge of books.

At this point in their exchange, Sidney realised that the power in his machine was dwindling, and he hastily thanked Sonia for the news she'd delivered and promised her that he would get back to her when he'd decided what to do – so that she could report back to Dorothy, and to Ted and Marc as well. Then it was turn-off time, and time to talk to his in-house friend, time to share his thoughts – and his bemusement – with Hazeem. He'd been listening to the exchange himself, and now looked not quite as bemused as Sidney, but rather more… well, intrigued.

'Well,' Sidney opened, 'what do you make of that? And of my chances of meandering through a battle line to start a new life in… *Écosse*? Would even a smuggler take on such a challenge?'

'If he had the right support,' responded Hazeem. 'I mean, the right friend. One who might just know how to get to, say, RAF Cosford. And one who might want to repay him for saving his life…'

11.

For Sidney, the first day of September was proving to be a day like no other before. Not only were the other residents of Hope Farm either absent or dead, but Hope Farm had an uninvited guest, and he was an English-speaking smuggler from north of the border. Then there was the prospect of an invasion to take account of, to say nothing of an unexpected invitation to visit Scotland – which, although it might constitute a lifeline, was impossible to accept. It simply wasn't feasible to travel maybe 250 miles through unknown territory against what was likely to be a flood of belligerent migrants moving south. Even with the help of a friendly smuggler, one who now appeared to be exploring the practicalities of exactly such a trip.

'What state is the wagon in?' Hazeem asked. 'Could it do a long journey?'

Sidney shook his head. He could barely believe what Hazeem was asking. However, having no wish to appear rude, he did provide his smuggler friend with a response to his questions. 'It's… well, sound. I mean, very sound. But as regards a long journey, I just don't know. It's never done one. And anyway, I just don't—'

'And the mule?' interrupted Hazeem. 'I mean, I assume there's a mule.'

'Yes. Kaalki. He's a great mule, but…'

'Wouldn't clap out after a few miles?'

'No. Well, I don't think so. I mean, he rarely does other than local stuff. But, Hazeem, this is all irrelevant. The idea of—'

Hazeem made his third interruption in a row, not to ask a question, but to make a statement – about RAF Cosford. 'I know RAF Cosford. I've been there. It's a dump. I mean, a real rubbish dump. Has been for as long as I can remember. But that's not important. What is important is that I know my way there. And I reckon, with a good wagon and a good mule, we could get there in about three days.'

Sidney shook his head again. '*We?* Hazeem, we aren't joined at the hip. As soon as your ankle is OK, you can be off to the Vale of Evesham or wherever else you want to be off to. I mean, the idea of your coming with me—'

'Is a great one, I know.'

Sidney regarded the northerner before him. He could see Hazeem was being deadly serious; that he had in mind a joint trip to the north – an absurd joint trip to the north.

Sidney needed to persuade him otherwise. 'What you're suggesting is very noble, and I thank you sincerely for your offer. But what you're suggesting, as well as being noble, is completely mad. I mean, the idea of Rishi lending us his wagon and then our heading north with Kaalki to maybe find someone we don't know in… in a rubbish dump is preposterous beyond words. And there's also the small matter of that swarm of guys poised on the border – to say nothing of the fact that I'm white, and they're not. And they might just notice that. Which could be another minor problem.

'I mean, Hazeem, I don't want to sound completely negative, but this just isn't a runner. We wouldn't get a yard beyond the border. And then we probably wouldn't get a great deal older. Or at least I wouldn't.'

Hazeem smiled. He wasn't a big man, and with that grin on his thin face, he put Sidney in mind of an imp: a devilish imp with some devilish ideas. And he now addressed Sidney's misgivings. 'You're right, of course. It's all preposterous beyond words. Us heading north in a wagon would be a complete waste of time, and it would probably cost us our lives.'

And here his tone changed. 'But what are our alternatives? How practical – or preposterous – might they be?'

'*Our* alternatives?' queried Sidney. 'I think you've forgotten what I said. You're a free agent. As soon as that ankle can bear your weight, you can be off to wherever you want. And you certainly don't want to be weighed down by me.'

'You let me decide that,' retorted Hazeem firmly. 'And at least for the sake of this argument, let's stick with "our". In which case, I ask you again: what are *our* alternatives?'

Sidney capitulated and gave a resigned sigh. 'Well… it's obvious. We both go south. We outrun the invasion. Or… I mean, if you're going to set yourself up as—'

'You said "obvious", Sidney. Obvious. And what did your friend Marc say?'

Sidney hesitated before replying to Hazeem's interruption. 'I know he said, "Don't do the obvious," but he didn't mean, "Don't do what is obviously sensible, but instead do what is absolutely crazy." That wasn't on his mind.'

'Sidney, have you ever in your life had the offer of a refuge – from one of your own kind? Have you ever been presented with the possibility of not living as a serf – completely cut off from people like yourself? Well, have you?'

'No,' responded Sidney rather sullenly, 'I haven't.'

'OK, I know you still think I'm mad, but may I ask a favour?'

'Of course.'

'Humour me. Just pretend for the rest of the day that the idea of us heading off north isn't preposterous, and then work out what you might like to take with you when we go. And what we might need to take to feed ourselves on the way. And how we might collect all this stuff together. How we might prepare for our looney expedition to this fabled *Écosse* place. I mean, it doesn't look as though we can stay around here, does it? So it might not be such a bad idea to give all this stuff some proper thought anyway. And while you're doing that, I intend to find myself a makeshift crutch and have myself a little wander around. I want to see where the murderer of my two friends has been spending his time.'

Sidney capitulated again. He promised to give some thought to the preparations required for a trip – to anywhere – and he also made no attempt to dissuade Hazeem from his plan to explore Home Farm and wherever else he intended to wander.

*

And thus the day passed, with Sidney inside the cabin, contemplating both what the immediate future might hold and how he would deal with abandoning his home, and Hazeem hobbling around outside, for most of the time well out of sight of the cabin. It wasn't until late afternoon that he returned – barely needing his makeshift crutch anymore and looking more impish than ever. And not, Sidney thought, just because he'd returned with a haul of cooked chicken liberated from the farmhouse kitchen.

At first, Sidney was appalled that Hazeem had done this. After all, when Rishi and Farid returned and discovered the theft of this most valuable food, they would go crazy. Sidney just knew it. And then all hell would break loose. But 'so what' he then thought? All hell was about to break loose anyway, so what was the point in worrying? Better to get on and eat the spoils, and then hide the evidence of the crime. That way, this early dose of hell might be deferred or even avoided completely. And he hadn't tasted chicken for years…

*

After the meal, Sidney showed Hazeem a list he'd made of what he thought might be essential to take on any journey, and was first of all delighted – but not surprised – to discover that Hazeem could read. Hazeem was clearly delighted himself that Sidney had acceded to his request – and more than delighted to spot that the list contained an *A-Z of Britain*, an ancient map book of the entire country, now probably more than a century old but, presumably, still in one piece. It was. Battered and yellow, but still in one piece, still intact, and still usable. It would be absolutely ideal for an excursion to the north.

It was now early evening, and after Sidney had shown Hazeem a handful of the other books he'd put on his 'to take with us' list, Hazeem announced he was going out again. He said he wanted to take a look at the wagon and the mule – when Rishi and Farid arrived back from wherever they'd been. And, now he was mobile – and for Sidney's sake – he also wanted to keep away from Sidney whilst he could. Better, if he were discovered, that he was discovered alone than with his protector. And that meant he wanted Sidney to stay in the cabin until he returned, which might not be until he was satisfied that Rishi and Farid had bedded down for the night. Only then would he come back to join Sidney in his cabin.

Sidney thought that Hazeem, having wandered around God knows where during the day, was again taking unnecessary risks. However, he now appreciated that this is what Hazeem did as part of his 'profession', and there was no point whatsoever in dissuading him from his plan.

In any event, Sidney thought, when he sees the wagon, he might have second thoughts about employing it for a long-distance trip, even assuming the impossible happened, and its owners offered it up for his use. Having first of all forgiven him for his stealing their chicken.

When he'd gone, Ted came through on the radio. Sidney had spoken to him earlier in the day to bring him up to date on the developing situation, but it now seemed that Ted had something *he* wished to impart. It was a piece of very specific advice, and it concerned a weapon.

'Sid, my old mate,' he began, 'I know what a decent sort of chap you are, and that normally you wouldn't hurt a fly. But take it from me; sometimes you have to be prepared to hurt not just a fly – but anything that gets in the way of your staying alive. I know. I've had to do it myself. And on more than one occasion, what was getting in the way of my staying alive was on two legs and was not a native of this land – if you get my drift. And Sidney, I've admitted this to no one before, but I thought I should admit it to you now, not just to alert you to the dangers you may be about to face but also to advise you how you might best deal with these dangers. And that's with a knife. Get the nastiest, sharpest knife you can find and keep it about you at all times. Because it can be a literal lifesaver, and you should never be without it.

'I hope I'm being a bit over the top here, but I suspect I'm not. Arm yourself, Sidney, and arm yourself with something very sharp – and be prepared to use it. Nobody will thank you for being restrained in its use when you're dead.'

Sidney was shocked. Not so much by the advice – which echoed that given by Marc – but that Ted had just admitted to more than one killing. And he'd killed his victims with a knife. He'd got to with inches of them, and then either plunged a blade into their flesh or ripped it open with a blade. Up-close, gory stuff. And whilst he clearly couldn't afford to be squeamish as a snake catcher, depriving a fellow human of his life in that way was taking things to a different level. One that Ted was now suggesting should be embraced by a diffident Sid.

He tried not to reveal his shock as he acknowledged Ted's advice. Instead, he made it very clear that he would take the advice and get himself 'a big one' – one that, as he dramatically described, would need only one thrust.

When the exchange was then concluded, Sidney asked himself who he was trying to fool. He doubted he could even scratch someone with his fingernails, let alone stab him with a knife. And he well remembered how awkward he'd felt even with just a blunt sickle. However, these thoughts were filling his head just minutes before Hazeem returned from his recce, which meant they would soon have to make room for some very different thoughts.

*

Hazeem had walked into the cabin without his improvised crutch. It looked as though his ankle was more or less mended. Sidney was just about to confirm with him that this was the case when his northern guest announced he had some news.

'Sidney, I think we have a wagon. Oh, and that Kaalki's a sweetie, isn't he? And powerful. He'll be ideal for the job.'

'You think we have a wagon? What do you mean? And don't tell me Rishi agreed to your having it. Or Farid, for that matter. I just won't believe it.'

'No, they didn't agree. Because I didn't ask them.'

'*You've stolen it?*'

'No, Sidney. I haven't stolen it. It's over by the farm now, and Kaalki is in his stable.'

'I don't understand.'

'Sidney, Rishi and Farid are dead. I killed them. With a knife I found earlier today. They were both dead before they knew it.'

'*What?*'

'Rishi killed my friends. Farid killed your friend. And, more importantly, we need a wagon and a mule. And I don't think those two murderers would have given up either very willingly. So, they had to go. Justice and deliverance with two simple cuts to the throat. And they didn't even have a chance to find out I'd nicked their chicken.'

Sidney realised his mouth was almost painfully dry. There was now no question that his life was about to change. Indeed, it had already changed. He was harbouring the killer of his masters, and it seemed that he now had little option other than to throw in his lot with this man – a man on whom he had set eyes only the previous day. And it was Rishi and Farid who this chap had killed! His owner and his owner's vicious son. No wonder his mouth was so dry – and no wonder he was literally speechless.

'Anyway,' Hazeem continued, 'our two dear departed chums will, of course, be aiding us in our expedition north, but I'll leave it until tomorrow to explain exactly how. Because, I have to say, it looks to me as though you're probably not in receiving mode at the moment. You look a little bit shell-shocked.'

Sidney was more than a little bit shell-shocked, but he finally managed a few words: 'You really have killed them, haven't you?'

'Yes, Sidney. It's not the sort of thing I'd joke about. And before you pass sentence on me, remember two things. One is that piece advice from your mate in France – to be ruthless – which is all I've been. And two, well, these two guys had it coming to them. I haven't just murdered two innocents. I've murdered two murderers, two good-for-nothing monsters who had blood on their hands. Well, they've now got more of it around their necks, and I can only say it rather suits them.'

Sidney let out a sigh, bowed his head and then raised it again to look Hazeem straight in the eyes. 'You'll have to forgive me, Hazeem, but it's not every day that someone tells me that they've just killed my masters. Even if they both deserved to be killed. And nor is it every day that someone insists on trying to save my life by risking his own. Which – as you well know – is exactly what you're doing. So, I'm more than just a little bit shell-shocked. I admit it. And certainly far too shell-shocked to conceive how Rishi and Farid are somehow going to help us on our… on our "expedition", any more than I can conceive that we really are going to embark on such an expedition at all. Maybe I'm just dreaming.'

'No, Sidney, you're not dreaming. But make quite sure you have sweet dreams tonight. You'll need all the rest you can get for what awaits us tomorrow and over the next few days. And while you're absorbing this advice, I have to ask you to excuse me. I have one last job to attend to before I settle down for the night.'

And with that request, Hazeem left his friend in the cabin – to do all the absorbing he needed to do – and disappeared in the direction of the farmhouse. He didn't tell Sidney, but he'd gone off to attend to his friends.

By the time he returned, Sidney had fallen into a deep sleep, and he wasn't having nightmares.

Kuldeep, 2112

Sullen. Both of them sullen. But they should understand. That it's right. That's it's for their own good. That they'll be with their own. All happy together. A new type of place. A new type of life. A new challenge. And they were given notice. Two weeks ago. Plenty of time to come to terms. To accept. To prepare. To pack. Yet still sullen. Still clearly resentful. Barely even civil.

Kuldeep had seen it before. Seen how resistant his clients could be. Even when he helped them. Even when he helped them with their stuff. No gratitude. No manners. No appreciation of his efforts. And it was nothing personal. It wasn't his doing. It wasn't his idea to shift them. It was what had been agreed. What had been laid down. What was necessary. What was vital if he and his kind were to have the space they so needed. Space no longer needed by those who'd be moved. Who'd be planted in a new space. A new space with their own kith and kin. Just for them. A haven. A refuge. A sanctuary. Somewhere they could really call their own. Where they could thrive. Where they could flourish. Where they could prosper again.

So why cry? Why, when the door was closed and locked, were there tears on her face? Why did her husband have to hold her? It was wrong. It was stupid. It was uncalled for. And it wouldn't be of any use. It wouldn't get Kuldeep to change his mind. It wouldn't make him give back their flat. How could it? It wasn't his decision. It wasn't his call to make. He was just doing his job. Just moving people on. Just helping people with a new start in life. Just doing what was best for them. If only they'd see this. If only they'd see it was good. And yet all they would do was cry.

In the truck, it was silent. Nobody spoke. Nobody passed the time. Nobody even cried any more. Still just sullen. And still ungrateful. No thanks for Kuldeep's help. For Kuldeep's kindness. And no thanks for being ferried in a truck! A real truck. A real working truck. Not a wagon. Not a beat-up cart. But a rare working truck. Just for them. Just for these two ungracious clients. It made Kuldeep cross. It's not what he'd have done. Not if he'd been saved from pushing a handcart. Saved from having to make his own way to a new life. Saved from indignity and, instead, given a grand ride. No wonder it had been decided to give these people their own place. To give them a chance to live together. To live with their own kind. With their own ungracious kind.

And there they were. Thousands of them. Thousands of brand-new citizens in a brand-new world. A world set apart. A world set apart from the world they'd once controlled. The world that was no longer theirs. Some were in the fields. Some were in their tents. And others were gathered at the entrance. Ready to process the new arrivals. The new fortunate few who could now carve out a new life on an untouched square mile of land. Theirs to be farmed. Theirs to be built on as they wished. And theirs to be run as they wished. As a world set apart.

She was crying again. He was holding her again. What were they thinking? How could they behave in that way? How could they not be excited? How could they not be thrilled? Now that they'd seen their new home. Now that they'd caught sight of their new world. And a world where quite soon, they'd be bringing into being a new life. Where, quite soon, she'd be losing that bump on her front and gifting her new friends a new bundle of joy. Surely a cause for celebration. For jubilation. For delight. And for rapture if it were a boy. Even a boy with one of those strange English names. Not Kuldeep or Aadesh or Saadhik or Jasprit, but Walter or Albert or Simon – or possibly Sidney.

Not that this Kuldeep would ever know or ever much care.

12.

Hazeem looked despondent. The imp no longer looked impish. And with good reason. It was the dawn of 2 September, but as Sidney was about to find out, it wasn't the prospect of an implausible trip to the north that was making his co-conspirator appear morose; instead, it was the need for some overdue care for his friends.

'They left them on a pile of rubble,' he announced to Sidney. 'One on top of the other. I mean, how could they do that?'

It wasn't what Sidney had expected as his start to the day. And he immediately felt a wave of guilt. Not only had he dismissed from his mind the murder of two wrongly accused men – probably due to all the other concerns on his mind – but he'd also given no thought whatsoever to how their remains had or hadn't been dealt with. Well, now he had to because his despondent new friend had just informed him that their remains had been disrespected. That they had been treated as if they were garbage; thrown onto a pile of bricks and stones to rot away or to be eaten by vermin.

It was why, he learnt, Hazeem had disappeared the previous evening. He'd gone to remove them from the debris, and to wash their bodies and wrap them in a shroud, ready for the interment they were due. However, not surprisingly, that was all he'd managed to do. As he explained to Sidney, with an imperfect ankle and not nearly enough strength, the task of digging two graves had been completely beyond him.

Sidney could well understand this. Indeed, he was amazed that Hazeem had even been able to do what he'd done. He really was a diminutive character, and to have dragged two bodies off the rubble, then to have washed them – three times, apparently – before wrapping them up as required must have taken an enormous amount of effort. To then contemplate using a spade – in Hope Farm's challenging ground – was simply inconceivable.

After acknowledging Hazeem's disgust at the treatment of his friends, it was this challenging nature of Hope Farm's soil that Sidney addressed. 'It's three-oxen soil,' he announced. 'It sometimes needs a pickaxe.'

Hazeem looked quizzical.

Sidney needed to explain. 'It's very heavy clay soil around here – so heavy it was reckoned that you'd need at least three oxen to plough it. And I know you're not planning to do any ploughing, but believe me, if you're planning to dig two graves, it will take you all day. Or when I help you, then maybe just the morning. And if you don't let me help you, I'll feel very insulted. Almost as insulted as you must feel that what might have happened to your two friends' bodies didn't even cross my mind.'

'Why would it?' replied Hazeem. 'If I were you, I think it would have been pretty low down on my list of concerns. And if I'm honest, it didn't occur to me straightaway. It was only when I was poking around yesterday that I gave it any proper thought. So, don't feel guilty. Please. You shouldn't. Although if that might help your digging, maybe you should. And I have found two spades...'

Hazeem looked despondent no more. Sidney's expression of contrition and his offer of help had clearly turned his mood to one of determination.

This, blended with a sense of urgency they now shared, meant that they were soon outside, digging energetically and sweating profusely. As Hazeem suggested after the first few minutes with the spade, he could not believe that only three oxen would have been needed for this ground. It would surely have taken four if not five. It was as hard as concrete.

Between them, they had chosen a site for the graves at the far end of the pond. It was a site that was unlikely to be disturbed – no matter what might soon engulf Hope Farm – and it was relatively out of sight of the main farm building. If any uninvited guests arrived this morning, it wasn't overly likely that they would spot two amateur gravediggers going about their business. Even if they did, Hazeem would have time to conceal himself whilst Sidney went off to 'head them off at the pass'. And in any event, whatever risk they were running by exposing themselves to discovery seemed minor when compared to the shoal of risks they would soon have to face.

By noon, the job was done. Hazeem's two friends had been committed to the ground, and although Hazeem had a forgivable ignorance of any of the rituals surrounding the interment of those of his faith, he managed a few heartfelt words above their sealed resting place, which were probably a great deal better than any of those stipulated for such a solemn occasion. Sidney was moved – almost to tears.

Then the imp returned. With his companions now properly laid to rest, Hazeem was clearly keen to use the remainder of the day to look after the living – in particular, his new white friend and himself. And there was little doubt that he regarded a lively approach to what he saw as the tasks at hand as the best way to complete them. Even if it meant a somewhat lighthearted approach to the treatment of two other bodies – as was immediately apparent when he addressed his fellow gravedigger.

'OK,' he said, 'as for your friend… er, Viraj… I think his body must have been taken away. I've seen no sign of it anywhere. And I can only hope that it's being dealt with as it should be, somewhere else in the village. Which, of course, leaves us with just two bodies to deal with ourselves: those of your dear departed betters, otherwise known as Rishi and Farid.'

'We can't build a funeral pyre. And why—?'

'Sidney,' interrupted Hazeem. 'How, by putting these guys on a funeral pyre, would they be able to aid our expedition? I mean, you can't have forgotten that I told you they'd have a role in our making our way north.'

Sidney wasn't sure what to say – because he wasn't sure what to think. Hazeem was talking about two cadavers. How could they possibly play a part in his and Hazeem's improbable flight to unknown lands?

So, in the absence of a response from his friend, Hazeem proceeded to educate him on the useful employment of two dead bodies – which were already beginning to spoil. 'Look,' he said sharply, 'our lives are at stake. We've got to do anything we can to survive. Even if it means crossing a few lines.'

'Crossing a few lines…?'

'Yes. Like slitting people's throats, for example. Or maybe using their stinking bodies to mask the presence of another body, a living one belonging to this white guy I know who, as he's admitted himself, wouldn't get more than a few yards beyond a certain border without his being discovered and probably killed. On the spot.'

'I don't—'

'OK, I'll spell it out for you. You're going to gather together what you think we need for our trip to the rubbish dump at Cosford. Meanwhile, I'll use a few more of those sheets I found for my friends' bodies to wrap up Rishi's and Farid's bodies. Then we'll load them onto the wagon, ready for when we need to leave – at which point you'll be wrapped in a sheet to play the part of another niffy stiff, all on their way back to get a proper and fitting comital in… let's say, somewhere near Stoke-on-Trent – or anywhere north of Cosford, come to that.'

Sidney's eyes widened and his mouth dropped open. When he finally closed it, he then managed to speak. 'Hang on, are you suggesting that I bounce around on the back of a wagon, next to two rotting corpses, wrapped up like… well, like a corpse myself? And for maybe as long as… what? Three days?'

'Yes,' confirmed Hazeem firmly. 'Or have you a better idea?'

Sidney spluttered, but he failed to find an actual word, let alone a proper response to this confirmation.

So, Hazeem carried on, 'Sidney, you're white. However much we tried to hide it, that whiteness would almost certainly be noticed. And remember, we're not planning a ride to market; we're planning a ride through a whole load of what might be some very aggressive and very jumpy members of my clan. Guys who'll probably take more than a passing interest in a wagon heading north – given that they're heading south. There just isn't any other way.'

Sidney had now gathered himself – just enough to pose a reasonable question. 'I thought your lot had to bury your dead within twenty-four hours? I'm sure I read it in one of my books. So, how will anybody believe a story about you carting bodies up to Stoke?'

'Twenty-four hours used to be the aim – years ago. But realistically, it was just "as soon as possible". And that's drifted out even more. Now, it's more likely to be within a few days. Or in extraordinary circumstances – such as when the bodies of some brave scouts are being returned to their homes – it can be however many days it takes. No one will question it, I can tell you. And nobody will even want to get that close. I mean, it won't be long after we've set out that anyone who might be interested in us will smell us before they see us. Think rotting meat, raw sewage and a drop of really cheap perfume – and you're not even close to how bad it'll get.'

'And I'm supposed to stand that for three days?'

'Better than being dead forever. And anyway, what do I really know? It's not as though I've ever encountered a rotting body myself. I mean, how could I? I'm just a simple smuggler.'

Sidney didn't pursue this rhetorical question. The hint of a grin on Hazeem's face said more than his words. In any event, Sidney had another question. 'Hazeem, did I ever actually *specifically* agree to this madcap idea of travelling north? Because if I did, I think I'd remember.'

'Stress can take a terrible toll on one's memory,' responded Hazeem. 'And of course you've had an awful lot of stress to deal with in the last couple of days.'

That impish grin was now wider than ever, and Sidney knew that whether he'd specifically accepted Hazeem's daredevil plan or not, the plan would soon be put into action. Even the fact that its execution would entail his sharing his life with the stinking, putrefying remains of both his former master and his master's evil son wouldn't change that. Nor would the fact that it would mean leaving so many of his cherished belongings – including his prized radio. That would be more difficult than his sharing a wagon with two corpses – or so it seemed to him now.

It was time, thought Sidney, to just get on with things. To ignore the fact that he'd been seduced into a foolhardy scheme by someone he still barely knew – and rather than contemplating the hideous challenges of the scheme, to make a start on collecting together what he'd put on that list; the few possessions he just couldn't afford to part with – which, inevitably, meant a number of books. Including, of course, that A–Z.

*

It took all afternoon, but by early evening, the wagon was loaded and ready to go. Just behind the driver's bench, next to two water containers and a couple of blankets, was a store of fodder for Kaalki, and hidden beneath this, in a number of sacks, was fodder for Hazeem and Sidney. It comprised various foodstuffs they'd found in the house and quite a lot of other foodstuffs they'd liberated from the veg plot. None of it promised to be particularly appetising.

Behind these provisions, lying lengthways in the wagon, were three 'bodies'. Two of these were the remains of Rishi and Farid, wrapped in off-white linen, and the third was a body-shaped package, similarly wrapped in fabric but made up of sacks containing some of Sidney's most-cherished tomes and possessions. Hazeem had been insistent that Sidney took all this stuff with him, just as he'd been insistent that, before they might have to take flight, Sidney should use his magic radio equipment to have a final chat with his friends around the world – as well as using it to confirm that a journey to RAF Cosford was now imminent and that everyone who needed to know this did indeed know it – especially the mystery contact who would hopefully meet them at RAF Cosford.

Sidney found every aspect of this task very difficult. Because it entailed what he knew would probably be his last ever discussions with three people who had, for years, kept him sane and given him the will to live. Their loss was going to be terrible – as Sidney's departure from their world would be. He knew he was as important to them as they were to him, and this would soon become more than evident when he initiated an exchange with Sonia.

To start with, it wasn't too bad. It simply involved being scolded by Sonia for not getting back to her sooner. And didn't he realise that she'd been up most of the night trying to raise him? Then it was down to business. The name of the man at RAF Cosford, she told him, was Stephen, and Stephen would be on the lookout for a visitor from the south, whatever time of day or night that visitor might arrive. Furthermore, Stephen would be ready to move off with this visitor and guide him all the way to Dorothy's place, however difficult that journey to the far north might prove – and despite his being over eighty years old.

Sidney digested this information – even the revelation of Stephen's age – and then commenced to tell Sonia that he would indeed be setting off for Cosford – in a mule-drawn wagon, and with 'a friend' (although he didn't tell her what this friend had done with his knife). If all went to plan, he continued, they should arrive at Cosford sometime in the next few days. And if all didn't go to plan, then they almost certainly would never get there – or anywhere near Scotland for that matter. But, in any event, could she relay this information back to Dorothy and ask Dorothy to somehow pass the information on to Stephen – by carrier pigeon or whatever other means of communication she had.

Sonia assured Sidney that she would, and at this point in the exchange, she remembered to tell Sidney that Dorothy communicated with Stephen using ground-wave propagation (her radio equipment, it appeared, was both sophisticated and adaptable). So, there would be no problem in letting Stephen know what was going on, and when Sidney got to Cosford, he would even be able to speak to Dorothy directly. *And wouldn't that be good?*

Sidney had only just agreed that it would, indeed, be very good, when Sonia started to quiz him on the identity of his friend. When he then enlightened her about his friend's northerner and smuggler credentials, she sounded more than delighted, and Sidney could only assume that she was very relieved that he'd found a capable minder. Just as he could only assume that, like Ted, she had no problem whatsoever with any of Hazeem's credentials.

Then it all got very awkward. With the business out of the way, it was time to recognise that there was a farewell to deal with – and probably not just an *au revoir*. This, however, was very difficult to acknowledge, and both parties to the exchange found it easier to ignore the likelihood that the formidable problems to be faced on a journey to Scotland might prove insurmountable, and that this might be the last time they would ever speak to each other. Therefore, Sonia went out of her way to sound optimistic about Sidney's chances – to the extent of assuming a totally successful outcome to his venture – and Sidney responded in a similar manner.

'It'll be a piece of cake,' he assured her.

And this approach delivered all that both parties had hoped for, right up until Sonia burst into tears.

Sidney could deal with this even less ably than he could deal with the prospect of a radical change to his life – or the potential end to his life. But he did the best he could, and he promised that, as soon as he was safe with Dorothy, Sonia would be the first person he would call. Meanwhile, she would have to make do with a remote radio-ham kiss – the first kiss he had ever delivered, either over the airwaves or for real (other than to his parents). It was the only thing he could do, albeit he doubted he would be doing the same with either Ted or Marc.

When Sonia finally signed off, it was Ted he called next. Sidney first of all filled him in on what Hazeem had put together – and what he'd done to reduce the population of Hope Farm – and then he assured Ted that, as advised, he'd equipped himself with a very sharp knife. It wasn't the biggest knife he'd been able to find, but it was one he could carry on his person and one that would be able to puncture or rip as required. (If its new owner could ever find sufficient bottle.)

Sidney couldn't see Ted's face – obviously – but he could hear in his voice that he was lifted by the news he was hearing and that he wasn't in the least bit shocked by Hazeem's work on Rishi and Farid (or how he planned to use their remains). Sidney formed the distinct impression that Ted and Hazeem had access to the same handbook, and that when circumstances demanded, they both simply applied the measures contained therein. As in, kill and be damned, and don't have any qualms about using dead bodies to avoid being killed yourself.

This all made Sidney feel very good. It seemed he was doing the right thing. Or at least Hazeem was doing the right thing, and Sidney wasn't stopping him. But then feeling good had to take a back seat when it came time to say what might well be his final goodbye to his friend in Windhoek. It was the Sonia farewell all over again – without a kiss, but with the feeling that he was losing not just a friend but a rock; someone on whom he could rely for guidance and good sense whenever these were needed. He hoped desperately that he would be able to talk to Ted again – and that, right now, he wouldn't blubber before he dispatched his last few words through the ether and cut off the link to Namibia. He didn't blubber, but he did have to collect himself before he called up his friend in France.

It was good that this was the last of the three calls he made, because Marc had clearly decided to remain Marc. To begin with, he didn't just accept the news about the killing at Hope Farm and the unconventional use of the deceased, but he welcomed it, almost as tasty bit of gossip and even as something to be celebrated. After all, justice had been delivered – along with the useful by-product of two life-saving cadavers. What more could one want? And, of course, there was no question that it wouldn't all work. That, with the help of a very handy mate, Sidney wouldn't break free from a life of servitude and make it to the sunny uplands of freedom. Or at least to the rain-drenched uplands of freedom in southern Scotland. How could he fail?

Sidney knew, of course, that Marc was a bit of a bullshitter and that he was probably working overtime to hide his true thoughts and his true feelings. But that was OK. There was only so much earnestness Sidney could take, and some of Marc's confidence – whether genuine or fake – couldn't fail to rub off and put Sidney into the best of moods. He was even able to get through the goodbye routine with only a hint of emotion from either side. And it was only when their exchange had ended and Sidney had stood down his equipment, maybe for the last time ever, that he was overwhelmed with emotion and began to feel tears streaming down his face.

Five minutes later, he had wiped them away and had left the cabin to find Hazeem. Sidney found him feeding Kaalki and, at the same time, talking to him gently – in English. It almost brought on a new stream of tears.

Syed, 2134

Their bad fortune. But Syed's good fortune. So why not accept it? Why not make the most of a gift such as this?

It wasn't his fault. It wasn't his fault the town folk were leaving. Had been leaving for years. And out of desperation. Out of the need for food. For the food no longer shipped in. For the food no longer in the markets. No surpluses any more. No food to sell. Just too many people. Too many people consuming all they were growing. So, the town folk had to join them. Leave and find a patch of ground. A patch of ground anywhere. Anywhere where crops would grow. A neglected meadow. An overgrown orchard. A roadside verge. Or maybe one of those reservations. One of those indulged reservations. One of those indulged reservations wasted on a load of indulged and undeserving aliens. Much better to cast them off, and divide up the land for those in need. For those no longer able to stay in their towns. And forget the buildings. Forget all the houses and apartments. For what mattered now was just land. Land where ex-townies could grow their own food. And if that created a problem for the aliens, then so be it. Not least because it created an opportunity for the likes of Syed...

The one he had in mind was in Herefordshire. Just ten miles from his place. And it was just bursting with people who were in need of a good home. Or just a home. Just anywhere that would provide them with what they needed to live. Just as long as they were prepared to work for it. And just as long as they didn't cause any problems. Syed didn't want that. He just wanted some new helping hands. Submissive new hands. Submissive new hands who really knew their place and wouldn't cause him grief.

It had to be them. It had to be those three there. Tall, all three of them. Even the woman. And her husband looked strong. Even stronger than his grown-up son. But no matter. With the work they would all have to do, they would, all of them, soon be quite strong enough and more. And grateful. How could they not be? Syed was giving each one of them not just a job but a home. A place where they could soon forget this wretched reservation. Where they could soon learn to be more grateful still. Grateful that a hero like Syed had appeared in their lives to save them. To ease their passage through life. To ensure that they wouldn't go hungry – or forget how to work.

He'd even forgive them. Forgive them for their scowls. For their frowns. For their looks of contempt and their looks of disdain. And for the young one's look of horror. He'd just put it down to upheaval. To losing what they'd known for some years. For what they'd invested in for some years. And for what they were now having to leave. To make room for those townies. To make room for those townies who were already crowding round to take their place. To take over their land to feed themselves and their kids.

It was life. It was no more than that. And they should see this. That their move was just a feature of change. Just a feature of inevitable change. And that their bad fortune – even if it were really bad fortune – could have been a fortune a great deal worse. It could have been a very bad fortune indeed. If Syed hadn't arrived in their lives to protect them. To feed them. To clothe them. To house them. And in return, to ask them for so very little. For just so very little work. And just every day. And of course, when necessary, just every waking hour.

Yes, they'd soon see. They'd soon see – with Syed's help – their bad fortune turning into one that was good...

13.

It was Sidney's birthday. It was 3 September 2154, and he was now forty-two years old.

When he awoke to this unsung anniversary, it first occurred to him that he was, in all likelihood, the only person on the planet to know it was this anniversary. The only people who had ever celebrated his birthdays had been his parents, and with their demise, nobody had taken over the task. Rishi and his family had never even enquired how old he was, let alone on which day of the year he moved from one year to the next. But now, he had in front of him a birthday he would never forget – for however long he might be granted the time to forget it. Hazeem had assured him that, with the whistle blown for that exodus from the north on 2 September, it would be on this day that the exodus made its way through his little part of the world. There was no question, he'd said, that at some time during this day, there would be a flood of those northern interlopers making their way past, and possibly through, Hope Farm. The only question that remained was quite when on this day would the flood arrive.

This was quite an important question. Because Hazeem's plan – of shipping bodies northwards – had to be timed to perfection. If they started off too early, they might run into any number of the local villagers or some other folk from the south, and this would almost certainly provide them with an insurmountable problem – not to say the probable end to their lives. However, if they started off too late, meaning that, when the folk from the north arrived, there were only three shrouded forms on the back of their wagon and one unshrouded white guy who was clearly far from being dead, they might have a similarly awkward situation to deal with. No, they had to leave when they were confident that all the southerners had left and just as the large tide of northerners was beginning to crash onto the Worcestershire shore. That way, with one live whitie no longer in evidence, Hazeem's story would make some sort of sense, and they might stand some sort of chance of actually making it to the fabled north.

It was why Hazeem had insisted they both made an early start to the day – and why Sidney found Hazeem attending to the chickens when he joined him at the farmhouse at six-thirty in the morning. Hazeem had also insisted that, whilst Sidney spent his last night at

Hope Farm in his cabin, he would spend the night in Rishi's bed. Not only would this enable him to relish the comfort of a real bed, as opposed to the discomfort of a hard cabin floor, but it would also distance him from Sidney if there were any uninvited guests in the night. Plus, he could also make an early start on the farm's poultry.

By the time Sidney joined him, he had dispatched three unfortunate birds – to join the modest stock of victuals for their journey north – and was busy coaxing their more fortunate sisters out of the coop, where they would have to learn to live wild, whilst, at the same time, avoiding the attentions of a multitude of hungry humans from the north. As Sidney watched them embarking on their road to freedom – and danger – he began to wonder whether they stood any more chance of being alive in just a few days' time than he and his friend did. But he failed to make up his mind. And anyway, his thoughts were soon on other matters – such as the timing of the start of their expedition and quite how soon he would have to be wrapped up in a shroud to share the back of a wagon with two festering corpses. But then Hazeem spotted that Sidney had arrived to join him, and Sidney's thoughts were immediately overtaken by the need to respond to an enthusiastic greeting.

'Sidney! You're up. I hope you slept well, and I hope you *are* well. And maybe even a bit excited?'

'Morning, Hazeem. I am well, thanks, but I'm not sure I'm exactly excited. Maybe more… well, you know, terrified. You have to remember that I'm not a smuggler and never have been. And come to think of it, I've never been a smuggler's contraband either – and wrapped up like a mummy as well.'

Hazeem laughed. 'That's OK. I've never smuggled a whitie before. Or any stiffs, come to that. So don't feel you're the only one who'll be learning on the job. Even if all you've got to do is play dead – while I play the considerate returner of the slain. Probably over and over again.'

Sidney rolled his eyes. 'You're not exactly filling me with confidence,' he observed.

'I'm just joshing you, Sidney. It's going to be a piece of piss. Believe me. Just as long as we set off when we should. And to make sure we do, I'm going to leave you here while I hide myself somewhere near the road. That way, I'll be able to see when your lot have gone – completely. And meanwhile, I suggest you make sure Kaalki has had a good feed and that you've got everything we need on the wagon. Oh, and that you've sorted out your clothes for the trip. You know, that bed sheet. You'll find it on the table in the kitchen.'

Here, Hazeem supplied Sidney with a wicked grin, before then advising Sidney that he'd already had his breakfast – one of raw carrots – and that he might want to do the same. And that Sidney might also want to keep a lookout for any of the locals who decided to make a crafty entrance into Hope Farm on their way south, and have a suitable story to tell them if they maybe questioned the whereabouts of his masters. Or if they got uppity, to be prepared to get as aggressive and as violent as required. After all, Hazeem reminded him, the new world order was already in place, and the imperative was no longer to mind one's manners or to be in the least bit servile. It was to survive – and to do whatever it took to do so.

Sidney tried his best to digest this advice – without much success – and when Hazeem had disappeared, he quickly distracted himself by investigating the inside of the farmhouse. He'd been allowed into only part of it before and not into that part where his masters had relaxed – and slept. So, having first inspected his designated bed-sheet outfit, he made his way into the family's personal living quarters, only to find that their private accommodation was as austere as their nature. Unadorned and with little in the way of comfort, it was actually much less attractive than his scruffy old cabin, and of course it held no reading material and no way of communicating with the outside world.

His cabin still did; his lovely, dilapidated cabin that he would soon be abandoning for all time. The thought suddenly grabbed him by the throat and made him feel sick. How could he leave all those books? All those books he hadn't been able to stash on the wagon? And how could he leave his treasured radio kit? He must be mad. He must be out of his mind. It just wasn't possible.

He shook his head in disbelief at what he was doing, and then he shook his head again – this time in disbelief that he was being so stupid. He had no choice, he told himself. He couldn't stay here, no matter what happened. And he couldn't indulge himself in any more doubts or any more hesitations. All he could do now was accept the reality of his situation and, before that reality dictated the rest of the day, get himself back to his cabin for one last time in order to bid it a fond, and probably tearful, farewell.

This is what he did. He returned to his shabby haven, and for five minutes, he soaked up its atmosphere as best he could. He stroked some of the books he'd be leaving, and he then ran his fingers over the buttons and dials of his radio kit in a way he'd never done before – and with a guilt he'd never felt before. It was, he tried to tell himself, just an inanimate pile of metal, but nevertheless, it had sustained him and comforted him – for years – and now he was forsaking it. If only, rather than abandoning it, he could be taking it with him. But that, he knew, was out of the question. As was his lingering for any longer in his precious retreat. Hazeem might be back at the farmhouse at any time. Or he, Sidney, might have some unwelcome visitors to deal with at any time. So, he had to go. He had to step over the cabin's threshold for one last time, take in the smooth surface of the pond for one last time – and then not look back. But instead, look to the future and whatever that held in store. Not immediately, but after he'd spent however long was needed in a grubby bed sheet.

Well, with tears in his eyes, he did manage to leave his cabin for that last time and to take in one last view of the pond, but when Hazeem reappeared just before noon, Sidney was still consumed with what he was abandoning and not with what the future might have in store. Even fussing over Kaalki and checking over and over again that they'd collected together everything they might need for their trip hadn't succeeded in diverting his thoughts from what he was losing. That would have to be done by Hazeem – and what he had to report as soon as his friend was in earshot.

'*So far, so bloody good,*' Hazeem shouted. '*In fact, it couldn't have gone any better.*'

Sidney's attention was captured immediately. He wanted to know why Hazeem was beaming quite so much and what he meant by those opening words. '*Meaning?*' he yelled back.

'Meaning,' responded Hazeem as he approached Sidney, 'that we're now in no-man's land. Your lot have gone. Completely. I'm sure of it. And I must say, whatever defence arrangements they'd been putting in place, well, they must have crumbled away in very short order. Although that's hardly a great surprise. I mean, they must have realised pretty damn soon that they didn't stand a chance. That there would be just too many of my lot to deal with, and all they could do was scarper. And pretty damn quickly.'

'You've seen them? Going past?'

'I certainly have. But not that many. I think most of them must have made off towards the M5. I mean south and west. And those around Redditch must have gone due south towards the Vale of Evesham. So, we've been sort of missed out. There's been no more than a few hundred all morning; first, in dribs and drabs – and then not even in dribs and drabs. I'm sure there's no more to come.'

This was all more than credible. There were no settlements of any great size north of Hope Farm, as places like Bromsgrove and Redditch had long ago virtually shrivelled away, when most of their residents had chosen a rural life over an urban one in order to keep themselves alive. So, there really were only a small number of southerners nearer the border, and not nearly as many as the huge number of northerners who must now have breached that border. Nevertheless, no matter how small their number, they appeared to have slipped past Hope Farm without making any noise whatsoever, a point Sidney now put to Hazeem.

'I didn't hear anybody.'

'Yeah, the silent retreat. Refugees, it seems, don't make any noise. They just keep their heads down and plod slowly on. And I can't say I blame them. They'll all be in shock, remember. And anyway, being chased out of your home isn't the sort of thing to make you very talkative, is it?'

'They've really just upped sticks and melted away? Without a fight and without even a shout?'

'Yeah,' confirmed Hazeem, but then he corrected himself.

'Mind, there were a couple of guys who needed a push.'

'What?'

'Two guys were planning to pay you a visit. Probably locals who knew there was a wagon here and thought it was worth seeing whether it was still around.'

'Nobody's been here. I haven't seen a soul.'

'I said they were planning to pay you a visit – and their plans were changed when I frightened them out of their skins. Didn't even need to shout at them. Two well-aimed rocks, and they were off down the road like a pair of rabbits with their tails on fire. Talk about spooked! I mean, if all your lot are like that pair, it's no surprise they've not put up a fight. And I wonder whether they ever will? Hell, they'll have to turn and stand their ground somewhere. Or before very long, they'll all be wading into the English Channel, and my chances of finding a new border to work on will be next door to zero.'

'I thought you'd given up that idea.'

'Not given it up, Sidney, only deferred it. Until such time, that is, as I've made quite sure you're entirely safe. Which reminds me, it's time for a snack, after which I think it might be time to "wrap up", as it were. No point in hanging around any longer, and the sooner we get our show on the road, the more likely it is that we'll get some useful miles under our belts before nightfall.'

Sidney didn't much care for that allusion to his forthcoming swaddling, but he was relieved that nothing had yet gone wrong, and that, sooner rather than later, they would be on their way. Waiting around to start, he'd decided, was infinitely worse than the prospect of actually starting.

*

In the event, he had to wait for only half an hour. By then, he and Hazeem had fed themselves, Kaalki had been fed and harnessed, and the wagon was ready to receive its final piece of cargo.

Sidney had worked out that, in order to adopt the role of a swathed cadaver on the back of the wagon, it would make sense to climb onto it *sans* bed sheet, and then let Hazeem swathe him in it *in situ*. That way, he wouldn't have to wriggle onto the vehicle like a giant cocooned insect. This worked quite well, and it wasn't long before the wagon held its planned complement of four bodies: two dead ones side by side, and between these and one live one, a false one made up principally of books and keepsakes. Sidney had demanded this arrangement, as he had no desire to literally rub shoulders with a stiff. After all, it was quite bad enough to be anywhere near one. And even now, they were both beginning to smell – of something far worse than rotten eggs – and the smell was bound to get worse. A lot worse.

'Right,' announced Hazeem. 'I think we're ready to go – or at least I am. How about you?'

He was sitting on the bench at the front of the wagon, with Kaalki's reins in his hands and just behind him, hidden between Kaalki's fodder and one of the water containers, was the ancient A–Z. Behind the fodder was Sidney, who was trying desperately to come to terms with being bound head to foot, with only one carefully positioned slit in the enveloping fabric to enable him to breathe and, with some difficulty, to mumble.

'I can't wait,' was his muffled response to Hazeem's question.

And as Hazeem acknowledged this response, Sidney felt the wagon lurch forwards, resulting in what – if all went well – would be the first of several thousand jolts to his body. Hazeem and Sidney were embarking on their journey through what would likely be hostile territory. Sidney's body was embarking on a journey through what would likely be a purgatory on earth.

It wasn't long before Sidney was attempting to rearrange his position, and what had started off as a partially-on-his-side attitude was soon replaced by a completely-on-his-back attitude. This was marginally more comfortable, and it was a little easier to breathe – as much as possible through his mouth. The jarring of dead bodies, he learnt within minutes, was not without an impact on the intensity of the smells they emitted.

He would also learn within minutes that Hazeem's madcap scheme might not be quite as madcap as he'd thought. This was when, after no more than ten minutes, Hazeem announced that they were just about to meet their first visitors from the north. It was time, he reminded Sidney, to play dead – as convincingly as possible – and to leave it to the driver to be as convincing as possible with his story.

Sidney didn't need to be told twice. As Hazeem drew the wagon to a halt, he lay as still as he could and began to take the shallowest breaths he could. Then he heard Hazeem greeting his fellow northerners in Urdu, and then chatting on in this same language, no doubt to enlist their assistance in returning their four brothers' bodies for a fit, if overdue, burial – by letting him continue on his way unheeded.

It took less than a minute. And it worked! According to Hazeem, absolutely beautifully. There had been nearly a dozen young men in the road, and only one of them had taken just the slightest peek at what was on the back of the wagon. And this was a result, Hazeem claimed, of his unsurpassable powers of persuasion and pretence, possibly aided, he admitted, by the scent-power of putrefaction. Indeed, he informed Sidney, all his fellow northerners had displayed a certain discomfort at what they were smelling, and this aspect of his chosen subterfuge could, he believed, only get better.

Sidney agreed, but he almost wept at the thought. Maybe, when they stopped for the night, he should make it a priority to find something to stuff up his nose?

However, if they did get that far on their journey, that possible remedy for his suffering was still hours away. Before then, there were countless jolts to his body to endure and a whole procession of meetings with groups of invaders to be dealt with – professionally and successfully by his talented driver. He, this talented driver, was a really good liar. Indeed, arguably as good as were the deterrent qualities of a nasal assault – something that was more than welcome in one sense, but not in another. The smell in the back of the wagon was now just so bad that Sidney was beginning to believe it might actually threaten their continued progress north. However, just as he was beginning to think that he might have to discuss his unendurable situation with the man at the front of the wagon, this man announced that they were about to join the M5!

Although it wasn't much more than four miles from Hope Farm, Sidney had seen the M5 only once before. This had been twelve years ago when he'd travelled from his former home to his new home with Rishi. They'd crossed this old motorway on a bridge, and Sidney had been astounded to see that what had once been one of the country's major roads was now no more than a linear slum. People lived on it – and farmed its sloping verges. They lived in simple shacks or in ancient abandoned vehicles, so that the six clear lanes of the past had now been reduced to a narrow, meandering lane through these makeshift homes – and the surface of this lane was anything but smooth. It was more potholed and rutted than some of the lanes around Hope Farm.

Hence, here was something to draw his attention away from the stink in his nose (and the pressure in his bladder), and he clutched at it like a sinking man might clutch at a straw. Because he really wanted to see whether the M5 was still as he remembered it – when, at last, a halt for the night might allow this.

*

It would indeed prove to be a long wait. The M5's 'single-lane-way' was full of folk streaming south, with all too many of them taking at least a passing interest in the wagon heading north, thus causing it to stop seemingly at intervals of two-hundred yards. However, Hazeem seemed not at all perturbed by this constant interruption to their progress, and he dealt with each interruption swiftly and successfully. If asked, he could, thought Sidney, have smuggled the devil into heaven.

Nevertheless, Sidney was now at the very end of his tether, and he knew that, if Hazeem didn't soon announce an end to their journey for the day, he just wouldn't be able to cope. He'd be ripping off his bed sheet even if it meant risking a very abrupt end to their joint endeavour.

However, Hazeem could apparently read minds, because just before this rebellious act could be embarked on by the prisoner in linen, Sidney felt the wagon drawing to a halt – but this time without the usual accompaniment of Hazeem's silver tones. Instead, when it was finally stationary, there was an immediate announcement from the front of the wagon that Kaalki had now brought them to where all three of them would be spending the night – or should that be all five of them?

'Resourceful' was clearly Hazeem's unspoken middle name. He'd brought their carriage to the end of the 'populated' part of the M5, just before an empty stretch of it climbed its way up to what had once been the crowded Birmingham / Black Country conurbation – and the border with the north. And a couple of yards away was what had once been a pale-blue lorry trailer, but was now a large, oblong, bleached-with-traces-of-blue box-on-wheels. This, it seemed, would be Sidney's lodging for the night.

Sidney discovered this as soon as he'd been unwrapped. And after some much-needed unloading of liquid, he then discovered he wouldn't be allowed to relish a view of the motorway slum through which they had just passed, because he needed to secrete himself in the trailer as soon as possible, and as soon as he'd had his vegan dinner within, he needed to get some sleep. As Hazeem was keen to point out, they would need to make a very early start in the morning.

Sidney, not surprisingly, did challenge these arrangements. He particularly wanted to know how Hazeem himself would rest for the night. After all, he could hardly just go to sleep and leave the wagon and Kaalki unattended. So far, the visitors from the north had behaved themselves perfectly when faced with a mule-drawn hearse, but would they be quite so respectful and circumspect when they encountered an unguarded vehicle and its attractive power unit? Might they not think their needs were greater than those of a handful of stiffs?

Hazeem, of course, had it all under control. It was now nearly nine o'clock in the evening. But even at this late hour, northerners were still passing by on their way south, not enough of them to prevent Sidney making his way to his bedroom unnoticed, but certainly enough of them to provide Hazeem with at least one soul who, in return for some food, would play nightwatchman until the morning.

In the event, he found two: a young man and his wife. Hazeem would later tell Sidney that he could discern they were a pious pair (as well as a hungry pair), and that they would take their night-guarding duties very seriously. Which is why, he was also able to report, he had enjoyed an undisturbed night whilst they kept watch over Kaalki and the wagon – and why he woke feeling far more refreshed than Sidney.

As Sidney would later tell Hazeem, his less restful night was probably something to do with his body having been bludgeoned for hours on end, his sleeping in a strange place for the first time in years, and the prospect of being wrapped up in linen again – to endure not just a further physical assault on his body but what, at the same time, might be an unbearable assault on his sense of smell.

But that was all for later. For now, as he tried to drop off to sleep, Sidney could comfort himself with the fact that he was still alive, still on track for a new life (maybe), and still in the company of the most capable (and likable) smuggler he was ever likely to meet. Oh, and one who already felt like a friend.

14.

Despite it starting off with a significant victory, Sidney would look back on the morning of 4 September as one of the worst in his life.

The victory concerned his bed sheet and its use as a shroud. He'd eventually persuaded Hazeem that it didn't need to be of the tightly wrapped variety, and that it could instead be of a variety that would allow him to breathe more easily, speak more easily, adjust his position more easily, and when necessary, pee through the slats of the wagon. When it was safe to do so, his new looser-fitting shroud would even allow him to have a drink or a snack, and maybe a peek over the sides of the wagon to see where he was.

He had a strong case in his favour. As he made very clear to Hazeem, he couldn't possibly spend a whole day trussed up as he'd been on the first leg of their journey. It was just inconceivable for so many practical reasons. Furthermore, as Hazeem had to concede, not one of the northerners they'd encountered so far had shown any desire to investigate the contents of the wagon. Their noses had given them all the confirmation they needed as to what the contents were, and the last thing Sidney could imagine was their conducting a close-up inspection of any one of the shrouds. They wouldn't come anywhere near them.

So, it was a good start. And with the night-watch people having been sent away soon after first light (with half a chicken), and with Kaalki and his passengers having been fed and watered, Sidney was able to climb onto the back of the wagon and there envelop himself in his bed sheet – firmly enough to mirror the appearance of his three partners, but loosely enough to allow him to cope with the day. Or so he thought.

*

Then it began: one of the worst mornings of his life. To kick off with, it was horribly apparent that the deterrent quality of the scent pervading the wagon had now shifted to the offensive (in both senses of the word). It was not only disgusting but it was also very distinctly in attack mode, and with cabbage and garlic now joining forces with 'rotten-eggs-plus', it was assaulting Sidney's senses like never before. It was purely awful. And having found nothing to shove up his nose to alleviate its effects, it seemed to Sidney that he would simply have to endure it for as long as it took. If he could.

He would also have to endure a very 'challenging' ride. The initial, empty stretch of the motorway was just a patchwork of warped and cracked tarmac. And this made for a very bumpy ride – and also for a very slow ride, one made slower still by the constant stops required to assure the procession of northerners coming south that the wagon they were meeting had legitimate business going north.

Then there was Kaalki's lack of enthusiasm for hills. It really was quite an incline up to Birmingham / Black Country-land, which was something Kaalki had never encountered before. Indeed, his enthusiasm ultimately disappeared entirely, and he simply refused to pull the wagon any further. Only when Hazeem abandoned his driving seat to use Kaalki's reins to pull him forwards did he deign to budge. Albeit not quite at the speed his passengers would have chosen, but more at a speed well below the minimum requirement that had once been enforced on this highway. Very well below it.

The result of all this – the smell, the bumps, the repeated stops and the overall snail's pace – was becoming more than Sidney could endure. Even in his more 'easy-fit' shroud. So much so that he began to make his predicament known to Hazeem in no uncertain terms. He, Hazeem, was now back in earshot on the driving seat, Kaalki having resumed his normal willingness to pull a wagon after reaching the top of that unwelcome gradient. He could therefore hardly ignore his friend's fervent entreaties – even if he wanted to.

'Hazeem,' Sidney started. 'You may have guessed this already, but I'm really suffering back here. It feels as though this wagon's got square wheels. And the smell… well, I don't know what it's like up there, but where I am, it's becoming intolerable. I'd be better off spending the whole day collecting shit. Much better off. I mean, I don't know how much longer I can take this.'

'How about an hour?'

'An hour! What do you mean, an hour? Christ, we're not going to be at Cosford in an hour.'

'No, Sidney. We won't be there today and maybe not even tomorrow. But I have in mind somewhere else a little nearer, somewhere where I might be able to find you something that will "ease the load". And I mean ease the load on your sense of smell. I can't do much about the square wheels, but I may be able to do something about… well, about what's getting up your nose.'

'Like what?'

'You'll see. Just give me an hour, and you might just find you'll no longer be bothered by smells. Not even sweet ones.'

'I don't understand.'

'You're not supposed to. You're just supposed to trust me. That's all. And all I need is an hour.'

Sidney gave in. He was now feeling too groggy to push Hazeem any further, and he decided he would indeed put his trust in his friend – again – and just hope that it wasn't misplaced.

*

It wasn't. Over the next hour, Hazeem conducted a number of further brief conversations with curious northerners, then they left what remained of the motorway (before it ended where once it had been an elevated section), following which they then embarked on their journey through a warren of crumbling roads in what were apparently the southernmost reaches of the Black Country. This was part of Hazeem's home patch. He knew it well. And he knew where within it there were still some residents, with some of them making a living from farming (there were even now some green spaces between the carpet of decaying buildings), and others of them making a living through different pursuits. Pursuits that were not quite so honest or laudable.

Sidney had been aware that they'd entered what had once been a built-up area, and he understood that Hazeem had left the motorway because the motorway no longer existed a little further north, but that was about all he was aware of. In any event, he was more consumed by the presence of the intolerable smell than he was with their route. Indeed, he only took any proper notice of where they were when, at the end of that promised hour, he could see through the linen of his shroud that Hazeem was guiding the wagon into a covered space. The wagon was then brought to a halt and Hazeem addressed him, 'Right. Stay here. I've someone to see. I won't be more than a few minutes. And don't worry, nobody's going to bother you. You have my word.'

And with that, he was off the wagon, and Sidney heard him moving away to who knew where. This was his cue to sit up and take a look around. After all, nobody was going to bother him here. He'd been assured of that. And he really did want to see where he was.

It was in a warehouse, a warehouse the condition of which was clearly teetering on the edge of 'extremely hazardous'. There was more of its roof left than there was of its walls. And, as it transpired, it was a warehouse that belonged to a man who lived in a windowless, brick-built blockhouse at its far end – and who dealt in drugs.

In a few minutes, Hazeem was back as promised. And a good few minutes after that, he had finally convinced Sidney that the particular knockout drug he was offering him wasn't addictive, but that it carried such a punch that even if Rishi came over and embraced him on the back of the wagon, he wouldn't notice – and he certainly wouldn't smell him. Moreover, its effects would wear off within just a few hours, and all being well, Sidney's return to the real world would coincide with when they stopped to bed down for the night. What could be more perfect, and what could be more irresistible?

*

It was a pity in a way. Sidney would have found the achingly slow trip through the Black Country quite interesting – had he been in any fit state to peek out from beneath his shroud and to use his eyesight or any other of his senses. So, he completely missed the acres of dilapidation that surrounded the progress of the wagon; the utter destruction of what had once been a thriving, if not particularly beautiful, part of England; and the squalor of the hovels and make-do shacks that housed the tiny number of people who still called this place their home. And who, without exception, took no interest whatsoever in a passing wagon. Even one they could probably smell before they saw it.

He felt a little peculiar when he came around, but it wasn't long before all his senses had returned. And with his sense of sight, he was able to see that Hazeem had found another very-past-its-best warehouse in which he'd parked the wagon, that Kaalki was tucking into his supper, and that there was more colour in the shrouds of two of his companions than there had been earlier in the day. This didn't surprise him, as another sense that had returned was now shouting at the top of its voice that it was being mugged by a smell that could only be described as ghastly. If anybody wanted to know why dead people were buried or burnt, thought Sidney, then they only needed to join him here on the back of this wagon. Then he realised it would be far better if he were nowhere near this wagon. So, after casting his bed sheet aside, he leapt quickly to the ground and almost ran to where Hazeem was tending a small fire – just far enough away from the wagon to be beyond its wretched, sickly reach.

'Ah,' Hazeem said, as he spotted Sidney. 'You're… awake. I hope you had some sweet dreams.'

Sidney blinked at him. His senses had returned, but not yet his equilibrium. It took him more than a few seconds to make a response. 'Well...' he began falteringly, 'I'm not sure...'

And then he stopped and made another start. 'You got any more of that stuff? Or have I had it all?'

'There's plenty more where that came from,' assured Hazeem. 'If you don't want to, I don't think you'll have to endure too much more of that stink.'

'*If I don't want to?* Do you think I'm mad? I'd rather swap places with Kaalki than miss out on more of that stuff.'

'Mmm, a pretty quick recovery. Some people take forever. You know, to come back from that other world.'

'I don't blame them,' said Sidney. 'They might wake up next to a couple of stiffs.'

Hazeem laughed, and Sidney joined him. And then he remembered to ask Hazeem where they were and whether he had been a little rash to emerge from the wagon quite so eagerly and brazenly.

Hazeem then told him that they were in 'a property he knew', in what had once been Dudley, and that it was the sort of property that never got any visitors – partly because of its location and partly because it was a property that had the appearance of a building about to collapse. Sidney had therefore not been either brazen or reckless in his behaviour. In any event, if there had been any prospect of his putting them both in danger, he wouldn't have been allowed to because he would have been given another dose of 'that drug'. They were safe here, Hazeem assured him, and they could now not only relax but they could also dine on a couple of chicken legs. And they might, he suggested, even have a chat.

It was the first time they'd been together without tasks to attend to and without the fear of being disturbed or assailed. It was also a welcome intermission in what might prove to be a very long-running adventure. That being the case, it was no great surprise that what Hazeem had suggested was soon taking place. And initially, their shared discussion consisted of Hazeem asking Sidney about his life to date: where he was born, what his parents did, what had happened to his parents, how he'd ended up at Hope Farm, and how he'd acquired all his books and his precious radio kit. Sidney was more than happy to answer all Hazeem's questions, and he even went on to tell him a little more about his radio-ham acquaintances around the world.

However, there came a point in the discussion when Sidney thought it was time to turn the tables – in the interests not only of courtesy but also of satisfying his own curiosity. What exactly was the background of his unlikely saviour?

Well, Hazeem had been left as an orphan. That was how, just over thirty years ago, his life story had started. And, as he went on to explain, being an orphan in his culture meant being raised by an uncle, which, in his case, meant being raised by a childless uncle who was known for his outstanding righteousness. In fact, according to Hazeem, this uncle often attacked people with his righteousness, and if you were unfortunate enough to have him as a guardian, he could mug you with it every day. He might even round off one of these muggings with a few blows from either his cosh of piety or his cosh of virtue – whichever first came to hand. And the result of all this faith-driven 'goodness' was a child who soon learnt that most of his brethren were very likely suspect, no matter how much they professed their decency and their desire to show care, and that he'd better look to his own resources to survive, and conduct most of his business with his fellow men on a transactional basis, with the first part of the transaction being a cautious exchange of trust. It's what he still did in his business now, and why, he claimed, he had learnt in whom he could place complete trust and to whom he could never offer even a scrap of provisional trust. Of course, as he was quick to point out, Sidney was at the extreme end of the trust spectrum – the right end of the trust spectrum. He'd known this even before he'd been helped into Sidney's cabin. It was why they were now here in this warehouse. Mutual trust, he proposed, could lead to all sorts of genuine good, and it could even be a lifesaver.

These revelations made Sidney want to know more about his friend. And given what he'd read about the embracing nature of his friend's faith, he particularly wanted to know what his view was of a 'higher power', and if he believed in one, how this affected his approach to life in general – beyond the problem he had with trust. He found it difficult to put into words the questions he had in mind, but it really didn't matter. Hazeem seemed more than willing to enlighten his friend on his views on all matters concerning beliefs and behaviours. And he started off with that divine being…

'There isn't one,' he stated flatly. 'He's just something that people like my uncle dreamt up years and years ago as an excuse for some of their more questionable habits – especially as regards women – and as a sort of scapegoat. You know, when things went wrong, it was just "divine will" or the outcome of "fate": something that was always conveniently outside their control and instead predetermined by their imagined and entirely non-existent deity. A pretty good ruse, if you can get away with it – and just about every organised religion has been getting away with it for hundreds of years. Duping all those suckers who haven't got the sense to see through the hoax.

'But not me. My uncle may not have made me a good man, but he did make me see the truth. That what he and his like were spouting – and, of course, imposing on others – was no more than a load of nonsense. A giant con, as well as an affront to the intellect of our species.'

Sidney could barely believe what he was hearing, but before he had a chance to add anything to Hazeem's denial of the existence of God, that reference he'd just made to his own species had led his friend to launch another assault, this one on the behaviour of his fellow representatives of *Homo sapiens.*

'The intellect of our species,' he began, a wry smile now spreading across his face. 'We don't seem to get it out of its box very often, do we?'

'I'm sorry?'

'We don't often use it, do we? I mean, not only do rather too many of us lap up all this God nonsense, but we take no responsibility for our actions. And we never have. I mean, look around you. We're sitting in a shithole – a shithole surrounded by acres of shit. And whilst it's all I've ever known, I do still know that it's shit. That not that long ago, this area was full of people making things and living in proper houses and moving around on proper roads – and leading a life very different to our own. But we've destroyed that life. Just as we've destroyed the whole fucking world. I've not read books like you have, Sidney, but I'm not unaware that the world used to be a very different place. That it used to have all sorts of birds and animals and so, so much. That our species used to occupy this planet along with thousands or more likely hundreds of thousands of other creatures, and not just the rats and the lice we have now.'

At this point, Hazeem laughed out loud. 'And they still pray to God. And they still think that they're the most important thing on the planet. The whole reason the planet is here: to give them a home. The fact that they've trashed it doesn't ever cross their minds. Nor the fact that their intellect is still sitting unused in that box, and not very long from now, if they don't finally take it out, it will cost them their lives. Not only will they have wrecked the whole bloody world but they'll also have wrecked any possible chance of their surviving.'

'I assume you're talking about some of the current farming practices?'

'Yes, I am. But that's just the end game. I'm much more disgusted by what we've done with our "mastery" of the world, and how we've screwed it all up – while, all the time, making quite sure that stuff like fate, worship, rituals – and glorified ignorance – always took preference over wisdom and what we saw with our own eyes. I mean, how have we been so blind for so long?'

For a brief second, Sidney thought he must be suffering the after-effects of that drug and that he hadn't really heard such an incisive tirade from… well, from a northerner of all people. But then he only had to focus on Hazeem's face to confirm that what he'd heard were the genuine beliefs of someone who probably had few, if any, opportunities to reveal what he thought of the world and how his fellow men had ruined it with a combination of ignorance and brainless piety. He therefore responded to Hazeem's tirade, not with one of his own but, instead, with the assurance that his friend would find no one in this warehouse who would take issue with anything he'd said. And that almost certainly included Kaalki.

Sidney knew this assurance was unnecessary, as Hazeem would already have formed the impression that Sidney wasn't a religious man or a stupid man. Had he not, he wouldn't have opened up as he had. Nevertheless, Sidney was keen to make sure that Hazeem knew he had a friend who held almost identical views to his own concerning the catastrophic impact on the world of that upright, naked ape that was now threatening to inflict a further catastrophe on itself.

Hazeem accepted Sidney's words with grace and probably with a *soupçon* of relief. After all, he hadn't held back, and he could have overstepped the mark. The fact that he now knew he hadn't clearly pleased him immensely, and it caused him to move the conversation towards a much sunnier destination – one where they might share some laughs before they retired for the night. And having done this – by telling Sidney some tales of 'smuggling ventures gone wrong' – they did then retire for the night. Both of them clearly happy and both of them clearly more attuned to each other than ever.

They were now a real team: Sidney, Hazeem and a very content-looking Kaalki.

15.

It might have been the first time in his life that Sidney had been awoken by a smell. But, by early morning, the stench from the wagon had colonised the whole of the warehouse, and it had certainly found its way into Sidney's nose. He sat up from his blanket bed, not sure for a second of where he was, but then that terrible smell propelled him into full consciousness, and he let out a wistful sigh. It had struck him immediately that he would once again have to engage with the realty of his situation and whatever this might mean in terms of danger and discomfort. And even though he was one of a proper team now, it wasn't a prospect he relished.

Hazeem was already up, tending to Kaalki, and when he saw that Sidney was awake, he offered him a greeting. 'Good morning,' he sang. 'I hope you slept well and I hope you're ready for another day on the road.'

Sidney couldn't possibly match Hazeem's cheeriness, but he did try to sound at least a little bit sunny. 'Good morning to you. And, yes, I slept very well, thank you, and I'm ready for anything – as long as it doesn't involve staying in this warehouse for a minute more than we have to.'

'Yes, it is getting a touch whiffy in here, isn't it? The sooner we're away the better.'

And within twenty minutes, they *were* away. Over a tasteless breakfast, Hazeem had laid out what they would be doing today, which would largely be a replay of what they'd done yesterday. And he'd also explained that the only significant differences would be their direction of travel, which would be north-west towards Albrighton, and the dose of the knockout drug to be provided to Sidney, which would be double the dose he'd received yesterday – to take account of the need for a whole day of oblivion. Half of this dose would be administered when Sidney had installed himself on the back of the wagon, and the other half when he emerged from his trance in the middle of the day.

So by the time Kaalki dragged the wagon out of the warehouse to begin the next stage of its journey, Sidney was already unconscious again, and Hazeem looked as though he wished he were as well. Even with a scarf wrapped around his face, it was all too obvious that he too was now suffering from the terrible smell that clung to the wagon. And as he would confess to Sidney later that day, this smell not only made him feel slightly nauseous but it also made him feel a little guilty. Was it really acceptable, Hazeem had asked himself, to so abuse the remains of two people – no matter how bad they might have been – simply to facilitate the escape of two others? It was a difficult question to answer – for both of the escapees – in spite of the fact that they knew Rishi and Farid's bodies had clearly served them well as perfect passports, and without them, their travel plans would almost certainly have been disrupted – and then probably discontinued.

*

In the meantime, Sidney came to in what he would learn from Hazeem were the outer reaches of old Wolverhampton. There, he would also learn that he hadn't missed much. It was now early afternoon, and the morning journey had seen the wagon passing through just more desolation, with a noticeably reduced number of stops due to the attention of curious northerners. There were, according to Hazeem, far fewer of them on the move than there had been yesterday, and as had been observed yesterday, those locals who weren't on the move were simply not curious at all. It seemed surviving in the devastation that was once Wolverhampton left little time for curiosity or, indeed, little time to consider joining that mass migration to the south – at least for the present.

Hazeem had a similar story to report when Sidney woke again in the evening after his second dose had worn off. That said, Sidney could see for himself that they'd now arrived in 'open countryside', or as open as any countryside remained these days. Hazeem had parked the wagon near the remains of a farmhouse and well away from any roads. And from the vantage point this situation provided, Sidney could see that they were surrounded by fields of sickly looking crops and other fields bereft of any sort of crops at all. And, dotted amongst these fields were the same sort of small, cobbled-together shelters that now exemplified the majority of British rural architecture. It was a dismal scene, and one that soon encouraged him to focus on his dinner and on another resuscitating chat with Hazeem.

This one encompassed their views on their respective circumstances either side of the north/south border, and how each of them had dealt with the problems these had caused. Sidney wasn't surprised to learn that Hazeem had developed a way to 'dance across the top' of any problem he might encounter, whilst, at the same time, remaining true to his own exceptional brand of fair play. (Even if few of his fellow northerners had been brought up to even recognise this term.) In many ways, his life had been a great deal harder than Sidney's. After all, Sidney's hadn't involved his having to subscribe to beliefs in which he didn't believe. Or at least to pretend to subscribe to such beliefs.

However, in a few hours' time, there would be another day to contend with, and accordingly, Hazeem drew their discussion to a conclusion by changing its subject to one that dealt with the practicalities of the day to come. They were now only a couple of miles away from RAF Cosford, and if all went well, they would be there by mid-morning tomorrow at the latest. And they needed to prepare themselves for finding – or being found by – a very old man by the name of Stephen, who would probably be somewhere in the middle of a giant rubbish dump – and who might possibly be armed.

'After all,' as Hazeem pointed out, 'if he's managing to survive in such inhospitable surroundings, he might not be burdened with entirely pacifist ideals.'

*

In the event, this consideration of the possibly hostile habits of their unknown contact proved rather more than relevant. Because when, the next day, they began to make their way into the gigantic spread of rubbish that was RAF Cosford, they were soon met with a noise, and this noise was that of a pair of gunshots. Although whether these shots were from a gun owned by Stephen and whether they'd been directed at them or at somebody else, they didn't know. All they did know – both of them – was that they should pretty damn quickly not present themselves as targets for any further shots to come.

Sidney hadn't been drugged this morning, so he'd divided his time on the relatively short journey to their destination between gagging and swooning. But now, as he hid under the wagon with Hazeem, his focus wasn't on a smell but instead on the threat posed by fast-moving munitions. Those gunshots had been unnervingly close, and it was even more unnerving that they'd coincided with their arrival at this former air base. And what the hell should they do now? Wait here under the wagon and hope for the best – or something else? But if something else, quite what else? And when? And what risk might it involve?

In the event, they did nothing. They waited and they listened. And then they heard it: the sound of someone approaching. Then Sidney saw him – or at least his bottom half along with, hanging down by his right leg, the barrel of a rifle. Sidney nudged Hazeem to warn him that the shooter was now very close, but the warning proved completely redundant.

Within just a second or so, the shooter announced his arrival – first, with a groan of disgust, and then with some words. 'Jeez, I assume you've got a reason for that stink. An' hell, it must be a good 'un.'

Sidney glanced at his fellow traveller and smiled. He was as sure as he could be that they'd found Stephen – or rather, Stephen had found them. But it was something they needed to confirm. So with no hesitation whatsoever, they both began to climb out from under the wagon, and this was when they were both presented with their first ever view of the whole of Stephen's body – and its exceptional appearance.

He was a small man, and he was wearing clothes Sidney had never seen before: a blue denim shirt and a pair of blue denim jeans, both of which were probably older than Sidney himself. They were fraying everywhere and they were covered in patches. In contrast to these ancient garments, he had on his feet some substantial, military-looking boots that were in first-class condition, and on his head he wore a blue-grey beret pulled down to one side. It looked completely out of place on a man with a long, grey beard and a series of wrinkles above that beard formed into the shape of a face. Sidney thought he looked more like a man who'd reached the age of a hundred rather than someone who was merely on a journey through his eighties.

He was such a startling apparition – armed with a deadly weapon – that Sidney could find no words of greeting, and before Hazeem could come to his aid, Stephen offered not a greeting but an observation. He didn't sound overly friendly, and he ignored Hazeem entirely as he addressed only Sidney.

'You're Sidney, I assume. And this man with you, is he your "friend"?'

Sidney bristled. Stephen's tone of voice said so much, and none of it was at all welcome. He therefore responded firmly to the question posed, and in a way that would leave Stephen in no doubt as to how he regarded his 'friend': 'Yes, he is my friend. A good friend. And more than that, he is the man who has saved my life and delivered me here. Without him, I would almost certainly be dead, and I wouldn't now be hearing you showing him so much disrespect.'

Stephen chuckled. 'Good. Just wanted to get things straight. And now, why don't you introduce me? We two know each other's names, but I haven't had the pleasure…'

Disarmed and relieved within an instant, Sidney proceeded to introduce Hazeem to Stephen. And Stephen proceeded to apologise for his bad manners, craving their understanding for his behaviour. 'After all,' he told them, 'I live under constant threat from people who look just like Hazeem – and, in fact, no more than five minutes ago, I had to kill two of them to prevent them killing me.'

On a number of occasions since he and the rest of his team had set out from Hope Farm, Sidney had tried to imagine what their meeting with Stephen might be like. However, nowhere in those imagined scenarios had there been anyone quite as novel as the Stephen they'd now met, and in none of them had the meeting taken place shortly after the dispatch of two humans. It was no surprise, then, that the revelation of the double killing – by this clearly capable octogenarian before him – left him again without any words. It would be Hazeem who would have to acknowledge this unexpected piece of information. 'They were going to kill you?' he asked quietly.

'Yeah, they were,' Stephen confirmed. 'Another damn ambush. But just like all the rest, they hadn't reckoned on a bullet. They can wave their talwars and their kukris around as much as they want, but that won't stop them getting a present from an SA80. And they always look surprised. I suppose because they are…'

'Just like all the rest?'

'Yeah, since the start of the year, I must have had about a dozen. Or, come to think of it, maybe a few more. I mean, there were those four of them back in the spring. You know, in one go.'

'I had no idea,' managed a shocked-looking Hazeem.

'Why would you?' countered Stephen.

'Well, I'm sort of local. You know, Black Country. I'm sure—'

'I don't advertise it. And anyway, I think most of them come from the west. Not very bright, some of them out there.'

'What are they after?'

'What's anyone after these days? Food. A way of surviving. Any way of surviving. Even if it means killing an old fool like m'self. S'pose you can't really blame 'em. Or me. For trying to keep m'self alive.'

Hazeem shook his head. Sidney just stared in amazement. This guy sounded more ruthless than Hazeem, and possibly even more ruthless than Ted over in Windhoek. And he was so old!

'Anyway,' Stephen continued, 'smells as though you might have been doing a little bit of self-preservation yourselves. Or is my nose deceiving me, and are those three bundles on the back of your wagon stuffed with just a whole load of nosegays?'

Although Hazeem had no idea what a nosegay was, he responded to Stephen's query by telling him exactly what was in two of the three bundles, and how they'd assisted him in bringing Sidney this far north. When Stephen then asked him how he'd equipped himself with two such useful assets, he freely admitted that he'd killed them – and he explained why. It was a revelation that generated not just a nod of approval from Stephen but also an unspoken and unmistakable hike in his respect for this unusual northerner. It was just so obvious in his eyes. As obvious as the need for Sidney to abandon his oath of silence. No longer could he leave all the talking to Hazeem, so he finally thought of something to say – something about the two bodies.

'Can we build a couple of pyres? You know, for the two bodies. They didn't choose to, but they've really helped us. And it just seems right...' but then he had second thoughts: '...but of course, if the smoke might be seen...'

'This is a giant rubbish dump, young man. Hardly used at all now. But fires often break out. Nobody pays any attention. And you're right. We should do good by them. Even if, from what I've heard, they were a couple of real bastards. And when we've done that... well, we can use their shrouds for my two. Pretty good timing, eh? Just as one lot gets overripe, another steps in to take their place. And I'm sure they won't mind a journey further north. Better than being interred in a rubbish dump – like I've had to do with all the others.'

Sidney had to tell himself that he wasn't in some terrible nightmare, one where old corpses were renewed with fresh ones when they'd served their purpose, and where the soon-to-be-stinking remains of the new ones constituted the perfect permit for further onward travel.

Just as long as the level of their stink didn't become completely intolerable.

This self-instruction worked, and he was soon fit enough to participate in leading Kaalki and the wagon between towering heaps of refuse – to a spot where Stephen believed there was room for a couple of funeral pyres. He even managed to help in the unloading of Rishi and Farid from the wagon, and in due course, the building of the pyres and their subsequent use. Then, before all three of the living attended to the pair of replacement cadavers, Sidney was in for a respite. Stephen had invited him and Hazeem to visit his bunker.

*

On their way there, having been freed from both the effects of shock and the demands of funeral duties, Sidney began a detailed inspection of the waste all around them. He was more than interested to see what had been dumped on this former airbase. And it wasn't just interesting but also really fascinating. Because it wasn't just common or garden refuse by any means; instead, there was every sort of thrown-away stuff one could imagine, from the remains of cars and the remains of animals to barbed-wire, bottles, broken toys – and books. And so, so much more. It was, thought Sidney, a cemetery for a lost civilisation, and one that had been here for many, many years.

Wherever he looked, it was clear that this stuff hadn't found its way here in the last few days. It had been here for maybe decades – an observation that was confirmed by Stephen when he informed his guests that, since the disappearance of powered trucks, the dump was now barely used. It was too far away from those who might want to use it, and they now, he suspected, just discarded their waste closer to their homes; something Sidney found no trouble in believing, given what he'd witnessed going on around Hope Farm. In any event, Stephen continued, with the demise of cars and trucks – and settees and 'white goods' – there weren't nearly as many 'big-ticket' items to be disposed of these days. As a dump, RAF Cosford was now effectively redundant. So too was its still-elegant hangar.

As Stephen explained as they approached the hangar, it was the giant edifice built to house a collection of military aeroplanes when the base had been transformed from an active base into an air-force museum. And it still housed these planes – albeit, as Stephen was sad to report, most of them were now rotting away or, years ago, had already been severely damaged by any number of thoughtless intruders. It was therefore more than fortunate, he explained, that these intruders hadn't bothered much with the museum's collection of old radio kit – and that, more recently, nobody had been given the slightest opportunity to interfere with the giant antenna that he himself had managed to erect on the hangar's tall roof.

And there it was, pointing to the sky – and perfect, no doubt, for Stephen's ground-wave communications with Dorothy. And the fact that it had been installed by

Stephen himself, presumably when he was fit enough to scale this giant building, pointed to the fact that he had been here a very long time indeed – and revealed the possibility that he'd been exterminating unwanted visitors for a very long time as well. Was this year's bag of a dozen or more, thought Sidney, a bumper year or a lean year? Just how many people had this guy killed? Well, maybe he would get around to asking him. But first, there was a mule to attend to and then a bunker to take in.

Unsurprisingly, this bunker was beneath the old hangar, and its access was well hidden from view – behind a large piece of fuselage decorated with a pig...

Stephen led his guests past this curiously decorated panel and down a flight of steps to a large metal door. This he opened to allow them into a short passage, at the end of which was another metal door. This one he opened with some difficulty before inviting Sidney and Hazeem to step into his inner sanctum, an inner sanctum that had in it one bed, one chest of drawers, one table, one hard chair, one easy chair, one (large) bank of bookshelves, one (not quite so large) bank of assorted radio kit – and a smell of smoked meat.

*

In due course, when Stephen had finished feeding his guests, the source of the smoked-meat smell would be made known. It was, in fact, smoked rat-meat, some of which they'd just eaten – and enjoyed. It was, explained

Stephen, a wonderful source of protein, and a plentiful source of protein. There were apparently countless thousands of rats living at RAF Cosford, and Stephen was now an accomplished ratcatcher – and meat-smoker. And, as he went on to promise, he would make quite sure that, by morning, he'd sorted out his entire current stock of smoked rats, so they could be added to whatever other food stores had been assembled for the long journey north. Indeed, he would make a start on this task just as soon as he'd got Dorothy on the radio, and Sidney had been given the opportunity to talk to her directly for the first time.

There was just so much that Sidney's life to date had left him unprepared for. His forty-two years on this earth had not been easy, by any means, but they'd largely been without unforeseen events, and there had certainly never before been a whole series of unforeseen events. But now, well, killings followed by more killings, the urgent abandonment of his home (with a northerner!), the unspeakable horror of sharing a wagon with a load of decomposing flesh, yet more killings, and now the prospect of having to sound collected when talking to a woman in Scotland, having just been informed that he'd recently dined on rat! He really wasn't sure he could do it, but Stephen was already firing up his equipment, and there seemed no way that Sidney could ask for an adjournment. He would simply have to get on with it and exchange his first few words with the enigmatic Dot. And remember to call her Dorothy, not Dot. Dot was a diminutive that not even Sonia had used.

*

As it turned out, it wasn't too bad. This was principally because it was a very short discussion, and his role in this discussion had largely been to listen and to say barely a word. After all, it had essentially been about receiving instructions and nothing else. Certainly nothing that would diminish Dorothy's enigmatic nature, over and above her actually revealing her voice. (Which was, in Sidney's opinion, refined, if a little sharp and unmistakably that of an older woman, and therefore not of a potential girlfriend, whether blonde or brunette.)

The instructions were basically to leave RAF Cosford as soon as was practical – with Stephen (that was essential) – and to make for a place that Stephen would know not far from a town called Lockerbie (a settlement situated, as would be discovered from a perusal of Sidney's A–Z, just over the old border with Scotland). And there, 'somebody would collect them'.

Dorothy did wish Sidney well at the conclusion of this briefing, but she invited no questions and merely asked to be handed back to Stephen, with whom she apparently wanted some private final words. Sidney had been dismissed, and he couldn't help thinking that not only were events piling on top of him almost faster than he could manage but also that he might not welcome any further events whatsoever. Such as events that might arise on a two-hundred-mile journey north. Did he really want to go to somewhere near a place called Lockerbie – to meet a woman who had been so impersonal and so, well, so dismissive?

The answer, he decided – after sharing the contents of his short radio session with Hazeem – was a slightly reluctant 'yes'. He knew he couldn't let Hazeem down now, after all he had done. And he couldn't let himself down – by staying here and probably ending up dead. He couldn't even let down the guy who'd just fed him rat. And he certainly couldn't refuse a request made a little later in the day to help this old codger package up the two new bodies for the wagon. This was something Stephen wanted to do today, rather than leaving it for the morning when they should be looking to make a very early start.

'And anyway,' he said, 'I don't like leaving corpses just lying around. It makes the dump look untidy.'

*

Stephen, it appeared, had a very dark side to his nature. Sidney had learnt that much by the time he and Hazeem had bedded down on the bunker floor, whilst, across the room, Stephen enjoyed his last night in his battered and creaky bed. He had also learnt that this man could kill, smoke rats, operate a ham radio and eat without getting food in his long beard – but that was about all he'd learnt. Stephen was as enigmatic as his contact in Scotland, and he'd made quite sure throughout the whole evening that the conversation had focused on Sidney and Hazeem – and their lives and their recent history – to the exclusion of anything about himself. Whenever Sidney or Hazeem had attempted to prise open the coffer marked 'Stephen', he'd sat on its lid and stopped them opening it even an inch.

Maybe, thought Sidney, as he finally dropped off, he and Hazeem might get a peek inside that coffer at some point. And with two-hundred miles of shared travelling due to start tomorrow, there would be plenty of opportunities to do so. And plenty of opportunities to adjust to the idea of consuming rats. One thing Stephen had disclosed was that he had more than eighty of the smoked little beasties to take on the trip.

16.

The team now had four members: one to pull the wagon and three to ride on it. And this trio were now in various positions on the wagon – with various roles.

Hazeem was back on the wagon's driving bench with the driver's reins in his hands, but he now had the company of an ageing father – otherwise known as Stephen – a very old gentleman whose role had involved him equipping himself with some traditional clothing, including a very generous cowl over his head. With his long beard and with his deeply wrinkled face, now dressed with a light covering of charcoal-impregnated grease, he really looked the part, and it would no doubt take a very sharp-eyed northerner to recognise that Stephen wasn't a northerner himself.

Behind Hazeem and Stephen, and wrapped up in

his hateful shroud, was Sidney, playing his normal role of an unburied corpse. However, his situation wasn't anything like as dire as that he'd endured recently, in that he wasn't wrapped up tightly and he wasn't sharing the back of the wagon with an intolerable smell. This was because, on the other side of the 'books and souvenirs' corpse (now a more corpulent corpse after the addition of a couple of Stephen's books and what he emphasised were a number of his 'essential' files), were the two 'fresh' corpses, both of them wrapped not just in linen but in some plastic sheeting beneath it. Stephen had supplied this, and he'd assured his two wagon-riders that this would serve to contain any smell that might develop over the initial days of their journey north. So at six-thirty in the morning, when the journey began, Sidney had been in receipt of no pharmaceutical assistance whatsoever.

If leaving RAF Cosford was at all distressing for Stephen, he hid it well. In fact, Sidney thought he'd detected a sense of relief on Stephen's part as they'd made their final preparations to board the wagon. And thereafter, all he became aware of was Stephen whistling as Kaalki pulled the wagon along. There were certainly no signs of regret and no indication that Stephen was doing anything other than enjoying the trip. In fact, it wasn't long before he was chirruping away about what he was seeing all around him: a landscape he'd clearly not seen for many long years.

'God, will you look at that? Used to be rolling fields around here. With quite a few trees if I remember. Not a bloody desert. Not a bloody wall-to-wall shit-scape, with a shitload of shit-awful hovels.' Here, he chuckled. 'Hell, I'm not surprised there's no effing food. What a way to treat good, fertile land. And what a way to treat the world. I mean, you couldn't make it uglier if you tried.'

'Got me on that one, old man,' responded Hazeem. 'And you're right. It didn't take any effort at all. As in, nobody had to try. All they had to do was ignore the consequences of their actions.'

Sidney couldn't easily take part in this exchange, but he did hear Stephen chuckling again before he then posed a question to the northerner beside him: 'You old enough to remember the green? And the trees?'

'No,' replied Hazeem immediately, 'but I can just about imagine it, and I can just about feel the loss. Not as much as you can, I'm sure. But enough...'

'Enough?'

'Enough to know that I shouldn't attempt to defend what has happened. And I'm sorry; I really am.'

Stephen didn't chuckle any more, and it was some time before he started to whistle again. Indeed, when he did, he'd left himself only a few minutes to do so. Because Kaalki, having pulled the wagon east along the old M54 for quite a few miles, had now turned north up the old A-road towards Stafford – down which were coming a good number of those inquisitive northerners. And whistling would have been seen as a very inappropriate pastime for a pious old man accompanying a consignment of his fallen brethren.

Hazeem was excellent. He hadn't lost his knack. With his 'aged father' next to him, he may even have upped his game. Hardly any of the curious northerners delayed him for more than a minute, and certainly none of them showed any interest in auditing the contents of the wagon. Even though these contents weren't yet able to confirm their credentials with the help of an appropriate scent.

Sidney had even begun to think that, whatever their journey north might entail, it wouldn't entail the consequences of their being discovered as frauds. But that was before mid-afternoon – before something happened that would radically change his view.

*

It started with a mumbled conversation between Hazeem and Stephen, which was rounded off by an emphatic command from Stephen – for Sidney's attention – to 'Lie still and shut up.'

This was unique. Up until now, the normal warning of the need to play dead was in the form of the wagon slowing as Hazeem prepared to convince another group of northerners of the nature of his mission. On this occasion, after Stephen's advice, the wagon did indeed start to slow, and within just a few seconds, it was stationary, but then Sidney became aware of some shouting in what must have been Urdu. This was like none of the encounters with northerners they'd had up to now. Nor was the attempted-placatory tone of

Hazeem's responses to these shouts. Sidney had no idea what Hazeem was saying, but it was clear he was trying to defuse what was some sort of very threatening situation.

Sidney did as he'd been commanded. He lay still. Then he heard a very animated conversation between Hazeem and what must have been two very close-by northerners – and he decided it was probably now the time to disobey the command and add his presence to the confrontation.

It was like Viraj's murder all over again – in that he was just too late again. Before he had even begun to free himself from his shroud, there were two very loud shots, and the wagon lurched forwards, no doubt as a result of Kaalki reacting to the unexpected gunfire. Then there was silence for a couple of seconds.

And this was only brought to an end when Stephen spoke quietly to inform Hazeem, that 'We'd better get them off the road. Now.'

At this point, Sidney threw caution to the wind and quickly rose to a standing position. This was when he saw them: two more bodies, both of them lying on the broken surface of the road, both of them with talwars in their dead hands and both of them with clear evidence of a lethal wound to the head. Even Sidney was able to deduce that they must have been dead before they'd hit the ground.

Maybe he was becoming accustomed to sudden death or maybe he was in shock, but Sidney's reaction to what he saw was simply to join in the task of removing the two bodies from the highway and 'laying them to rest' in a ditch. He did notice they were the bodies of two very young men, but as far as he was concerned, that was something of an irrelevance. What was more important was that these two young northerners had clearly intended to hijack the wagon and do whatever was necessary to achieve this end – and whilst their failure was a matter for some celebration, it was now necessary simply to focus on the practical – and immediately. Only by doing this would those still in possession of the wagon be able to continue on their way.

This they did, as soon as possible and before there was any time to debrief Sidney on what had just happened. Not that he really needed a debrief. As he already suspected – and as would be confirmed in due course – Stephen had used a pistol concealed within his traditional garb to end the lives of the two bushwhackers before they'd been given any opportunity to demonstrate their proficiency with a talwar. Hazeem, sitting between Stephen and the putative assailants, had apparently provided the necessary masking of Stephen's preparations for this task, but not a shield against its consequent outcome. Stephen had fired his RAF-issued Glock pistol with more than enough skill to miss Hazeem's body – by merely inches – but not the foreheads of the two unsuspecting bandits. And it had all happened so quickly. As Sidney had noticed as he'd helped to cart their bodies to the ditch, they didn't even have a look of surprise on their faces. They just hadn't had the time.

It was a good move – to have proceeded so promptly. While the bodies were being dealt with, people had emerged from their hovels to establish the source of the two gunshots, and others were also coming down the road who must have heard or seen what had happened. However, nobody had been given the time to replace understandable caution with what might prove to be reckless curiosity. Indeed, it would definitely have been far from prudent to have stayed around. Better to get away immediately and, if possible, find somewhere to hide – just in case anybody did finally overcome that caution and decided to mount a pursuit. And fortunately, no more than a mile up the road there was somewhere to hide. It was in a place called Gailey, and although it looked like another rubbish dump, it was in fact a graveyard for numerous examples of a particular reminder of long-lost England: caravans.

As Hazeem would explain, this place had – many, many years ago – been a huge outlet for caravans and vehicles called 'motorhomes'. However, that was before the influx of new citizens had begun to requisition whatever could be used as a dwelling, and the large caravan lot had soon become a caravan town – but not for long. Potentially flammable homes crammed together and filled with people making open fires weren't destined to remain homes for more than a few months, and caravan town soon moved on to its next manifestation: the burnt-out residue of caravan town – and a place to dump more of these clearly suspect relics of English culture. These weren't the only unwanted relics to be dumped here, but for reasons that were far from clear, they constituted the largest part of what had been dragged to this site, and their remains were now everywhere – and far from intact. Indeed, as a graveyard, this was a graveyard full of desecration. But it was also encouragingly empty of people.

This was why Hazeem had chosen to come here. He knew it was very unlikely that he and his friends would be bothered here. And he also knew there was nowhere just to the north that would provide quite so much privacy as this location. It was therefore soon decided that, even though it was early and they hadn't covered the distance they'd hoped to on this first day, they should make camp here and wait until the morning to move on. Furthermore, when were they ever likely to have an opportunity to be surrounded by so much evidence of a way of life that would never return?

*

With food preparation underway, it was the subject of two human lives that would never return that first dominated the conversation. This was when Sidney's suspicions about what had happened as a result of Stephen's sharp-shooting were confirmed – and when he learnt a little more about the armaments with which Kaalki's wagon had now been equipped. He knew Stephen had brought along his rifle and a store of ammunition for this weapon, but only now did he discover that Stephen and Hazeem each had, concealed about their bodies, a loaded Glock pistol and some spare pistol ammunition. Furthermore, in a metal case that had been sneaked onto the back of the wagon by Stephen and Hazeem and then hidden beneath Kaalki's forage, was one further Glock pistol and even more ammunition.

When quizzed by Sidney as to why he hadn't been told about this additional weaponry and, in particular, why he hadn't been given that third pistol at the outset of their journey, Stephen countered by asking him whether he would have been comfortable as the custodian of a lethal weapon and whether he would ever have considered it appropriate to engage its lethal powers. Sidney had to confess that he wouldn't have been comfortable, and as he'd never killed anybody in his life, he would no doubt have had a real problem in pulling the weapon's trigger. (Just as he would have a real problem in putting into aggressive use the knife that, following Ted's advice, was now fixed to his leg.) However, he admitted that now he'd witnessed what had been the vital use of lethal power, he had an entirely different view. This journey, he'd realised, wasn't necessarily going to be straightforward, and it was more than likely that his 'team' would have further recourse to pistol or rifle power, in which case he simply had to play his part. He couldn't expect his companions to do all the shooting that might be required.

This admission brought smiles to the faces of both Stephen and Hazeem, and there was even a smile on Sidney's face when Stephen presented him with that third gun. It didn't last long, though. It was soon replaced by a look of concern and consternation as Stephen went on to explain where on the gun Sidney would find the safety, the trigger and the end of its barrel. Nevertheless, he himself was now armed with more than just a knife, and it wouldn't be too long before he would begin to feel exposed without that pistol about his person. Such was the world in which he now lived.

However, there was only so much of a late afternoon and evening that could be devoted to guns and their use, and the conversation eventually turned away from armaments and towards the 'lost civilisation' aspect of their surroundings. It was Sidney who turned the wheel in this direction, and he did this by asking Stephen whether he'd ever been in a caravan – or in one of those motorised caravans. And if so, what was it like?

Stephen took his time to respond to Sidney's questions. It seemed to Sidney that he was checking with himself whether he could supply any answers that wouldn't reveal too much about his past life – or about himself full stop.

When he did respond, it was carefully and not with any particular eagerness on his part. 'I remember a camper van—'

'A what?' interrupted Sidney.

'A camper van. A van you could camp in. With beds and a place to cook. That sort of thing. Just a small van, but… well, big enough.'

'Big enough for what?'

Stephen didn't look happy, but he responded to Sidney's question. 'Big enough for a small family.'

'Your family?'

'Yes, my family.'

'And…?'

'We had to get rid of it. There was no room for it – when we were moved.'

Hazeem began to look uncomfortable. He would undoubtedly have liked Sidney to have turned the wheel in a less hazardous direction. Little did he know that Sidney was now going to turn it so hard in the original direction that it ran the risk of threatening their whole mission.

It might have been the adrenalin still pumping through his body or it might have been the result of now owning a gun, but Sidney had been riled by Stephen's obvious reluctance to talk about his experience of caravans – on top of his obvious disinclination to disclose anything about himself the previous evening. They were a team! A team in which each member would, in all likelihood, have to depend on the other team members to preserve his life. And the latest member of the team – who'd been plucked from his hidey hole as ordered and at the cost of a serious diversion – wasn't prepared to do what each of his 'rescuers' had done, which was to willingly open up about himself and his previous life.

Well, it just wasn't good enough, and it was time to make this known to this latest member of the team – in no uncertain terms.

'Right,' announced Sidney. 'That's a good start. We now know you had a small family – who owned a camper van – and that the camper van had to go when you were all moved. Now all we need to know is the rest of your life history so we know as much about you as you know about us. I mean, the stuff we told you last night and the stuff all of us should know about each other. And if I haven't made myself clear, let me just say that I'm sure Hazeem, just like me, would prefer not to be facing the next few days with a "man of mystery". If either of us has to save your life, we'd like to know just a little about the life we'd be saving.'

At the end of this challenge to Stephen, Sidney wondered whether the shock he felt from what he'd just said was apparent on his face, and if it were, whether it was quite so apparent as the shock that was on Hazeem's face. He no longer looked uncomfortable but completely incredulous. Just as Stephen, below all those wrinkles, looked sheepish and maybe a little remorseful.

Then Stephen spoke. 'I thought you were the softie. You've taken me by surprise.'

'And myself,' confessed Sidney.

'Yeah, well, you're right, of course. And I've got no excuse. Other than when you've been a hermit for quite as long as I have, it's not so easy to abandon your cave. Even if you might manage it physically, you're still reluctant to give it up mentally. You hide inside your head. And that means you do what I've done: lock people out, lock them out by revealing nothing about yourself. Even when there's probably no reason to do this.

'Well, I suppose it's about time I undid that lock and gave you a brief rundown of what I've been doing for the last eighty-six years. And don't worry, it won't take that long. Hermits, by their nature, lead very uneventful lives.'

There was now a smile in the middle of all those wrinkles, and after checking that his audience really did want to hear a precis of his life story, he began it. And he was right: it took very little time at all.

'OK. Born outskirts of Bristol 2068. Only child of two parents – who owned a camper van...' Here, his smile broadened. '*Relocated* in 2079 to a flat near the centre of Bristol. Two years later joined the Royal Air Force – or what was left of it—'

'You flew aeroplanes?' interjected Sidney.

'No. I trained as a maintenance engineer. While they still had anything to maintain. And when they didn't – in... I think it was 2088, I joined a commune in Dorset. I mean a group of people about my age who were trying to live off the land and went about this by sharing everything they had. It was a bit of a throwback existence, but it kept me going for quite a while, right up until I realised I wanted to be on my own.

'I wanted to be able to move around, maybe meet other people, and... well, come to terms with what was happening to my life and to the lives of so many other people in Britain. Remember, I'm talking about the early nineties here – a time when, if you were native English, your life was increasingly no longer your own. Unless, maybe, you 'dropped out', as I did, and began to live on your wits.

'Anyway, that's what I did until, in 2118 – when I'd reached fifty – I washed up on the rat-infested shores of what would become my home for the next thirty-six years. Right up until you guys came along and paddled me out to sea again in that wagon over there. Which I think brings us right up to date.'

'I suppose Cosford—' began Hazeem.

'...had a supply of protein, a few places around and about where I could grow my own food, lots of familiar kit from my days in the RAF, a perfect hermit cave in the shape of that bunker – and complete solitude. If, of course, you don't count the odd unwanted visitor, who I sometimes had to shoot.'

'Where did you get the weapons?'

'There was a stash of them in a storeroom, along with loads of ammunition. I couldn't believe it when I found them. Thought they had to be decommissioned and that the ammo was dummy. But no, it was all good stuff. Just overlooked, I suppose, and just waiting for someone like me to find it.'

'And the radio kit?' challenged Sidney.

'That, I had to get working. Museum stuff. All of it. But... well, I soon got it to work. And with the aerial I put up, I was soon surfing the airwaves.'

'And finding Dorothy?'

'Eventually. Although, in true hermit style, for years, I just listened in to her conversations. You know, with other hams. In fact, we've only been on talking terms, as it were, for about ten or so years.'

'And is she your only contact?'

'Yes. Just Dorothy.'

'Stephen,' asked Hazeem nervously, 'what do hermits

do? I mean, how have you filled your days for so many years? Talking to that lady in Scotland and shooting intruders couldn't have taken all your time.'

Stephen frowned, and when he spoke, he sounded distinctly irritated. 'I existed. I stayed alive. And I found that to be a full-time occupation. How the hell could I not?'

Hazeem's eyes widened. Stephen's sharp response had clearly taken him by surprise, just as clearly as he now needed Sidney to come to his aid.

This Sidney did before Hazeem had a chance to mount his own defence. 'How the hell indeed,' he opened. 'And who's ever heard of a part-time hermit?' And then, turning to Hazeem, 'Come on, Hazeem, Stephen's just told us more about himself than he's told anybody in decades, and then you go and press him for more. I mean, how could you?'

Hazeem grasped the offered assistance eagerly, and immediately presented Stephen with an apology. 'Sorry, Stephen. I mean, I really am sorry. I wasn't thinking. And I didn't mean any offence. You know that, don't you? I mean, I hope you do anyway.'

'Of course I do. Just as I didn't mean you any offence… But, well, it's been a bit of a day, and when you get as old as I am, you can get more than just a little bit cranky at the drop of a hat. So… well, I'm sorry too, Hazeem, and next time I'll try and remember who my friends are – the first ones I've had for a very long time.'

Sidney felt a huge wave of relief. His intervention had worked just as he'd hoped. Indeed, it was even better than he'd hoped. That open admission of friendship had been a real bonus, and one he and Hazeem would never forget. No more than they'd forget that there were still limits to Stephen's openness.

After all, what indeed had their new companion been doing for the last thirty-six six years at RAF Cosford? And would they ever find out?

17.

In the early morning light, the remains of caravan town looked bleak and ugly. In sharp contrast, Kaalki, standing within their midst, looked as handsome as any thoroughbred – and as happy and contented as any stalwart mule could ever look. In fact, to Sidney, he just seemed to radiate fulfilment and even a mulish air of serenity. As though he knew he was now a vital part of his closest friend's well-being – and that of his two new friends as well.

'All in the mind,' Sidney told himself. But nevertheless, as he delivered some breakfast fodder to his four-footed companion, there was something in Kaalki's eyes that cemented his belief that the division between humans and other animals wasn't just suspect but completely wrong. Kaalki couldn't speak, but he could express himself in other ways. And right now, he was confirming that, without a shadow of doubt, he was not only relishing his new responsibilities but he was also eager to do whatever was required of him to fulfil these responsibilities. (Even if it meant tackling further demanding inclines.)

He still had this air of purpose about him as he finally left the caravan dump behind and was directed by Hazeem to make his way to what remained of the M6. Once again, sitting behind him, he had Hazeem with the reins in his hands, and Stephen wrapped in layers of fabric – and both with pistols about their person. And behind these two fellows was his long-time friend, along with two real cadavers and one false one and, like his two living companions, his friend had his own loaded pistol jammed into his belt. Kaalki would have been unaware of all this detail of the disposition of the living, the dead, the fake – and the weaponry – as much as Sidney was only too aware of the fact that he was now the owner of something that could dispatch another's life; a possession, he realised, that made him feel not just assured but also somewhat alarmed. Would he ever be able to use it if called upon to do so? He really wasn't sure.

Nevertheless, as soon as Hazeem announced from the front that they'd made it onto the motorway – or what was left of it – Sidney realised he already had his hand resting on the pistol's handle. Then, when the wagon began to slow to accommodate the first of a number of challenges from those on their way south, he found his index finger had moved to the weapon's trigger.

At least, he thought, he might have lost his fear of this thing, even if he was still by no means confident that he could ever exert any pressure on that trigger – if it would mean a bullet leaving the pistol's chamber and ending up in a human's body.

It was just as well, then, that Hazeem's standard explanation of the purpose of their journey north was still working well. Right up until it failed spectacularly.

*

It was now nearly midday, and Kaalki had pulled the wagon a good number of miles along the broken motorway. This was when Sidney felt his carriage slowing once again, but he then heard Hazeem issue a strained warning to lie low and still. His driver-guardian had clearly seen the signs of impending trouble, and he hadn't been mistaken.

Within seconds, there were voices all around the front of the wagon, and none of them sounded calm or friendly. In fact, they were quite the reverse. They sounded threatening and combative. Sidney couldn't understand what was being said, as the voices were all those of Urdu speakers. However, he could tell that Hazeem had, for a second time, been unsuccessful in keeping the inquisitive at bay, and on this occasion, the inquisitive were being not only confrontational but also very determined. And what they were determined to do was take control of the wagon. There was no doubt about it.

Sidney gripped his pistol tightly and attempted to decide what to do: to stay concealed or to leap into action. Then he did decide. He would leap into action. So, he began to pull himself up and, at the same time, poke his head out of the shroud. And this is when he saw that his minders were already taking care of the situation. For there was Hazeem, throwing one marauder off the front of the wagon and now squaring up to attack another about to climb aboard it; a stocky gentleman, who, despite his holding a very large talwar in his right hand, now looked more alarmed than brave. And while this physical action was being played out, another lacking close contact was underway as well. This was Stephen demonstrating to another six assailants that if they got any closer to the wagon or its patient mule, they would discover to their cost that the weapon he was holding in his hands was loaded – and they would probably end up with their heads blown off. It was a challenge that needed no common language. And it worked. Despite all six assailants being armed with knives or talwars, not one of them came any closer to the vehicle.

Nor did either of Hazeem's uninvited guests make a move to join him on the wagon. Instead, they stood with their mouths open, looking even less enthusiastic than their colleagues to resume any interaction with a couple of mad men. It therefore took only some quietly delivered advice from Hazeem to see all of them readopting their southerly course, so that within five minutes of their unwelcome visit, they were well on their way down the motorway and not even looking back. Furthermore, much to the relief of all those still in possession of the wagon, this desirable outcome had been achieved without the discharge of a weapon, and therefore without alerting others to the presence of projectile-firing armaments – and what this might mean regarding the identity of these armaments' owners.

Those coming down the motorway and those living in nearby shacks may have been aware of a slight contretemps having taken place, but this was evidently not an uncommon occurrence in these times, and people had learnt to mind their own business as a matter of course. Nobody wanted to play police officer – especially when the unruly were total strangers who might not take kindly to an uncalled-for intervention. In fact, those still coming down the road seemed not only to be showing little interest in the wagon that was now on its way further north but they may also even have been studiously avoiding showing any interest in it whatsoever.

Stephen made that observation when Hazeem had brought the wagon to a halt about two miles further on in order to give Kaalki a rest. He also noted the fact that he wasn't confident that there wouldn't be further awkward confrontations, and so they needed to be on their guard – all three of them, including Sidney.

Sidney agreed immediately, but he was keen to point out that it might be better if his companions chose a trigger word to advise him that he should swap his prone position for one that would enable him to be more than just on his guard, and instead be actively involved in dealing with any of these awkward confrontations. They concurred, and the word they chose was 'Lazarus'. Little did they know then that less than half an hour later, after they'd set off north again, it would be put into use – loudly and urgently by Hazeem.

*

It was another ambush; this time, by more than a dozen men. And they'd given barely any warning to Hazeem and Stephen of their hostile intentions. They'd simply walked up to the wagon as Hazeem had begun to slow it, and as one of them grabbed Kaalki's bridle, the others began to surround the vehicle.

On this occasion, there was no time for Hazeem to get physical, but there was still just enough time to make the enemy aware of the combined firepower aboard the wagon. And it wasn't just Hazeem and Stephen who had drawn their guns. It was Sidney as well.

He could barely believe it, but on hearing that 'Lazarus' command, he'd got out of his shroud and on his feet in an instant, and he was now pointing a gun at the head of a very tall youth who had wisely decided that pulling himself onto the back of the wagon was no longer a good idea. Hazeem, at the front of the wagon, had trained his weapon on the man who still had Kaalki's bridle in his hands. And Stephen, beside him, wasn't aiming his gun at anyone. He was just cradling it in his lap – and smiling.

Then he spoke.

'Any of you gentlemen speak English?'

This question didn't elicit an immediate response, but it did cause a clear wave of consternation in his audience. An English voice emanating from that darkened, wrinkly face was obviously as shocking as it was unexpected. It may even have been more shocking than the appearance of the guns. So shocking, in fact, that it took what seemed like an age for one of the raiding gang to confess in a very shaky voice that he did know a few words of this foreign tongue.

'Splendid,' began Stephen, 'because I want you and all your chums to know that I and my two friends are not having a very good day.' And here he stopped, presumably for dramatic effect.

'However,' he continued, 'compared to how your day might shape up, you could say we're not having too bad a day at all. I mean, we won't all be dead in the next few seconds, which you and your friends will be if you don't all leave us alone and continue on your way without further ado. And if you haven't understood all that, the basic message is that you and your fellow pirates should get out of our sight pronto. And that means now!'

The man he addressed was now nodding his head – vigorously. And whilst he started to mumble something to his compatriots, he was clearly wasting his time. They had no doubt all comprehended only too well that their continued presence was not welcome, and that if they chose to ignore this fact, then it might be the last choice they'd ever make.

In no time at all, they were all shuffling off south, and Sidney was coming to terms with his first 'use' of an offensive weapon. Which, he registered, seemed to involve his acquiring two very sweaty palms and a slight feeling of weakness in his knees. But all being well, neither Hazeem nor Stephen would be aware of these attendant phenomena.

They didn't seem to be, and when, a few hours later, they stopped for the night somewhere near the abandoned sprawl of Stoke-on-Trent, Stephen actually made quite a point of praising Sidney's rapid reactions – and his willingness to deploy his weapon. 'Like a natural,' he said. 'And I couldn't be more delighted – although I'm not particularly surprised. I always thought you'd measure up when you had to. And you've certainly done that. So, well done. And welcome to the club.'

Sidney had no idea how to react to this unexpected tribute, but he did know he felt more like a fraud than a genuine novice warrior. After all, he'd merely pointed a gun at someone's head, and he hadn't fired it. That was hardly the same as the behaviour of his companions who had, when they'd needed to, robbed a number of people of their lives. He just hoped that neither Stephen nor Hazeem had overestimated his combative credentials, ones that might still be found to be distinctly suspect when put to a more rigorous test. And that was still very much a possibility.

However, that was the future. For now, after such a demanding day, exhaustion had seen all three of Kaalki's charges eager to have an early night. Therefore, the little time they spent before retiring was filled with just feeding themselves and their faithful mule, and discussing little more than how to approach the forthcoming day. Should they continue on the old motorway and run the risk of more threatening encounters, or should they try to follow the route of the motorway on smaller roads and tracks to stand a better chance of avoiding further trouble? Hazeem, as a dyed-in-the-wool smuggler, used to seeking out hidden ways, was the keenest to consider this less direct route to Scotland. But even he was concerned that such a course would take far longer than staying with the M6, and there was no guarantee that there wouldn't be other brigands waiting to do their worst on the back lanes of modern Britain. Indeed, there might be even more of them there, and they might be even more desperate. There was, of course, no way of knowing, and therefore no way Hazeem could convince himself, let alone his companions, that they should abandon the M6.

So that was that. It would be another day on the main thoroughfare north, and another day of possible confrontations. It wasn't an encouraging prospect, and as Sidney took the first watch as Hazeem and Stephen bedded down under the wagon, he couldn't help thinking about his fraudulent 'warrior' designation, and how it would be revealed as such when it made its first contact with genuine, kill-or-be-killed combat.

These thoughts even kept him awake when it was his turn to sleep, and they were still there with him in the morning. In fact, it took another comforting man-to-mule interaction to finally chase them away, so that when Sidney had finished feeding Kaalki, he was at least focused more on the now-familiar practicalities of travel – in his shroud – than he was on the prospect of imminent danger.

*

Not long after they had set off once again, Sidney was even thinking that, as so often, things seem worse at night, and that there was no real reason that Hazeem's persuasive powers wouldn't just carry on working. That those two incidents yesterday had been aberrations – merely two unfortunate lapses in the trio's good fortune that were unlikely ever to happen again. However, his comforting musings were then washed away in an instant.

Hazeem had just shouted the word 'Lazarus' for a second time, and Sidney needed to be on his feet – with his gun in his hand.

He nearly tripped over as he was getting up, and then he almost let out a gasp as he found his feet. Only fear held it in his throat. Because there before him wasn't a gang of bandits but a small army of them, and at the front of the assembled throng were three full-bellied men, each with a pistol of his own, and each pointing it at his armed counterpart on the wagon. Sidney's man-marker was chewing something, and to either side of his corpulent frame were a number of grinning, mostly bearded men, armed not with more guns but instead with knives and what looked like home-made cudgels. These 'members of the chorus' and the mastication habits of the guy with the gun weren't, Sidney decided quickly, the most significant features of his and his friends' predicament. It was the fact that the gang's three principals had weapons to match their own and that these three were backed up by a whole host of willing helpers, who could no doubt overwhelm the wagon and its passengers within seconds. Or of course, just kill the passengers if they so chose.

That didn't seem to be what the phalanx of bushwhackers had in mind to do – at least not yet – because one of their gun-toting members was now addressing Hazeem, and as far as Sidney could tell, this apparent gang leader was ordering him to accept his situation. This being that he and his two friends were in a hopeless position, and whatever they did with their own weapons, they would soon simply be inundated by the gang members, and soon after that, they would be dead.

It was interesting, thought Sidney, that even in times of acute stress one can discern what is going on from just tone of voice and facial expression.

And he wasn't wrong. Hazeem was clearly being given an ultimatum, and if it wasn't accepted, it would be the end of his and his two friends' trip north – and probably their lives.

Hazeem looked crestfallen, and now, stooping down like a completely broken man, he threw his gun to the ground and then began to dismount the wagon slowly. As his feet hit the ground, he then leapt at the chief brigand, and with a knife that had appeared from nowhere, he soon had the man in a painful armlock with the knife at his throat. It had all happened so rapidly that Sidney could barely believe it had happened at all. Nor could he comprehend how eager all the leader's men were to avoid that knife being used to open up their leader's throat and so dispatch him to his maker.

Even without a command from Hazeem, they all seemed to take a step back, and as their leader dropped his gun, the other two armed with similar weapons lowered theirs and looked as likely to use them as Sidney was to use his.

There was then a hiatus. Hazeem simply stared at the two who still had guns in their hands, and they too then dropped them to the ground. There then followed a total disarmament exercise, where knives, talwars, cudgels and the odd machete were let fall, until Hazeem and his friends were surrounded by a host of sheepish-looking and entirely unarmed peasants. If it were a world that still handed out medals, Hazeem would have been in line for one of the most distinguished. It wasn't, but his actions did mean that Kaalki and his human cargo would be allowed to go on their way unharmed. Even if, for the first mile further north, they had to take the principal peasant with them, his throat never too far away from the blade of Hazeem's knife.

This did give Hazeem a chance to have a brief chat with their hostage, who, it transpired, had once been the police chief in this area – before the remnants of a police force had disappeared completely – and who, along with his two deputies, now earned a living in a very different way. With their three possibly serviceable firearms, this trio of ex-cops now led a group of ne'er-do-wells who preyed on passing travellers – particularly those who appeared to have something worth stealing, but not the ability to protect themselves or their property. Most of the time, he admitted, this alternative occupation provided him and his minions with a passable living, and the worst that had happened to date was their finding that some of those they'd 'delayed' had nothing 'to offer'. Never before, he confessed, had anything like this happened. And he had no idea how much his reputation might have been dented or whether it might even have been so bent out of shape that he would now find it difficult, if not impossible, to exert any authority over his troops ever again. He might never 'work' again.

Hazeem recounted the details of this conversation when, at the end of a long day and hours after they'd left the dented copper at the side of the road, they'd stopped for the night. It provided a welcome spell of merriment in what was otherwise an evening of concern and uncertainty. After all, whilst our three aliens had survived another day in foreign parts, they knew full well that there were more foreign parts to come, and in all likelihood, there would be other incidents to disrupt their progress or even bring it to an early conclusion. Therefore, it wasn't long before the debate once again turned to the wisdom of sticking to the motorway and thereby putting themselves in the path of all sorts of danger.

It wasn't, however, a long debate. They would soon be approaching the old conurbation of Manchester, and as far as Hazeem was aware, the whole of the area up ahead was now a maze of small settlements, linked together with tracks, which in all probability constituted a greater threat to any travellers who passed through them than that inherent in a further slog up the M6. Even if the travellers in question were carrying with them two cadavers, both of which were now beginning to make their presence known, even through an envelope of thick, odour-containing plastic.

So, it was concluded it would be more motorway in the morning, and Sidney would just have to accept this as his fate. Just as he would have to accept that Hazeem's talents were so much more advanced than his own in so many ways, which was both comforting and disturbing at the same time. And especially disturbing if one dwelt on one's continued virginal status as a real warrior.

Would tomorrow, with its inevitable transit through the promised Mancunian badlands, perhaps finally bring his innocence to an end?

18.

Sidney knew it was all too easy to become blasé about squalor. When one had lived a lifetime with the dismal results of rampant neglect all around one, one couldn't help but become desensitised to all but the worst examples of filth and decay. One's default setting was 'total indifference'. However, this morning, as he and his friends were preparing to leave their overnight stopping place, all three of them were captured by the acute desolation that surrounded them. From their vantage point near the top of a motorway turn-off, they could see a landscape that had been completely disfigured by humans and largely buried under the spoils of their careless behaviour.

They hadn't been unaware of it the previous evening, but now, in the early morning light, they could observe it in all its horror; a huge expanse of squalor, a panorama of muck and grime spreading out from the motorway, liberally studded with a hideous mix of hovels, huts, make-do tents and 'workshops'. The latter more accurately being soot-coated shacks that must have housed all manner of making and mending activities – none of which, it appeared, could be conducted without adding to the abject degradation of this man-made hell on earth.

'British industry,' observed Stephen with a wry smile on his face. 'This is what it's come to. A shit-scape of shitty little enterprises. And they live with it. All those people live with the excrement of their toil. It's extraordinary, and terrible, and… well, I don't know. But I think I'd choose my dump back at Cosford any day of the week. This place just stinks. And it goes on forever. I mean, how do people exist here? How do they stand it?'

'No choice,' answered Hazeem. 'They're stuck with it. It's all they've ever known. It's all they can do: make stuff, and just about enough stuff to get by. And if that means living in a shithole…'

'You've been here before?' queried Stephen.

'No, I haven't, but I've known about this place for years. Although, I must say, I didn't know it was quite this extensive – or quite this awful. It beats anything in my neck of the woods by miles.'

'But why here?' asked Sidney. 'I mean, we're nowhere near what used to be Manchester, and there's no way this was ever part of that city. No way at all.'

'Correct,' confirmed Hazeem, 'and it never will be. Not while Manchester – and everywhere between Manchester and Liverpool – is run by guys who speak Bengali.'

'*What?*' interjected Stephen. 'You mean…'

'I mean, Stephen, that as we make our way further north, you might want to prepare yourself for some voices that are not of the Urdu variety. After all, what was the old urban north-west is now little more than the capital of Bengali-land…'

'*Bengali-land?*'

'Yeah, but don't worry. I do know Bengali. At least just about enough to get us through.'

'I can't believe it.'

'Can't believe what?'

'That you neglected to tell us that we have an even higher hurdle to clear. That we're about to pass through an area that's probably even more dangerous than the one we'd expected. I mean, you're now telling us that we're about to try to bluff our way through a friggin' foreign country. One where you might *just about* know enough of the foreign lingo to get us through – or maybe not.'

'Hey, it wasn't me who told the Bengalis where to set up home. And if they're in our way, then there's nothing we can do about it other than to carry on. Remember, if it all goes wrong, it's my life on the line as well, which I can tell you now is way more than enough to make me do my very best to get us through – all of us – and preferably in one piece.'

Stephen looked a little chastened, and lost no time in offering an apology. 'You're quite right, Hazeem. I was well out of order there. It's just that I had no idea...'

'No problem, and you're right to be concerned. Whoever is living in the remains of the north-west, those remains go on forever. And I'd be lying if I said we didn't have something of a challenge ahead of us. In fact, to tell you the truth, I can't quite believe that we won't find ourselves in more than a little bit of trouble.'

'Well, maybe,' agreed a grinning Stephen. 'But... well, I have to say, trouble – as you may have noticed – hasn't got the better of us yet.'

'Precisely. And anyway, Sidney can't wait for another bit of trouble.' And then turning to Sidney. 'Isn't that right, Sidney? And all being well, one where you can pull the trigger on that gun of yours.'

Sidney's eyes widened into discs, but then he realised Hazeem was smiling broadly, and that his reference to impatience and the discharging of a firearm was just Hazeem's way of bringing a touch of levity to his exchange with Stephen and, at the same time, bringing it to a conclusion.

It worked. Stephen began to chuckle, and Sidney soon found himself offering up a 'Yeah, just let me at 'em.'

And just one minute after this shared exchange, all three of them were back on the wagon and back on the motorway, and Kaalki was pulling it along through Hades to take it ever closer to the realm of the Bengali-speakers. Sidney was probably not the only one aboard it who was now consumed with that unwelcome duo of 'fear and trepidation'.

*

To begin with, the journey proved uneventful, with no more than a rerun of what they'd experienced before. They still stood out by being one of the few vehicles on the move (most people had to rely on their feet) and by being the only vehicle moving north. They were still very markedly swimming against the tide and therefore still attracting the attention of any number of southward-bound pedestrians, some of whom wanted an explanation for their unusual conduct. In the first hour alone, Sidney counted seven occasions on which Hazeem had to justify their novel behaviour, now helped by a distinct smell of putrefaction emanating from the back of the wagon. This stink was very unwelcome, to say the least, but it was probably preferable to running into any of that likely trouble, something that might yet happen – especially now that Hazeem had just announced quietly that he'd picked up the sound of some Bengali-speakers at the side of the road. They were almost certainly, he reported, already on the southern outskirts of Bengali-land – which meant, thought Sidney, that they were maybe just about to leave "uneventful" behind.

As usual, lying beneath his shroud, Sidney could see nothing of this new area and had to rely on a whispered report from Stephen that it was rather more open in its nature than the industrial area to its south, but no less shitty. In fact, he suggested, he had yet to see anywhere that held out more appeal than his former home in Cosford. And he certainly didn't like the look of some of the locals. Or the way they were looking at him.

He didn't expand on this observation, but Sidney soon became aware of a mumbled conversation between his two companions at the front of the wagon, and there was definitely some concern in those mumbles. Then came a command from Hazeem for Sidney to lie low and remain still – just before the wagon began to slow.

Sidney wrapped his finger around the trigger of his pistol. It had to be another challenge to the manner and direction of their travel, but this time from one or more Bengali-speakers. And who knew how such an encounter would turn out? Would Hazeem be up to the job of persuading a 'foreigner'?

Well, the wagon was now stationary, and Hazeem was already offering a greeting to whoever had decided to make their business his business. And whoever it was, he wasn't using Urdu to discover the nature of this business. He was definitely addressing Hazeem in Bengali.

Hazeem responded in Bengali, and a conversation developed between the two. It seemed to Sidney to be a friendly enough conversation, and he heard no other voices. Could this be a lone challenger or just a lone inquisitive local who would soon let them on their way, and be the cause of no more than a brief interruption to their progress? After all, not every interaction with another human had to be a threat.

Sidney continued to listen intently, trying to pick up the slightest hint of what might be going on. It was difficult. But then, there it was: an exchange that he could not understand but one that sounded like a final exchange – complete with what could only be the tones of some thanks and some amiable farewells. It seemed that the first interaction in this new land – with what could only have been one individual – had gone exceedingly well, and to underline this assumption, Hazeem was now putting Kaalki into gear, and the wagon immediately began to move.

A few seconds later, as the wagon rumbled on, Hazeem began to tell Stephen and Sidney what the Bengali stranger had told him – and what it would mean for their immediate future. 'It's the viaduct up ahead. I don't know whether you've ever heard of it, but it's the huge one that carries the motorway over the canal. You know, the big Manchester Ship Canal. Well, it's still standing, but unfortunately, that old geezer has just told me it's now a bit of a problem. Because it's in the hands of… well, the same sort of characters who bushwhacked us yesterday. Only there's a whole swarm of them, and they don't just pick on one or two passing travellers, but they have a go at every traveller they can – by levying a toll. You can't get over that viaduct without coughing up some loot. Not, apparently, a huge amount if you're on foot, but rather a lot more if you're in, let's say, a wagon. Then the toll might be as much as the whole bloody wagon and whatever's pulling it. And just to top off the good news, the guy also said that the fact we're going in the wrong direction might mean that we could lose not just the wagon and Kaalki, but—'

'…our lives,' finished Stephen.

'Got it in one,' confirmed Hazeem. 'If we try to get over that viaduct, we've had it. We will be completely fucked.'

'Erm, that's not a particularly attractive prospect,' observed Stephen in a world-weary tone. 'I suppose it means we'll have to get over this wretched canal some other way.'

'Got it in one again. And as luck would have it, my old Bengali mucker has just told me exactly how to do this. I mean, how we might get to the other side of that big waterway with our transport and our lives intact. And, as we all know, there's nothing quite like local knowledge. Not least when you're trying to keep yourself alive.'

'OK,' interjected Stephen. 'That's all very drole, but exactly what do we do? And I mean exactly where do we ask Kaalki to take us?'

'To Warrington.'

'Eh?'

'Well, towards Warrington. Off the motorway to the west – and then we apparently keep going until we come across the canal where there's some sort of… well, some sort of *home-made* bridge. And, all being well, we should be able to cross there. Even if it might cost us some food or some other sort of levy – but not the whole wagon and not, of course, our lives.'

Sidney had eased himself out of his shroud to better engage with this revelation by Hazeem, but he still couldn't see his friends' faces and was still reliant on listening to their exchange to gauge where it might lead.

At this point, it was leading to some serious scepticism. And this was being expressed by Stephen. 'You believe this chap?'

'Well, yes, but I didn't have much of a choice.'

'Uh-huh, and he reckons we can get across this home-made-bridge thing by giving its keepers a few carrots. Or maybe a lot of carrots?'

'Well, that's what he said. And why wouldn't I believe him? Hell, he may have just saved our lives.'

'What do you think, Sidney? Do you think we've just had a visit from a saint, and that he's just directed us to the promised land – over some sort of safe crossing?'

Sidney was taken by surprise. He hadn't expected Stephen to ask him for his opinion – and in such a direct manner. But when he'd gathered himself, he managed a fairly good attempt at a decisive-sounding answer. 'We have to go with the home-made solution. The viaduct idea sounds... well, nothing short of suicide.'

'I agree,' responded Stephen firmly. 'Not least because we haven't really got a choice. Even if that saint was more a sinner, we've got to follow his advice. Which means, I think, we now need to look for a turn-off to Warrington. And start saying our prayers.'

*

In the event, no invocations were offered up by the wagon's three occupants, but after a mile or so, they did find a crumbling turn-off from the motorway that they reckoned would take them west towards Warrington and, in due course, over a canal. In fact, to start with, it even provided them with a route through a deserted part of Bengali-land that had nobody around to challenge their progress. It began to look as though that saint could turn up to collect his saintly-guidance-award any time he liked. But that, of course, was before Kaalki pulled the wagon into some sort of traffic underpass. This was a disintegrating piece of highway architecture, about sixty yards in length and, as it transpired, well supplied with a natural or man-made gas, strong enough to make Kaalki stumble but not quite lose consciousness – but easily strong enough to render the three humans on his wagon unconscious within seconds. The saint, it appeared, was no saint at all, and certainly not one deserving of any sort of awards.

*

Nevertheless, in due course, there was some really good news. When Hazeem, Stephen and Sidney came to – which, as far as they could tell, was later the same day – they were actually able to come to. That is to say, they were still alive. They may no longer have been the owners of a wagon – or of anything other than their clothes – and Kaalki and their firearms could be anywhere, but whoever had caught them in that gas trap hadn't left them there and hadn't added murder to the crime of outrageous daylight robbery. Maybe they still had some scruples that had stopped them from going quite that far.

Sidney was actually the first of the new pedestrians to regain consciousness, and therefore the first to see that they had been dumped into a not-very-large deserted-looking quarry – along with the two cadavers from the back of the wagon. They'd both been partially unwrapped and were now providing a background scent to the quarry that would encourage those within it who were still alive to quit it as soon as they could.

Accordingly, when Hazeem and Stephen finally came around, they quickly concurred with Sidney that the best place to be was anywhere other than in the quarry. And even before they worked out any sort of plan, they all agreed they had no choice but to neglect their interment duties and instead climb up the side of the quarry, where, once out of nose range of the corpses, they'd decide what to do next – and that this decision might well depend on where they found themselves after they'd made that ascent.

So far so good. Even though all three of them had discovered they'd been relieved of not just their guns but their knives as well. Nevertheless, they'd now made it to a sweeter-smelling part of Bengali-land – at the lip of the quarry – and having established that they were all uninjured, albeit a little woozy, they then tried to work out where they might be and how they should possibly proceed. This wasn't easy because it soon became apparent that they could be anywhere. And without transport, firearms, food or water – and with no compass – they couldn't even start to work out where to go and certainly not how they might resume their journey north. That now just seemed like a pipe dream.

However, Hazeem then began to wander around – maybe to find some inspiration – but he found instead some wheel tracks and the tracks of what could only be a healthy mule. And the tracks led off into the distance and continued into the distance. Their abductors, it seemed, had left them a trail to follow.

'But why,' he asked his companions, 'would they do that? Why would they leave themselves open to the possibility of being tracked down?'

'Complacency, stupidity, some other congenital deficiency or maybe they thought we would die,' suggested Stephen.

'Or maybe something simpler,' offered Sidney. 'Like they knew they'd soon be too far away for us ever to reach them. Even if those tracks don't just run out at some point.'

'Mmm, I like the congenital-deficiency theory more,' observed Hazeem. 'Plenty of that round here, I'm sure. And anyway, whatever made them give us a trail, it doesn't really matter, does it? Because we all know we're going to follow it, aren't we? How can we not go and rescue our missing team member? And when we find him, we might even be able to take back our wagon.'

That observation caused smiles all round. And when the smiles had been stowed away, it was time to unpack some determination and begin what might prove to be a very long hike – in the hope that they might just be able to get themselves back into business. And maybe even settle the odd account…

19.

They all knew they were running a big risk. Not only were they in unknown territory but Sidney was no longer wrapped in a shroud. He was on foot, and all he had to conceal his white identity was a strip of fabric ripped from Stephen's cape and fashioned into an odd-looking hood. It would fail as a disguise the moment anybody got anywhere near him. However, there was no choice. Borrowing anything more substantial from the two corpses in the quarry was ruled out as being pretty much unthinkable, and the three of them could hardly wait for nightfall to act as a cloak. There was, after all, no way they could follow the tracks in the dark. So, armed with that recently unpacked determination, they set out on their quest – and they just hoped for the best. Which initially, at least, is exactly what they got.

To begin with, there was nobody around. It seemed they'd been dumped in a very out-of-the-way place that was even lacking in the normal ubiquitous hovels and was little more than a landscape of empty fields. In fact, it was just the sort of place one might want to discard some unwanted victims of one's crimes.

Next, after no more than a couple of miles of trudging, they found a small stream where they were able to get themselves a drink. This was very good news. As was the fact that, as they were supping from this small watercourse, Sidney announced that he'd just spotted something that was better news still – much better, in fact, than an absence of prying eyes and this access to water. It was something standing in a field of stubble; a mule, and one that was looking more than a little relaxed, not least because he was without his harness. There wasn't so much as a collar or a strap about his person, and Sidney thought that, as well as looking relaxed, he also looked elegant beyond words.

Sidney had to stop himself shrieking with delight. He managed to do this, and when – instead of shrieking – he'd pointed out their fourth team member to his companions, he offered up a firm opinion. 'He did that himself. I don't know how, but he's slipped his harness. I mean, there's no way they'd have let him go. Hell, he's worth more to them than the wagon is. He's just—'

'I think you're right,' interrupted a grinning Hazeem, and then he chuckled. 'Heh, maybe he didn't like them. Maybe he knew what they'd done?'

'Bloody right, he knew what they'd done.'

And as soon as Sidney had made this remark, Kaalki turned his head, looked towards the three new people in the distance, and then began to make his way towards them.

'That's my boy,' managed a now nearly tearful Sidney. 'That's my Kaalki all right.'

Within only a minute, there had been a properly tearful reunion, with even Stephen looking a tad emotional. And when they'd all gathered themselves again, it was the practical that forced itself to the fore, assisted on this occasion by Sidney. This he did by offering the opinion that a wagon without a mule wouldn't have got very far, so it might be a good idea to go and look for it now – particularly as the sun was low in the sky, and they might soon add another recruit to their cause in the shape of failing light.

Nobody disagreed with this view, and it wasn't long before three humans and a mule were again following the tracks of the wagon, with the firm intention of reclaiming some stolen property and possibly meting out some justice at the same time.

Hazeem, with the unspoken agreement of the others in the party, led the way. So, it was him who signalled them to stop as they came to where their route curved to the left past a grassy bank. And he'd gestured them to stop here because he'd seen up ahead the engineless wagon, and when he'd managed to get himself a little better look, he was able to report that it had, for company, six obvious villains – all gathered around a fire.

He quickly formed a conclave with his friends and suggested to them that it was now time to formulate a plan. In particular, a plan that might just allow three unarmed individuals to overcome six others who were, no doubt, now in possession of at least four firearms and three knives. This, he admitted, wouldn't be easy, and Stephen agreed. Even with the element of surprise on their side, to say nothing of the sort of motivation coming from a desire to continue their journey north – other than on foot – they did need a little more.

They needed, Stephen said, at least one firearm of their own – and preferably his treasured rifle. With this, he assured his friends, their plan would be simple. It would involve nothing more than him shooting each of the villains in turn – in the same way he'd shot countless other antagonists in the past.

Sidney couldn't think of a better plan. Neither could Hazeem. Both knew Stephen was quite capable of doing exactly what he'd said. However, Hazeem was adamant that, to stand any chance of providing themselves with the required rifle, they first needed to know exactly how their adversaries were disposed – and where precisely all four stolen firearms were disposed. His brief recce hadn't allowed him to collect that information, and to remedy that situation he proposed that what was now needed was a much more detailed recce – before it got dark.

This proposition was debated, but for only a few minutes. Hazeem was clearly right. So he further proposed it was now time for his skills – learnt over a lifetime of smuggling – to again be brought into play. He would, he announced, get as close to the camped bandits as he could, observe them as best he could and, indeed, spend however long it took there to work out the precise location of the three pistols and the one, all-important rifle – plus the location of any other firearms that the bandits might possess. Then, if he hadn't been detected, he would report back in the hope that the information he returned with could be used to work out exactly how the rifle could be redeemed and how it might be subsequently used. Meanwhile, Sidney and Stephen, who couldn't argue with Hazeem's suitability for the chosen role, would remain where they were – and probably worry. Or, there again, they might distract themselves by trying to find something to feed to Kaalki…

So, when Hazeem disappeared – with their best wishes and with their earnest requests that he take great care – his two stay-at-home companions embarked on a hunt for some fodder for Kaalki, and maybe even somewhere where he and they might have a welcome drink.

With a great deal of effort, they were able to gather enough spiky grass together to make a meal for their mule, and they even found a tiny pool where Kaalki and his carers were all able to quench their thirst. And it was near this pool that they also found some old fence posts that they decided might serve as useful clubs – if such weapons were ever needed. They selected two of these posts, each adorned with a snag of barbed wire near its top, which, Stephen suggested, might make them more effective – in all sorts of ways.

With these jobs done, it was then time to resume their waiting for Hazeem's return – and time to really worry. Their furtive friend might well avoid detection – but he might not. Sidney knew this only too well. Just as he knew that, right now, he would give everything to have a chat with just one of his fellow hams – one of those three people from a time that now seemed lost in the past and with whom he could share his thoughts and concerns.

Marc, he knew, would be suitably flippant about his situation – to conceal his concern – but he might well have offered some useful advice, advice that for once, might not have involved the concoction of an alcoholic beverage. Ted would simply have sought to stiffen his resolve – and emphasised the need to be ruthless when required. And Sonia would have offered sympathy and her heartfelt hope that he made it out of his awkward situation – and maybe all the way to Saskatoon.

But knowing what each of them would say wasn't like hearing them saying it. It couldn't be. He just so wished he could hear their voices through the ether – now – and not just to give him support but also to remind him that he'd once had a life that didn't involve sharing the back of a wagon with a succession of corpses and one that might now involve his getting killed – along with two other people whom he'd now come to regard as his brothers. If only he had a radio, and if only Hazeem would return from his perilous mission…

And there he was, like a creature of the night appearing through the gloom but smiling in a way that no real creature of the night would ever smile.

He walked slowly to where Sidney was sitting – next to a dozing Stephen – and whispered an announcement, 'Sidney, I could do with a drink, and I'll tell you right now that those lot back there could do with one good brain between them. Talk about a bunch of blockheads!'

Once Stephen had been raised from his slumbers, this announcement was expanded to enquire as to whether his friends had found any drinking water close at hand and to assure his two friends that their adversaries were as stupid as they might ever have hoped for. He'd apparently been listening to their inane exchanges for over two hours and had been unable to detect a spark of wit or acuity in any one of them.

Sidney informed him that they had indeed found some water, and after leading him there for a drink, both returned to where Stephen and Kaalki were waiting. Hazeem then began to address the main course of his report. This concerned not the limited intellect of the Bengali highwaymen but where they'd settled their carcasses and where they'd positioned the single rifle and the three Glock pistols. To do this, Hazeem found a small twig and scored in the earth a simple map of the enemy's ad hoc camp. This showed where each of the robbers was sitting, and where, as far as he could tell, they'd placed those stolen firearms, which were – again, as far as he could tell – the only firearms they had. Prior to that recent bushwhacking, it seemed that they'd not had one shooter between them.

This was all good news. However, as Sidney realised, it meant that Hazeem would again have to adopt his smuggler-learnt stealth skills and return to the camp, not to check that the rifle hadn't been moved but to extract it and bring it to Stephen. He would have to creep into the lions' den and somehow relieve them of one of their prized possessions – without getting eaten. Like Stephen, Sidney knew that only Hazeem could possibly do this. But even for him, it would be far from easy, and to stand any chance of success, he needed to wait until they could assume that the majority of the bad guys were asleep and whoever might be left on guard was nearly asleep himself. That pointed to an early-hours launch of Hazeem's mission, and in the meantime, Sidney and Stephen would have an opportunity to distract Hazeem by quizzing him on the content of the bad guys' discussion. What had they talked about for two hours and what exactly had they said that had led Hazeem to decide that they weren't burdened with an overload of intellect?

Hazeem seemed to welcome this distraction, and he willingly supplied them with the information they sought: 'Well, their leader is an example of… er, how can I put it? That particular breed of *religious* that doesn't just lead to blindness, but somehow allows people to arrive at a very strange interpretation of what's right and what's wrong. As in, it's quite OK to gas other people in order to steal their possessions before dumping them in a quarry, but not OK to kill them. Even though, without their possessions, there's a pretty good chance in these current times that they'll end up dead anyway. And I kid you not. For most of the time, he sounded more like a mullah on speed than the nasty thief that he is. And he'd certainly give mullahs a bad name.

'Anyway, this damn fool demigod has gathered around him five gullible and even more stupid followers who seem to believe his every word – and who would certainly never cross him. And who can talk about little other than how their fortunes will be made with the help of our wagon, and how something evil must have robbed them of their newly acquired mule, "Because animals have no minds of their own – and, of course, they can be easily possessed."

'While I was listening to them, I couldn't help thinking what they might have made of your two radios, and whether they would have thought these had been possessed as well. Although, there again, maybe they'd not be able to formulate any thoughts at all. At least, not without the help of their moronic messiah.'

'Well,' observed Stephen. 'I'm all for moronic messiahs if they inadvertently save our lives – and even more so if they haven't the sense to get their followers to check whether they're being tailed. Much better any day to come up against ignorance and idiocy rather than cunning and competence. As I hope we will soon discover.'

'These followers,' asked Sidney, 'do they include our saintly guide – the bloke who led us into the trap?'

'No, I'm afraid not,' responded Hazeem. 'Maybe he's just on commission or something. Or maybe he's got more sense than to be mixed up with a bunch of dummies. And, I must say, he did sound a great deal more *normal* than any of the dummies around that fire. In fact, I'm quite pleased he won't be there to help them. Or maybe to spot me making off with a rifle... Talking of which, I think I'll just go off and get myself another drink, and then get myself ready.'

This he did, and ten minutes later, he'd crept off in the direction of the enemy's camp, and Sidney and Stephen were left to worry again.

Twenty minutes passed, and there was no sign of their friend's return. After thirty minutes, there was still nothing. So when over forty minutes had passed, Sidney was about to suggest to Stephen that he went to find out what had happened to Hazeem – only to be stopped from doing so by their tame smuggler appearing through the dark – and in possession of Stephen's treasured rifle.

'It's been fired,' he announced quietly. 'And I couldn't find another magazine.'

'*What?*' exclaimed Stephen. 'You mean the magazine's empty?'

'No. There are two rounds in it, but I think even you couldn't swat six guys with just a pair of bullets. We may need a plan B.'

'Shit. What the hell were they shooting?'

'Who knows? Probably the sky. I told you they were bloody idiots, didn't I?'

Stephen sighed, and then he clearly remembered what Hazeem had achieved. The rifle he'd extracted from that lions' den might not have arrived with a full magazine, but it had arrived – courtesy of a remarkably talented and remarkably brave man. And this was worth acknowledging.

'Hazeem, you've done brilliantly. And even with just two rounds to play with, we can now join the game. And it's a game we can win. I guarantee it.'

Sidney added his own congratulations and thanks to their extraordinary friend, and then all three of them addressed the issue of plan B. How would they now proceed, now that Stephen had a rifle not with the hoped-for twenty rounds in its magazine but instead just two? It didn't take them long to work out what they would do. And as soon as Sidney had delivered another bundle of fodder to Kaalki – and an instruction that he should not move from where he was – all three of them began to make their way towards the camp – to take up their agreed positions.

As Sidney walked through the dark, he couldn't help thinking about Hazeem and what he now felt for this smuggler turned self-taught commando. He was, Sidney decided, more in awe than ever of his friend's capabilities, and more thankful than ever that their paths had crossed when they had. That fortuitous coming together was the only reason he was still alive. Even if he were now about to risk his life like he never had before.

*

Fifteen minutes later, Sidney was now thinking not of Hazeem but of what was required of him when he heard the first rifle shot. He would have to be off his feet like a demented sprinter to make it from his hiding place to where his chosen victim was lying so as to arrive before his victim had a chance to get up. It wouldn't be easy, but probably a lot easier than using his fence post as a club.

Then it happened. There was a rifle shot, and one of the prone figures nearest to the smouldering fire jerked into life only to collapse into a motionless death. One down, and five to go, and that meant Sidney was already running towards the deceased's neighbour, whose Glock pistol was easily within his reach.

This was when time slowed down. The faster he ran, the more slowly Sidney perceived what was going on. So, it seemed like an age before he swung his fence post at his target – who was now just reaching for the pistol – and managed to miss his head by a foot. As he followed this ill-judged swing by toppling over in slow motion, he became aware of a second shot ringing out and, at the same time, of a knife sticking out of the ground. He had more than enough time in this slowed-down experience to know that if he grabbed the knife, rolled over as he landed and then thrust the knife to his right, he would achieve what he'd failed to do with his cumbersome club. And so this is what he did.

Time only returned to its normal pace when he felt the blade of the knife entering his victim's chest. And that was before his victim had the opportunity to fire the pistol that was now in his hand, and before Sidney then realised that the knife must have entered his victim's heart. It was as though he'd stunned him rather than stabbed him. He was as dead as could be within seconds.

Sidney felt confused, but he still registered further gunfire, and then total silence. There were no more sounds of gunfire and no more sounds of conflict.

And why would there be? Stephen had killed two of the thieves with his rifle. Hazeem had killed two more – one with his club and one with a recovered pistol. Sidney had extinguished the life of another with a knife (in fact, as it turned out, with his own knife), and the remaining member of the dirty half-dozen had run off into the night, presumably quite relieved that he was still able to run.

Sidney's confusion began to ease, but it was replaced with some involuntary shaking. He was trying to come to terms with the fact that he'd just killed somebody – by plunging a metal blade into his heart – and in the full knowledge that this somebody, whatever else he'd done and just like his fellow thieves, hadn't sought to kill him and his friends. He'd been aware of this overreaction aspect of their deadly plan before he'd embarked on it – as they'd all been. But as they'd all agreed, they'd had no option. It was either a disproportionate response to their misfortune, or some guaranteed further misfortune – and no wagon. However, now, after he'd taken another human's life, this asymmetric aspect of their conduct only emphasised the horror of what he'd done – to another individual. He knew already it would take him quite some time to come to terms with what he now was: a killer.

Nevertheless, that sort of self-indulgent introspection would have to wait because Hazeem had just shouted to him – to tell him that Stephen had been hit...

It seemed that, in that short flurry of gunfire, the villain whom Hazeem had shot with his own pistol had first fired it in the direction of the rifle shots, and had quite improbably – but definitely – hit his intended target.

Stephen had a dreadful stomach wound, and it was bleeding heavily.

All of them had hoped for the best – and, to start with, this is what they had found. But now, even with the recovery of their wagon, they were having to come to terms with the fact that they would have to settle for something far removed from the best. And that, for Stephen, the outcome could hardly be worse.

20.

Sidney surprised himself by taking the lead in attending to Stephen's wound.

It was still dark, and he was having to work with only the light of the moon and a dim glow from a dying fire – but he was working. With linen taken from one of the dead robbers, he was binding Stephen's torso and, at the same time, supplying him with a stream of comforting words. He was far from sure that the words were doing any good at all, but the tightly bound linen did seem to be having an effect. Stephen's blood was now not flowing freely but was instead just colouring the make-do dressing, and if nothing else, Stephen hadn't lost consciousness. Far from it. Indeed, he was still very responsive and clearly very annoyed that he'd let himself get shot. However, as light was returning from the east, what must have been the shock of the wound, together with the lateness of the hour, finally overcame him, and he fell into a fitful sleep.

This gave Sidney and Hazeem their first real chance to assess their shared situation, and they immediately applied themselves to this task. What had they been able to recover? Where might they be? And what did Stephen's injury mean for their continuing their journey north? If indeed, they were able to continue at all.

Well, in the first place, they'd recovered most of what the robbers had taken. They had their wagon back – and Kaalki back – both of which constituted the best news possible. Furthermore, their store of food and fodder was mostly intact, and they'd recovered their all-important weapons and a good stock of ammunition. Adding in the fact that they'd already worked out which direction was north – and, of course, that they had yet another supply of fresh corpses – it seemed that they might well be back in business. Always assuming, that is, that Stephen could withstand being bounced around in the back of a wagon – and that Sidney could be sufficiently disguised to take Stephen's place on the front seat of the wagon. Neither might be possible. In particular, it might prove deadly for Stephen to be moved any distance at all.

Nevertheless, it seemed like nothing more than common sense to ready the wagon for travel whilst Stephen dozed on. So, everything that needed to be loaded onto it was loaded onto it, including the bodies of two of the bandits, wrapped around with the garments of all five of the departed – before the three who were to be left behind were 'buried' in a ditch. In the circumstances, it was the best that Sidney and Hazeem could manage.

There was also the faux corpse to be loaded: the one made up of mostly books and files. However, this corpse first needed to be reconstituted. Its contents had been spilt onto the ground – and some of these contents had quite clearly been used as fuel for the bandits' fire. It was consequently now a much thinner corpse, and whilst it still contained the majority of Sidney's books, it was soon discovered that it contained none of Stephen's 'essential' files. These, it seemed, being more easily flammable than the bound books, must have been used as kindling, and there was now not a single one of them left. They had all been turned into ashes.

Given Stephen's condition, this was news that his two friends thought he could well do without. But ultimately, the time arrived to discuss with him how he was and what his thoughts were on being moved, and as Sidney suspected, the loss of his files was a subject that couldn't be avoided indefinitely.

*

Stephen had woken up mid-morning, and Sidney had used the full light of the day to re-dress his wound and to make him as comfortable as possible. And now it was time to decide, with Stephen's input, what they should do next. Or as Stephen himself put it, to decide whether they should resume their journey north or stay where they were and pray for a miracle cure for his injury – taking account of the fact that he had it on very good authority that miracles were in desperately short supply these days.

It was Stephen's way of recognising the inevitable, and of relieving his two friends of any guilt they might feel about the consequences of pursuing the inevitable. As he put it so succinctly himself: 'Being bounced to death is probably not the worst way to go, and it certainly beats just twiddling one's thumbs and waiting for the Grim Reaper to turn up – and particularly here. I mean, we're somewhere near Warrington, of all places!'

So that was it. They would load Stephen onto the back of the wagon, do their best to make Sidney look like anything other than a white Caucasian (something that, understandably, had been discounted as impossible at the beginning of their odyssey), and then point Kaalki in the direction of Scotland. But not before Sidney had been obliged to respond to Stephen's enquiry concerning the now-extinguished fire.

'What,' Stephen asked, 'did those bastards use for fuel?'

Sidney had no option other than to confess to Stephen that his files had been amongst the principal casualties of their assailants' incendiary activities. That, in fact, all his files had probably been used to start the fire and that they no longer existed. Whatever they'd contained was now lost for all time.

On hearing this, although he'd probably been expecting it, Stephen's expression became one of acute distress – instantly. It was obvious to both Sidney and Hazeem that the pain of his wound was as nothing compared to the pain of losing what had been in those files. Indeed, his expression was one of such acute anguish that Sidney became truly concerned that his aged friend might not be travelling north with him and Hazeem after all – because he might expire on the spot. This didn't happen. In fact, Stephen soon managed to gather himself and at least give the appearance of someone who was now reconciled to a bit of bad news. And that this was all it was: just some unwelcome tidings about some lost sheets of paper covered in words, which hardly constituted the end of the world. And that, as he then made clear to his companions, what really mattered now was getting on with whatever needed to be done – which probably involved his being loaded onto a wagon to join two real stiffs and another not-so-real one that was presently burdened with rather less paper than it had been before.

And so it was done. Within minutes of Stephen being loaded onto the back of the wagon, Hazeem was guiding Kaalki along a dirt track that seemed to lead north, whilst beside him, Sidney was fiddling with a makeshift hood that virtually obscured his grease-and-ash-coated face. He might, he thought, no longer look like a pale Caucasian, but instead more like a recluse – a filthy recluse recently prised from his recluse's filthy hovel. He just hoped it would do the job, and that he didn't become the cause of any further problems for his two companions.

*

To begin with, all was well. There was still nobody about – on what were little more than lanes through a desolate and deserted countryside – and when they did encounter their first humans of the day, these humans were far too preoccupied with their stunted crops to pay much heed to any sort of passing traffic. Indeed, it wasn't until late in the day, just when they caught sight of the M6 up ahead – somewhere near Wigan, they thought – that they had their first exchange with some curious locals. However, their leader addressed Hazeem in Urdu, which was a good start, and it took only a minute for Hazeem's well-worn story of repatriating corpses to be accepted by them all.

So, when it had been decided that Kaalki had done all the pulling that could be expected of him for the day and they should look for a place to camp overnight, Sidney was beginning to believe that his disguise might not warrant too much concern. Certainly not when he had sitting beside him, someone who needed no disguise and who had shown he could successfully deal with any number of curious strangers, no matter how curious or, indeed, how intrusively inquisitive they might be.

Stephen was another matter. The wagon had now been drawn into the cover of a half-hidden derelict barn, and Sidney and Hazeem, having helped him to dismount the vehicle, were now together tending to his wound – and to his condition.

The wound was proving the easier of the two. Despite it being put to the test by the wagon's constant bumping, it now wasn't bleeding at all, and there were no signs of any infection – at least as far as the two amateur medics could tell. However, Stephen's mood was far from good, and whilst he no longer looked as though he was in acute distress, he did appear to be settling in to some sort of chronic despair. And not, Sidney suspected, because of that injury to his person, but because of the loss of his precious files. In which case, Sidney decided, he would have to find out what those files contained. It might be the only way to alleviate Stephen's despair – and give him a fighting chance of being able to cope with the physical damage he'd incurred. Such an enquiry might all go wrong, Sidney realised, but he knew he had no option. He had to ask Stephen directly what was so important about those files that their loss was so clearly devastating.

It was OK. Sidney's question elicited only a smile from Stephen and an acknowledgement that he'd already been toying with the idea of telling both of them what his collection of files had contained – if for no other reason than to let the two people he was sharing his life with also share the knowledge of what he'd been doing with his life for so long – when he hadn't been busy just surviving at RAF Cosford or shooting unwanted intruders.

So he did it. He began to 'reveal all' and in doing so, he first addressed Hazeem: 'You asked me what hermits do when they're not being hermits. Remember? You wanted to know how I spent my idle time at Cosford when I wasn't being reclusive or, in the case of unwanted guests, being rather antisocial. Well, I'll tell you. I was filling up those files, and I was filling them up with a history of Britain, a history of this country largely based on what I'd learnt from all those people I'd encountered on my travels. You know, back in the last century when my life was moving around and meeting people, some of whom might just be able to tell me how my country had become what it was: no longer my country at all.'

Hazeem winced. Sidney almost heard it.

However, Stephen was quick to come to his aid. 'Hazeem, you must realise that I like you. And that I respect you. Greatly. And you must accept that what I am saying has nothing to do with you personally. Nothing at all. In fact, the loss of *my* country has a great deal to do with… well, let's call them the "natives" of my country… and in fact, very little to do with… well, with any of your lot. And you'll have to forgive me for the use of such a thoughtless expression, but it's just that I'm not feeling quite at my best at the moment, and a more acceptable expression, for the moment, eludes me.'

'You mean us… sub-continentals,' assisted Hazeem. 'The people you're having to pretend to be to make your way north.'

'Correct,' confirmed Stephen. 'Our *replacement population*.'

Hazeem was clearly not sure how to follow that statement, and it was left to Sidney to make a contribution to the discussion.

He did this by asking Stephen a question. 'You'll think I'm a fool for asking this, Stephen, but I thought what happened to Britain over the past century or so was more or less known. So what was in this history of yours that made it so... unique – and so much of a loss?'

'Good question, young man. And I can give you an easy answer. You see, it may be common knowledge that this country underwent a complexion change – even if a lot of the detail's been lost along the way. But how many people know why it happened and how it happened? Why a country with a settled population – and a largely homogeneous population – offered itself up to such radical change – one that would ultimately see it transformed out of all recognition and, of course, much to the detriment of its former residents? And how did it go about this? I mean, do you know? Do you know why all us turkeys voted for Christmas and how we all ended up in the oven?'

'Er,' started Sidney, only to be interrupted by Stephen.

'Sorry. Turkeys and Christmas. Ancient traditions. Something else that was the victim of radical change. But all I meant was do you have any idea why we – us whities – so easily let go of what we had and how we did it, so that – only decades on, as Hazeem has just pointed out – we'd be having to pretend to be other than who we were? Because I suspect you don't. And that's why those files were so important, or at least to me. They may be… Sorry, they might have been the only comprehensive account of why and how our lot threw in the towel, without even waiting for the first bell—'

'The first bell?' interjected Hazeem.

'Sorry. That's another allusion in the same category as turkey and Christmas. I just mean we gave up without much of a fight, and alarmingly quickly. But why? And how? Why would any settled population do that, and how would they go about it?'

'This history,' questioned Sidney, 'is it why Dorothy wants you to join her? Does she want to learn about the why and the how – and does she know you're the only person who has the answers?'

Stephen smiled broadly. 'Goodness, no. She has no idea about my little hobby. You're the only two people I've ever told. Not, of course, that this means a great deal now. Now that my files have gone up in flames…'

'But,' interrupted Hazeem, 'she was obviously very keen for you to join her. And I mean really keen. So if…'

'She didn't want me to die on my own,' re-interrupted Stephen. 'She wanted me to have some company as I slid into oblivion. And then, presumably, a few people around who could bury me. You know, so that I wouldn't end up as a rats' dinner back in Shropshire.'

'Hey, you're not going to die,' promised Sidney. 'You might have a bullet in you at the moment, but that can be sorted. And it will be – as soon as we get to Scotland.'

'Maybe, but I doubt that there'll be anybody there who can sort out my other little problem.'

'What other little problem?' squeaked a surprised-looking Sidney.

'The one that's been grinding me down for weeks, the one that'll soon see me off. If, of course, that bullet doesn't do the job first.'

'What are you talking about?' demanded Sidney, his voice now edged with panic.

'Could be any number of things. Probably one of those things they used to be able to cure, but can't any more.'

'You mean—'

'I don't know.' Stephen shrugged. 'I ain't no doctor, but I know I'm done for. And I know for a fact that I've been losing weight and I've got all this… discomfort. Lots of… discomfort. And that I'm really tired all the time. And more and more tired every day.'

'But how can you be sure?' pressed Hazeem. 'It could be anything.'

'I just know it,' insisted Stephen. 'I can feel it. I can feel it's there. And I know I've hidden it from you pretty well. In fact, I must have hidden it very well. But believe me, every day is becoming more difficult. I used to have all the energy I needed and then some, but now I have to scrape it from wherever I can. And I really don't think there's much more to scrape.'

'Even so—' Sidney began.

'Even so nothing,' cut in Stephen. 'I'm not long for this world, whatever way you look at it. If the bullet doesn't do for me, well, my… my little problem will. I know it. And I'm old. Or have you two forgotten? And, of course, old people die. They die all the time. And it just so happens that it's now my time to die. And I reckon pretty damn soon...'

And here he hesitated, and then he went on. 'Although, I do have to say, it would have been nice to have finally met Dorothy.'

'You'll meet her all right,' insisted Sidney. 'And when you do, you can tell her all about your history...'

And here Sidney hesitated. He'd just been struck by a thought.

Then he put the thought into words: 'And I tell you what. While they're fixing you up, you can tell me about it as well. I'm a scribe, remember? And if that history is still in your head – and it has to be – then you just have to recount it to me, and I'll write it down. Your history, my dear Stephen, will not be lost – certainly not while I've got anything to do with it.'

Stephen managed a weak smile, but gave no response to Sidney's surprise suggestion. Instead, in a very matter-of-fact way, he simply informed his friends that it would probably be best if he now had a rest.

It seemed to Sidney that Stephen had convinced himself that his life *and* his history of Britain were both lost causes, and all he wanted to do now was to have some respite from these two inevitabilities – by dropping off to sleep. Hazeem seemed to be thinking the same thoughts. So both his carers burdened him with no further questions nor any further plans for the future – but one of them did begin to consider the practicalities of reconstructing the contents of some lost files – and whether or not he should wait until they made it to their destination to embark on that task.

21.

When Sidney awoke in the morning, he first asked himself whether he was dreaming. Could he really have swapped a life of drudgery and tedium for another that was full of so much more – everything from apprehension and real fear to violence, bloodshed and death? Perhaps he'd eaten a mouldy chapati, and he was now in a toxin-induced coma, with this nightmare journey simply playing on a reel in his head. He'd heard of things like this before; how a delusion could so easily become a convincing reality. So how could he be sure he wasn't completely deluded now and in reality, he was lying on his bed back in his cabin, probably being cursed by Rishi for not attending to his chores?

He shook his head. No, this was real all right. No question about it. After all, no nightmare would include forming an unbreakable bond with two of its principal participants; two very tangible characters who, along with his three fellow hams, had now become the most important people in his life. And if it were all a delusion, how could he now be feeling so concerned about one of those characters? The one whose life was teetering on the edge of eternity and whose life's work had actually dropped over that edge. At least, that's the way it had looked before Sidney had come to its rescue with his plan, one that had now been adapted overnight to take account of Stephen's fragile condition. It still needed a little polishing, but that he would do during the morning's trip north, ready for its launch later in the day. If, indeed, he had the courage to launch it.

Before then, however, there was more of the mundane to attend to, and the aforementioned character's violated body to tend to as well. So, whilst Hazeem sorted out breakfast for Kaalki, himself and his two companions, and then made sure everything was ready for their journey further north, Sidney again played nurse to his injured friend.

Given what his patient had been through, Stephen seemed to be in remarkably good spirits, and he didn't even complain about what must have been a serious level of pain. He didn't even react to some inept fumbling by Sidney as he went about changing Stephen's dressing. Sidney knew that, if it had been the other way around and it were he who was having a hole in his stomach inexpertly dealt with, he would have been squeaking like a child. Maybe, thought Sidney, the way Stephen had spent much of his life had so hardened him that pain was something his body would simply not acknowledge. Whether it was the pain from a wound or the clearly understated 'discomfort' from his mystery illness. Or maybe old age inured one to suffering. Maybe it was as simple as that.

But for whatever reason, Stephen was displaying some of the very best tough-as-old-boots qualities Sidney had ever seen, and he even failed to show any signs of discomfort when Sidney and Hazeem manhandled him onto the back of the wagon. Furthermore, as their journey got underway, he proved once again to be the perfect uncomplaining passenger. Sidney was greatly impressed – but not really surprised.

He was also greatly impressed with Hazeem's continuing management of the curious. Before they stopped at midday, he'd dealt with another seven enquiries from people passing by – on the latest stretch of the decaying M6 motorway.

One of these enquiries had been made by a gang of youths from whom Sidney had expected all sorts of trouble. Every one of them was carrying a knife or a club, and their leader looked not only combative but also slightly unhinged. But no matter. Within just a minute, Hazeem had convinced them all that there was 'nothing of interest here', and they had let him go on his way without even a question about the odd appearance of his companion. Hazeem was clearly becoming a doyen of deception. Sidney just hoped that he himself could now match this impressive ability in the arena of well-meant persuasion.

*

Kaalki was chomping on his fodder, and his three human comrades were nibbling on their chosen carrots. It was, after all, to be a very light lunchtime meal. And straight after Hazeem had proffered his opinion on how much further they could hope to travel today, Sidney took his chance – and began to roll out his slightly revised plan, nervously and rather awkwardly.

'Stephen,' he began, 'those files of yours: I am right in assuming you can remember most of what they contained?'

Stephen looked taken aback, as though 'those files' were from a different age; another time that had now been lost for all time. But he seemed to collect himself, and he managed to respond to Sidney's question. 'Yes, you are right. I can. I can remember a lot of it. But not all. I mean, there was so much detail. I hadn't just relied on all those people I'd talked to, but I'd done some research as well. You know, in libraries – when libraries were still around – and even in some old newspapers, some old back copies I'd found in a warehouse near Bath—'

'Newspapers?' interjected Hazeem.

'Old-school communication on paper,' clarified Stephen. 'Lots of stuff about what was going on in the world, presented on big sheets of paper – every day. Quite useful stuff for a… historian.'

'Yes. A historian,' echoed Sidney. 'A student of history. A chronicler. A compiler of what happened in the past. An important person. And someone who should never betray his calling.'

Stephen had clearly smelt a rat. It was so apparent in his response to Sidney's observation: 'Well, Sidney, we're not just having some sort of academic discussion here, are we? Some sort of exploration of the indispensability of historians and chroniclers. We're setting somebody up – i.e. me – to agree to your idea of recreating my history by using your services as a scribe.'

'You remember?'

'Of course, I remember. How could I not? And how could I not think it was a great idea? Or it would be if only you weren't intending to wait until we got to Scotland. After all, I might not make it to Scotland, and then your plan rather falls apart, doesn't it?'

Sidney couldn't believe what he'd just heard. He'd been gearing himself up all morning to broach the idea of capturing Stephen's history whilst they were still travelling north, and yes, whilst Stephen was still alive. Because whatever his 'little problem' was, his bigger problem just now was a bullet wound, and this wound could prove fatal at any time. Stephen clearly knew this as well, and just as clearly, this is why he'd surprised both his friends by suggesting that a start should be made as soon as possible on what would probably be a highly abridged version of his history.

'You mean you want us to start *now*?' managed a delighted Sidney. 'You're prepared to start recounting your history… well, this evening? Or tomorrow, maybe? I can't believe it.'

Stephen smiled and assured Sidney that he should believe it – and that he might want to consider some of the practicalities of documenting this history whilst on the move. 'For example,' he suggested, 'there might be a need for some paper and some writing implements, and I'm not aware that the wagon carries either.'

Sidney responded to this observation with a smile of his own – and then some information: 'Well, you'll no doubt remember – because I reminded you last night – that when I wasn't emptying pots of shit or digging up carrots, I was a scribe. And I do still have my writing implements: three pens secreted in the spines of three of my books – three of them that have fortuitously survived.'

'And paper?' enquired a now unmistakably interested Hazeem.

'My books have flyleaves and margins – and I can write very small. And I mean very small indeed. And that means I have plenty of blank paper. Probably not enough to recreate all Stephen's files, by any means, but more than enough to document at least an outline of his definitive history of Britain. No question about it.'

At this point in the exchange, Stephen asked an inevitable question. 'Uh, OK, paper and pens in place. And I hope I'm not being rude here, but what about the mechanics of the task? I mean, you're not planning to write down my words as I speak, are you? Because I don't think I can speak that slowly. And if you're not, and instead you're going to document them after the event, how on earth are you going to remember them all? There will, I can tell you, be quite a lot of words to remember.'

'I've got a great memory, Stephen – or at least the sort of memory that will allow me to file stuff away overnight for writing up the next day. I haven't had to use this "skill" for some time, but I'm sure I'll be able to dust it off and put it to good use. Whenever you want to start.'

Stephen looked pensive. It was as though he hadn't heard Sidney's last words and was now thinking about something else. Then suddenly his mood and his manner changed – rather abruptly.

'No, it won't work,' he announced. 'And I'm not even sure I want to do it anyway. I mean, who the hell is interested in the past? And who the hell deserves to know about the past? And it's over. The past is gone. It's dead. It doesn't mean shit. And why I even bothered over all those years… well, I've no idea.'

Sidney looked as though he'd been struck in the face. It had all been going so well. But now this dramatic U-turn, one that represented a genuine threat to the project he'd planned and the project Stephen had more than endorsed. He had to respond – firmly and immediately.

'Because it was worth it,' he whispered. 'And because you knew it was worth it. And you *still* know it was worth it. And that it would be criminal if you threw away—'

'*Criminal?*' spat Stephen. 'Maybe I should be the judge of that. It is, after all, my history – mine to recall or abandon as I wish.'

Up to now, Hazeem had contributed little to the interaction between his friends. But with this pained declaration from Stephen, he clearly thought it was time to contribute something more – by pouring a little oil on these suddenly troubled waters. He therefore made a well-timed – and effective – intervention.

'Er, tell you what. Why don't you, Sidney, just shut up for the moment? And why don't you, Stephen, as we make our way to Preston, think a little bit more about whether you want to… er, recall or abandon your history? Because, that way, peace will no doubt descend pretty damn quickly, and the two of you might even find some common ground later today. When we stop to take in the famous vista of Preston from the M6.'

'You can actually see Preston from the motorway?' asked a surprised-sounding Sidney.

'No, you can't,' responded Hazeem. 'Any more than *you* can see that you seem to have ended up pressuring Stephen into doing something he needs to think about – and something he might never want to do.'

'But it was his idea. He—'

'Quiet. And back off. Just remember that our friend here has an unwelcome opening in his body – which might mean he could well do without your insistence that he does anything at all. Even something he might appear to have agreed to. Especially something that will involve him regurgitating a comprehensive history of Britain – to order.'

That hit home, and Sidney was soon in repentant mode, starting with a straightforward apology to Stephen. 'Sorry, Stephen. It's just that—'

'…you care about things,' concluded Stephen. 'And there's no harm in that – not usually. But I just think that, in this case…'

'I've got you,' assured Sidney. 'A precis of the history of Britain is now off the agenda until such time as you want to put it back on again. And if that's never, then that's OK with me. Hell, it's not as though it's my history of Britain. As you've just said, it's yours. And if you don't think anybody deserves to see it, then I can well understand that. In fact, I can understand that very well indeed. And I should have taken that into account before I—'

'No harm done,' interrupted Stephen again. 'And I do promise to… let's say, reconsider the proposal in hand – on our way to Preston. After all, the mountain air will no doubt clear my mind.'

'Mountain air?' queried Sidney. 'I had no idea…'

'No, you don't, do you?' chuckled Hazeem, 'You have no idea at all.'

And after his amusement had been shared with Stephen, who didn't so much chuckle as guffaw, Hazeem made ready to get them all on the move, and in no time at all they were once again on their way north.

*

Any discussion about history was shelved for the next five and a half hours, five and a half hours that were so lacking in any challenge from passers-by that Sidney found them really very tedious. There wasn't even a hint of adrenalin to make the time pass by more quickly. But eventually, they'd pitched their overnight camp – next to a huge culvert under the motorway – and as soon as Stephen had been unloaded from the wagon, the damaged team member provided Sidney with a bigger rush than any adrenalin could ever have achieved. And he did this by asking Sidney to spell out precisely how his plan to save the history of Britain might actually work. It was clearly a question based on his renewed acceptance of Sidney's plan.

Sidney could hardly believe it. Stephen had changed his mind again. There was no doubt about it. Whilst being bounced about in the back of the wagon, he had somehow re-embraced Sidney's proposal – and he now wanted to engage with its practical implications: how exactly he should relay to his willing scribe what was in his lost life's work, and how his scribe would commit this to paper.

Sidney, although shocked by Stephen's latest U-turn, was nonetheless well prepared to answer his questions. Because he'd already worked out, in some detail, how his scheme might work – as would soon be made clear. But not before he'd acknowledged Stephen's second change of mind.

'Stephen,' Sidney gushed, 'you don't know how happy—'

'Yes, yes,' interrupted Stephen. 'I know all about that. But what I want to know now is—'

'…how. How are we going to do it.'

'Yes. How you're somehow going to distil several thousand sheets of words into a lot less than that, and how you're going to manage the whole process.'

'Easy. First, you're going to have to put your history into… well, let's call them "precised episodes". And each episode should be short enough for you to narrate it in an evening – when we've pitched camp for the night – and also short enough for me to write it up when we have a midday break the following day.'

'*What?*'

'Well, as I said—'

'Look,' Stephen interjected. 'I can probably sort out these "episodes" as you call them, but are you really going to be able to remember what I've said if you wait until the next day to write it up? It doesn't sound possible.'

'And neither does your idea of taking time off in the middle of the day to get to work with a pen,' added Hazeem.

In response to these challenges, Sidney gave his two companions a look of mild exasperation and then enlightened them on the method in his madness – and on his facility to store and retrieve information. 'Gentlemen,' he declared, 'as I thought I'd made clear earlier today, I'm not just a good listener; I'm also a very good "rememberer". I can assure you, Stephen, that whatever you tell me at the end of each day... well, most of it – and I do mean the vast majority of it – will still be there in my brain twelve hours thereafter – if not for a lot longer. And I won't even have to take notes. I might not recall every detail, but if you can precis your work, then believe me, I can document that precis better than any scribe you're ever likely to meet. And if I get anything wrong, then I'm sure you'll correct me. Not that I will.'

'That's all very impressive,' commented Hazeem. 'But you're going to need time to work this miracle of recollection, aren't you? In the middle of the day. When we should be making our way north.'

'We'll start out half an hour earlier each morning. And if we give Kaalki a really good rest in the middle of the day, I'm sure he won't complain if we ask him to finish his day half an hour later.'

'You've got it all worked out,' conceded Hazeem, a rueful smile spreading across his face, 'and I suppose you're already looking to shoot down any other concern I might have – or indeed that Stephen might have.'

'There can't be any more concerns,' responded a smiling Sidney. 'I really have worked it all out. Just like you said, and—'

'You've more than made your case,' finished Stephen, 'as you very well know.'

He then turned to address Hazeem. 'It's not worth wasting any more breath – at least not until his plan doesn't work, and he forgets everything I've told him. Although that's not going to happen, is it? Instead, he'll no doubt end up producing what will be a pleasingly concise – and therefore readable – history of Britain, which is something I should have done myself. I mean, who the hell was ever going to wade through hundreds of thousands of words? Nobody, that's who. But an abridged version? Well, that's an entirely different matter. And a bit of a no-brainer. In fact, those robbing bastards might have done me a really good turn by burning my files. They'll make me think about what was really important in all those words – and those are the ones I'll keep. As for the rest… well, they can stay lost in the ashes.'

Here, Stephen turned to Sidney again, and delivered the conclusion to his coming to terms with the loss of his original work: 'Yes, this could all work out very well. After all, I've yet to come across a distillation process that doesn't provide a rewarding product, and indeed the more intense the distillation, the better the product.'

Sidney nodded in agreement. It was an assertion that Marc in faraway Toulon would have understood very well. Even if the product, on this occasion, wouldn't be the sort of thing you could unload onto gullible peasants.

22.

As confidently predicted, a view of Preston from the motorway never did present itself. In any event, on the morning of the next day, taking in any of the local scenery was not a priority. Instead, all three travellers were more interested in pressing on north as soon as they could. Stephen had told his colleagues that it wouldn't be long before they encountered some serious gradients in the motorway, and that meant Kaalki – even if he didn't need some extra encouragement – would need some extra time. It would be slow progress today, and they certainly didn't have time to linger if they wanted to get up towards Lancaster by the end of the day.

So, they conducted their usual morning routine as expeditiously as they could, taking account of the need to tend to Stephen and to make sure he was as comfortable as possible before they moved off for another extended period of bumping and bouncing.

When they did move off, to start with, they made very good progress. So much so that Sidney began to think that Kaalki, having pulled the wagon for so many days, must now have been a much fitter animal than he'd been at the outset of their trek. This thought was then reinforced when Kaalki began to tackle his first stretch of inclined M6, as he appeared quite capable of maintaining his pace, and without any signs of distress. Indeed, he seemed to be almost relishing the challenge – and with no need for any encouragement whatsoever.

Consequently, when they stopped for a midday break – having been challenged by the curious (and having seen off these challenges) on only two occasions – they reckoned they had covered more than half their hoped-for mileage for the day. And Kaalki was still as spirited as a red-blooded colt.

The afternoon proved to be a repeat of the morning: just two fended-off challenges (and very few people on the road) and Kaalki still on top form. So when it was decided that he'd done enough for the day – near to a turn-off to the east of Lancaster – it was still late afternoon, and Kaalki could now look forward to a really worthwhile period of rest. And his companions could look forward to a similarly worthwhile period of rest, and maybe a worthwhile tranche of British history as well.

First, though, Stephen's wound needed to be checked and so too did his willingness to go ahead with

Sidney's ambitious plan. Had his wound continued to stay closed and uninfected, and had his commitment to play narrator remained intact?

It was fine. The wound looked good, and Stephen sounded almost eager to embark on his oral account of the events that, in his opinion, had led to the transformation of his country. Just as soon, that is, as he'd had his dinner.

*

Finally, he was ready. In the gloom of what may once have been a cowbarn – big enough to provide a trio of humans and a single mule with shelter from what was now a very rainy evening – Stephen geared himself up to pass on his knowledge to an impatient Sidney. Hazeem was there as well, of course, and all three of them were gathered around the embers of the fire they'd used to cook dinner. It was an improbable setting for a lecture, albeit no more improbable than Stephen's opening remarks, remarks that would address events that took place in the very long-distant past.

'OK,' he began, 'If you're ready, Sidney, I'm going to make a start on… on, you know, on what we agreed. And bear with me, but that means I need to take you back to the fifteenth century.'

'The fifteenth century!' squawked Sidney. 'Why do you—?'

'Yes, the fifteenth century,' confirmed Stephen. 'And you'll just have to learn to be patient. If you manage that, you might just understand why I'm starting all that time ago. Which reminds me. As you suggested, I've divided my history lesson into "episodes", four of them; one for this evening and three for the next three evenings. And this is episode one. And it's… well, it's going to deal with the… er, well, with the first of the "ingredients" we British managed to get our hands on, the first we managed to collect along the way, which would eventually enable us to cook up our own demise. Or maybe, to use more academically acceptable language, the first aspect of our history that, along with other aspects, would lead to our country's ultimate downfall – or at least to its downfall as the country that had existed for hundreds of years.

'So, with your permission – and, as far as possible, with your silence – I'll now start this first episode – by talking about the "Age of Discovery". Which, it is generally accepted, began sometime in the fifteenth century.'

Sidney wasn't about to interrupt again, but his face betrayed a certain disbelief that the transformation of Britain in the last century could really have involved any events that took place such a long time ago. And would it really be worth committing such events to paper? He was about to find out.

'Right,' continued Stephen. 'And do please bear with me because I need to give you a bit of *context*. You know, a bit of an idea of what was going on all those years ago that set us off on our path to disaster. And what was going on then was an age of exploration – an

"Age of Discovery" – conducted, for the most part, by a bunch of guys from Spain and Portugal. And what these guys did was explore the globe, and, of course, as much as they could, exploit what they found, and so start the process of establishing some overseas empires. Yes, they were the first colonists, and the sort of wealth they were generating from their colonial habits began to make some others rather envious, not least the French, the Dutch – and… us.

'Well, as far as I can work out, the way *we* assuaged this envy was to develop a taste for piracy. Whatever wealth the Spanish and Portuguese were squeezing out of their overseas possessions in the New World – you know, the Americas – it had to be brought back to Europe in ships, and those ships could be attacked and the wealth they were carrying removed. And this all added up to a fairly rewarding business, even if there were certain risks involved – such as being sliced in half with a cutlass or discovering your ship was sinking beneath you.

'However, things were about to change. And they did change when, in 1588, we managed to give the Spanish Armada a bit of a thumping—'

'The Spanish Armada?' asked a puzzled Hazeem.

'Yes. Sorry, Hazeem. What I mean is in that year we inflicted a big defeat on a whole bunch of Spanish ships, and by capturing some of these ships and a few Portuguese ones as well, we opened up the possibility of travelling the globe; not to attack other countries' ships – well, not exclusively – but to go in search of riches ourselves. To replicate what the Spanish and Portuguese, and, by then, the Dutch had done, and make every effort to fill our pockets with whatever we could find. Not necessarily through plunder but through trade.'

Sidney couldn't help himself. He had some inkling of what Stephen was presenting as a story of the past – from what he'd been taught by his mother – but he did have some misgivings about the accuracy of Stephen's tale. He had to challenge him before he went on. 'Stephen, how certain are you of what you've just told us?'

Stephen didn't hesitate in his answer. 'Not certain at all. But I do know for a fact that – within the historical context I've just described, accurately or otherwise – a group of London merchants petitioned a certain Queen Elizabeth – the reigning monarch of this country at the time – to be allowed to sail to the Far East with the prime intention of knocking out what remained of Spanish and Portuguese trade in that area, and grabbing it for themselves. Well, the petition was granted in 1591. Two ships were then sent off and… well, the chaps on board them sort of reverted to type, and they simply preyed on Spanish and Portuguese ships before returning to London with more plundered loot, but without making much, if any, attempt to initiate what might be regarded as trade.

'Nevertheless, they came back not just with all sorts of stolen goodies but also with something taken from a Portuguese ship called a "mariner's handbook". And this was a handbook that contained vital information on trade routes to places such as China, Japan and India, just what was needed to make a proper start on some proper trade.

'So....' (And here Stephen tried to introduce a slightly dramatic tone to his lecture.) '... in 1599, a further group of merchants, together with some sailors and some explorer types, met to discuss the potential of initiating what they called an "East India venture", under the auspices of a royal charter. And what that means is that they were now seeking Queen Elizabeth's support for this project, and some more besides. Yes, with the right charter, they also wanted to be granted a total monopoly over all English trade conducted with the Indian subcontinent and Southeast Asia, and later on with East Asia – which sort of adds up to the whole of Asia...'

Here, Stephen paused in his address to take time for a smile and maybe to gauge how said address was going. Having apparently satisfied himself that it was going well enough to hold the attention of his audience of two, he then carried on. 'Right. Well, what we're talking about here is something called the East India Company. Because those merchants did get their charter, and with some quite large funds behind them, they did get their East India venture underway. Not that successfully to start with, it has to be said. The Dutch had a well-established set up in the Far East, not to mention that, quite often, the Dutch – and the Portuguese – would give them a fight, and they'd quite often win. In fact, the Dutch, for some time, were the wealthiest commercial operators in the world, and the rivalry this created led ultimately to a series of Anglo-Dutch wars in the seventeenth and eighteenth centuries—'

'Stephen,' interrupted Sidney, 'are you sure all this is necessary? And all these dates? I'll remember most of what you're telling us, but there are limits. Especially when there are dates to remember, and especially if what I'm trying to remember isn't necessarily very relevant.'

'Patience,' admonished Stephen. 'I'm almost there. Because what I want to make plain now is that, despite those pesky Dutch, the merchants' East India Company went from strength to strength. So much so that Charles II – who was the king of England in the middle of the seventeenth century – granted the EIC – the East India Company – a series of very important rights. And these rights were the right to "autonomous territorial acquisitions", the right to mint money, the right to "command fortresses and troops", the right to form alliances and to make war and peace, and the right to "exercise both civil and criminal jurisdiction over any land acquired".'

'That makes it sound as though this East India Company was like a country itself,' observed Sidney, 'with all the powers of a country to take over other countries.'

'Spot on, young man. That's what I've been coming to. I mean, this EIC set-up, which would go on to assemble its own army of 250,000 men, had already made huge inroads into India by doing deals with its rulers and setting up fortresses and trading posts, and it was well on its way to establishing more of these "forts and factories" throughout the rest of Asia. Its power and reach were now both so extensive that any monarch of this country couldn't ignore it – any less than he could ignore its potential to enrich the whole country. And this, I might add, was at a time when its activities had helped stimulate a taste for our creating some serious overseas possessions, possessions that would match any of those Spanish and Portuguese ones that you might just remember I mentioned at the outset of this lecture.'

'So, what you're saying—' attempted Sidney.

'…is that the East India Company, in many ways, provided a template for this country's overseas ambitions, and despite setbacks in North America – when those ungrateful new Americans decided they would be better off without us – this country then used that template to furnish itself with even more overseas possessions, some of them in the bit of Asia beyond India, and more of them in Africa and the Pacific. And after we defeated the French in the Napoleonic Wars – that was at the beginning of the nineteenth century – we became the principal naval and imperial power in the world, and not surprisingly, we expanded our *imperial holdings* even more. We'd equipped ourselves with the British Empire – the biggest empire the world had ever seen, and one that looked as though it might go on forever. Which, of course, it did not. Although it did last for quite some time.'

'And the relevance of all this?' asked Sidney.

'Don't you remember?' replied Stephen. 'What I'm talking about is the first "ingredient"; the first component we collected on our way to constructing our destruction, the first feature of our history that would lead to the end of our history – as a long-standing, predominantly white nation that was at ease with itself and that had much to be proud of.'

'And should it have been proud of its empire?' challenged Hazeem. 'From what you've just told us, it hardly sounds as though all those countries were… you know, acquired for the benefit of their inhabitants.'

This was a well-moderated challenge. Hazeem's tone wasn't aggressive. And it received an equally temperate response from Stephen, and one that was introduced with a statement of gratitude: 'Hazeem, I am genuinely very pleased that you've asked me that. Because how the empire came to be regarded back at the beginning of the twenty-first century is integral to understanding how this first *ingredient* got incorporated into the mix. And I'm not going to jump ahead of myself here, but what I will do is give you the benefit of my thoughts on how we, as a species, have behaved ourselves since we stood up on two feet, and I'll then let you come to your own decision as to whether the empire was something to be proud of or not – and whether it was good, bad or just plain inevitable.

'You see, my firm belief is that we, as a species, are not a particularly nice lot. We can be nice to each other when we want to be, and thank goodness for that. But as often as not, when we want something we haven't got, we can then become pretty unpleasant. And that's why, for the whole of our history, we've consistently been abusing our fellow humans. When we haven't been murdering them, we've been enslaving them, raping them, subjugating them or sometimes wiping them out in their droves. And even if that might be a very sour view of our natural behaviour, you'll never convince me that our hallmark is forbearance, and we certainly rarely hesitate in exploiting others for our own reward when we want that reward. It's simply how our species has conducted itself forever and, I might say, still does.

'So, if one arrives at a point in human history when technological advances in one part of the world mean that the inhabitants of that part of the world can travel all over the world – armed with their clearly superior technology – it would be perverse in the extreme if they didn't use their advantage *to* their advantage. I'm bloody certain that, if the boot were on the other foot, and Africa had won out on the comparative development race, we'd have had an African Empire spanning the world, with the whole of Europe having been colonised and exploited. Quite simply, it's not as though we – and the other colonial powers – were bad, and all those countries colonised were full of saints. It's just that we Europeans had the sort of opportunity that nobody in history had been given before, and we made the most of that opportunity. Yes, thanks to the East India Company and our… well, our grab-it-if-you-can attitude – probably cultivated in the days when we robbed Spanish galleons – lumped together with a few bloody good wins against other European powers, a healthy dose of undeserved good luck and, not to be forgotten, a lot of deserved good luck that we engineered ourselves through our ingenuity and our… well, our engineering, we ended up making the very best of the opportunity – and with an empire, the likes of which had never been seen before – or since.

'And one, I might say, that did provide to all its subjugated people quite a lot of benefits – not least loads of infrastructure and various ready-made systems of government and justice, all of which would remain in place long after we'd gone. And we were quite good at getting rid of some fairly unpleasant practices as well, such as eating your neighbours or insisting on your wife joining you on your funeral pyre.'

'You're making that up,' remarked Hazeem.

'No, I'm not,' responded Stephen. 'Although it hardly justifies exercising political control over millions of people who haven't asked for that control. And getting rid of nasty habits certainly wasn't our motive for assembling an empire. This was, as I've said, our desire to take advantage of an irresistible opportunity – in the same way that anybody else in our situation would have done. Not knowing at the time, of course, how our colonial habits might be mixed with some other ingredients yet to be found, which would lead to a very unpalatable outcome. Which is, I think, where we came in. And I doubt I should tax our scribe with any more words of wisdom just now, no matter how well his memory might work. As I'm sure you'll agree.'

'That's it for the evening then?' confirmed Sidney.

'It certainly is. And anyway, I'm knackered. It's been a long day, and giving lectures is surprisingly tiring. Maybe for those receiving them as well.'

Sidney chuckled. 'Maybe more perplexing than tiring, but I'm sure all will become clear when we get episodes two to four. And I'm certainly already intrigued.'

'So am I,' added Hazeem. 'Not least because I'm not unaware that I'm a sort of coloniser myself; probably part of that end result you've been referring to. And does that make me good or bad?'

This last sentence was delivered with a smile, and it earned from Stephen his final words as a teacher for the evening. 'You're a good student, Hazeem. You learn fast. I look forward to filling your brain with more… stuff tomorrow. If I'm still alive.'

And with that reminder of the fragility of their teacher, Hazeem and Sidney made haste to get Stephen comfortable for the night, before they both retired for the night themselves. This would no doubt be with Hazeem digesting what their teacher had told them, and Sidney committing to memory, as best he could, everything Stephen had told them – especially the dates.

23.

In accordance with Sidney's new regime, the three pilgrims and their faithful mule were already on their way up the remnants of the M6 soon after seven. And the particular stretch of motorway they were tackling now was indeed little more than just remnants. Through what must have been a combination of the impact of harsh weather in the area and no maintenance whatsoever, it was in a terrible condition, with parts of it now overgrown with grass and small shrubs.

This meant that they made very slow progress and also that they met very few curious travellers coming down from the north. Indeed, they met only two. The first was a solo traveller who must have left all his curiosity at home, as all he did was try to make friends with Kaalki before wishing Hazeem and his bundled-up companion a safe trip further north. And the second was another solo traveller who must have seen through Sidney's far-from-perfect disguise within seconds, so causing him to seek to pull Sidney from his seat on the wagon, and Hazeem to shoot him in the head as he was doing so. He was, after all, brandishing a large knife as he attempted to unseat Sidney and, according to Hazeem, accompanying his assault with some unmistakable death threats in Urdu. Hazeem had to act as he did. And whilst he and his two friends would have liked to have known why the man had such a strong dislike for badly disguised white people, they settled for not knowing at all but remaining a party of three, none of whom were either further injured or slain.

It was a very unwelcome episode in an otherwise trouble-free if slow-moving morning (and a more than unwelcome event for the guy who was now lying at rest beneath a hawthorn bush), and it did remind Sidney that his disguise was no more than very amateurish and that he was, in fact, far more exposed to danger than when he'd been wrapped up in a shroud. That wasn't an option now, but he was grateful that not only had he started this journey in that manner but also that he'd just received a very powerful reminder to keep his face as much hidden from view as possible. His home-made skin-colour change would fool nobody who took even the slightest interest in his features.

*

Fortunately, when they stopped at midday, there was nobody around to take any interest in him or in the other two occupants of the wagon, and although he was still recovering from witnessing another death – at close range – Sidney knew he would be safe to make a start on recording what Stephen had narrated last night. And he also knew that doing this would provide him with a very welcome distraction from the continuing very unwelcome reality of their journey to Scotland.

It took him a little over an hour to complete his task – albeit it took much less time than this to discover how difficult a task it would be. First, there were the complaints from his arthritic writing hand. Then, although remembering what Stephen had recounted wasn't a problem, finding enough blank spaces on the flyleaves and margins of his books certainly was. He'd overestimated how much blank space he would have at his disposal, and he'd also overestimated his skills in condensing his handwriting into a suitably Lilliputian script. Nevertheless, the job was eventually completed, and he promised himself that he would definitely see the whole job done, even if it entailed much more pain in his hand and his having to overwrite much of the text in any number of his books. And, of course, it would also necessitate no other assassins attempting to take his life as he moved further north.

*

None did. At least, not for the rest of the day. And with Kaalki putting in another impressive performance, despite the almost-absent-road conditions, Hazeem brought the wagon to a stop, next to a lake, in the late afternoon.

Stephen was soon unloaded from their conveyance, and soon after this, he was having his wound inspected. It still looked OK. And with this task completed, Hazeem got on with preparing some dinner (one of more roasted rat), Sidney sorted out some grazing for Kaalki on the shore of the lake, and Stephen tried to remember the name of the lake – but failed. All he could recollect was that it was a lake that had given its name to a now-disappeared motorway service station, and that this meant they were somewhere near Kendal or whatever remained of Kendal.

A little while later – after feeding and watering had been concluded – he was being charged to recollect a lot more. Specifically, he was being asked to remember the second episode of his history of Britain and to relate this to his two students, one of whom would again be committing it to memory. When he'd been made comfortable with the help of a blanket and a moss-covered bank, he began his address: 'Right, do either of you two know anything about World War II? You know, the big war that took place towards the middle of the twentieth century?'

'Wow!' exclaimed a smiling Sidney. 'We've moved on a bit from the Age of Discovery, haven't we? I thought we'd be hearing about the eighteenth and nineteenth centuries. Or the... er, the Industrial Revolution. You know, when we became... What was it called? Er, the...'

'...workshop of the world,' finished Stephen. 'Which was all very interesting – and your knowledge of it does prove you know something of the past – but it isn't relevant to my story of Britain's downfall. Whereas something that was set in motion during World War II is. Which is why I asked both of you whether you knew anything about that war.'

Hazeem shook his head. He appeared to have not even heard of it. However, Sidney had; he said so. He knew that Britain was on the winning side at its end and that on the losing side there'd been a guy called Hitler. 'But as regards a lot of the detail,' he admitted, 'well, there are quite a few gaps in my knowledge.'

'OK,' resumed Stephen. 'Well, all you need to know about it for the purpose of my story is that the war effort called for lots of sacrifices to be made by the people of this country. So many, in fact, that even while the war was still in progress, these people made it very well known that when the war was over, they wanted a very different Britain, a Britain that would... well, look after its citizens – in a way that they'd never been looked after before.'

Hazeem now had a look of bewilderment on his face, and Sidney sported a look of confusion. What could Stephen mean by Britain looking after its citizens? How could that possibly be a realistic idea? And why would anybody even consider it? They were about to find out.

'You see, before the war, people in this country had to more or less look after themselves. Like we've had to do all our lives. But after those sacrifices they'd made... well, they wanted a payback, and the payback was the creation of a state that cared for its citizens and was duty bound to care for them. So while the war was still being waged, something called the Beveridge Report was published. And the author of this report – this Beveridge bloke – well, he was a liberal economist who wanted to introduce a system of what he called "social welfare", which would be designed to address five "giants on the road to reconstruction" as he called them. And these five giants were, if I can remember all five: "want", "disease", "ignorance", "squalor" and... er, what's the fifth? Ah, I know: "idleness".'

'Blimey,' observed Hazeem. 'And he was taken seriously?'

'Yes, he was,' confirmed Stephen. 'And largely, I suspect, because if this social welfare stuff wasn't promised – and the promise kept – there might well have been lots of trouble. And I mean real trouble. Like a class war. You know, a sort of British revolution.'

'So, what you're saying is that they did actually introduce this stuff?' offered Sidney. 'At the end of the war.'

'Yes, soon after 1945. And to my mind, not as some sort of noble gesture but more as a pragmatic response to a looming problem. And this was the start of what was called the "British Welfare State"—'

'The Welfare State?' interrupted Hazeem. 'Meaning what exactly?'

'Well, I think the official definition is something along the lines of the state taking an interest in the well-being of its citizens, based on some sort of *fair* distribution of wealth and, maybe most important of all, a public responsibility for those of its citizens who couldn't provide for themselves.'

'*What?* You mean... you know, anybody who needed it was given money... or, well, maybe food?' asked an incredulous Hazeem.

'And health care. And help with housing. And help with finding a job.'

'I can't believe it! How can that possibly work? Where does the money and food come from? And who pays for the doctors? And who decides who gets what?'

Stephen smiled. 'All very valid questions. To which I am not going to supply any answers just yet. Because that would be getting ahead of myself, and what I want you to remember from this bit of my history lesson is that we've just collected another ingredient that would prove to be essential—'

'...in our cooking up our demise,' finished Sidney.

Stephen's smile broadened immediately. 'Correct. We'd shown to the door stuff like frugality, self-control and self-responsibility, and we'd welcomed in in its place dependency, expectation and any number of... well, let's call them "unfortunate opportunities" that hadn't existed before. And there's more. Because in this time of liberal zeal, there were two further ingredients that we would go on to gather. And the first of these was something called "The Universal Declaration of Human

Rights", which was an international document adopted by the UN General Assembly in 1948 "enshrining the rights and freedoms of all human beings".'

'What's this UN Assembly thing?' asked Hazeem.

'Sorry, I keep assuming,' apologised Stephen, 'but the UN was the United Nations. And the United Nations was a collection of most of the world's countries, which came together in a vain attempt to solve some of the world's bigger problems. And sometimes they held general assemblies, where leaders of these countries would… well, assemble and agree on things… such as the rights of all humans.'

'Sounds mad,' observed Hazeem. 'Why would anyone think they should have any rights at all – other than the right to live a bloody tough life? And as for freedoms… well, what do they mean? And anyway, how did any of this stuff actually happen? You can get as many people as you like agreeing something between themselves, but that doesn't mean anything will actually get done.'

'Well, things did get done, Hazeem. Through lots of laws being developed and these laws then being incorporated into things like international treaties, national laws and national legal codes. So, it wasn't long before everybody on the planet could claim they had a load of *inherent* human rights, rights that could no longer be ignored – no matter where they lived, and no matter what their status, religion, gender, ethnic origin or… Well, you get the general idea. Everybody was suddenly the recipient of a whole pile of rights that they'd never enjoyed in the past—'

'...which in some way yet to be revealed provides us with our third ingredient,' suggested Sidney.

'Excellent. You're making my job very easy. And don't be concerned, I will come back to these rights – and to the Welfare State – to illustrate how these two ingredients were blended into the mix. Which might well entail my telling you how both of these "liberal steps forward" had what might be called some serious unintended consequences. But first, to conclude my lecture for the evening, I want to talk about a third ingredient collected in this post-war period.'

'Just before you do,' interrupted Sidney, 'will you be telling us how these human rights things and the Welfare State all disappeared? I mean, I don't even remember my mum talking about them, and they've certainly never come my way – ever.'

'No. Mine neither,' added Hazeem. 'And no surprise. They both sound so crazy, I'm surprised they ever existed at all.'

'Well, they did,' responded Stephen. 'And to answer your question, Sidney, I'm sure you'll be able to work out why they disappeared when I cover some of those unintended consequences – tomorrow evening. But first, as I said, there's one more ingredient to deal with, and this was something else that was concocted after the war, and it was called "The Convention Relating to the Status of Refugees", also known to its close friends as "The 1951 Refugee Convention". And this was yet another cracker dreamt up by the UN, which not only defined who could claim to be a refugee but also set out the rights of these refugees to be granted asylum in whichever country they sought it.'

'You've lost me there,' interjected Hazeem.

'And me,' added Sidney. 'What's this "asylum"?'

Stephen sighed. He clearly realised he was still assuming too much, that he was expecting two people who knew little of the past to be aware of features of the past they knew nothing of at all.

'OK. It's just after the war. Remember? And just after the war, at the start of the Cold War (something that needn't concern you at all), there were people – refugees – who were fleeing persecution by Communist Russia. And forget the Communist bit as well. But what's important to remember is that there was a real desire – in both Europe and America – to protect from this Russian threat people who were primarily Europeans. These guys were running away from Russian control and seeking *asylum* – or *sanctuary* or *shelter* – in another country, which was all quite understandable. And the convention was meant to protect these guys, and only these guys. But unfortunately, someone had the bright idea to include in the convention the ability of any country to declare that the provisions applying to Europeans could be extended to cover refugees from anywhere on the planet! Which in plain English means that, all that time ago, we – and a string of other naïve countries – were opening our doors to anyone who cared to come in. Just as long as they could declare that they were refugees, we would be obliged to offer them asylum.

And we were specifically banned from returning them to the country from which they'd fled.'

Hazeem's eyes widened. 'So, my lot… we had a right. Even if we hadn't actually been invited.'

'Well, sort of,' responded Stephen with a smile, 'but sort of not. And you'll just have to wait for my next lecture to understand what I mean.'

Sidney's face was now a study in absorbed contemplation. And what he was contemplating was what this asylum stuff would have meant for the security – and the autonomy – of any country that had existed in the past. Then he put the immediate results of this contemplation into words: 'Stephen, how did any country back then… well, look after itself. Or its own people? How did it retain its…? I'm not sure I know the word.'

'Its sovereignty,' assisted Stephen. 'Its authority to govern itself – and to choose, amongst other things, who to allow into its territory.'

'Yeah,' confirmed Sidney. 'If you let anybody in—'

'You end up with what you've got now.' suggested Hazeem, a slightly awkward smile spreading across his face.

'Hang on,' pronounced Stephen. 'We're getting a bit ahead of ourselves again. And I want to deal with the consequences of this asylum stuff tomorrow – along with the fallout from the other ingredients I've listed. But what I will tell you now is that, as a result of the Refugee Convention, the concept of a nation's sovereignty had now been holed below the waterline and it would soon sink out of sight.'

'Below the waterline?' asked a puzzled-looking Hazeem – just before Sidney expressed a desire to know how a concept could sink out of sight.

Stephen had done it again, and he needed to explain what these references to a past world actually meant. 'It all relates to a ship. You know, those big things that floated on water and that could sail around the world. Well, if they were hit below the waterline – by a bomb, say – they wouldn't float any more. They'd sink. They'd be gone. Just like the concept of a nation's sovereignty was gone.'

Hazeem still looked slightly puzzled, but it was Sidney who spoke first. 'Maybe it would be easier for us—'

Stephen jumped in: 'Yes. Got it. No more metaphors from the past. And no more lecturing for tonight. I suspect we've all had enough. And again, I don't want to overburden our memory-man here. In fact, all I want to do is go to sleep. Suddenly, I feel very weary indeed.'

This, thought Sidney, was hardly surprising. Stephen was an old man, a sick man, and an injured man. The fact that he was still managing the journey – and the lectures – was quite remarkable. And there was no question at all that he should now be allowed to sleep.

Accordingly, Stephen was soon bedded down, and only a few minutes later, Sidney and Hazeem retired for the night as well. They too were tired, but Sidney's tiredness couldn't overcome his further contemplation of what he'd heard from Stephen tonight, nor his thoughts as to how he might relay these revelations to his three ham friends around the world. If, of course, he was ever able to talk to them again.

These thoughts took him on a downward spiral, and he was soon wondering whether it was simply stupid to believe there was any chance at all that he'd ever again be clearing the airwaves with archaic but polite requests in order to make contact with three special people dotted around the world. That was part of a life that had now disappeared, only to be replaced by a life full of more fear and uncertainty than he'd ever experienced before – and by the occasional ending of a life. And not just a brutal occasional ending of a life, but also a 'matter-of-fact' occasional ending of a life. It was, after all, only hours after the death of that guy who'd attacked him, and he'd almost forgotten it had happened – even though it had happened within only feet of where he was sitting, and he'd seen at close quarters a hole being made in the poor fellow's head.

At this stage of his musings, Sidney began to feel very morose indeed. It was just fortunate then that fatigue finally overwhelmed his maudlin meditation, and he dropped off to sleep. Now it was only his dreams that would be disturbed by the huge uncalled-for upheaval in his life – and with luck, he might not even remember these dreams in the morning.

24.

When Sidney awoke in the morning, it wasn't properly light, and Hazeem and Stephen were still sleeping. This was unusual. Hazeem was almost always the first to face the day, and Sidney would usually wake to see him having some 'bonding time' with Kaalki. He'd clearly become just as attached to their very special mule as Sidney had been for years. However, this morning, it would be Sidney who would go to rub the animal's nose and put his arms around his neck.

Kaalki didn't seem to mind. How could he? Despite Hazeem's affection and his constant attention, Kaalki hadn't forgotten who was his oldest – and closest – friend. So when Sidney moved off to take a look at the lake, Kaalki no doubt didn't feel abandoned, but only happy that he had the company of three two-legged animals who all seemed to like him – a lot. After all, even the sometimes-brusque Stephen had shown him only kindness. He therefore, as he watched Sidney walk to the shore of the lake, had in his eyes rather more than just of a hint of contentment, maybe tinged with a *soupçon* of bliss.

No such feelings could be detected in Sidney's eyes. They were now scanning the surface of the lake and taking in its lack of life. Like virtually all bodies of water in the country, this one had been dead for years. Even algae couldn't cope with the abuse it had suffered, and it was now more like a large expanse of liquid desolation than something that still deserved the title of 'lake'. In the early morning light, its beauty wasn't just superficial but also deceptive – and a reminder of what had been wreaked on every natural feature of this country. Sidney, of course, had known nothing other than the wreckage of what once had been, but he did know it was wreckage, and he was soon as morose as he'd been before he'd dropped off to sleep. And then he became truly despondent.

What were he and his friends doing, he asked himself? And was any of what they were doing worth anything at all? Where would it all lead? Was it really worth the effort? And the constant gnawing uncertainty? And the killings? Even with the task of documenting a history of Britain – which would probably be read by no one and about which no one would care – was it worth carrying on? Maybe they should all just accept that their world had fallen apart and that in no way was it going to be mended. In which case, they might as well give up now and simply walk into that dead lake – and get it over and done with as soon as they could.

It was at this point in his descent into terminal despair that Kaalki reminded Sidney of his presence. He did this with a soft whimper that, without waking up Hazeem or Stephen, certainly woke up Sidney's sense of responsibility. Not only was he prompted to remember that he had an inescapable responsibility for this wonderful animal, but he also had a compelling responsibility not to indulge in melodramatic musings. They certainly wouldn't help his companions in the pursuit of their goal. No matter how futile that goal might appear.

*

So, when, just a few minutes later, his two companions awoke, they were both met with a smiling Sidney, and together, they were all able to assemble some enthusiasm for the day ahead; a day that would see them travelling through some of the least populated and, consequently, the least devastated stretches of northern Britain. They were now, after all, skirting the eastern edges of the Lake District, an area from which it was difficult to make a living and that had been colonised by only a few hardy herders – none of whom were to make themselves apparent today.

This all boiled down to a slow journey north – as Kaalki tackled more inclines on the broken motorway –

and a journey interrupted by only two encounters with others during the whole of the day. One was before their midday stop, and was with a group of young men who showed no interest whatsoever in either of the wagon's two passengers. And the other, which happened after this stop, was with a group of older men, only one of whom took any interest in the odd chap to Hazeem's left. He stared at Sidney for quite some time, and having stared long enough, he then just winked at him. He must have known that Sidney was not quite what he pretended to be, but he must either not have cared or have just been a kind old guy who had no wish to cause needless trouble.

In any event, Sidney was definitely more than happy when the wagon moved on from this latter encounter, and he could relish in peace the fact that he'd successfully documented the second episode of Stephen's history just one hour before. It had again been difficult to find those much-needed blank spaces in his books, but he had found them and he had covered them in enough of his tiny writing to capture in words everything Stephen had told him the previous evening. And if Stephen dispensed a similar consignment of knowledge this coming evening, he knew he would be able to make a similar record of this as well. Indeed, he could barely wait to discover what the forthcoming lecture would reveal about all those ingredients Stephen had identified. And were there any more ingredients to come?

*

Well, he now had only seconds to wait. The three wandering *hombres* and their faithful *mula* had stopped for the night in what was a close relative of the middle of nowhere, Stephen's wound had been attended to, the stomachs of all four of them were now pleasingly full, and the three *hombres* were gathered around a smouldering fire – one smelling strongly of heather and singed moss – and Stephen was preparing to speak.

Then he made a start. 'Right, if you cast your minds back to last night, you might remember that the much-admired definitive history of Britain had reached that time, just after the Second World War, when there was a shift in expectations in much of the world, together with some radical rewriting of a number of the world's rules.'

Stephen accompanied this introduction with a smile, and not for the first time, Sidney could see that these lectures were proving to be a tonic for his injured friend. No matter how much pain he was still enduring – and not admitting to – and no matter how frail he was becoming, his being charged with educating his two helpers on the genesis of Britain's transformation was clearly galvanising him so much that it was difficult to think he was anything other than entirely healthy.

And this welcome invigoration of mind and body was still very much in evidence as he continued his talk: 'OK, we'll now focus on just Britain in this post-war period and what the builders of the promised new Britain were faced with. Because it was all very well creating this caring-for-all Welfare State – and ladling out all these human rights to people – but essentially, Britain was in a pretty sorry state. It was bust – from the cost of the war. It was battered – from its role in the war. And it certainly wasn't a country with an impressive empire any more. That was quickly crumbling away, and all Britain could do was look on with a sickly smile as its empire melted into something called "the Commonwealth" – or in other words, an association of now-independent former colonies. And not to be ignored is the fact that these former colonies were initially granted special rights, including – most importantly of all – the right of their citizens to come and live in Britain if they so wished—'

'And that would include Pakistan,' interjected Hazeem.

'Correct, it would. And indeed, some people from the whole of the subcontinent and a load more from the Caribbean did begin to arrive "to help us rebuild Britain" – which, I suppose, is what they did. Although, for the life of me, I still don't understand how, after the war, we couldn't sort things out for ourselves in the same way that other European countries did. And as for Germany and Japan, both of which had been careless enough to end up on the losing side of the war, well, they did get some post-war reconstruction help, but in the form of money, not in the form of people from overseas – who would then stay around indefinitely. I suppose, if I had to guess, I'd say it was just that we had a pool of cheap foreign labour – left over from empire – and we tapped it. We took the easiest route we could and never thought about the consequences.'

'This was quite a flood of people then?' asked an already-enthralled Sidney.

'No,' responded Stephen, 'it wasn't much more than a trickle. We Brits still had what was called a "work ethic" back then, and we shouldered most of the post-war rebuilding ourselves. And I must just say it was this work ethic – shared by what was, back then, a very homogeneous population – that saw the Welfare State get off to a bloody good start. It was widely accepted that the state was now there to help, but only for as long as was needed. As soon as you could stand on your own two feet, you did, and you didn't then look to the state for any more help. Permanent dependency on the state hadn't yet established itself as the norm, and although it eventually would, it was still very much the old order in Britain – with a bit of added kindness. In other words, we had a country predominantly full of white, self-reliant people, who tolerated a trickle of immigrants in the same way they'd tolerated – and welcomed – immigrants for centuries. Only now these immigrants weren't coming from some of our neighbours in Europe, but from much farther afield. And from places with some very different cultures.'

Hazeem gave an involuntary nod of his head at this point, but said nothing, and Stephen carried on: 'OK, now the story turns a little sour. And that's because that trickle of immigrants from the old empire was becoming a larger trickle, and the white population of this country – in the age-old tradition of tribal behaviour – began to see the new citizens of this country, wherever they came from, as a distinctly different tribe, and a tribe that was muscling in on its own patch. The fact that the members of this different tribe were doing jobs here and still "helping us" didn't really come into it. And resentment began to grow all across the country.'

'People could still come in as they pleased?' asked Sidney.

'Not after 1971, they couldn't,' replied Stephen. 'By that time, the trickle had become a stream, and an act was passed – the 1971 Immigration Act – which, some might say, not before time, made a distinction between the rights of UK-born citizens and the citizens of former British colonies. No longer could these ex-colonials just hop on a plane and come here. Now, they had to submit themselves to a set of immigration controls – designed, of course, to cut down their numbers – and I mean cut them down very significantly.'

'And did they?' queried Sidney.

'What do you think?' grinned Stephen. 'And remember, that trickle had now become a stream.'

'Erm, I suspect they didn't.'

'You suspect right. And it's not too difficult to work out why. After all, what we're talking about here is a combination of two powerful forces: the forces acting on those choosing to come here that existed in their own countries – that is, the "push forces"; and the forces in this country that were now attracting them here – that is, the "pull forces".'

He was about to lose them. Hazeem was shaking his head to indicate his state of confusion. Sidney merely smiled weakly and tipped his head to one side. Stephen got the message.

He closed his eyes, took a deep breath and then continued, 'OK, let's start with the *push* forces, and let's think about what might be going on in those ex-colonies. I mean, few if any of them – especially in the sub-continent and in the Caribbean – could offer a standard of living to their citizens anything like the one that existed in places such as Britain. And that's even taking account of the fact that, in the case of Britain, it was still in what you might call a recovery stage. And if the idea of a standard of living is a bit nebulous, what might be clearer is the fact that in these ex-colonies, jobs were increasingly hard to come by, and even if you could get a job, you weren't going to be earning a great deal of money. And there's nothing like poverty and a zero chance of escaping that poverty to make you think of maybe going somewhere else. It's the biggest push force of the lot. For some, it has to be admitted, what could have been encouraging them to leave might also have included suffering at the hands of a brutal regime, or being part of an oppressed minority or even their having… well, let's call it an "*unpopular* sexuality". But generally, it was the poverty. That was the biggest of the push forces by far.

'In fact, I should underline the importance of poverty as the principal push force by pointing out that being poor wasn't unconnected with what was happening all around the world at that time – which was an unprecedented growth in the world's population. And particularly in places such as… well, Pakistan and India, where lots of people were trying to make do with a lot less space and a lot fewer resources than they'd had in the past. Which was inevitably leading to poverty. And Sidney, do take note of this point because it's very important. India, as an example, was now on its way to tripling its immediate post-war population. And more and more people were looking to escape the overcrowding and get to a place that seemed to offer so much more – in all sorts of ways.

'Anyway, before either of you interrupt me, I want to mention some of the *pull forces* here that combined with the *push forces* 'over there' – wherever 'over there' was – and made Britain such an attractive place, and our job of stemming the flow just about impossible. And to start with, there was that welfare system that I've talked about, which would, of course, guarantee that all those poor people coming here would end up with a much better standard of living than they'd had before, even if they didn't get a job here. And then there's the fact that many of those who were eager to leave their home countries would by now have relatives here – which was a distinct pull force. As was our having a language with which many of them would already be well acquainted.

'Anyway, what was probably the biggest pull force of all was the desire of many employers in this country to retain that source of cheap, willing labour I've referred to – and I can't stress this enough. You see, the local children of the Welfare State might no longer want to work in a foundry – but eager young souls from Pakistan or Yemen were only too willing. So why on earth would you want to stop them?'

Stephen certainly wasn't expecting an answer to that rhetorical question, and after a brief pause, he moved on to another aspect of this last of his pull forces. 'OK. Now, this enthusiasm for foreign workers leads us to consider something else that you need to understand – something that, by this time, had entrenched itself in this country – and this was the marked dichotomy of thinking in Britain—'

'Dichotomy?' interjected Hazeem.

Stephen hesitated before responding to Hazeem's incomprehension. 'Migrants were increasingly seen as something bad, something threatening. But at the same time, people in this country simply wouldn't countenance doing lots of jobs that were now almost exclusively the preserve of recent immigrants. And, although they wouldn't admit it to themselves, they were quite happy to see all sorts of darker-skinned workers labouring away in kitchens and crappy factories – because thanks to the workings of the Welfare State, they could never be forced to do these jobs themselves. They now had the attractive option of letting others do all the dirty work for them – and these others were the very people they didn't want here. Which I think, Hazeem, gets us pretty close to understanding the meaning of dichotomy.'

'So, what you're saying—' began Sidney.

'...is,' continued Stephen, 'that there were some very strong forces at work – of both the push and pull varieties – and these forces were always going to overcome any controls put in place. And I'll go on to say that the controls that were put in place *were* overcome, and fairly easily. And mostly through legitimate means – such as people claiming family ties here, or by their getting certain classes of work visa, or even by their playing the human rights card. And that had now become almost a trump—'

'A what?' interjected Hazeem.

Stephen hesitated again, drew breath and carried on. 'Hazeem, in the unlikely event that I live long enough and I can get my hands on a pack of cards, I'll teach you how to play a card game called bridge, and you'll then understand what a "trump" is. But in the meantime, please forget about the word completely. Instead, just remember what I told you about human rights last night and how they could now be successfully employed by any individual in the world – especially when the individual in question might be attempting to enter a country that had embraced human rights so closely to its bosom.'

'You mean there were guys who were using human rights as a way to come here?'

'Yes. Just as lots more who couldn't find a legitimate way here would use their rights as asylum seekers to get in. Although I should stress that we're still in the period here where that route in was a minority undertaking.

Most of the stream who were evading the dam designed to stem it were using *legitimate* means. And despite more and more unrest about the size of the stream, it continued to flow.

'Of course, it began to pool into lots of self-contained ghettos in any number of cities, and this made these new citizens of Britain even more unpalatable to its established citizens. Those same citizens who, through their unspoken acceptance of these *foreigners* doing the nasty jobs, were acting as the handmaidens to the demise of their own long-established country, together with its long-established culture – and complexion.'

'You're saying we… whities are the principal culprits in our country's… transformation from what it was?' asked a concerned-looking Sidney.

'You bet,' confirmed Stephen. 'If I were a poor farmer in the Punjab back in that period, I'd be doing everything in my power to get me and my family over to Britain. Even if I knew I might end up with a job as a street cleaner, I'd still be much better off than as a Punjabi farmer. And my kids would get an education, my whole family would get free healthcare, and I wouldn't even have to adopt any of the local culture. I could still eat, dress, behave, speak and worship just like I had before – because that was my human right. And nobody could take that from me.

'So, why the hell would I not come? And therefore, how could I be anything other than an innocent in this tale? Just as the real culprit in this tale can only be the lazy, blind, complacent, spoilt and, ultimately, doomed British people who, not content with losing their empire, were now set on losing their own bloody country – and through the very process they'd used to win that empire. We had colonised a third of the world, but that third of the world – plus a bit more – was now in the process of colonising us. And as much as these Brits moaned and whined, they allowed this process to continue – and, by doing so, they set themselves up for a surge in this process that would see the beginning of their total demise – and which will be the subject of my address for tomorrow evening.'

This was a sudden end to Stephen's lecture, but one that drew an immediate observation from Hazeem.

'So, we really weren't the bad guys,' he observed. 'We were just an inevitable—'

'...consequence of a country losing not just its empire but its self-confidence, the belief that its values and its culture deserved to be protected and cherished. And not just traded in for an easy life where someone else would have to deal with all the shit.'

Stephen delivered this statement with an unmissable tone of regret – or was that bitterness? In any event, it was the last statement he delivered this evening, and now he was just asking to be helped to his makeshift bed. What had energised him to start with – the third episode of his history – had now clearly drained him, and he looked to Sidney as though he were on the point of collapse. Accordingly, he was soon helped to retire, and it was left to Sidney and Hazeem to close down their little camp for the night – and to retire into their own thoughts about what they had just been told.

For Sidney, this involved his thinking about what he would have done – as one of the 'guilty whites' all those years ago – and whether it would have been any different from what the rest of the indigenous population had done back then. He soon decided he would have gone with the crowd, which is why he and Stephen were now in the company of one of the new Britons, trying to make their way to what was probably a remnant population of some of the old ones. It was also why he began to feel a little of the guilt of his forebears for their surrender of their country – with so little fight and, as pointed out by Stephen, with so little confidence in themselves and their culture.

He suspected he wouldn't feel a great deal less guilty in the morning.

25.

Despite their being ambushed in the middle of the afternoon, by late afternoon, the three men and a mule had got to within a mile or so of what had once been Carlisle. This was where they had planned to be when they'd set off on their journey about ten hours before.

The ambush had come out of the blue, and had been mounted on a stretch of the motorway that had looked to be as deserted – and as unthreatening – as any other length of this top end of the old M6. This far north, there were very few people around and only a handful on the highway, none of whom had made any attempt to approach the wagon.

Hazeem and Sidney had talked about this absence of people and other travellers, and they could only conclude it was due to there being so few people living hereabouts, no doubt because making a living from this unforgiving part of Cumbria would have been a real challenge. But, on top of that, suggested Sidney, maybe whichever people in Scotland who'd wanted to seek their salvation in England had left there quite some time ago, which would mean that most of the migrants going south had now passed them, and there were few if any more to come. That would certainly fit with what they'd previously learnt from Dorothy. However, whilst this all seemed to make sense, it did ignore the possibility that not all of those who'd been made desperate by the worsening conditions in the country would either end up as migrants or stay put and hope for the best. Some, such as those villains back in Warrington, might resort to thievery – and to unrestrained violence.

There had been nine of them, all armed with either a club or a blade, and they had rushed at the wagon in a way that indicated they wouldn't be making any demands of its occupants, but instead that they'd be attempting to dispatch these occupants with their weapons. This was so obvious that even Sidney hadn't hesitated to take out his gun. He may even have fired at the charging group before Hazeem had. In that way, he did down one of them as Hazeem got on with ending the lives of three of the others. That was enough for the remaining five. They turned tail and made off across a tussock-covered expanse of Cumbria as fast as they could. And no way would they be back.

The incident was all over within a couple of minutes, but it took much longer than two minutes for Sidney to recover from the shock of the event, not least that part of it involving his putting a bullet in someone's body. In fact, in that someone's head. Nevertheless, after a little while, he was able to engage with Hazeem – and with Stephen, who was now propped up in the back of the wagon – to discuss what this unexpected attack might mean for their further progress north.

Hazeem didn't appear to be too bothered. It was, he thought, just another attack, no different from the others they'd had before. And this one had been pretty easy to deal with.

But Stephen wasn't so sanguine. He was concerned about the locals. As he was keen to point out, if any hope of these people finding a way out of their dire predicament was disappearing as fast as their food stocks, they might be beginning to do whatever they needed to do to stay alive: fighting with their neighbours, robbing their neighbours, killing their neighbours and, of course, robbing and killing anybody naïve enough to stray into their part of Britain. In fact, he was seriously worried that what they'd just experienced was their first taste of the lawlessness and chaos that comes with acute desperation. So much so that he suggested that, before they moved off again, they should dispose of not only the recently departed but also the not-so-recently departed in the back of the wagon – who were now beginning to impose their presence through their scent. He argued – very successfully – that their continued tenancy might prove more of a difficult-to-explain complication than an aid to further progress north.

Nobody disagreed. All six corpses were soon dealt with – not perfectly, but at least respectfully.

When they did move off, Sidney reminded himself that he hadn't been convinced by Stephen's pessimistic views on the mayhem that might now await them. After all, just an hour previously, hadn't he been writing up more of Stephen's history of Britain in the middle of some of the most idyllic and most 'peaceful' scenery he'd ever seen? And that recent burst of violence must therefore have been some sort of aberration, and one that would certainly not be experienced again. Furthermore, in no way did it prove that the whole area they were entering had fallen into some sort of deadly disorder.

*

Nevertheless, when their journey for the day finally came to an end, he was more than a little relieved when Stephen insisted that they should find somewhere very secure for the night, and even more relieved when Hazeem then found such a place. It was a derelict stone farmhouse, just big enough to conceal a wagon, a mule and three weary travellers – one of whom declared that he wasn't too weary to talk further on the subject of Britain's history, and two of whom were plainly not too weary to listen. And so the fourth and final episode of Stephen's chronicle of Britain's downfall got underway…

'Right,' he kicked off. 'There's nothing like a history lesson to take your mind off a dose of bloodshed – and bloodshed, I should emphasise, that was completely unavoidable. The only way it wouldn't have happened was if those guys hadn't made it their business to try to shed *our* blood. So, well done, you two. And don't feel any guilt. Instead, just pin back your ears, and get ready for another thrilling instalment of British history.'

This was a good opener. Sidney and Hazeem were both nodding their appreciation for Stephen's well-chosen words, which he then followed up with an awful lot more.

'OK. Let's start by reminding ourselves of those four ingredients we Brits had gathered by the end of the twentieth century in order to cook up our demise. And I know I didn't refer to them in specific terms last night, but I'm sure you're well able to remember what they were – and to begin to work out how our imperial past, our acceptance of the concept of both human rights and the rights of refugees, together with our tasty Welfare State, were being combined to provide us with the sort of mix that would eventually lead to our undoing. As in it would kill us as a nation.'

Sidney couldn't help himself. He had to interrupt. 'Surely someone could have seen what was happening? I mean, there must have been loads of people shouting for something to be done – to stop what was going on.'

'Yes. There were plenty of people, Sidney. In fact, the majority of the country were shouting for something to be done. But what *could* be done? I mean, we couldn't erase our history, could we? We couldn't deny that we'd once had an empire. Which meant that we couldn't get rid of the hangover of empire. And, of course, one of the features of this hangover was all those people from the old empire wanting to come and live here. And more and more of them did want to come. Remember, things weren't getting any better in lots of those ex-colonial countries – and nor were their populations shrinking. In fact, quite the reverse. They were experiencing the sort of population growth they couldn't cope with – and that was encouraging more and more people to look to Britain as an ideal destination.'

'But, even so, there were those immigration controls,' suggested Sidney.

'Useless,' responded Stephen. 'People were still being let in for all sorts of so-called *legitimate* reasons, and we still had those human rights and the rights of refugees. And these rights, I might say, meant that immigration was turning into a nice little earner for a whole army of lawyers. So much so that representing the rights of immigrants – particularly the illegal ones – became a full-blown industry, and a giant one at that. Funded, incidentally, by all those suckers who'd rather have seen the flow stemmed, if not stopped entirely.'

'Why didn't the country, you know, just junk all this rights stuff?,' asked Hazeem, 'Why didn't they just leave those two conventions: the human rights one and the refugee one? I mean, what was to stop them?'

Stephen chuckled and smiled. 'If I knew the answer to that, I'd have myself a history that people might be prepared to pay for. But I don't. I can only think that those in charge of this country had tired of its indigenous population and wanted to replace it with another; a more deserving one. And withdrawing from either of those conventions wouldn't have helped them in their cause.'

This answer wasn't good enough for Sidney, and he made this known: 'You can't believe that.'

'Sidney,' responded Stephen. 'Don't forget we're at the end of the twentieth century. The Refugee Convention was from another time; it had been drafted almost half a century before – when the world had been a very different place. It was totally unfit for purpose, but nobody – here or anywhere else in the world – dared to question it. Or maybe they didn't want to. And maybe, in this country, there was a desire to see it do its very worst. And I can make as much sense of that as you can. Which is why I made that cynical observation about the worth of the indigenous natives and how we had maybe passed our time. It's as good an observation as any.'

'And the human rights stuff?' pushed Sidney.

'Same thing. It doesn't take a genius to realise that human rights are a chimera—'

'A what?' interjected Hazeem.

'An illusion; something that might be hoped for, but that will never be achieved. I mean, the only rights that have any meaning at all are *civil* rights. Because civil rights are those rights conferred on the citizens of a society *by* that society – that nation – and that nation not only has to believe in them but it also has to be prepared to police them. And these sorts of rights used to exist in this country. Right up until the concept of universal *human* rights came along and swept them all away. And that was bloody awful. Because human rights, remember, unlike civil rights, are inherent. One doesn't have to work to get them or to protect them – and they come with the very attractive feature of their having no matching responsibilities. Because they're *inherent,* aren't they? So, what you've done, in a place like Britain, which already had well-honed, *enforceable* civil rights, is replace them with nebulous *aspirations,* but not that nebulous that they can't be used to undermine a society that worked well with just its *civil* rights.

'And, I can tell you, there were lots of cases where, by employing human rights, some real toerags got the better of loads of people who were far more aware of all their responsibilities than they were of any of their rights.

'So, search me why we didn't junk this stuff as well. Unless, of course, there really was a plan to replace us – or maybe that mix of ingredients was already proving toxic?'

'And we couldn't do anything about the Welfare State?' queried Sidney.

'No. It couldn't possibly be dismantled. It had long ceased to work as intended: as a safety net for those on hard times. Now, it was more like a nicely plumped cushion – and being used as a cushion by a sizable proportion of the population. In fact, if you include the role of what was called the "National Health Service" in the welfare system, virtually everybody had now become dependent on the state, and the idea of going back to a pre-Welfare State was just about unthinkable.

I mean, apart from anything else, *expectation* was now a fundamental part of what people were, just as self-dependency and self-respect were quickly becoming endangered species. So, at that time, the Welfare State was a fixture that would remain a fixture for some time to come – before everything started to fall apart. And back then, that meant it continued to be a real attraction to all those souls overseas who were languishing in a country that didn't have similarly generous arrangements – and let's just say that it certainly wasn't putting people off from coming here.

'OK, so what does all this mean? Well, it means that those four ingredients of mine couldn't be taken back to the shop. We were stuck with them. And anyway, we were now about to mix them up properly and, in doing so, make something that was already pretty dangerous a hell of a lot worse. Yes, we got on with giving these ingredients a really good stir at the very beginning of the twenty-first century. And if the ingredients themselves weren't highly toxic, then the concoction we produced by blending them together certainly was. Because, in retrospect, this blended mix made us entirely crazy. In fact, from my reading of lots of stuff from that period, I think quite a few people thought our behaviour was crazy at the time, but they couldn't seem to do anything about it.'

'Will we think it was crazy?' asked Sidney.

'Almost certainly,' replied Stephen, 'because it was the behaviour of a mad man – as I will now explain. You see, whilst we'd already begun to question our self-worth as a nation – and our self-worth as individuals – we now took every step we could to actually *eradicate* both our national self-worth and our personal self-worth. All this along with the pride in our culture, the pride in our achievements, the pride in our values and, very importantly, the pride in our history – the history that, over centuries, had made us what we were. And we did all this by engaging in a veritable orgy of self-loathing, an orgy that was as totally destructive as it was completely unjustified.

'I can't tell you just how stupid this was and just how *diligent* we were in convincing ourselves how awful we were. But what I can tell you is that it was that wonderful empire we'd had that was now to be used as the engine of our self-abasement. After all, we were guilty, weren't we? Actually, guilty of doing no more than any other nation would have done, given the same opportunity. But that didn't matter. No more than our empire building was no worse and, in many ways, much better than all that raping and pillaging that has characterised human behaviour from the beginning of time. No, all that mattered was that we were guilty of the despicable crime of "having had an empire". And maybe it helped that, unlike any of those horrible beasts from the distant past, we – the beasts who had run an empire – were still around. And not just still around but also more than willing to take the flak for our intolerable behaviour. Flak, I might say, that was quite often provided by people who'd come to share in the rewards of this earlier, now indisputably egregious, conduct.

'And might I also say that this warped, caricatured view of our history, centred on violence and oppression, managed to push to the side – and then over the side – all our many achievements in stuff such as science, medicine, technology, the arts, sport and quite a few other areas of human endeavour – all of which meant that, in reality, we had far, far more to be proud of than ashamed of.'

'There was that… slavery stuff,' ventured Sidney.

Stephen indulged himself in an enormous grin. 'Oh yes. There was all that slavery stuff, wasn't there? In fact, a fundamental part of our orgy of self-hating was to equate the Empire with slavery. The two became almost interchangeable. But how much do you actually know about slavery, Sidney?'

'You mean *historical* slavery. Not—'

'Yes, I mean the historical stuff, not what you've endured yourself.'

'Well, not a lot. Other than we took a lot of slaves from Africa, and a lot of them were taken to the Caribbean.'

'Correct. There's no denying that and no way of defending it either. It was a disgusting practice. But here's the point: in this time of self-humiliation at the beginning of the twenty-first century, it became more and more an accepted fact that we had invented slavery – and we most certainly had not. Slavery is as old as human history. It's been going on around the planet forever – and of course, it still is. So when we arrived off the coast of Africa, it didn't take us too long to discover that the Africans had been enslaving other Africans – probably for countless centuries – and either using them themselves or flogging them off to the Arabs. And it didn't take the Africans too long to realise that they now had a new promising export market for their slaves, and one they needed to get on and exploit as soon as they could.

'Sidney, we simply plugged into an existing arrangement, in a time when abusing other people like this was seen as morally acceptable. Hell, just think about it. We didn't bring any of these African slaves back here, did we? And we didn't because, of course, we didn't need to – on account of the fact that, in our domestic society, we already had slaves: otherwise known as the domestic workforce. Remember, we were getting into that famous Industrial Revolution back then – on our way to becoming the workshop of the world – which might as well have been called the "sweatshop of the world". So, if, in this country, we were sending worthless oiks up chimneys or down mines, or we were shackling them to looms or various other bits of machinery that would guarantee them a miserable life and an early death, why the hell would we get all soft and cuddly when we were offered further cheap labour in faraway lands? Especially if they were being offered by willing sellers, and there was a desperate need for them in our new plantations in the Caribbean. It just wouldn't have made sense. No more than it made any sense 150 years ago to conflate this slavery stuff with our empire building. It was, of course, part of our empire story, but only a part – and although detestable, certainly not a major part.

'And two other points. No, three other points. One: we were the ones who brought the slave trade to an end. It involved a hero called William Wilberforce and a lot of effort after the event to enforce its abolition.

'Two: 150 years ago, slavery was still alive and well – in other parts of Africa and elsewhere. However, that didn't seem to matter to us or to the people who were cheering along our orgy of self-loathing. And it wouldn't, of course, have helped much in establishing us white people as the scourge of the earth.

'And three: I keep using the words "we" and "us", as though it were the same *we* and *us* who lived at the beginning of the twenty-first century as those who lived during our so-called "slaving past". But of course, it was a completely different set of *we* and *us*. So, even if you can't write off all that despicable behaviour from the past, why would you want to pin the blame for that behaviour on people who hadn't even been born then? Or, to put it another way, why would any rational being want to take responsibility for something done a very long time in the past by one bunch of people to another bunch of people, when he or she knew none of those who were either the perpetrators or the victims, and who, on top of that, could do sod all about whatever might have happened anyway? And what I mean is that slavery wasn't the fault of those misguided idiots at the beginning of the twenty-first century, and all the shame they were made to feel was just plain wrong, because it's quite simply impossible for anyone to inherit shame. And why this fact wasn't shouted from the rooftops back in that sackcloth age, I'll never understand.'

'Yeah, I see what you mean,' observed Hazeem.

And then after a thoughtful pause, he went on. 'I must say, Stephen, you do seem to know an awful lot about the beginning of the last century.'

'I do,' confirmed Stephen. 'It might even deserve its own book. I mean, it was probably the most critical time in our cooking up our downfall – and by that, of course, I mean the downfall of us whities.

'You see, the established thinking became: "whites are guilty of a terrible past and deserve only contempt; whereas black and brown people deserve all they desire – and should be granted all they desire." After all, they were the survivors of a history of oppression and exploitation. And what this meant in practice was that whites were now not just a real problem, but *the* problem, and so they should accept this and just get out of the way. Indeed, they could be helped to get out of the way if every institution and every bloody enterprise in the country embraced the two new gods that had been set up on the altar of our demise: the two new deities known as diversity and inclusion.'

'*What?*' This was Sidney making his incomprehension known, and this incomprehension called for an explanation by the master.

'All these institutions and companies began to introduce *targets* for the proportion of non-whites they employed. They knew that, if they didn't have a *diverse* workforce and one that displayed their *inclusive* credentials, they would be pilloried and, worse of all, be called out as *racist*.'

'But,' queried Sidney, 'if you have these targets for non-whites, then that must mean that some whites get a bad deal – as in "no job", for example. Which sounds sort of... well, racist.'

Stephen smiled broadly. 'Not in the upside-down thinking of that time. And do bear in mind that racism – against brown and black people – was, at that time, about the worse crime you could commit. It could get you into all sorts of trouble, and it could certainly lose you your business or your job, or ruin your career. But there was more...

'Not only was an indigenous view of this country now irredeemably seen as a racist view, but no aspect of life could be allowed to remain the province of just these indigenous saddos. So, *our* culture had to be made... well, let's call it common property – with, of course, as an absolute minimum, an *adequate* degree of participation by you know who. And, at the same time, television and radio – which I realise you might have trouble imagining – were being overtaken by... overrepresentation. I've read a lot about this, and it seems that diversity was such an imperative in the world of broadcasting, that brown people were hugely overrepresented in areas such as the news, and in adverts – which were bits of film they used to sell things, and from which most of the broadcasters made money; well, black people were all over them. So much so that it's reckoned that if a visitor from another planet came to Britain and watched its TV channels or listened to its radio channels, they'd soon conclude that white people were in a minority in this country. And, of course, this was well before they ended up that way. And I reckon the fact that they did must largely be the result of the whites in this country going completely crazy in this crazy period and somehow coming to the opinion that Britain was no longer their legitimate home. And taking account of their disgusting behaviour in the past, the best they could hope for was some sort of squatters' rights – as long, of course, as they kept well out of the way.'

'You're making this up,' interrupted Sidney.

'I wish I were,' countered Stephen, 'but I'm not. Hell, there was a public broadcaster then called the BBC, which was a pillar of our society and had been for years. And "BBC" originally stood for the "British Broadcasting Corporation", but not for long. It was soon referred to by those who hadn't bought into this crazy world as the "Black and Brown Corporation", and not without cause. I mean, this BBC wasn't just advocating unrestrained diversity – which meant more and more non-white faces and voices and as few white ones as it could manage – but it was also an enthusiastic convert to the idea that white people had to be *re-educated*.'

'Re-educated?' queried Hazeem.

'Yes. You see, at this stage in our glorious history, somebody – probably a third-rate academic at a third-rate university – had discovered that we whities had something called "unconscious bias". And this unconscious bias was essentially the theory that all of us have a natural tendency to form stereotyped ideas – and often, not very nice ideas – about people outside our social group. Which, in plain English, means that lots of people in the white tribe might not be overly comfortable with people in other tribes, especially if these people had different habits and values and held different beliefs. And this was clearly wrong, and they therefore had to be subjected to something called, not surprisingly, "unconscious bias training", in order to be shown the error of their ways.'

'You're joking,' interjected Hazeem.

'No, straight up. The BBC – and loads of other organisations – would insist that their staff were brainwashed – I'm sorry, I mean "trained" – to supress their normal reactions to what they might see as a threatening tribe, so they would willingly embrace the members of this new tribe, and so live happily ever after.

'Oh, and these ignorant whities would also be taught about something called "white privilege", which was the inherent advantages they possessed as white people – even though they were white people in a land that, whilst still predominantly white, was being overwhelmed by people who were not white.

'And we mustn't forget the idea being pushed at the time that a multicoloured society was far superior to that old monochrome variety, and that whities should therefore welcome with open arms all the diversity on offer and then some more. The more diversity the better – with, if possible, no cap. And if we could somehow achieve this, then we could build the perfect society in which there was no unconscious bias remaining and no chance that white privilege would raise its ugly head ever again. Plus, if you were one of those sad white types – who were in the cross hairs of this new enlightened thinking – then you should just remember that you were *the* problem, and the sooner you stepped aside the better.'

'You are joking,' Hazeem insisted.

'I really wish I were, but I'm not. It was all part of an incredible self-flagellation by the indigenous population of this country at the outset of the twenty-first century, which also saw institutions "decolonising" themselves. That is to say, getting rid of any connection with our old empire in any way they could, and for no good reason. Then there were other institutions bending over backwards to practice "positive discrimination", which I know I've touched on before in talking about targets, but that ended up with even revered institutions, such as my beloved RAF, announcing that a specified – and large – proportion of its intake had to be from ethnic minorities.

'And let's not forget the opprobrium that was heaped on anybody at the time who tried to point out that this was all a load of self-destructive nonsense. Had such views been expressed several centuries before, they would have been burning these folk at the stake every week. Lots of them. But in these more modern times, they just condemned them, ignored them or sometimes charged them with a hate crime.'

'So,' asked Sidney, 'what happened next?'

'Well, with our indigenous society having been successfully emasculated—'

'What?' queried Hazeem.

'It'd had its balls cut off, Hazeem.'

'Ah, right.'

'Yes, well, with our society having been well and truly emasculated, and with its government having been impregnated with a generous helping of diversity, our defences were down, and the door was open to more and more diversity.

'You probably know most of this, but illegal immigration soon started to outpace legal immigration – and in a big way. What had started off as a stream of people coming here across the English Channel in small boats soon became, with the help of those friendly Russians, a much bigger stream. Hundreds and sometimes thousands of migrants were arriving on the east coast every day. Then, of course, when the earth began to really warm up and things began to fall apart all around the world, somebody had the bright idea of using not just small boats or dinghies to get here, but big boats. And I mean really big boats – as in, ships – lots of which were parked off the coast of India, Pakistan and Bangladesh, waiting there to be broken up but still seaworthy – just. So why not load these vessels with… well, tens of thousands of poor souls, and sail them off to Europe. Or even better, to Britain – where they spoke English, where there was a nice welfare system and already lots of people from the subcontinent – many of them in positions of power – and where the residual indigenous population was so supine that it wouldn't even ask you to wipe your boots when you stepped ashore. And that was it. We were stuffed.'

Sidney looked dismayed. He half-knew what had happened in his country in the last century, but never before had it been laid out in such stark terms.

And it was while he was digesting what Stephen had just told him that Hazeem asked Stephen a question. 'Why was it just… us… and all those Indians? What happened to people from the Middle East and Africa?'

'Purely numbers,' responded Stephen. 'Tens of millions of people all over Africa and a good chunk of Asia were desperate to leave their homes. After all, with what was happening with climate change – and other things – they couldn't survive there any more. However, in the subcontinent, there were *hundreds* of millions in this situation, and they had the will and the means – and the numbers – to overwhelm the mere tens of millions and so colonise not just this country but most of Europe. And in that process, they would see off any other folk who might want to come here – and even those who were already here; all those guys from Africa and other parts of Asia who were soon *encouraged* to leave. Then, of course, the subcontinent crowd became more and more entrenched, and more and more able to hold what they'd taken – particularly when they'd set about *organising* the rump population of whites, those unfortunate natives who hadn't left for another country and had been dwindling away by giving up on the habit of breeding.'

'You're talking about how we took their homes, and moved them onto reservations—'

'...and then took the reservations,' finished Stephen. 'Yes. So, we eventually ended up as either a tiny residue of chattels such as Sidney or maybe as hermits like m'self.'

'Wow!' observed Hazeem. 'I'm surprised you haven't shot me.'

Stephen laughed loudly, and there was a smile on his face when he then acknowledged Hazeem's declaration.

'Hazeem, you may have forgotten, but I've already told you that I like you and that I admire you, and I'm hardly going to shoot you – certainly not after what you and Sidney have done for me. And furthermore, I know I've also told you that you and all the millions of your fellow Asians are not responsible for what has happened to this country. That was down to us white folk – and particularly those of us who lived at the beginning of the twenty-first century. If they'd started off the century with just a fraction of the confidence their forebears had displayed when they built that odious empire, and if they hadn't indulged in such an extended period of self-loathing, matched only by their desire to abandon common sense, then maybe it would have been different. Unlikely, I know, given the huge numbers of people with this country in their sights. But they might at least have had a say in how the country would be shared.

'Anyway, what I'm trying to say – and I know I've said this before – is that our downfall as the white tenants of this country was more a self-inflicted act than it was an unforgivable act on the part of your lot. In their situation – in India or Pakistan – I would have done just the same. I'd have got on a ship and got myself to England to give myself – and my family – a chance to survive. In fact, what you, me and Sidney are doing now isn't really any different. We're just giving ourselves a chance to survive – even if, for one of us, that might not mean surviving for too long.'

The smile on Stephen's face had now weakened, and Sidney recognised this – as did Hazeem, it appeared. Indeed, it was Hazeem who began to apologise to Stephen for not realising that he'd spoken for such a long time this evening and who then told him that he must now not speak any more, but instead get himself to bed.

This Stephen did, without any further encouragement. And soon he – and Sidney and Hazeem – had all retired for the night, both of his pupils a lot wiser than they had been when they'd first awoken, and with at least one of them not entirely sure how to deal with his new-found wisdom. If, indeed, discovering how your forebears had gone about undermining your life before your life had even begun could ever be regarded as anything to do with wisdom.

26.

Yesterday, Stephen had expressed his concern that, although they were now moving through a barely populated area, there might well be real danger about. The probable desperate circumstances of the locals might lead to them taking equally desperate measures – such as attacking anything that came within attacking range. And today, he would be proved right – albeit not until Kaalki had hauled the wagon and its occupants over the old border into Scotland.

It wasn't immediately apparent to anyone on the wagon that they'd entered the domain of this former northern nation. Whatever signs had once existed to announce the demarcation between it and its southern neighbour had long since disappeared, and it was only Sidney's scrutiny of his battered A–Z that allowed all three of them to indulge in a brief celebration of their 'foreign situation' and what this meant in terms of their long journey north: that they were now reaching its end. And the celebration was necessarily brief because it was brought to an early conclusion by the arrival of three bearded 'gentlemen' who had appeared out of nowhere and who were clearly intent on greeting the newcomers to this land with a selection of bladed weapons.

They were quick. One of them was nearly within striking distance of Hazeem before he was shot in the chest by his intended victim, and another was so close to Sidney when Sidney discovered his pistol had jammed, that Sidney had barely a second to unstrap his knife from his leg and even less time to decide where to plant it in his assailant for the optimum effect. In the event, almost as a reflex action, he didn't so much plant it as bury it in the left temple of the gentleman's head. The result was messy but immediate, and Sidney even registered the fact that the poor bloke had expired before Hazeem let loose a second shot that ensured all three attackers were now on their way to oblivion.

Then Sidney registered two other facts in quick succession. The first was that his knife had saved him for a second time, and if he ever got the chance, he would thank Ted profusely for his insistence that Sidney arm himself with such a device. Knives, he now realised, never jammed, and without this one, he would be dead.

The other fact, which soon overtook its predecessor, was that killing people was becoming too much a habit – and too much matter-of-fact. Something that only a fortnight ago would have left him devastated had now become just the forerunner of dealing with the dead, of the chore of disposing, as respectfully as possible, of people who were recently alive. This wasn't good. He wasn't just becoming desensitised to killing – and death – but he was also becoming somebody else. And he didn't much like it. As much as he admired Stephen and Hazeem and their ability to regard the elimination of human life as a pragmatic act of self-preservation, he hoped he wasn't following them down the same path. He knew he was being a hypocrite, and that he wouldn't be alive if it weren't for their pragmatic behaviour, but he still wanted to be someone he recognised as himself; the someone he'd been before he'd set out on this terrible road trip, the someone who was sickened by killing – even the killing of a couple of intruders from the north whom he'd never had the chance to meet whilst still alive.

With that final musing about what now seemed like ancient history – the murder of Hazeem's original companions – Sidney returned his thoughts to the present, and the needs of the present. There were three bodies to deal with, to say nothing of checking on Stephen. And then there was the small matter of getting quite a few more miles under their collective belts as soon as possible, together with committing to paper the final episode of Stephen's history of Britain. Feeling upset about his transition from a timorous beastie to a sometimes brutal beast would just have to wait.

*

It was done, at least as well as it could be done. The three men had been stowed out of sight in the shelter of a stand of dark conifers (of which there were many hereabouts), and Hazeem had said a few words over their bodies – words that recognised they weren't necessarily bad men, but just unfortunate men; unfortunate to be the victims of very hard times, and unfortunate to have chosen the wrong route out of their misfortune – one that involved a combination of more firepower and more determination than they'd expected.

Stephen hadn't attended this committal. He'd been told to stay resting on the wagon. Even though he appeared more chipper than ever, he was now going to get all the cosseting he could manage and then some more. Sidney and Hazeem had been insistent about this. Just as they were insistent that he did absolutely nothing when Kaalki was brought to a stop for their midday break. Their faithful mule had now pulled them a good way along the old M74 (without their encountering any further greetings from the locals), and it was time for Hazeem to sort out some victuals, for Stephen to give his body a rest from the constant bumping, and for Sidney to embark on some serious scribing. After all, Stephen's lecture last night had been a long one, and there were a good many words to be squeezed onto the pages of his books before they set off once again.

*

This they finally did, but not before Stephen had summoned his two friends to come to his side so as to receive some very important information. It was a summons that sounded urgent, as though it might be the last summons Stephen could muster before he succumbed to either his wound or his ills. He did look a lot less chipper than he had just three hours before.

Nevertheless, his voice was still strong, and he used it to impart some vital information to his two companions: 'I'm stupid – really friggin' stupid. I mean, what if I'd been killed? What if that bullet had landed in my head and not in my stomach? And... well, what if I peg out at any moment?'

'You're not going to peg out at any moment,' replied Hazeem, 'and whatever you've got to tell us, well, you've got all the time in the world.'

Stephen smiled, and he was still smiling as he responded to Hazeem's reassurance. 'Thanks, Hazeem. If only you were right. If only I did have all that time. But just for the moment, let's assume that I don't, that I really might be on the edge of you know what. In which case, you wouldn't be bidding me a fond farewell if I hadn't got round to telling you where "just outside Lockerbie" you're supposed to be going.'

Sidney's eyes widened, and then he noticed that Hazeem looked similarly aghast. And why wouldn't both of them feel shocked – and stupid? After days on the road, it had occurred to neither of them to ask Stephen where their journey was to end, where 'just outside Lockerbie' Dorothy had designated as their terminus 'where somebody would collect them'. And here they were – with the only member of their team in possession of that information in what might best be described as a fragile state – still not knowing where they were supposed to end their arduous journey north. 'Just outside Lockerbie' could be any number of locations, and finding the right one by chance would probably be impossible. Needless to say, this realisation made them listen carefully to what Stephen was about to reveal.

'OK, I seem to have your attention,' Stephen continued. 'And just in case I'm a few breaths away from my last, I'll tell you now… it's a place called Samye Ling, which is just outside a tiny place called Eskdalemuir. That's where we've got to go.'

'Sammy what?' queried Hazeem. 'That doesn't sound… you know, very Scottish.'

'That's because it isn't. After all, it's a… sorry, I mean, it *was* a Tibetan Buddhist monastery. One of the biggest in what used to be called the Western world.'

'You're having us on. You're having a go at us for not having asked you where we were going. And now you're just having a joke. I mean, I was once told about this Buddhist stuff, and I'm bloody certain they were never here. Not in Britain.'

'They weren't – at least not in any numbers. But when our Chinese cousins elbowed themselves into Tibet more than two hundred years ago, some Buddhists had to make themselves scarce. And a few of them landed up in Scotland, and then they set about building what would become one of the biggest Tibetan Buddhist monasteries outside Tibet – one with a full-blown Buddhist temple at its core. It was a very famous place. Although, I suspect, its fame wasn't universally known. After all, Buddhists weren't known for shouting their achievements – or their beliefs – from the rooftops.'

'Wow!' offered Sidney. 'Who'd have thought? I mean, who'd have thought—'

'...that an abandoned monastery in the middle of nowhere would provide the perfect place for a covert pick-up?' finished Stephen. 'Or, of course, it might be a great deal more than that. I mean, for all I know, it's no longer abandoned, and it's now where Dorothy and her group are holed up. After all, if it was a good enough place for some exiled Tibetans to set up home, it might be an equally good place for some exiled whities to do the same.'

'It's in the middle of nowhere, then?' asked a now entranced-looking Sidney. 'Somewhere well off the beaten track?'

'Well, about as far off the beaten track as you can get in this crowded isle,' responded Stephen. 'Although, if you look in that ancient A–Z of yours, I think you'll find it marked. It should be shown in little red letters, just north of that village I mentioned: Eskdalemuir. And as your A–Z will also show you, you get to it by taking a road that runs north-east out of Lockerbie, and then by turning left when you get to Eskdalemuir. Then I doubt you'll be able to miss it.'

'Wow!' exclaimed Sidney for a second time. 'I can't

believe we have such a... well, such an exotic destination – and one that's not that far away. I mean, all being well, we should get there tomorrow.'

'I can't believe we never asked where we were going,' mused Hazeem. And then, theatrically ignoring Stephen to look directly at Sidney, and with a big grin on his face, he added to this statement: 'I know we've got the company of one helluva indestructible bastard, but just imagine what a mess we'd be in if, against all the odds, he did get destructed. And what fools we'd both feel. Talk about a pair of idiots!'

'Well,' assured a suitably amused Stephen, 'you've had plenty more on your minds to think about, so don't be too harsh on yourselves. And, anyway, you do know where you're going now. And if you do want to get there tomorrow, I suggest we conclude this brief revelation session and ask our kind friend at the front of that there wagon to pull us a bit further north. I promise not to tell him that two of his friends were so dim they didn't even think to find out where they were leading him.'

That observation by Stephen caused a round of laughter and, within only a couple of minutes, Kaalki was back on what was left of the M74 and heading further north. And Sidney was dreaming up a number of questions about Buddhism, in readiness – along with those he already had on the newly revealed history of Britain – to be posed to Stephen when they stopped for the night.

*

They did this in a nondescript part of the countryside just south of Lockerbie, which had one very desirable feature: a mostly-still-complete stone sheepfold. It would provide a little bit of cover for the wagon and at least a little defence for the three travellers and their mule if more of the natives detected and then objected to their presence.

It wasn't too long before these travellers and their mule had been fed and watered within the sheepfold, and Sidney was preparing to put some of those questions he'd formulated to a very-contented-looking Stephen. (So contented-looking, Sidney thought, because he knew that his precious history was now in the care of another.)

However, it seemed that Hazeem had a bundle of questions of his own, and it was Hazeem who got to play question-master first. And the subject of his quiz was exclusively the re-formation of Britain and, in particular, certain specific aspects of it that he either didn't understand or that he simply wanted to know more about. Sidney was happy to let Hazeem take the lead in this way, not least because he believed Hazeem's questions on Britain might reflect a slightly different perspective to his own, and this could only be good. He thought it would almost certainly mean the revelation of further insights into the past that he might otherwise have missed. And it did.

Through listening to Stephen's answers to a whole series of Hazeem's questions, Sidney learnt a lot more about how the 'exaggeration' of the black population in Britain in the early twenty-first century was inevitably exploited to its disadvantage; how that population was ultimately removed in its entirety; how the reality and perception of most aspects of the changing racial mix in the country were kept well apart – this time to the disadvantage of the white population; how the political control of the country slipped so easily out of white hands; and how the gang of southerners eventually took over the whole country, albeit only for three short years. And these, of course, were the three years that led up to the partition, when the southerners were forced to acknowledge that the northerners were already the *de facto* 'owners' of the northern half of the country. That, mirroring what had happened on the subcontinent many years before, Britain would be sliced in two, with a new border running through what had once been Birmingham, keeping the two South-Asian tribes apart for all time – or at least until everything began to fall down around their ears.

Sidney found all this stuff quite fascinating, and when Hazeem seemed to have exhausted his store of questions, Sidney could well have asked some more – all concerning British history. However, he was conscious of the evening getting late and of the limits of Stephen's stamina. His wounded friend would soon need to sleep. So when he assumed the role of quizmaster himself, he immediately switched the subject to Buddhism and he started off with a question about the nature of Buddhism – assuming, without thinking about it much, that Stephen would know the answer. After all, he knew so much about so many things.

'Stephen,' he asked, 'this Buddhism stuff. I have read about it, and from what I've read, it wasn't much like Islam or Hinduism – or Christianity. And I've never been able to pin down quite what set it apart. And I was wondering whether you knew.'

'Well, I'm no expert on religions, but from what I remember, Buddhism was just a little less... well, less forceful than those other religions, and it was also a lot less sure of itself. And what I mean by that is it didn't have the certainty of the other brands. None of this "We are right, and you are wrong." It was more... well, "Everything we believe in might be bollocks, but if you live your life as a Buddhist, you won't be doing anybody or anything any harm." And that's quite a selling point – even if the beliefs *are* all bollocks. And may I just stress that I'm not an expert on any religion, and any Buddhist worth his salt would probably inform me in no uncertain terms that I am simply talking through my arse.

'However, I do know that a central principle of Buddhist ethics is that you shouldn't create suffering, and you should seek to reduce suffering wherever you can – which translates into not doing any harm. And that's all to do with what I think they called the "four noble truths", the first of which is that life is suffering. And then I think the second is that suffering is due to desire, and the third is that the *cure* is letting go – of all sorts of desires. And I can't quite remember what the fourth is.'

'I can go along with that first one,' declared Hazeem. 'Life *is* bloody suffering. But I'm not so sure I buy into the desire thing. That sounds a lot less credible.'

'Erm, I suspect you might not buy into their ideas on reincarnation either...' Stephen suggested.

'*Reincarnation?*'

'Yes, Buddhists believe that, when you die, you'll be born again as something different, and what you're born as depends on your actions in your previous life.'

'You mean—'

'Yes, I'll probably be reborn as a rat, and you, Hazeem, might be due for a swap with Kaalki. I mean, I think he's well overdue for a promotion, whereas you and me... well, I'm not so sure we are – if you get my drift?'

Hazeem did get his drift. So too did Sidney – as evidenced by both of them becoming convulsed with laughter. And only when the laughter had subsided did Stephen offer an open apology to all the remaining Buddhists in the world for misrepresenting their beliefs so badly and for seeking to use their beliefs to entertain his companions. And he was serious. Sidney could see that he clearly thought Buddhism had a great deal more to offer than any of the world's dominant cults, and that it was deserving of the ultimate respect. This he underlined by telling his two friends that, if they discovered tomorrow that Dorothy and her friends weren't just occupying whatever remained of the Buddhist monastery but were themselves Buddhists, he would be delighted beyond words. Furthermore, he would join up there and then – even if it meant accepting that his next life would be as one of those rats back on that giant spoil-heap at RAF Cosford.

He went on to concede that Dorothy had never indicated that she was a Buddhist, and he also conceded that finding any living Buddhists – anywhere on this unhappy island off the coast of Europe – was next to inconceivable.

However, from what he'd just said, even with these concessions, Sidney formed the impression that Stephen was now not just content but also optimistic. That he hadn't in any way 'let go' now that his legacy was in the hands of someone he trusted, but that he was really looking forward to a new life – for however long – with not just rats and intruders for company, but with people like… well, like the people he remembered from his youth; his people, people who shared his heritage and his views.

So, when Sidney retired for the night – enfolded by a broken ring of stones – he hoped against hope that Stephen's wound would remain quiescent until it could be dealt with by Dorothy's group, and that his illness – whatever it was – would bide its time indefinitely.

His next life – whatever he returned as – would just have to wait.

27.

Before setting off in the morning, Sidney – having referred to his battered A–Z – had expressed the concern that their route to the Samye Ling monastery would lead them through the centre of Lockerbie, and that this might not be the best route to take. 'Might it not be better,' he suggested, 'to give any settlement of any size a wide berth? Surely we can find another way to get to where we're going?'

Stephen admitted that they might be running a risk by taking a direct route through the town, but he maintained that, if Lockerbie were anything like most other settlements in modern Britain, it would have few, if any, residents, and furthermore, whichever route they took would involve some risks. Hazeem then backed up Stephen's views by pointing out that, from his perusal of that A–Z, the local countryside didn't appear to be endowed with too many roads or tracks, so giving Lockerbie a wide berth might prove to be completely impractical, and it might even mean they wouldn't reach their destination by nightfall.

So that was it. Sidney gave in gracefully – and with the assurance that the wagon would roll into Lockerbie in 'combative mode'. He and Hazeem would have their pistols on display, and Stephen, in the back of the wagon, would brandish his rifle as best he could. Such an approach, they all agreed, would dissuade any of the local residents from hindering their progress.

Nevertheless, when Lockerbie came into view just thirty minutes later, Sidney began to feel nervous and to think that the decision they'd made might not be just risky but also reckless. Who was to say that the residents of this town didn't have their own guns – and a willingness to use them?

The closer they got to the town, the more apprehensive Sidney became. Right up until Hazeem observed that there didn't seem to be much of the town left, and he wouldn't be too surprised if, as Stephen had predicted, there were about as many people living in Lockerbie as they'd seen on their approach to Lockerbie – which was none. Lockerbie, he proposed, might be a virtual ghost town. And ghosts, he declared with a wry smile, rarely if ever discharge firearms.

As Kaalki then pulled the wagon into Lockerbie proper, it became only too apparent that what had once been a town was now little more than an ancient ruin, and that all of Lockerbie's former residents had probably abandoned this Scottish settlement long ago – albeit it looked as though they'd taken much of it with them when they'd left. Many of the (once) pink stone houses had no roofs, and quite a few of them had barely any stones. No doubt various bits of Lockerbie had ended up as parts of simpler dwellings in the surrounding countryside, anywhere where some sort of living could be scratched from the near-barren land. So, all that was left of a once-stone-solid community was a collection of torn and tattered buildings, now green with algae and moss – and home to not a single person. Lockerbie had essentially died.

Sidney was relieved but sad. And he was just about to put these thoughts into words, when Stephen made an announcement from the back of the wagon. It concerned the history of the town.

'This place was famous once,' he announced, 'but not for a good reason.'

'Sorry?' questioned Sidney.

'It was back towards the end of the twentieth century. A big aeroplane – and I mean a *really* big aeroplane – landed on it. And when I say landed, I mean it fell out of the sky and was completely obliterated – along with the lives of two or three hundred people. I think it happened just before Christmas.'

'Do they know why?' asked Sidney. 'You know, why it crashed.'

'Yes. It was blown up. In flight. Somebody had put some explosives aboard it, and these explosives were detonated as it flew over this part of Scotland.'

'Why?' interjected Hazeem. 'Why would anyone want to do that?'

Stephen sighed, and then answered Hazeem's question as best he could. 'Because one lot of people thought that the world would be a better place if they killed another lot of people. Which wasn't exactly a new idea back then, just one that you could organise pretty easily. Particularly when innocent people were flying through the air in metal tubes, and other people with the required twisted motives could convince themselves they were doing the work of God, or some other such bloody nonsense. Never for a moment questioning whether they might themselves be somewhat misguided or, more likely, just plain fucking evil.'

'I don't understand,' pushed Hazeem.

'Probably because it isn't comprehensible,' countered Stephen. 'And I'm bloody sure I never understood it. But I do know it happened – just here. Although looking at the place right now, I doubt you'd notice any damage if ten planes came crashing down. There's just so little left to destroy.'

And on that rather bleak observation, Stephen now 'rested his eyes', and the wagon rolled on through the abandoned Lockerbie without any further conversation – and without any fear of an armed confrontation. This place really was completely empty. Probably even of ghosts.

At the end of the remains of the town, there was a turn to the right that promised to be the road that would lead to Eskdalemuir and the monastery beyond.

Hazeem directed Kaalki to take it, and soon he and Sidney discovered that what had once been a narrow road leading north-east was now a narrow, uneven track leading north-east. Furthermore, within a couple of miles, this track came to an end where its route took it across a bridge. This was because the bridge was no longer a bridge, but just a ribbon of rubble across the bed of a not inconsiderable river.

This was a new experience for the migrants from the south. Whatever hurdles they'd had to overcome this far, they hadn't included torrents of water. It was one of the benefits of having kept to decaying motorways. Nevertheless, it was a hurdle they now had to confront – and deal with.

This meant that, with Stephen's encouragement, both Sidney and Hazeem were soon in the flood, leading a very wary Kaalki to its far bank over that ribbon of rubble. A lesser mule, Sidney decided, wouldn't have let himself be led in this way. And a lesser mule, when this audacious escapade had been successfully completed, wouldn't have given the impression that he pulled wagons across rivers every day of his life. He looked so completely at ease and almost bored that Sidney was obliged to announce to his friends that they were fortunate enough to have with them the best mule in the world. Full stop. And Hazeem and Stephen could only agree.

On the other side of the river, the track was more like the road it had once been, and it wasn't too long before Kaalki was pulling the wagon into the remnants of the tiny hamlet of Boreland. It was just like Lockerbie, only much smaller and even more desolate. It made Sidney begin to wonder where all the people who used to live in this area were now living – whether it was somewhere in the surrounding hills or on an embankment of a motorway far to the south. They'd seen nobody anywhere, which did tend to point to a mass emigration, and to the land around here having been entirely abandoned. In fact, Hazeem proffered such a view himself. The road had been climbing since they'd left Lockerbie, and the elevated area they'd now entered looked very unforgiving and very unwilling to provide much of a living to anyone.

As Hazeem remarked, it looked a lot like grade-A starvation territory to him, and he would have been out of here just as soon as he could.

It was the same when they arrived in Eskdalemuir, a small cluster of more domestic ruins and a still-intact but sad-looking chapel, which had probably looked just as sad the day it was built. It seemed, Sidney thought, to reflect so well the desolate nature of the whole of this upland patch of Scotland.

'Well, we're nearly there,' announced Hazeem. 'According to the map, this Samye Ling place should be just down the road. No more than a mile away, I reckon. So, I think we should have a bite to eat here and then press on. I mean, no point in putting off our date with paradise…'

'Paradise!' exclaimed Sidney. 'You don't know what we'll find. And you certainly shouldn't—'

'Let him indulge himself,' interrupted a hearty-sounding Stephen. 'We've come this far, and I reckon we're now close enough to envisage whatever we want. So what's wrong with envisaging paradise? It can't do any harm.'

Sidney conceded defeat and joined in Hazeem's optimistic anticipation of what would soon be revealed. He even managed to sustain this optimism as the wagon resumed its progress towards the monastery and when what could only be the monastery came into sight. Not that there was much of a monastery to see. It was more a stand of various ancient trees – within the first rank of which was something monumental – and white.

Hazeem directed Kaalki off the road to a clear area at the approach to the trees, and brought the wagon to a halt. Soon, he and Sidney had dismounted, and while Sidney peered through the trees in an attempt to identify the nature of the white construction, Hazeem went to the back of the wagon to attend to Stephen and to help him to the ground. However Stephen might be feeling at the moment, both his companions knew he would want to accompany them on their exploration of the monastery. He'd also, of course, want to participate in their much-awaited rendezvous with either Dorothy or, more likely, with whoever from her group had been stationed here to greet them.

Sidney was still looking towards the trees when he heard Hazeem gasp – and then wail. It was a sound he'd never heard anybody make before, and it caused him to turn his gaze to the wagon – where he straightaway caught sight of Hazeem kneeling on its rear, crying. He knew instantly what had happened, and why it had happened – now. After all, Stephen had not only seen his history delivered into safe hands, but he had also just seen his friends delivered safely to their destination, and he no longer needed to 'hang on'. He could leave behind his pain and he could leave behind the prospect of further pain to come. And, as he would have pointed out himself, 'Old people die – and I'm older than most.' Maybe Sidney should have expected him to go.

Sidney wasn't used to comforting people. However, after checking that Stephen really was dead, he did his best with Hazeem. And, at the same time, Hazeem tried to comfort him, but it wasn't going to work. Even though Hazeem revealed that, only yesterday, Stephen had confided in him that he hoped the bullet inside him would soon act as a rough and ready form of euthanasia. Such was his fear of suffering a horrible, lingering death from the illness he'd been hosting.

Yet despite that hope being realised, it would take some time for both of those who remained alive to come to terms with what had happened, and even now, they knew that whatever the future held in store, it would forever grieve them that Stephen had lost his life at such a critical point in their own lives.

For nearly thirty minutes, they just sat with their fallen friend. They spoke little other than to recognise how suddenly life could be snatched away and replaced by death, and how cruel this theft could be; cruel enough, it seemed, to cause those who were left behind to lose the will to do anything at all. Which, in Sidney and Hazeem's case, meant their doing nothing that would cause them to abandon Stephen's body. Not for a second.

But inevitably, one of them – and it was Hazeem – gave voice to the fact that Stephen would hardly have wanted them to keep him company indefinitely, and not, instead, seek whatever reception awaited them. Probably somewhere beyond those trees. So, having covered up Stephen's body and having left strict instructions with Kaalki that he now had to undertake the start of a vigil for their lost friend, they began to make their way towards the trees and, in particular, towards that white structure within them.

*

When they reached it, they discovered it was a huge bell-shaped building, still mostly intact and with the remains of a covered walkway at its rear. This, thought Sidney, must, in times long past, have had a connection with the building itself. However, neither he nor Hazeem could hazard a guess at what this connection might have been. And after they'd examined the inside of the building – which was empty – nor could they imagine what purpose both structures might have served. Nevertheless, the very peculiarity of the 'bell' and its obvious foreignness confirmed in their minds that they had indeed arrived at the designated Buddhist monastery and that they should therefore continue their exploration in the hope of locating more of it and maybe, within it, a friendly reception committee.

This they did by heading deeper into the stand of trees and thereby discovering first a toppled sculpture, which served to cement their belief that they were in the right place. After all, where else but in a Buddhist monastery would one encounter the still recognisable shape of a seated figure with, towering above it, a giant snake's head? And despite that snake – and despite the ravages of time – the expression on the seated figure's face was still discernible as one of obvious serenity.

Discernible also, just a little further on, was what once must have been a large greenhouse, one now in pieces and surrounded by brambles, bushes and ranks of some sort of willowherb.

'Maybe,' Sidney suggested to Hazeem, 'this is where the monks once grew some food.'

It was a suggestion that would never be confirmed, but that a nearby river had furnished the monks with their water was beyond doubt.

'And this river must mean,' announced Hazeem, 'that the main part of the monastery has to be close. Maybe just through those trees over there.'

It was. As they passed through those trees, Sidney and Hazeem began to make out the shape of a large, brick-built building with the remains of a strange ornate porch at its front. On passing through these remains, they entered the building proper and discovered it was just a shell, but a shell that formed one side of a giant quadrangle. And facing them across the quadrangle and constituting its opposite side was what had no doubt once been the monastery's central feature: its Buddhist temple.

This was still standing, although much of it looked as though it has been scavenged, and whatever windows it once had were now just holes in its walls – to match the holes in the walls of the two flanking buildings. It must, thought Sidney, have been an astonishing sight when it was pristine, and even though it was now no more than a relic of those better times, he was keen to explore its interior. So too was Hazeem, and without a pause they both made their way across the littered floor of the quadrangle, then up a broad set of littered stairs and then into the temple.

Sidney had expected to find some evidence of its former life, some shreds of what the temple had once been used for, or maybe there'd be just a remnant of its original decoration. But all that he and Hazeem found was another shell, its roof half gone and whatever had once adorned its interior now not even a memory. It was as demoralising as it was ugly. And its loss – the loss of its purpose and its very identity – prompted him to return to the loss of their precious companion, and he suddenly felt more desolate than he'd ever felt before.

He had to get out of this corpse of a temple – and quickly. And it seemed that Hazeem had the same thought. The two of them arrived at the threshold of the edifice together, and in that way, they both became aware of the other occupants of the quadrangle at exactly the same time. There were four of them: four heavily bearded men in traditional northerner clothing, and all of them were carrying a gun. Two of these guns were aimed at Hazeem and two of them at Sidney.

This wasn't the reception Sidney had hoped for.

28.

As he watched all four gunmen approach, Sidney suddenly recalled a dream he'd had just the previous night. It was a dream in which there'd been… well, gunmen.

There hadn't been four of them, but maybe a dozen – and they were all northerners. They'd ambushed him and his two friends as they'd entered some ruins. Stephen and Hazeem had been shot and killed almost immediately, but Sidney had evaded their bullets and, in the way that only happens in dreams, he'd then found himself not in the ruins any more, but at the side of a fast-flowing river. Looking across it, he'd then caught sight of his mother and father. What happened after that, he couldn't remember. But he now began to think that he'd maybe had a somewhat inaccurate premonition of what had been in store for him today, and that, far from finding a sanctuary in Scotland, he and Hazeem had found themselves a pile of trouble. It seemed they were in a terrible predicament that could only get worse.

It wouldn't take too long for his fears to be confirmed or otherwise. One of the four northerners had now climbed the steps of the temple and was no more than six feet away from where he and Hazeem were standing, both of them with their pistols still stowed in their belts.

Then this northerner addressed Sidney – in English and with an unmistakably English accent. 'Sorry,' he said, as he lowered his gun, 'but I needed to get a proper look at you. And now I have… well, I assume, you must be Sidney, and you…' and here he turned to face Hazeem, '…you must be Hazeem.'

Not for the first time, Sidney's mouth adopted its open condition. He just couldn't help himself, but he did at least catch the northerner's next words – which were: 'Well, my name's Peter, and before I introduce you to my fellow bushwhackers, may I just say that we're all really sorry about Stephen.' Here, he hesitated for just a second before going on. 'I mean, that is Stephen in the wagon, isn't it? And, of course, we're so very sorry he didn't make it.'

Sidney's mouth was still open and not of much use, and it was therefore left to Hazeem to respond to Peter's condolences. 'Yes, we thought he'd make it. I mean, he was still alive only an hour or so ago, but… well, a bullet… it did for him. And he wasn't a very well man to start with…'

Here, Hazeem's response tailed off. It was clearly not only Sidney who was having trouble coming to terms with their new situation and the future this situation promised – a future that for both of them, possibly in very different ways, might be nothing like they'd ever experienced before.

Peter seemed to recognise that he was dealing with two people who needed time to adjust to their new reality, and after offering more condolences, he then introduced them to his three fellow bushwhackers, explaining as he did so that all four of them were, in fact, 'rangers', four of the 'community's' men who sometimes had to venture out from the 'community' – just as now. They were therefore required to grow large beards, which with the help of the right clothes and some suitable staining of the face, would allow them to pass themselves off as real northerners. Enough anyway, not to attract too much attention.

Sidney, who was now just about back in the real world, was more than impressed. Their face-staining was excellent; it was far better than his own amateurish efforts. And their beards were just as they should be, and so very convincing. It would take a very observant true northerner to spot that these guys were fakes, that they were non-northerners (and non-southerners, for that matter), who were normally to be found only within the confines of some 'community', the whereabouts and nature of which Sidney suspected might soon be revealed. After all, Peter had now announced that it was time to return to collect the wagon – and its patient mule – and to make a start on their journey 'home'. And it wasn't a good idea, he added, to linger around here any longer than one had to. That would be to invite all sorts of trouble.

There were no dissenters from this view, and it wasn't long before Peter and his fellow rangers had led Sidney and Hazeem back to their wagon, where Kaalki was clearly having his own coming-to-terms episode, evident in his wide-eyed look and his constantly shuffling feet, and brought about, no doubt, by the presence of five other mules. They were there with a fifth ranger, and their appearance must have filled Kaalki with a mix of astonishment and pleasure. There were other beasts just like him! And they were here with him now! *And just what might this mean?*

Well, being a champion mule, he had soon taken control of his excitement, and with Hazeem and Sidney again installed behind him, he immediately appeared more than ready to embark on another pull of his wagon, this time following five other four-legged creatures, each with one of those smaller two-legged creatures on its back. This was a new experience for him, but one he was only too pleased to engage with. This was only too obvious in both his gait and his general demeanour.

Kaalki, thought Sidney, was not just a champion mule but now a very happy mule. As happy as Sidney was relieved, if still a little apprehensive…

*

They were travelling back along the road from Boreland, and although Peter and his friends had been very… well, friendly, and although they'd made a passing reference to Dorothy, they'd said nothing about where they were taking Sidney and Hazeem. So, factoring in the return direction of travel and the general strangeness of the whole situation, there was still a lot to justify at least a little apprehension.

Then, after twenty minutes of travel, the leading quintet of mules made a right turn off the main road onto a rough track that led north and, within about three hundred yards, to two signs at the side of this track, both rendered in Urdu and both accompanied by an image of a skull-and-crossbones.

Hazeem anticipated the question that was just about to make it past Sidney's lips. He therefore informed his friend that one of the signs was a warning of the presence of mines, and the other of the presence of *anthrax*.

'Anthrax!' exclaimed Sidney. 'I've read about that. And… well, you'd be better off with the mines. I mean. What the hell?'

But before he could give voice to any further disquiet, Peter was there to set him and Hazeem at ease.

He'd pulled his mule to a stop, and now addressed them. 'Sorry,' he said to Hazeem. 'I forgot you'd understand them. But not to worry, they're both lies. There aren't any mines and there certainly isn't any anthrax, though you wouldn't believe how effective a combined threat of buried ordnance and a deadly disease can be in keeping out the neighbours. It's served us well for quite a few years now. Helped, I might add, by a handful of *corroborative disappearances*.'

Those last two words were given a wicked emphasis and were delivered with a disarming smile. Sidney was immediately very glad that Peter was on his side. He only wished Stephen had lived long enough to meet him.

Soon, however, his thoughts were elsewhere. The wagon and its leading escort were now getting deep into 'anthrax country', and it was a country empty of people and, indeed, of any signs of people, but it was instead filled with trees and then more trees. In fact, neither Sidney nor Hazeem had seen so many trees before, and were finding it difficult to believe that so many existed – anywhere. And the landscape was giving them something of a challenge as well. It was all so *wild* and so *uneven*, the complete antithesis of anything they'd known before. And so beautiful.

It was only a matter of time before Sidney put some of his thoughts into words. 'Hazeem,' he began, 'where the hell do you think we are? Have you any idea?'

'No,' answered Hazeem. 'I haven't a clue. I didn't think places like this still existed. And I'll tell you something else, young man…'

'What?' asked Sidney eagerly.

'I bet they don't see much in the way of smuggling round here. I mean, any smuggler would have a really lean time of it. He'd go bust in a week. And that, my dear Sidney, is a fact.'

Sidney dissolved into laughter, and Hazeem then joined him. Relief was morphing into pure delight, the sort of delight that comes from reaching a goal after a gruelling ordeal. Even if that goal hadn't been reached quite yet, and the ordeal had involved losing a cherished comrade along the way.

*

Indeed, in due course, Sidney began to feel more than a little guilty at the delight he was experiencing. After all, as the wagon rumbled on, he could hardly forget that behind him was the body of a man who'd fallen short of his goal; a man who would never savour any sort of delight again. There was nothing Sidney could do about that, he knew, but he also knew he could at least keep that man's memory alive – with the help of a unique account of British history. And he might be able to make a start on that task very soon because he'd just spotted something. It was a half-hidden lookout post, and it probably meant they were now very close to Dorothy's 'community'.

And there it was – or at least some of it. Because as the track curved to the left, it became apparent that, as well as the track having brought the newcomers to the summit of a ridge, beyond that ridge and disappearing into the distance was a huge valley, dotted here and there with fields, grazing animals and *houses*.

Hazeem had to pull Kaalki to a stop. Indeed, if he hadn't, Sidney would have asked him to do so – and with some urgency. He needed to take in this sight and savour it. For some time. Just as his friend was doing. And this was no dream in which he would end up spotting his parents on the other side of a river. No, this was for real. And that river was for real too!

Yes, he hadn't noticed it to start with. Rivers weren't something he was well acquainted with, and when there was something else calling for his attention, he could easily overlook them. Even when they were quite sizable and flowing at the bottom of a well-defined valley. And this one had a name. Peter, who'd now ridden back to joined his transfixed charges, informed them that it was the Skyffe and one of the bigger rivers here in the Southern Uplands.

So, here was a river that neither Sidney nor Hazeem had heard of, just as they'd never heard of the Southern Uplands – which were clearly, thought Sidney, not that far from the old border with England, but quite remote enough to provide a hidden community with a remarkable haven.

Indeed, as Peter went on to tell his guests, these Southern Uplands were very extensive as well and quite capable of accommodating a community that stretched far beyond this single valley – with far more fields, far more grazing animals and far more houses than could be seen from this first vantage point.

Dorothy, mused Sidney at this point, ran not just a community but a veritable realm.

And now it was time to move on and maybe see a little of this realm at close quarters. Probably down near that river.

*

It was better than Sidney could possibly have imagined. Between great stands of trees there were fields of some of the healthiest crops he'd ever seen. He didn't recognise most of them, but he did know what a sickly crop looked like and what a healthy crop looked like – and these were all in the rudest of health. Then there were other fields full of grazing grey-coated sheep, and yet others occupied by huge, shaggy-coated beasts with impressively long horns. In due course, he would learn that he'd just had his first ever view of Herdwick sheep and Highland cattle, but for now, there was something else to catch his attention: a modest farmhouse close to the river, and at its open door, a white woman!

The sight took his breath away. Other than his mother, she was the first white woman he'd seen since he left his life on the reservation. And now, coming around the corner of the farmhouse, was another white woman. This was all too much; it was just too much to take in.

Maybe, he thought, it was a dream after all.

But no. As the wagon rolled on, he convinced himself that the scores of other women (and men) – busy working in the fields or tending their beasts – were as real as his astonishment, an astonishment that only grew further when he spotted a series of pylons. They were on a ridge in the distance, and he knew immediately what they were for.

He had to tell Hazeem. 'Look, Hazeem!' he exclaimed. '*Aerials!* Aerials for you know what!'

Hazeem looked in the direction Sidney was pointing. 'I'm not sure...' he began hesitantly.

But Sidney went on, 'They're aerials for radio communication. They're Dorothy's aerials. They must be.'

Hazeem signalled his understanding with a long drawn-out, 'Aaaah.'

But Sidney was already thinking about what those aerials might mean: that, very soon, he might be able to make contact with his own little holy trinity – his three precious fellow hams who might be very relieved to learn their meek and mild Sidney had made it to a haven, and that he'd indulged in some real adventures on the way. And they would have to believe him. How could they not?

However, chatting through the ether would have to wait a while because Peter had just indicated that he was now leading Sidney and Hazeem to what would be their quarters for the night. It was a small wooden cabin, sitting on the valley's eastern wall and reached by a steep, narrow track. It was a modest sort of building, but Sidney had already decided that, for him, it would be the grandest building he'd ever stayed in. He suspected Hazeem would be coming to exactly the same decision.

When they finally arrived at its door, Peter explained that their lodging for the night was a sort of guest house. It was for the use of any newcomers, he said – without saying quite how often it was put into use. He also said that tomorrow would no doubt be a busy day, and that he would therefore leave Sidney and Hazeem to have a well-earned rest – whilst he himself dealt with Stephen's body. He would take it away in the wagon, this time pulled by his own mule, and he'd ensure it received its appropriate treatment until it could be respectfully interred.

No sooner had Peter informed the two current newcomers of the arrangements for Stephen than they informed him – in unison – that these weren't the arrangements they wanted. They made it clear that, instead, their first night in what had been the team's destination for so many gruelling days had to be a one shared by the whole of that team. And that would mean that not only would Kaalki be housed in a shelter to the side of the cabin but Stephen would be accommodated within the cabin, even if it meant he would occupy the only bed.

Of course, as well as there being no protest from Peter at his guests' proposal, it turned out there was more than one bed (along with everything else that newly arrived guests might need, including new sets of clothes). So, after cleaning, watering, feeding and reclothing themselves, and then spending a good half-hour helping each other come to terms with where they were, Sidney and Hazeem retired for the night – in two beautiful, real beds – whilst Stephen, in a third, began his own infinite and peaceful slumber.

And despite the comfort of his bed – and his relief at his being here to enjoy it – Sidney soon found that he had rarely felt sadder.

Needless to say, Hazeem felt the same.

29.

Dorothy was businesslike. However, that wasn't Sidney's opinion. He'd yet to meet her, and his only contact with her remained that short radio exchange back at RAF Cosford. No, it was her husband's opinion; Raymond's opinion. Albeit Raymond had gone on to proffer the view that, at heart, she was a real softie, and her businesslike nature was just the result of her having been pushed into a leadership role that she'd not really wanted.

Raymond, a tall guy of probably about sixty, had arrived at the 'guest cabin' the morning after its occupants' first night of rest – late enough not to disturb them and early enough not to cause them to think they'd been forgotten. He'd spent almost an hour with them on a bench outside the cabin, devoting most of this time not to revealing his thoughts on his wife but to filling them in on what they soon learnt was the community of 'Ginniegill', the community in which they were now safely ensconced.

It didn't amount to a full-blown lecture on the history and operation of the community, but it did provide Sidney and Hazeem with a basic understanding of how it had come about and how it now survived as a shelter from the increasingly chaotic world all around it.

It had started not as any sort of community but as just two houses at the upper end of the Skyffe valley, occupied by what Raymond called 'old-school types' who, more than a hundred years ago, had wanted to escape from what was happening to their country. Then, through a combination of pure chance, serendipity and some growing desperation – all seasoned with just a little local input from that Samye Ling monastery – the original old-school types were joined by more of their kind, and the embryo of a real, sustainable community was brought into life.

Of course, as Raymond explained, at that stage it was all a little touch and go. With the exponential growth of 'those without' – even here throughout southern Scotland – it was difficult to see how the embryo would survive, let alone thrive. And there were many times when it looked as though it was all over. There were raids and abductions and deaths – and on more than one occasion, it seemed that the whole nascent community was facing its doom. But then somebody came up with this bright idea of harnessing the threat of minefields and a deadly disease – and maybe even reinforcing this threat by dealing with persistent intruders in a not-necessarily-pacifist manner.

At this point in his presentation, Raymond indulged in a wicked grin before he then went on to explain how this pair of 'proven' deadly threats, when combined with the unpromising nature of this part of the Southern Uplands – and its resident population of Scottish biting midges – had managed to dissuade all but the most foolish outsiders from attempting to make it within. Indeed, he suggested, it may have been the biting midges that were the most effective element in this cobbled-together defence system – a far-from-serious statement that left his audience of two somewhat puzzled, as they were presently sitting outside their cabin at a time of the year when the worst of the midge season had long since concluded.

In any event, he went on to explain, the defences held – as they did even now – and that allowed the community to grow and to establish itself as an almost-self-sustaining society and, in due course, a society that would flourish – both organically and, over the years, with the help of a small but constant trickle of new members. As to how these new members found their way here, well, that was largely the result of one of the original members of the community having arrived here with a large consignment of unwanted radio kit and the knowledge of how to maintain and use it. This chap had then educated others in its maintenance and use, and when it was used, it gleaned not only new members directly (from the tiny residual radio-ham community in Britain), but quite a few more through word of mouth. There hadn't been a year in his life, he said, when a handful of new 'indigees', as he called them, hadn't found their way to Ginniegill and then been incorporated into the existing population. Which is why, he was proud to announce, the number of indigees currently living here was now almost four thousand. And with Sidney and Hazeem – who, of course, were also here as the result of the power of HF communication – it would now be even closer to four thousand.

At this point, Sidney couldn't help wondering what Hazeem might be thinking. After all, there was no way Hazeem fitted Raymond's definition of an indigee, and for Raymond to have conferred some sort of honorary indigee identity on him... well, it was either disingenuous or possibly calculating. He would have to wait and see – as would his now stony-faced friend.

The lesson was drawing to a close, and its closing elements included a brief rundown on the community's current form of government. This, Sidney decided, could be summed up as a 'democratic monarchy' – with an unwilling queen on the throne (Dorothy) – where each 'subject' of the monarch was subject to no more than his or her own sense of self-responsibility, tempered by the need to come to the assistance of a neighbour when this was required. It wasn't, by any means, a latter-day kibbutz, but instead an extremely benign version of the sort of society that had existed in Britain in the far distant past – made even more benign by the absence of stuff like famine, early death, misery, oppression and 'faith'.

And so the lesson was over, with Raymond having presumably decided that his pupils had been filled with quite enough information on the subject of Ginniegill. It was therefore time, it seemed, to change the subject, something Raymond did as carefully and as delicately as he could.

And he started with an apology: 'Look, I know I've gone on a bit, and I also know that you'll inevitably have something else on your mind at the moment. But what I didn't want to do when I arrived here this morning was adopt the role of undertaker. I did, as you might recall, offer my condolences. However, as regards what needs to be done with your lost friend… well, I didn't think it'd make for a good start to the day if I'd kicked off with the subject of Stephen's "arrangements". You'd have probably regarded me as being rather hasty and rather insensitive. So, I hope you'll understand why I've taken this detour through a sermon on Ginniegill before arriving at—'

'We do understand,' interrupted Sidney, 'and thank you. It was very thoughtful of you, but…'

'Yes,' said Raymond quietly, 'it's now time, isn't it? And might I just suggest that, to start with, you go and sort out the wagon and—'

'Kaalki,' assisted Sidney.

'Yes, exactly. Your invaluable mule. And while you're doing that, Hazeem and I will go and get Stephen ready for his trip.'

Neither Sidney nor Hazeem challenged this suggestion. They both knew they would soon be meeting Dorothy, and not only would it be some of Dorothy's people who would be charged with looking after Stephen's body, but it was also inconceivable that Dorothy herself wouldn't want to see the remains of someone with whom she'd been in contact for years – someone who, earlier than she'd wished, she'd now be laying to rest and in a decent grave, far away from all those rats back at RAF Cosford.

*

It was a long trip. Kaalki had to follow Raymond, who was riding his own mule, for well over an hour. And it was only when the little convoy had travelled along the whole length of the Skyffe valley to its head and then taken a track leading off to the east that Raymond indicated to Kaalki's passengers that they were approaching his and Dorothy's home.

It wasn't a palace. Indeed, it was just a wooden cottage, virtually indistinguishable from any of the other cottages the newcomers had encountered so far – albeit that it was possibly just a little bit larger than most.

Soon, they were at its door, and Raymond was announcing their presence to whoever was inside by shouting, '*We're hear, dear. Me and our two new guests.*'

This had the desired effect. Within a matter of seconds, a woman had opened the door and was now standing there with a smile on her face – and not even a hint in her demeanour that she was businesslike or, as Sidney had interpreted from his brief exchange with her days before, 'impersonal and dismissive'. No, this was a woman who radiated kindness, and a woman who looked as though she'd spent her first sixty years on this planet honing her body for the next sixty. She was slight but, Sidney suspected, tough as old boots, and more than well-suited for a life in the unforgiving surroundings of her realm.

She was now walking towards the wagon, prompting Sidney and Hazeem to climb down from their seat as quickly as possible, lest they encountered a regal matriarch from an elevated position – something they had no wish to do. So, their initial meeting was face to face – and warm. Dorothy seemed genuinely delighted that Sidney and Hazeem had made it to her haven. Nevertheless, her greeting was a short one because she soon excused herself and moved to the back of the wagon. On tip-toe, she looked over its side and, for more than a minute, she gazed at Stephen's remains and no doubt gave him a silent but heartfelt greeting.

When she then rejoined the living, she wasn't crying, but her eyes betrayed her emotions – and the fact that she was clearly distressed by having been denied the opportunity to finally meet her 'unknown' but long-cherished friend.

Nevertheless, a hint of businesslike soon replaced the veiled grief in her manner, and she lost no time at all in inviting Sidney and Hazeem to follow her into her home, within which Raymond was already busy preparing something to eat and drink. This would prove to be Sidney's first encounter with sweet cake and his first encounter with *beer* (albeit there would be a second encounter with the latter somewhat later this day.)

However, the refreshments were very much secondary to business, and that business involved Sidney and Hazeem giving Dorothy an abbreviated account of how they'd managed to get to Ginniegill – and how Stephen had failed to make it to the end of the course. It was only when Sidney described how Stephen had succumbed to the bullet, and then disclosed that he was already a very sick man, that Dorothy – much to the surprise of her guests – expressed her relief that the bullet had won.

'I wish I'd seen him – to talk to,' she said. 'I really do. But… well, he didn't have long to go. I could tell. Even over the airwaves and without seeing him. So I'm actually very relieved – that he's been relieved. You know, of so much pain and of so much suffering. In fact—'

'How did you know?' interrupted Sidney. 'How could you?'

'I knew,' Dorothy answered sharply. 'I just knew.'

It was a response that silenced Sidney immediately, and he only dared say another word when Dorothy's countenance transformed itself into one of unalloyed brightness as she asked Sidney whether he would like to talk to his friends around the world.

'I haven't,' she said, 'told your radio chums that you and your friend have arrived safely, because I wanted to leave that pleasure for you. As I'm sure you'll understand. Well, I reckon it's now time that you gave them the good news. There's all the radio kit you'll need in a room at the back of the cottage. So, I suggest you get in there and get on with calling them as soon as you like.'

At this offer, Sidney found his voice again – and immediately. 'I can think of nothing I'd rather do,' he said. And as he was saying this, he was already thinking that, although it was still early morning in Canada, it would be Sonia he would talk to first.

'Splendid!' observed Dorothy, rising from her seat. 'Just let Raymond and me go and sort out the kit, and then you can make a start. And while you're having your chats, I can have a chat with Hazeem, because I'm pretty sure he wants a chat with me.' She then disappeared from the room along with her husband.

As soon as she'd gone, Hazeem turned to Sidney and gave voice to his thoughts. 'They don't want me here, do they? But they want it to be my decision. They don't want to throw me out. They want me to choose to leave – of my own accord. I wonder how she'll go about it.'

'Hazeem, I don't—'

'Sidney,' interrupted Hazeem. 'It isn't a big deal. You know I never intended to stay. I said so at the outset. That I would deliver you to safety, and then I'd get back to my job. It's just that I'm fascinated to see how they might tie themselves up in knots convincing me to do what I've always planned to do – and will be doing anyway.'

Sidney's joy at the prospect of talking to his fellow hams had now dissolved into desolation. He knew what Hazeem had said at the outset of their journey. But that was then – before he and his northern travelling companion had forged a close friendship and before either of them had seen what their destination was like; not paradise, but just about as close to paradise as one could get in a largely miserable Britain. He had hoped desperately that Hazeem would have changed his mind, although he'd always feared that he wouldn't. It was why, during their journey north, he'd shied away from discussing with Hazeem anything to do with his future – and possibly discovering that he was indeed still intent on heading back south.

But now he had to say something – and before Dorothy returned. And rather than pointing out to Hazeem that returning to his life of smuggling would now be both impractical and probably suicidal, he simply said that he wanted him to stay. He, Sidney, Hazeem and Kaalki were still a team, he said, and Stephen would be dismayed if he knew that they planned to split up.

Hazeem didn't respond. He just looked a little unsure of himself, but only for a moment. Dorothy and Raymond were now returning to the room, and his expression immediately turned to one of suspicion.

There was nothing more that Sidney could do at this moment, so he pasted a smile onto his face and accepted the invitation to follow Raymond to the radio room whilst Dorothy remained behind to have her chat with her northerner guest.

*

When they reached the radio room, the likes of which Sidney had never seen before, Raymond soon left him alone. The room was full of all sorts of kit, and although it was all probably as old as his own back in Worcestershire, it looked to be in better condition and very well cared for. That part of it which he was about to use was already switched on, and as he'd promised, he would now use it to speak to Sonia first. Just as soon, that is, as he'd raised the spirits of HF communication through the normal series of incantations.

By the time he'd done this, his mood had recovered and it would soon be lifted to new hights. Just as soon, that is, as he'd heard Sonia's soft voice.

'Goodness gracious!' was her initial response to being contacted by Sidney so early in the Canadian morning. And then she started to cry. Indeed, she continued to cry throughout the whole of the ten minutes Sidney took to explain to her that, although they'd lost a dear companion on the way, he and Hazeem were now safe with Dorothy – and very safe because of the size of Dorothy's clan and the vast extent of its land. Whether all he told her got through, he couldn't tell, but that she was in a state of delight at the end of their exchange, he was sure. Just hearing Sidney's voice had obviously been all that Sonia needed to make her one of the happiest residents of beleaguered Saskatoon or indeed the whole of North America.

Ted was pretty happy as well, although he tried to pretend that he'd never had any doubts that his friend would make it to his destination in Scotland, just as he'd never had any doubts that, as and when required, his friend would be able to wield a knife to his life-saving advantage.

Sidney, of course, had been obliged to tell him about the use of his knife – and to thank him for insisting he carried one. So there was no way Ted wouldn't express such confidence in his mate's knife skills – even if, in all likelihood, he was actually astonished that bookish Sid had somehow managed to morph into lethal Sid the Impaler when the circumstances demanded – and that he hadn't instead simply stabbed himself by mistake.

To draw this exchange to a conclusion, Sidney promised that he'd call again soon and give Ted a chance to tell him what was going on in Windhoek – concluding that, if things weren't going too well there, maybe he should consider relocating to Scotland. Ted thanked him for this advice, but pointed out that, in the past, Sidney had come up with better ideas than suggesting to a snake catcher that he should up sticks and resettle himself in a country in which there were no snakes. Sidney could only agree – before he moved on to talk to French Marc.

'Scotland! Whisky! Real Scottish whisky! When do you plan to start?' Marc queried.

It was inevitable. Marc viewed the world through

the lens of distilled liquors, and clearly, anyone washed up on the shores of upland Scotland – and right next to a rushing river, apparently – should certainly lose no time at all in setting up a still to produce one of the finest drinks mankind has ever conceived. And furthermore, he added, there was bound to be a really healthy market for this product, as there was only so much fun you could have with a sheep before you wanted something that would really get your juices flowing.

Sidney was delighted that his French friend was still as impractical in his advice as he was irresponsible and incautious in his life, and he felt he had to promise Marc that he would embark on a search for a still and all the necessary ancillary equipment as soon as possible. He didn't, however, mention that the locals had an established competitor to whisky in the form of home-brewed beer. After all, in Marc's eyes, compared to distilled liquors, beer wasn't just a poor relative but a relative that, having first been castrated, should then be banished to distant shores and never spoken of again. And as everyone knew, it tasted of mud.

*

When, after his three short conversations, Sidney came back to join the others, he was smiling from ear to ear, and he didn't have to explain why. Nor, for the rest of the day, would there be anything to puncture his mood of almost pure euphoria. Stephen was being taken care of. Hazeem's future, whatever it was to be, wasn't even referred to. His own future was not marked out – other than in respect to his access to a radio. Peter and the other four rangers had arrived to help celebrate the safe arrival of the two newcomers. And together with Dorothy and Raymond, the five rangers, and two ladies who had appeared with mountains of food for a large evening meal, Sidney and Hazeem were able to revel in one of the best evenings they had ever spent in their entire lives.

In fact, if previously teetotal Sidney hadn't indulged in quite so much of that hateful beer, he might have better remembered just how good an evening it had been – and how he, Hazeem and Kaalki had got back to their cabin.

30.

Three months after his first ever hangover, Sidney was in his bothy, turning a blank sheet of home-produced paper into another page of what would become the first copy of Stephen Croft's *An Exposition on the Shaping of Modern Britain (as recounted to a scribe)*.

Sidney hadn't known Stephen's surname when he was still alive – as he'd not sought it – but in sorting through Stephen's remaining possessions, just two days after his death, he'd discovered it in the flyleaf of one of his books – and it had delighted him beyond reason. After all, 'Croft', he'd decided, was a surname just made for a man like Stephen, and furthermore, it was also a surname that would sit very well on the heavy basalt headstone down near the Skyffe where Stephen would soon be laid to rest…

There had been hundreds of people at his funeral, even though only Sidney and Hazeem – and, of course, Kaalki – had known him in person whilst alive. And it was Kaalki who had taken him on his very last journey in *that* wagon, and who – as Stephen had been lowered into the ground – had stood near the graveside, looking desperately forlorn. And no, that wasn't Sidney and Hazeem projecting their own feelings on to their favourite four-legged friend; that was all Kaalki and all genuine sadness on his part. After all, Sidney knew Kaalki very well, and Sidney could tell.

Sidney had, understandably, left the funeral with a heavy heart himself. However, from the short time he'd spent with his late friend, he knew that Stephen would have deplored a long period of mourning and would have expected everybody simply to get on with their lives without delay – and without any great burden of grief. And that's precisely what Sidney decided to do – just as soon, that is, as he'd decided what his life was to be and where exactly it would be spent.

In the event, these two decisions weren't too difficult to make, not after Dorothy had made it clear what it was that she wanted him to do and where, within the Ginniegill estate, he might want to set up home.

She wanted another teacher, she revealed. There were already three men and three women who spent much of their time educating the young ones as best they could, but through a combination of their advancing years and their limited knowledge, they were finding this job more and more difficult. What was needed, she went on to explain, was an energetic newcomer, steeped in 'bookery', who wasn't just able to bolster the efforts of the existing educators but also to build on their efforts with the aim of establishing a more formal system of education, and one that involved a much wider syllabus than the one that existed at present. She confessed it concerned her that, after receiving a number of years of the present form of Ginniegill education, few young people could tell her where in the world Scotland was situated or what part gravity played in ensuring that they stuck to it and didn't spend all their time just hovering above it.

If he'd been challenged to take on such a role only a month before, back in Worcestershire, Sidney would have refused it. He would have been terrified by the prospect of such a daunting responsibility. However, now that he'd undergone that journey north – and had survived that journey – his immediate reaction to Dorothy's offer was to grasp it with both hands. It seemed the fact that his existing knowledge of all sorts of things was sketchy at best and that his only responsibility to date had been for a vegetable patch no longer really mattered. He would cope. He just knew it. Just as he'd coped with taking the lives of others when he'd had to. Only, of course, introducing children to knowledge would, he recognised, be infinitely more gratifying than introducing any number of assailants to an infinite oblivion.

So, a deal was done. Sidney was to become Ginniegill's 'tutor-in-chief' – and as a welcome bonus, its *de facto* chief librarian as well. Because in making her offer of a teaching role, Dorothy had revealed that, in addition to the books Sidney had brought with him, there were many more already here, waiting to be sorted, organised, catalogued – and read. This was music to Sidney's ears, as he had no doubt that, with access to more volumes and to Stephen's yet-to-be-penned history of Britain, he could assemble just the sort of curriculum that Dorothy wanted. Even better, he would be able to do this in his very own one-man home; a currently unused bothy on the west side of the Skyffe, which was no more than two-hundred yards from the main schoolhouse on the river's east side and accessed by a cross-river plank-and-handrail construction that had yet to fail its users. That said, this not-quite-a-bridge would not be ideal for the job of transporting any of those books to the bothy – or for the job of transporting his very own radio kit to the bothy!

For it seemed that not only did the community have a sizable store of books, but it also had a surplus of the sort of radio kit that any radio ham might want in order to keep in contact with his fellow hams around the world. Sidney couldn't quite believe it, but his tiny bothy was to be set up as a rather more solid replica of his hut back at Hope Farm. Albeit that he would, of course, have to make do with a sparkling river outside his door and not a dark, placid pond – something he suspected he could quite easily manage.

In trying to digest so much good fortune, Sidney brought to mind something he'd read in one of his books many months before. It concerned a 'scientific' postulation on the existence of numerous parallel universes and how these multiple universes might be brought into existence. It was, he remembered, a postulation that was difficult to understand and even more difficult to take seriously, but he'd been fascinated by the idea that a new universe could be added to an existing universe every time a sentient being made a decision. And with sentient beings constantly making decisions, there would therefore be a constant stream of new universes – in some of which the decision-maker would experience a good outcome and in others of which he or she would experience a bad outcome.

Well, he thought, if what had been postulated in that book was real and was at work in his own life – now – he must, through all the decisions he'd made in the recent past, have ended up in the best parallel universe there was, somewhere he could not conceive he would ever have reached.

But he had. He had left a terrible life for one that held so much promise and so much of everything he wanted – including, of course, the ability to complete Stephen's book. And when this was done, he would then get some of his pupils to reproduce it. He was quite determined that everybody in Ginniegill should know why they had ended up where they were.

So, it was on with his work, only stopping when that blank sheet of paper was barely blank any more and he could instead indulge himself in a little bit of fine-tuning of one of his favourite aspects of Ginniegill's new curriculum: that part of it that dealt with the world's geography. And it was as he was tidying up what he'd already documented on the geography of South Asia, that his thoughts drifted towards his only friend with a South Asian heritage, and what this friend was doing now.

*

After only a week in Ginniegill, Hazeem had made up his mind to leave this Southern Uplands refuge and make his way back to England. There, he would either pick up his old life – wherever he could – or he would seek out any of the new opportunities that uncertain times always bring. And there was certainly no question that times were now more uncertain than ever. The handful of radio hams in England still in contact with Dorothy were reporting every day that the country was in a desperately chaotic state, and in some parts of the south of England, the northerners and the southerners were now engaged in open conflict.

Sidney had pleaded with Hazeem not to go, but he'd been adamant. He was a smuggler, he maintained. And smugglers had to follow their calling, or if they weren't able to do this, then they were required to use their smuggling skills in some other appropriately clandestine activity. This, he pointed out, would be near impossible in Ginniegill, but only too easy in a society 'in flux'. Indeed, he was more eager to point this out than he was to dwell on the other reason he didn't want to stay in this upland sanctuary, and that, quite obviously, was his having a darker complexion than any of Ginniegill's other residents. He knew he didn't fit in, and however much Dorothy – and Sidney – continued to assure him that this wasn't an issue, he clearly couldn't believe that he was really welcome.

'Why,' he challenged Sidney, 'would a bunch of white guys, secure in their impregnable bastion, want one of their enemies within its walls? If I leave, it would be best for me and best for you and all your kind. Surely you can see that?'

Well, Sidney couldn't – and neither could Dorothy, which is why she'd followed up her original chat with Hazeem with many more, and why she'd eventually asked him to help the rangers on one of their forthcoming missions before he headed off south. She told him they needed to scavenge some salt; a commodity not readily available in upland Scotland, but a store of which existed in a forgotten warehouse just outside what had once been Ayr. But the journey to this destination near the coast was through distinctly 'occupied lands', and the presence of someone in the party who not only looked and sounded like a genuine northerner but also *was* a genuine northerner would make what was a perilous expedition much less perilous.

Hazeem could hardly refuse this request. Dorothy had shown him only kindness and concern, so he owed her. Plus, not to be ignored was the fact that he was being offered a genuine slice of adventure and a task that might just call upon some of those smuggler-associated skills that very much needed to be kept in shape. Oh, and he'd never seen the sea before, and the prospect of visiting somewhere on the coast of Scotland and actually observing a stretch of what lay beyond this coast was simply irresistible. He decided to accept the request within seconds – and to defer his return to England until the salt had been safely delivered to Dorothy. After all, it would mean deferring his leaving Ginniegill for good by only a few days.

It all worked out well. Hazeem and four rangers – and their five mules – made it to the warehouse without incident, and only on the way back – loaded down with bags of salt – did they have any 'interactions' with the locals. To bring them to a safe conclusion, two of these required his authenticity, and the resolution of the third – to the locals' satisfaction – required the application of his guile, topped off with just a little of his acquaintance with deception. All four rangers were left in no doubt that, apart from being a good guy, Hazeem could prove to be an invaluable colleague.

It was no surprise then that, once they were back in Ginniegill, they asked him to reconsider his decision to leave and suggested that, whilst he was giving this decision its due consideration, it was only right that he should share their quarters. This was a rambling building just a stone's throw from Sidney's schoolhouse and right next to another rambling building that housed their treasured mules (now including one by the name of Kaalki, who had probably never believed he would have the company of so many of his own kind).

Inevitably, he had to accede to their request whilst, at the same time, making it eminently clear that he would never change his mind, and the deferral of his departure from Ginniegill was an act of courtesy and nothing more. Indeed, he maintained this assertion even after a second sortie with the rangers when they travelled all the way to the east coast of northern England to 'retrieve' one of Dorothy's ham contacts, whose situation was quickly becoming untenable. This guy had effectively come under siege, and he needed to be extracted and rehoused in Ginniegill as soon as possible.

In fact, it wasn't until the third such mission that Hazeem's resolve began to falter, and he finally admitted that maybe he should stay around for a while. And only when this 'while' was in its fifth day did he change his mind again and announce that he would, after all, be setting off south.

That was just a fortnight ago, since which time a combined assault by Dorothy, all the rangers, a good number of other residents, and Sidney, of course, had managed to get him to change his mind yet again. (And Sidney hadn't held back on that earlier appeal to his friend to maintain what remained of the team – just as Stephen would have wanted.)

So, Sidney was now a firm permanent resident of Ginniegill – with a home, a well-defined role in the community and an ongoing ability to talk to three long-standing friends around the globe. Kaalki was also a permanent resident who –as well as having a new role himself, as part of the 'ranger brigade'– also had a set of new friends, some with two legs and some with four. And as for Hazeem, well, he'd resigned himself to a sort of indefinite deferral of his departure, which gave Dorothy more time to talk to him and more time to convince him that the community in Ginniegill wanted to do no more than follow her country's traditional assimilation of 'others', as it had done for centuries, and that it didn't want to exclude anybody on the basis that they were 'different'. A few 'incomers', she explained, would always be welcomed. And as regards just one incomer, and one who had such special skills… well, he would be welcomed with open arms.

Nevertheless, Hazeem would continue to regard himself as not quite part of the Ginniegill community for well over a year. And it was only when he set up home with one of Dorothy's nieces that he finally admitted to Sidney – and to the wider community – that he was now a settled resident of this wild stretch of Scotland, and his smuggling career was at an end. He would now have to make do with a loving wife, the company of rangers and, in due course, the duties associated with fatherhood.

However, that was the future. The present, for Sidney, was still very much reading and writing: reading all the new books he'd been given to assist in his compilation of a new curriculum, and writing both this new curriculum and Stephen's history. It was a lot more satisfying than writing tedious letters for Sanjiv and the other illiterates who'd used his services back in Worcestershire. And as demanding of his time as it was, he still found time to engage with Kaalki most days – and to reengage with Sonia and with Ted and with Marc, providing the latter with a whole series of excuses for his failure to set up a still.

Life was finally good; very good. Often good enough to make him cry.

Ten years later

31.

There was a steep path behind Sidney's bothy that led to what had once been a logging track – when, in the distant past, Ginniegill had been a managed forest. This track was now barely discernible beneath a mix of birch, rowan and hazel, but there was one small clear space on the track where, if the biting midges weren't too active, Sidney would sometimes sit and take in the view of the Skyffe valley – either on his own or sometimes with Jo. On this late summer afternoon, he was here without his girlfriend, and he'd soon found himself thinking about that day, a full ten years ago, when he'd first come to Ginniegill, and how bittersweet that day had been. He, Hazeem and Kaalki had made it, but Stephen hadn't. And Stephen dying when he did – almost in sight of the promised land – still pained him acutely. If only, thought Sidney, he was here with him now. For if so, he mused, he'd learn how little the promised land had changed over the last ten years.

The Skyffe still snaked down the valley, never tiring of buffing its bed of smooth pebbles. There were still cattle and sheep dotted around the sides of the valley, and where the valley had been cultivated, men and women still worked in the fields. And directly below where Sidney sat, the schoolhouse still stood, looking much as it did the day he'd first entered it – as did the rangers' 'longhouse'. So too did the mules' accommodation and the paddock for the use of its residents, and there were still wagons parked between the stables and the rangers' place, wagons that were now needed more than ever before.

Sidney sighed. In thinking about how little had changed in Ginniegill, he was now slipping into a contemplative mood, one that would soon see him reflecting on what *had* changed in the last decade, both here in Ginniegill and beyond Ginniegill's borders. And he would start by reflecting on his own transformation from a naïve scribe – to an educator, a writer and, more recently, a lover.

As regards his role as an educator, he'd been able to do everything Dorothy had asked of him all those years before. By digesting the contents of countless books and, at the same time, formulating in his mind which of these contents shouldn't be denied to much younger minds, he'd developed a comprehensive curriculum for all the children of the Ginniegill community. This curriculum – which included, for the older children, Stephen's exposition on Britain – had then been adopted by his fellow teachers, with the result that not only did the young people of Ginniegill now know where Scotland was in the world and what part gravity played in ensuring they and their livestock didn't ever lose contact with it, but they also knew an admirable amount about subjects as diverse as chemistry, botany, the etiquette of radio communication and – most important of all – the nature of their past. And, of course, they could all read and write, and some of them could even tackle complicated sums.

However, Sidney didn't spend all his time as an amateur educationalist and as an amateur teacher in the classroom. He also found time to write – for himself. He'd begun with some essays that looked to amplify parts of Stephen's history. (There were certain books he'd inherited that provided further insights into what had happened in Britain in the last century.) But it wasn't long before these essays were joined by a few original short stories, intended to entertain the children, and following on from these came a succession of full-length novels, which ultimately ended up entertaining some of the grown-ups in Ginniegill. Not many of them, as each novel was in the form of one copy of a handwritten manuscript, and they all had to be handed around – slowly and carefully.

However, one grown-up was particularly entertained. So much so that, when out riding Kaalki one day, Sidney had been ambushed by this grown-up, and left in no doubt that he had one very admiring reader – and one very admiring… well, admirer. Her name was Jo, and it wouldn't be too long before he and Jo had formed rather more than a literary connection. Indeed, this relationship between a slightly arthritic schoolmaster and a noticeably younger and more attractive seamstress was now at a stage so advanced that Sidney's tenancy of the bothy could only be continued if he were somehow able to increase its size – and quite considerably. There was no way that, on top of all those books and all that radio kit, it could comfortably accommodate *two* people – or maybe even more. It was all a work in progress, of course, and bringing their relationship to the sort of completed state already achieved by Hazeem would still take some time.

Hazeem now lived in the next valley – close to where Jo currently did her sewing – and he lived there with a beautiful wife and two beautiful children. Indeed, one could suppose that he'd been domesticated. Although, if one did, one would be wrong.

He was still a ranger. And as a ranger, he'd been involved in virtually every 'extraction exercise' throughout the length and breadth of Britain, when there were still radio hams to collect from their hiding places and bring back to Ginniegill. That exercise, which was now complete, had taken over seven years, and Hazeem's participation in it had earned him the respect of the whole community. They'd come to learn just how skilful he was in every aspect of his covert profession, and how brave he was as well. Latterly, they'd come to learn how accomplished he was at leading the sometimes-perilous foraging expeditions that had now replaced the extraction sorties – and that required the increased use of the community's stock of wagons. Ginniegill was almost self-sufficient, but not quite. And there were always supplies of materials, bits of hardware, salt and other difficult-to-find commodities that needed to be located and brought back for the community's use. This wasn't easy, and it sometimes involved many days away in 'the wilderness', the wilderness that Britain had become since it had been emptied of people.

Yes, whilst very little had changed in Sidney's Shangri-La, the world outside this Shangri-La had changed out of all recognition. And that was the whole world, not just the lands of perfidious Albion.

It had taken a little time, but the full-blown battle that had developed between the northerners and southerners in Britain had first become a sideshow to a much more significant world event, and then it had been overtaken by that event. And the event was something that would exterminate the vast majority of mankind, taking no account of people's colour, race, age or gender or, indeed, whether they prayed to a god or to a devil or they didn't pray at all.

It was, of course, the final pandemic, the one for which the previous pandemics had been dry runs, and the one that would exploit a world brimming with people, none of whom had retained an acquaintance with any aspects of advanced science and technology, not least the science and technology that had formerly been used to develop vaccines. Impoverished and undernourished, the billions who'd recently been trashing the planet with their careless pursuits were soon merely fertilising it with their scrawny carcasses, and only a tiny few – on small islands or maybe in remote upland areas cut off from all those around them – had stood any chance of survival.

It was impossible to be certain, but from the reports of Dorothy's British hams – before they'd all been extracted – and from what Hazeem and his fellow ranger-foragers had learnt, it was thought that Ginniegill's population of about four thousand souls now constituted the entire population of what had once been Great Britain. Whether there was anybody in Ireland wasn't known, but that there was nobody in the old England, the old Wales and the rest of Scotland was almost beyond doubt.

There were also, of course, reports from those hams around the world who were still in contact with Dorothy – and Sidney – but not yet in contact with the pestilence. And they told a similar story – of countries being emptied of their entire stock of *Homo sapiens*, with only a handful of this species managing to huddle together for survival in various out-of-the-way places. In fact, from what had been learnt about this apocalyptic slimming-down process, Dorothy reckoned that there might be as few as eighty communities like her own dotted around the globe, and probably no more than double this at most. If so, that might mean that the world's human population was well below half a million. And it was certainly nowhere near enough to make a dent in the rapid recovery of a sorely damaged but resilient natural world that was now effectively free of its two-legged scourge. The wilderness beyond the borders of Ginniegill didn't stop at the English Channel. It went on and on, wherever the world's new climate would allow it.

Sidney now wondered – as he had done many times before – how many of these tiny communities, lost within the vast expanse of recovering wilds, were following a similar path to his own. Through radio contact, he knew of a few that certainly were and of none that had taken a different route. Which might mean, he thought, that mankind's recent history had led to the same result wherever mankind still existed. And this was the excising of the rapacious gene from its DNA. No longer was growth in its numbers – at the expense of other species and often to the cost of other members of its own species – the driving force in its conduct. Instead, its surviving members were content simply to continue to survive and to see their numbers maintained rather than increased, and they had no desire to leave those places that had sheltered them against the plague. However seemingly tempting, the world beyond the borders of these places would be left largely untouched.

This was certainly the case in Ginniegill, where the population was virtually the same size as it had been a decade ago, with no signs of it increasing, but instead it just rolling along at around the four thousand level for years to come and possibly indefinitely. It would also stay in its upland retreat, and limit its interaction with the rest of Britain to regular foraging runs. There were certainly no plans for a new Ginniegill in somewhere where the grass might be greener but not nearly so familiar.

For those folk with whom Sidney had shared his life back in Worcestershire, this lack of an ambition to spread further afield would have been incomprehensible. However, his community's lack of an appetite for more and more of their kind would have been regarded not just as incomprehensible but also as shameful – as something deserving of not just disdain but actual punishment. After all, how can the betrayal of one's primary role as a human – to produce as many more humans as one can – not attract the harshest of penalties? They would also, Sidney knew, have had more than a minor problem with the lack of a recognised religion in this accursed community. Trying to explain to them that the closest the inhabitants of Ginniegill came to a religion was their dabbling in a mix of various Buddhist and pagan beliefs (possibly to spice up their core beliefs of pragmatism and liberalism) would have been an impossible job. Indeed, one just as impossible as convincing them that their own beliefs and their own conduct had always been destined to lead to disaster. And if they suggested that abandoning the centuries-old behaviour of their kind would also mean abandoning any hope of 'progress', then they might be reminded about where 'progress' had led them: to almost total oblivion.

And it hadn't been a picnic for the world's fauna and flora either, and the remaining examples of all of them would take centuries to recover from the comprehensive kicking they'd received. And they were the lucky ones: the ones that had survived at all.

So, life in Ginniegill was admittedly very simple, and it could even be accused of being dull – but it wasn't really. It still had all the human interactions that make life really interesting, and on top of that, it had serenity, a rewarding intimacy with the improving natural world, plenty of gratifying hard work, a surprising number of challenges, and a distinct absence of certain features of the old way of living that made it a constant pleasure to be alive. And these absent features included disharmony, discord, antagonism, corruption, abuse, ill-treatment, exploitation and a whole list of the less enviable aspects of human nature. What Sidney had experienced every day at Hope Farm now found it impossible to make its way into his life in Ginniegill. And that wasn't dull at all.

At this point in his musings, the man on the hill indulged in a very satisfied sigh, and then he reminded himself that it was probably time to make his way down the path to his bothy and make use of his radio kit. It was time to talk to people in faraway places. Not three of them, but just two.

*

Nobody had been able to raise Sonia for almost five years now, and it finally had to be assumed that she'd either succumbed to the pestilence or to the tide of humanity that had been threatening Saskatoon for as long as Sidney could remember. It was sad; very sad. For Sidney, her loss brought back memories of the loss of his mother, and he could barely believe how much he could miss somebody whom he'd never met. But he did miss her – desperately. Even though he still often thought about her and even though she would live on in his memory for all time – and, of course, in the memories of Ted and Marc as well; his two ham chums who had, against all the odds, survived the apocalypse – and still had access to a radio.

Ted had found his route to salvation through a combination of intelligence and serendipity. The intelligence had been in the form of a very early warning of something very nasty about to arrive in Namibia – provided (unintentionally) by an extremely alarmed Chinese client who'd recently been sharing his house with two zebra snakes. And the serendipity had been in the form of his inclusion, just the next week, on a fishing trip out of Walvis Bay with two fellow snake catchers from that town. This had been due to last eight hours, but it ended up lasting the eight days it took their little boat to make it to St Helena. They didn't receive a very warm welcome on this island, but after a month in quarantine, they were allowed to stay and, ultimately, to become part of one of those communities that avoided obliteration.

Not that they could pursue their former profession. St Helena, like Scotland, has no snakes, which meant that two of them became farmers and Ted – using his knowledge of snakes and a number of other animals, and by studying a few old books – became an amateur vet, who specialised in tending to the needs of the island's numerous dogs, sheep and cattle. He also had a sideline: the mending of all sorts of electrical equipment, including radio kit. And this, of course, allowed him to put together his own radio and, after an interlude of some months, to resume his contact with Sidney and others.

Marc ended up on an island as well. It wasn't anywhere near as big as St Helena, and it wasn't in the Atlantic. It was just off the southern tip of Corsica, and it was called Cavallo. He'd gone there to attend the wedding of a former girlfriend – to a French drug lord who owned the island. Along with all the other guests, he'd decided to stay there in order to avoid the onslaught of the plague. This coincided with the fourth day of the celebrations, and it soon overtook the whole of France and, of course, the whole of Corsica. (Albeit Marc had always been a bit vague about which day it had been, blaming this vagueness on the arduous demands of said celebrations.)

However, the good news was that, despite the felonious nature of the majority of the wedding party, they all survived and very soon they all adopted a very different sort of life, one that offered them some much-needed redemption and one that would eventually see them becoming self-sufficient, principally by their learning how to fish and their discovering where, on neighbouring Corsica, they could gainfully forage.

Marc, of course, felt he could better contribute to the community's prosperity by avoiding all that fishing and foraging stuff, and instead by offering some of the more legitimate aspects of his medical knowledge to Cavallo's modest population, whilst, at the same time, running the ex-drug lord's radio kit – and, on top of these two activities, he also made something called *eau de vie myrte*. This was a local alcoholic tipple that, on good days, would apparently have some myrtle in it, and on bad days – in accordance with his standard practice – would have virtually anything that came to hand in it. So far, he had assured Sidney, none of his *eau de vie* customers had lost their sight – for more than a few hours anyway. And no doubt, if more serious problems arose from the imbibing of his questionable liquor, he would admit this to Sidney. And maybe that would be today – directly after Sidney had made contact with Ted.

*

Yes, Sidney was now back in his bothy, and he'd decided to contact his friend in St Helena first.

It took him only a few minutes of the normal radio-ham etiquette to conjure up a greeting from Ted that, not for the first time, sought to recognise Sidney's residence in Scotland.

'Ah, Sidney,' Ted began. 'Good to hear from ye. An' tell me, hoo's it gaun in bonny Scotland? An' haes ye got yersel a kilt yet? An' haes ye grown yersel a sporran yet?'

Sidney giggled. 'Well, I've heard tell that midges hibernate in kilts. And, as for the sporran… well, you know they only pop out of the ground in spring and soon die off. So, it's a no on both counts, I'm afraid. I'm as likely to get a kilt and a sporran as a cool customer such as yourself is likely to get your *broekies* in a knot.'

'Hey, I'm no Afrikaner, you know. My family was originally from Surrey.'

'That I can believe. Your attempt at a Scottish accent was dreadful. You sounded more like a Saint with a bad case of laryngitis.'

'If only,' responded Ted. 'I'll never be a true Saint – unless, of course, I can convince the locals that I was actually born here and maybe spirited away as a baby. But that's hardly likely. Although, there again, I'm not too concerned. The locals really aren't a bad bunch at all. And, especially when you've cured their dog of the mange.'

And so it went on; an exchange no longer filled with advice on how to survive a famine or how to pack a knife, but one filled with various references to the joys of living in settled communities, whether in the middle of the Atlantic or in the uplands of Scotland – and the particular joys of treating and healing animals rather than catching and ejecting them. Ted, even though he was still the Ted whom Sidney had known for years, had undergone something of a road-to-Damascus experience, and was now the friend of animals and not their bane. Furthermore, he seemed to like his new identity immensely, no doubt helped by the fact that he no longer had the Chinese as his clients, but instead was dealing exclusively with Saints – who weren't that much different from guys with a heritage in Surrey.

No sooner had Ted informed Sidney that he would have to sign off in order to deal with a Labrador with an ear infection, than Marc had been spirited out of the ether, and Sidney had asked him directly whether his myrtle product had yet robbed anybody of their sight – permanently. It was just possible that, by doing this, he would avoid the inevitable grilling about his continued failure to produce a distilled beverage – some Scotch whisky in particular.

However, the ploy didn't work. As soon as Marc had expressed his indignation that anybody should question the *relatively* wholesome nature of his *eau de vie myrte,* he challenged his radio correspondent on the persistent dereliction of his duties.

'Sidney,' he declared firmly, 'I know you 'ave certain responsibilities concerning the filling of the minds of young people, but you 'ave other responsibilities as well – concerning the filling of glasses with a liquid that will reflect the 'eritage of your community. Because, my friend, whisky izn't just a drink that was enjoyed by people in Scotland; it iz a drink that was enjoyed – for centuries – by people throughout the 'ole of Britain. It iz interval to your identity—'

'Integral,' corrected Sidney.

'Yes, integral to your identity as a Brit – and I mean the identity of your 'ole community as Brits. And I'm sure I don't 'ave to remind you that you're now the only

Brits there are. You are the only natives of Britain that remain. The 'ole place iz yours – and you should stamp your ownership on it with as much of your native 'eritage as you can. And that 'as to include drinking whisky!' Marc was very emphatic on this point, even if the point wasn't quite as valid as he would like to think.

It did, however, cause Sidney to make a not-very-convincing promise that he would finally get around to researching how one might go about setting up a working still in Ginniegill, one that would furnish the community with something rather more than just neat alcohol and might even merit the description of 'whisky'. Marc accepted this promise, but insisted that, after ten years of not even producing some gin, the research should certainly not take another ten years.

After the exchange on this topic, their shared conversation moved on to other topics as diverse as the true nature of democracy in self-contained communities and the use of conch shells as musical instruments, a developing pastime on Cavallo of which Marc heartily disapproved. And as he made clear, it certainly wasn't a recognition of his own community's heritage. It was just a new noise he could well do without.

For a little while after his conversation with Marc had come to an end, Sidney mused on the use of conch shells. He did know what they looked like because he'd seen illustrations of them in one of his books, but he hadn't realised that people cut holes in them and then blew into them to make sounds.

However, this musing on conch shells was short-lived, and as he made his way down to the mules' stables to share a little time with Kaalki, he began to consider what Marc had said about the people of Ginniegill now being the only inhabitants of Britain, and how – with the welcome exception of Hazeem – these inhabitants were now exclusively natives of Britain; indigenous people whose ancestors – going back centuries if not millennia – had, for the most part, been natives of this island themselves.

He'd been well aware of this fact ever since it had become accepted that the plague had wiped out everyone else in Britain. But Marc's reference to the fact had, for some reason, made him give it his focused attention for once and to consider whether it was something he should be pleased about or not. After all, the return of this country to its indigenous people had come about through the annihilation of millions of other humans, and even though his personal experience of just some of those humans hadn't been the best, he could hardly relish the loss of so many lives. He'd be inhuman if he did.

Nevertheless, bringing to mind that personal experience also brought to mind his present experience of a life without the subjugation and exploitation he'd known in the past, and one shared with people like himself. How, therefore, could he not conclude that he was well satisfied with how things had turned out, even though it had involved the deaths of millions of innocents in his country and billions of innocents around the world? All those people sacrificed just to deliver, here in his homeland, a good life for Sidney and for about four thousand other Brits. Or as Marc had referred to them, the remaining natives of this land: a people no longer needing to share it with others and no longer facing the threat of being overwhelmed by others.

This was sobering stuff, not least because Sidney couldn't help feeling a pang of guilt – for being alive and for being one of the very fortunate few, the very few who now constituted Britain's remaining population. He wondered whether Ted and Marc had similar feelings about their own situation.

And then he found himself in the stables and saw Kaalki looking at him from his stall. It was a sight that always warmed his heart, and on this occasion, it caused his thoughts to move on from carnage and guilt to pleasure – to the pleasure of a relationship with a faithful animal and the more general pleasure inherent in his living in Ginniegill. To his living – with a loving partner – in what was now a very much transformed Britain. (Albeit not transformed to the extent that radio hams couldn't still indulge their radio-ham habits…)